"Magary has created a fictional future as wildly enter-
taining as it is eerily foreboding. *The Postmortal* is as
funny, inventive, and outlandish as anything you'll read
this year. Or next. Assuming we're all still here."
       —David Goodwillie, author of *American Subversive*

"A darkly comic, totally gonzo, and effectively frighten-
ing population-bomb dystopia in the spirit of *Logan's
Run, Soylent Green,* and the best episodes of *The Twilight
Zone.*"
       —Neal Pollack, author of *Alternadad* and *Stretch*

"I suppose you could wait for the inevitable *Postmortal*
movie. But then you might miss Magary's rendering, his
word play, his singular sense of humor. A book that is, at
once bracingly funny and—get this, Deadspin Nation—
unmistakably poignant."
       —L. Jon Wertheim, coauthor of *Scorecasting*

"A startling leap forward. *The Postmortal* is dark, funny,
and terrifying. This book draws such a vivid, convincing
picture of immortality that it, quite literally, made me
want to die."
       —Will Leitch, author of *Are We Winning?*
       and *God Save the Fan*

PENGUIN BOOKS

THE POSTMORTAL

DREW MAGARY is a writer for Deadspin, NBC, *Maxim*, and Kissing Suzy Kolber. He's also written for *GQ*, *New York Magazine*, *Rolling Stone*, ESPN, Yahoo!, Comedy Central, *Playboy*, *Penthouse*, and various other media outlets. His first book, *Men with Balls*, was released in 2008. This is his first novel. He lives in Maryland with his wife and children.

You can contact the author at drew@deadspin.com or at twitter.com/drewmagary.

THE
POSTMORTAL

[A NOVEL]

Drew Magary

PENGUIN BOOKS

PENGUIN BOOKS
Published by the Penguin Group
Penguin Group (USA) Inc., 375 Hudson Street, New York, New York 10014, U.S.A.
Penguin Group (Canada), 90 Eglinton Avenue East, Suite 700,
Toronto, Ontario, Canada M4P 2Y3 (a division of Pearson Penguin Canada Inc.)
Penguin Books Ltd, 80 Strand, London WC2R 0RL, England
Penguin Ireland, 25 St Stephen's Green, Dublin 2, Ireland
(a division of Penguin Books Ltd)
Penguin Group (Australia), 250 Camberwell Road, Camberwell, Victoria 3124, Australia
(a division of Pearson Australia Group Pty Ltd)
Penguin Books India Pvt Ltd, 11 Community Centre,
Panchsheel Park, New Delhi – 110 017, India
Penguin Group (NZ), 67 Apollo Drive, Rosedale, Auckland 0632, New Zealand
(a division of Pearson New Zealand Ltd)
Penguin Books (South Africa) (Pty) Ltd, 24 Sturdee Avenue,
Rosebank, Johannesburg 2196, South Africa

Penguin Books Ltd, Registered Offices:
80 Strand, London WC2R 0RL, England

First published in Penguin Books 2011
1   3   5   7   9   10   8   6   4   2

PUBLISHER'S NOTE
This is a work of fiction. Names, characters, places, and incidents either are the product of
the author's imagination or are used fictitiously, and any resemblance to actual persons,
living or dead, business establishments, events, or locales is entirely coincidental.

LIBRARY OF CONGRESS CATALOGING IN PUBLICATION DATA
Magary, Drew.
The postmortal / Drew Magary.
p. cm.
ISBN 978-0-14-311982-1
1. Aging—Prevention—Social aspects—Fiction.   2. Longevity—Social aspects—
Fiction.   I. Title.
PS3613.A33P67 2011
813'.6—dc22   2011014531

Printed in the United States of America
Set in Minion Pro and DIN   •   Designed by Sabrina Bowers

TO MY WIFE AND CHILDREN

I was standing staring at the world. And I still can't see it.

—MASTODON, 2009

THE
POSTMORTAL

A Note about the Text:
From the Department of Containment,
United North American Territories

FEBRUARY 6, 2093

In March 2090, a worker for the Department of Containment named Anton Vyrin was conducting a routine sweep of an abandoned collectivist compound in rural Virginia when he stumbled upon an eighth-generation wireless-enabled projected-screening device (WEPS.8) that was still functional after charging. Stored inside the device's hard drive was a digital library containing sixty years' worth of text files written by a man who went by the screen name John Farrell.

The text files appear to have been written as posts for a blog or online journal. It's impossible to know which of these files Farrell actually published in a public forum, as all mentions of his name in the cloud as it now exists lead to sites whose servers were destroyed during the Great Correction. There is also no way of corroborating that John Farrell was a licensed end specialist for the United States government for twenty years prior to the Correction. All U.S. Department of Containment servers were destroyed in June 2079.

However, considering the level of painstaking detail and the highly personal nature of the entries, combined with many of the articles and interviews Farrell saved, his writing is itself evidence supporting its veracity. As such, his collected entries must be considered one of the definitive personal records of life in the former United States during the sixty-year period that followed the discovery of the cure for aging. It must also be considered the most important first-person account yet of the end specialization industry that thrived in America in the last part of the century.

Farrell was a remarkably fastidious record keeper. He used the LifeRecorder app to preserve and transcribe virtually every human interaction he had, and he incorporated many portions of those transcripts into his writing. In its entirety, the collection contains thousands of entries and several hundred thousand words, but for the sake of brevity and general readability, they have been edited and abridged into what we believe constitutes an essential narrative, and incontrovertible evidence that the cure for aging must never again be legalized.

NB: The whereabouts of Solara Beck are still unknown.

I

PROHIBITION:
JUNE 2019

"Immortality Will Kill Us All"

There are wild postings with that statement all along First Avenue. If you've been in Midtown recently, you've seen them. They're simple black-and-white posters. Just type. No fancy fonts or designs in the background. No web address. That one sentence is all they say, over and over again, down and across the hoardings. When I walked by them, they were clean, as if they had been posted the night before. But I noticed, as I got toward the end of the block, that one of them had already been defaced. Not on the lowest rung but the second from the bottom. Someone had used a cheap, blue ballpoint pen to write something underneath the slogan. It was small, but it was unmistakable: EXCEPT FOR ME.

The doctor I saw has an apartment located near the Fifty-ninth Street Bridge. I got the address from a banker friend. He told me 99 percent of the guys he knows in finance rushed to get the cure the moment it became available on the black market. So if you know a finance guy, it's not that hard to get the name of a doctor who can give it to you. Even now, after the arrests, and even after what happened in Oregon. In fact, it's much easier than getting weed, at least in my experience. All I needed was an address, a password, and a phone number on a scrap of paper. That was it.

I should have been required to do more to get it, like cross an ocean and fight off a tribe of bloodthirsty headhunters, or answer a series of complex riddles asked by an evil bridge troll, or defeat some really big guy using karate. Something like that. But I didn't need to do much of anything, and I didn't feel at all guilty about it. I still don't. Once I realized that I could get the cure, I instantly wanted it, more than I had ever wanted anything. More than any woman. More than any long-overdue sip of water.

Normally, any decision I confront is forced to navigate the seemingly endless bureaucracy of my conscience. Not this one. This impulse was allowed to bypass all that nonsense, to shoot through the gauzy tangle of second thoughts and emerge from me as pristine as when it first originated deep within the recesses of my mind. It was a want. A hunger. A naked compulsion that was bulletproof to logic and reason. No argument could be made against my profound interest in not dying.

The doctor's apartment is located in a doorman building, but the doorman wasn't exactly a palace guard. He didn't ask me to sign in. He didn't ask me who I was seeing. I'm not even sure he looked up from his racing form. I just walked into the elevator and pushed the button. All too easy.

I got out, walked down the hall, and knocked on the door of the apartment number I'd been given. A voice from the other side of the door, and seemingly from the opposite end of the apartment, asked me to identify myself. I said my name and that I was there to pick up Ella's toaster. There is no Ella, and she had not left a toaster at the apartment. I found this part of the process far more exciting than I should have.

I heard the doctor walking over to the door and I watched the knob turn. He didn't quite look the way I thought he would. He was middle-aged but still youthful looking. Tan. Sharp silver hair. He didn't look much older than forty. And more like a banker than a doctor. I expected someone a bit dweebier, with glasses and a lab coat and whatnot. Someone far more careful looking. I think I would have preferred that. He shook my hand without identifying himself and shepherded me through the door.

I have to say, visiting a doctor for illegal purposes is a far more satisfying consumer experience than going for legitimate purposes. You ring the bell, and, boom, there's the doctor. No hostile receptionist. No signing in. No presenting your insurance card. No forgetting to get your insurance card back after the hostile receptionist copies it. No eternal waiting. Hell, no waiting of any sort. It was lovely. I was tempted to ask the doctor if I could visit him like this for all my future ailments.

"So, John," he said, "you're here for the toaster."

"Yes."

"Okay, I need to see your driver's license."

"Okay." I handed him my ID. He began nodding.

"You're twenty-nine. Good. That's just about the perfect age. I don't give it to people over thirty-five."

"Why not?" I asked.

"Because it would be foolish. Here, sit."

He sat me down in a leather chair and took the seat opposite me. I didn't feel like I was talking to a doctor at all. He had the air of a very cool English professor.

"Now, do you know exactly how the cure works?"

I was briefly disappointed that he had stopped referring to the cure as "the toaster." I really wanted to see how long we could keep it up.

"Yes," I told him. "I think so. I mean, I know how it came about. And I've read everything about it that I could, like everyone has. Some of it conflicts. I'm not entirely certain what's true about it and what isn't."

"Do you know how gene therapy works?"

"Vaguely."

"Okay, well, I'm going to go over all this anyway, even if you know it. So, what this involves is me taking a sample of your DNA, then finding and altering—or, more precisely, deactivating—a specific gene in your DNA, and then reintroducing it into your body through what's known as a vector, or a carrier. In this case, that means a virus. So I'm going to take some blood from you today, isolate the gene, change it, create the vector virus, and then inject that vector back into your system at three distinct points: your inner thigh, your upper arm, and your neck. That's two weeks from now. And then we're done. After you go home, the virus will replicate the new gene code throughout your system. Within six months, it will be present in all your tissue, and the aging of your body will be permanently frozen where it is. The rest, after that, is up to you."

"Will it make me sick?"

"No. No side effects. No allergens."

"Is it guaranteed to work?"

"Well, I've had to reinject two or three people. But that's pretty rare, and it's never taken more than two tries to get it working. I won't charge you if I have to do it again."

"Can I still die afterward?"

"Yes. Of course you can. You can still catch a cold. You can still die of AIDS or a heart attack. You can still get cancer. People can still murder you. In fact, that's why I give people two weeks until they come back."

"What do you mean?"

He took a deep breath. "Well, you have to take a moment to consider what all this entails for you. When people come through my door, the first and only thing they think about is, 'Oh boy, I'm gonna live forever.' But they don't stop to consider what that means. They want to live forever, but they don't think about what they're going to have to live with. What they'll have to carry with them. And whether or not that's something they really, truly want. Let me ask you: Why do you want to do this? Is it out of vanity?"

"I don't think so. I'm just curious, I guess."

"Ah, but think about what curiosity is. Curiosity is seeking out answers to *your* questions. It's about satisfying everything you want to know about *you* or things around you. It's about your own personal fulfillment, isn't it? So, really, is there much difference between curiosity and vanity?"

He had me nailed there. I don't know why I tried to sugarcoat it for the doctor. I always lie to doctors. Maybe that's why I want to stay young forever and ever. So I can avoid situations where I inexplicably lie (poorly) to stern-looking medical professionals. I relented and gave him the raw truth.

"Okay," I confessed. "You got me. I don't want to die. I'm terrified of death. I fear there's nothing beyond it and that this existence is the only one I'll ever possess. That's why I'm here."

He patted my leg to give me reassurance. "That's why they're all here. Even the ones that believe in heaven and seventy-two virgins and every other good thing supposedly waiting for them in the afterlife. But again, this is no cure for death, even if everyone is calling it that. It's merely a cure for aging. In fact, if Malthus's theory is right, you certainly *will* die. It may be a hundred years from now. It may be ten thousand years from now. But it will happen. And not in a pleasant fashion, mind you. What this cure guarantees is that you will never die a natural, peaceful death. And you're going to have to spend the next two weeks asking yourself if it's worth all those extra years of knowing that your demise will inevitably come at the hands of disease, starvation, or a bullet."

I immediately pictured myself being gunned down in an alleyway, a smoking revolver barrel the last thing my eyes ever have a chance to focus on. Then the sliding door in my brain shifted and I was eighty-five years old on my deathbed, fat nurses sponging off my rotting skin.

"I don't think most people die natural, peaceful deaths," I said. "All the loved ones I've seen die have been sick, frail, and helpless. Undergoing chemo. Lying in hospitals. Soiling their beds. Two of my grandparents died alone, with no one to talk to. I don't think natural death offers much in the way of gentle relief. I think it's a slow, wrenching thing I'd like to try to get far, far away from."

"Okay."

He stood up and gestured to me to do the same.

"How many of your patients have come back after two weeks and decided they didn't want the cure?"

"Oh, I think you already know the answer to that. Come on. We'll take your blood in my lab."

He walked me over to the apartment's open kitchen. The cupboards and drawers were all white, painted ages ago and in a sloppy fashion, with big streaks of dripping paint frozen and hardened in place. Inside the cabinets, where you normally would see dishes, glasses, and assorted sundries, were medical supplies: swabs, gauze, syringes, scalpels, tongue depressors, etc. I marveled at the lack of food or items to help prepare it. He quickly got out everything he needed to extract the blood and slapped a tourniquet onto my arm.

"What do you do if you want to eat here?" I asked him.

"I never eat here. Tell me, what do you do for a living?"

"I'm a lawyer."

"Oh dear. Another lawyer? I should put a moratorium on you folks. Last thing we need are a bunch of godforsaken lawyers hanging around forever. Here comes the needle."

He pulled my arm toward him, gave a firm slap to the underside of my elbow, and drew one large vial of my blood. I'd never stopped to consider my own blood before. I'd only really thought of it as the fluid that occasionally seeps out of my body, causing me great alarm. Nothing deeper than that. Now I stared at the blood filling the vial, and it was that deep, rich, unmistakable red, the kind of red they try to reproduce in paint and in lipstick but can never quite match. It looked vital, as if it had its own pulse. Active. Alive. If all went according to plan, I thought, it would soon return to me even more so.

"Let me ask you something, Doc."

"Of course."

"What's your normal practice? What's your doctor day job?"

"Orthopedics."

"Ah."

"I almost went into plastic surgery, but I didn't. Thank goodness. Those guys will be doing nothing but sucking out fat from now on."

"So you run a successful practice, yes? I assume you make a nice living just through your day job."

"That I do."

"Then why do this? Why do more than what you need to do? Why risk losing your license to practice medicine by giving this out? Hell, you're risking your *life*. What's the benefit for you, besides making extra money you really don't need?"

He grinned. "Well, John, with this cure I have the power to grant anyone the ability to live thousands of years—possibly forever. Let's just say that it appeals to my curiosity."

He bandaged me up.

"This won't cause me to sprout fangs and sleep in a coffin, will it?"

"No, that's a different gene. Would you like me to alter that one?"

"No, no thank you."

"Well, you're all set. I have you in the books for the same time two weeks from now. Don't bother calling to confirm. Just show up with your money—no denominations higher than fifty dollars, please. I'll be here."

(Note: the total cost was seven thousand dollars. Not bad.)

I walked to the door. Four million more questions flooded into my brain. I felt the urge to ask all of them simultaneously. Instead, I offered only one.

"One last thing."

"Sure," he said.

"Have you given it to yourself?"

"Of course I have."

"But you're over thirty-five."

He shrugged. "Oh well. I'll live. I'll see you in two weeks, John."

A cursory wave goodbye and the door shut behind him. I walked back out into the street. A massive thunderstorm had come and gone while I was getting my blood drawn, and as I walked out, all that remained in the sky was that odd, sickly glow that happens when a thunderstorm clears out at summer twilight. It's an unsettling kind of light. Almost puce colored, as if the sky hasn't been feeling well. I was stuck between the violent darkness of the storm and the last flickering embers of daylight.

I rushed home. And now here I am, a day later, comfortably seated in immortality's waiting room.

DATE MODIFIED:
6/7/2019, 8:47 A.M.

"Death is the only thing keeping us in line"

I know it's mere coincidence, and yet I find it discomforting that the pope would officially come out and damn all postmortals to hell right in the middle of my mandatory deliberation period. This article posted ten minutes ago:

Vatican Threatens Cure Seekers with Excommunication

By Wyatt Dearborn

BUDAPEST (AP)—The pope today issued his strongest condemnation yet of the so-called cure for death, officially codifying it as a sin and promising to excommunicate permanently from the Roman Catholic Church anyone found to have received it, including priests.

Still on his weeklong goodwill tour of eastern Europe, the pontiff purposely chose to deliver his edict in the city of Budapest. Hungary is one of only four industrialized nations, including Russia, Brazil, and the Netherlands, that have officially legalized the cure.

"This cure is an affront to the Lord and His work," the pontiff told a crowd of nearly seventy-five thousand at Puskás Ferenc Stadium. "But more than that, it is an affront to our fellow man. What responsibility will we feel compelled to bear for one another if we know we can eternally put off facing the Lord's judgment? Death is what makes us humble before God—knowing that our lives will come to an end and that when that end arrives we will be forced to answer for them. If we answer not to Him, to whom do we answer? Death is the only thing keeping us in line."

The pope then went on to issue this warning: "You cannot avoid God's judgment. Not even if you live for another hundred thousand years. This planet and the sun that keeps it alight are all fleeting. There is no 'forever' down here and to believe so is a blasphemy. That's why, from this point forward, the Vatican officially condemns the taking of the cure as a sin and an excommunicable, unforgivable offense."

The pope's words were met mostly with silent reverence from the crowd. But thousands protested outside the stadium, nearly all of them in their teens and twenties.

"The pope hasn't condemned us," countered Sasha Delvic, a twenty-three-year-old student. "It's his church he's just condemned—to a life of obscurity. How can he expect the people of his faith to accept dying while everyone else out there goes on being happy and healthy? It's insane. He'll lose constituents by the millions.

"No one should listen to him," she added. "He's just a stupid old man."

It is believed the pope chose to deliver his address in Budapest as an attempt to pressure the Hungarian government to begin drafting anti-cure legislation. But thus far, here in one of the youngest countries on the planet according to median age, very few government officials appear willing to speak out in favor of doing so.

When I was a kid, I saw religion as insurance against death. It's what the preachers on TV used to say. You're better off believing in God, they'd warn you, *just in case.* Because you'd hate to arrive at the gates of heaven a nonbeliever and find out the Christians had been right all along. It was a pretty ingenious line of thinking. It almost made me want to go to church. Not enough to actually go, but still.

I wonder if we've completely flipped the script on that now. I wonder if the cure represents insurance against religion. Because what if the pope is wrong? If I forgo the cure and end up dying at seventy to please a Lord who turns out to not exist, I'm gonna feel like a real jackass. Isn't it better to live an extra thousand years or so, just in case?

I guess I'll find out at some point. Some very, very distant point. Twelve more days till the cure.

DATE MODIFIED:
6/8/2019, 7:05 P.M.

"I'm always gonna get my period"

Until the other night, I hadn't told anyone that I'm in the middle of getting the cure. I didn't tell my dad or my sister or anyone at work—didn't consult them either. They don't know I've done it, and I sure as hell don't know if they have. I didn't even tell the banker friend who gave me the address. For one thing, I haven't finished the process yet, so I'd feel a bit foolish telling everyone that I'm about to live forever, only to find out a week from now that my doctor has been caught and thrown in Rikers.

But more to the point, I have yet to meet a single person who has publicly admitted it. I think we've all collectively adopted the unspoken rule that you don't mention it out in the open. Like getting a nose job. Every discussion I've had about it has been conducted strictly in hypothetical terms. "Would you get it?" "What if it were legal? Would you get it then?" "Would you fly to Brazil and do it? I heard about a bunch of people at work who are taking sudden 'vacations' to Rio." Stuff like that. But no one has ever said to me, "Yes, I got it"—which is just so weird. Clearly, people are going to get it. If a random person like me can go and have it done, I have to assume that I'm not alone. But I suppose there's just too much uncertainty right now to go around parading the fact.

Anyway, I was more than happy to keep all this to myself. But Katy got it out of me. She's an interrogator, my roommate. Aggressively interested in other people. Present her with wine, and she'll pepper you with questions until you feel as if you're under a hot lamp. She delights in extracting key information from you and then playing with it—stretching it out and bouncing it against the walls until she grows bored with it.

We were sitting in our apartment, watching the news. They were doing their nightly cure story, and Katy turned to me, clear out of the blue. She was squinting one eye.

"Did you get it?"

"What? No."

"Oh my God," she said. "You are the absolute *worst* liar ever."

"I'm not lying."

"You fell dead silent when that report came on just now. Don't try to hide it. I have excellent cure-dar."

"Cure-dar?"

"Uh-huh. Remember when I said Jesse Padgett had it done? She totally did. You could tell because she'd clam right up whenever the subject was mentioned. Just like you did there. You should look in the mirror. Your face is so red right now. You look like a giant tomato."

"Aw, Jesus."

"You did it! You did it! You did it! I can't believe this. You slippery bastard!"

She got the confession in record time and beamed in delight at the accomplishment. Her eyes bugged and she smiled proudly. She has a snaggletooth and loves to flaunt it as a distinguishing feature.

"Don't go broadcasting this all over the place, all right?"

"Oh, I won't tell anyone," she said. "I promise you that. But you're gonna tell me everything."

"They haven't even finished yet."

"They haven't finished? What do they do to you? Tell me, tell me, tell me. I heard you get sixty shots, all in the armpit."

"No. They just took my blood, and then a week from now they give me three shots. That's it."

"That's it? Holy underwear. What did it cost?"

"Seven thousand bucks."

"*Seven grand?*"

"Shh!"

"That's nothing! That's less than nothing! I once expensed a tab at Lusardi's that was bigger than that! You have to tell me how to do it."

"I can't."

"Oh, bullshit."

"This doctor will only take direct referrals from a small circle of people he knows, and one of them happens to be a guy I know. No extra degrees of separation beyond that. It's like a drug dealer, I swear."

"So just give me your guy's name and I'll say I know him."

"I can't."

"Oh, please. Who made you guardian of the fountain? What—is this like your little boys' club? Do you all go get the cure and then take a naked swim together? Is that it?"

"I just don't want to get anyone in trouble. They asked me not to refer anyone."

"This is so unfair. Who's the guy you know? Is it Schilling? I bet it's Schilling."

"No . . ."

Another crooked, triumphant grin. "It is! This is amazing. I don't even need a polygraph. All I have to do is ask you a question and wait for your head to blow up."

"Regardless, you still need the address and phone number."

"Well, why hold it back? Honestly. Give me one good reason, apart from your little pinky swear not to, why I don't deserve the information and you do. I've never known you to be timid about anything. But I ask you about this and you turn into a mute. Come on. Don't be so annoying. It's not like people won't find out at some point that you've had it done. In fact, judging by how quickly I found out, the whole city should know by morning."

"Okay. Fine. I will give you all the information. *After* I've gotten the final shots a week from now. And you have to pay the cable bill for six months."

"What?"

"Referral fee," I said. "It's only fair."

"You're such a goddamn lawyer."

"Those are the terms. We have a deal?"

"We do. I can't believe you found it. Oh, I love you! Thank you, thank you, thank you, thank you! Yes! You know, I've been trying to find a curist for months now. I am so relieved. This is gonna be incredible. Except . . . You're sure this guy's legit, right?"

"Yes."

"Because you know about all the bogus ones out there, right? How do you know this guy isn't gonna inject you with Cascade? Remember the lady in Queens who had that done to her last week?"

"I'm certain it won't be Cascade. For one thing, this doctor has no dishes to wash."

"Okay, then I'll wait until you get your shots. And if you don't drop dead on the spot, I'm definitely calling him. I am so excited! I'm gonna be twenty-seven forever! And I don't have to go to São Paulo to do it!"

She sprung up and rushed to the kitchen, then froze halfway there.

"Oh, Christ," she said. "Do you know what I just realized? I'm always gonna get my period. That sucks."

"Seems like a minor sticking point."

"We could be roommates forever too. Do you want to sign a hundred-year lease?"

"No."

"Your loss, because I am gonna party my ass off until the year 5000!"

Then she poured a glass of Shiraz to the brim and danced on the sofa.

DATE MODIFIED:
6/13/2019, 10:02 A.M.

"Cake-batter mixes are one of the great food innovations of the past sixty years"

That's the kind of thing you hear when you talk to my dad for any considerable length of time. I don't want to say he goes off on tangents, because that would suggest that he has a main topic from which to deviate. I enjoy his company because he never answers any question with the phrase "I don't know." He either knows or he'll talk out his ass until he's convinced you he knows. It's a skill I've yet to master.

I'm due to get the cure finished off on Monday. I should be all excited at the prospect of beginning the rest of my indefinitely elongated life, but I've found myself increasingly impatient as I grow closer. All I've done the past few days is calculate population figures and think about death—mine and anyone else's. I don't enjoy thinking about death, which is one of the reasons I wanted the cure in the first place. Now, I seem to be obsessing over it. The irony of it all is infuriating.

All this ruminating and provocation was beginning to feel like a vise on my head. I was getting sick of endlessly talking about it with myself. I needed an outlet. Someone besides Katy. Any time I bring up the cure with her, she screams out in ecstasy and packs a bowl. She's got a fabulous attitude about the whole thing, but I needed to go a bit deeper. Besides, I was already visiting my dad for the weekend, and I would have burst like a grape if I didn't fess up.

My dad has lived in northwest Connecticut for the past fifteen years, in one of those towns you can only get to on Metro-North by switching trains at Bridgeport. Then you have to go all the way to Waterbury, at which point you feel as if you've been dumped off in a nuclear fallout zone. Towns around Waterbury are populated exclusively by elderly people and kids who took enough acid to permanently unmoor their brains. After more than five days in the vicinity, I have a hard time not wanting to tear off my own skin. Once you're in that part of the state, there is nothing to do except eat and drink. And that's how my old man has spent his retirement: eating and drinking.

He picked me up at the Waterbury station and drove me home. He had cold beer and a dish of mixed nuts waiting at the house for us. It was his way of entertaining the way my mom might have, way back when—of adding a nice little flourish to my arrival. I appreciated it greatly. Once we sat down, I couldn't hold back.

"I'm getting the cure."

"What?"

"I'm getting the cure. Final shots are on Monday."

"So it's real?"

"Far as I know."

"Well, I'll be damned."

He sat there. He had an inscrutable look on his face. I couldn't read him in the slightest.

"How did you get it?" he asked.

"I knew someone. It wasn't that hard. Do you want it? The doctor said he wouldn't give it to anyone over thirty-five, but I bet I could convince him otherwise, or find someone else to do it."

"Won't give it to anyone over thirty-five? Well, isn't that a bitch? I suppose I'm a member of the 'unluckiest generation' now. That's what they called it in the news report. 'The last to die,' they said. It's like the people who died just as TV was being invented. That had to have been aggravating. You spend your whole life sitting next to some giant radio. And when they finally get around to adding picture to the sound, you're dead as a doornail. Not really fair."

"Like I said, I still think I can get it for you."

"How much did it cost?"

"Seven thousand bucks."

"I don't know. Seems like a lot."

"It's eternal youth, Dad. It's not gonna cost the same as a gumball."

"No, you're probably right about that. It's just . . . I dunno. Look, I don't mean to sadden you. Because I'm happy as can be that you found something that will keep you healthy forever and ever. I really am. It's a comfort to me to know that you're not going to grow old and have crappy knees and hit a golf ball no more than eighty yards. But each day I'm down here is another day I'm away from your mother."

We sat quietly for moment. My mom died when I was fifteen years old, right after we moved from Buffalo. She died of cancer. For two years, she went through chemo and radiation. She aged forty years in a whisper. All her hair fell out. They kept going back to cut out parts of her again and again. And she stayed alive because she knew this was the only life she'd ever have. No reincarnation. No afterlife. Just this. That's all you get. By the time the cancer had colonized every inch of her frame, she'd dropped to ninety pounds and looked like a mummy preserved in oil. Just a skeleton with a tarp of skin stretched out over it. There was nothing about her dying that was good.

"You really think you'll see her again?" I asked him.

"Oh, I have no doubt of that."

"But she'll always be there. Why spend the next few years just sitting here waiting? Why not do something with the time you have?"

"I do plenty!"

He gestured to his railroad timetables. My dad collects them in bulk. Five times a year he'll drive to some random state and attend a timetable convention. He's the only person at those things who isn't dressed in overalls and a Fruit of the Loom T-shirt.

"I'm just saying that there may be places and people that you still have to discover. You may find a new passion, like antique boats or something."

"Antique boats? Why would I like antique boats? I've met those boating guys. They're all completely cheesy."

"It's just an example, Dad. It could be anything. I just don't think there's any need for you to sit here, waiting for the end."

He grew angry at that remark. "I'm not waiting for the end, John. I'm not in a rest home. I have a life, one I'm glad to have. I'm not some sad old thing you have to come and check on occasionally like a houseplant. But I have a date with your mom somewhere down the line, and I don't want to postpone it longer than I have to. I don't judge your decision to loiter around this planet forever, like a skateboarder outside a movie theater. And I would hope that you'd refrain from judging mine."

"I'm sorry. I didn't mean to make you mad or to judge you. I'm being selfish here. I know that. I just don't want to see you go."

"You're gonna have to. I'm sorry."

We sat quietly for another moment. I checked my watch. It was 9:19 P.M. When I was in grade school, a friend told me that every conversation pauses awkwardly at 20 and 40 minutes past the hour, because the ghosts are flying over your head. So in my head I rounded up to 9:20. For Mom's sake.

"I know it was hard to see your mom go," he said. "I was there. I wouldn't wish the anguish you, your sister, and I went through on anyone. I know why you'd want to hold on to me so fiercely after that. I really do. If your mom were still around, you can bet I'd turn over fourteen grand to your doc quick as lightning. But she isn't, and I've accomplished everything here that I wanted to do. I'm comfortable. So I don't want you to think this is some awful thing that's going to happen to me down the line. It's fine. Besides, I'm already old. I assume this thing doesn't take thirty years off your odometer, correct?"

"Yeah, unfortunately. It only puts you in park, not reverse."

"See, I don't want to stay old forever and ever. That's why everyone your age is probably rushing out to get it. It's not that people don't want to die. It's that they don't want to grow old. Well, I missed out on that chance."

"The unluckiest generation."

"The unluckiest generation." He sipped his drink. "You know I'm still due to be around here for a while, don't you? I drink red wine. I eat my asparagus. I'm going to be annoying you for quite some time."

"I wouldn't have it any other way."

"If everyone ends up your age, that's gonna be one hell of a party."

"Could be."

"What do we do about your birthday? Do we wish you a happy twenty-ninth birthday every year from here on out? Do we have to get you presents every year for the next thousand damn years?"

"I'll just take a cake."

"I can do that. I can bake a cake, you know. They have some incredible cake mixes in the store now. They have fudge ripples. Sprinkles. Everything. And they taste just as good as the ones people make from scratch. I'm telling you, cake-batter mixes are one of the great food innovations of the past sixty years. They are a fabulous, fabulous product. I suppose you'll still be around when they find a way to improve them."

"How will they do that?"

He thought for a moment. "They'll fly. In the future, you'll get to eat flying cake."

He poured me a glass of whiskey, and we proceeded to talk about the Bills and graham-cracker piecrusts and his ten-year crusade to have a stoplight put in at the intersection of Rand Avenue and Route 118. I happily would have stayed there, talking to him about anything and everything, for God knows how long.

DATE MODIFIED:
6/19/2019, 10:34 A.M.

The Woman in the Elevator

They changed the slogan on those First Avenue wild postings: DEATH BE PROUD. I don't think it's anywhere near as clever as the first one they tossed up there. Nearly all the posters had already been defaced by the time I saw them. There was one piece of graffiti that I particularly enjoyed. It had been done by someone who was clearly skilled with a can of spray-paint. It was the grim reaper, with his scythe plunged straight through his own back, impaling him and leaving him dangling in midair. He was stone dead.

Unlike two weeks ago, yesterday was an insanely gorgeous day. Razor-sharp blue sky, as if you were staring at it through polarized lenses. I took this as a good omen, and walked to the doctor's office from the subway using my finest New York walking technique: ass tight, legs churning, chin up, purposely avoiding eye contact with any people or objects. I can walk ten blocks like that in five minutes, even if you spring a tour bus group on me in the middle of it.

I had a faint trace of anxiety way in the back of my mind as I approached Dr. X's building. It had been two weeks. He could have been arrested or killed. Or he could have already fled the country for Brazil, taking with him thousands of dollars in cash (all in denominations under fifty dollars, of course). Or maybe those people decrying the cure as a giant hoax were onto something.

And the money. I'm not much of a cash person. I've never carried more than a hundred bucks on me at a time. Now I had 350 twenty-dollar bills to deal with (the clerk had no fifties). They wouldn't fit in my wallet, and I didn't want to keep them there anyway, since it would have bulged out and looked all too conspicuous. So I wadded the bills up and put them in my messenger bag. But my bag has roughly nine thousand pockets, and I'm the type of person who will put something somewhere and then immediately forget where the hell I put it. So on the subway ride there, I did this thing where I'd feel for the cash, only I'd feel the wrong pocket; then I'd quietly freak out and frisk the bag until I found the bulge. This happened at least three times.

But I was out of the subway now, and the crisp day quickly cleared all those niggling obsessions from my mind. It was nice out, and I was about to stay twenty-nine years old for the rest of my life. Nothing else mattered.

Again, the doorman let me sail right through to the elevator. I jammed the button and stared at the number glowing above the door as it moved progressively downward: eight, seven, six, five ... still on five ... still on five ... still on five ... Jesus, was someone herding buffalo into the car? It began moving again, finally settling on L.

The door opened, and out stepped an unreasonably attractive woman. My fervent urge to get in the elevator was instantly destroyed. She was nearly six feet tall (I'm six foot six), naturally tanned. California blonde. If she hadn't been standing before me, I'd have sworn she could only be created with Photoshop. She radiated like some kind of bright-shining beacon, welcoming all to a newly discovered paradise, a gateway to unimaginable happiness.

She saw me, gave a small smile, and said hi in a party girl's raspy voice. I said hi back. I think I said hi back. I may have simply mouthed it and forgotten to make an audible sound. That's probably what I did.

She walked right past me. I turned to look. So did the doorman. She was the promise of eternal youth made flesh. A feeling of incredible urgency lit up my system. The kind of instant love you know isn't the real thing but feels like it all the same. She had an impossible body, athletic and voluptuous all at once. Somehow. Some way. I have no idea. I immediately hoped she was coming from Dr. X's office. I've never wanted to live forever so badly.

She breezed out of the entranceway and turned to walk down the street, out of view. I carefully etched the outline of her body into the most easily accessed part of my brain. That accomplished, I turned to the elevator to get back to business. It had already closed and gone back up. Eight, seven, six, five . . . still on five . . . still on five . . . Christ.

I made it to Dr. X's door and knocked again. He let me in. His eyes were bloodshot. He beckoned me in and closed the door. I immediately handed him the cash, relieved that I no longer had to be its guardian.

"Oh, excellent," he said. "Thank you. Would you like a receipt?"

"You give receipts?"

"Oh, sure. I mean, they're not explicit. They don't say, 'Hey, I did something illegal.' But I've had more than my fair share of clients who have employers that would happily cover the cost for this kind of thing."

Scores was within ten blocks of the building. I immediately put two and two together.

"Before we get started," I said, "I have a question."

"Always with the questions. I like that you're so inquisitive."

"There was a blonde woman I saw walking out of the building. She was attractive. Highly attractive. Was she here just now, getting the cure?"

"I can't answer that question. You know that."

"But she was, right?"

"Again, I can't answer that."

He gave me a look that told me she was.

"Can I have her number?"

"What did I just say? Look, do you want these shots or not?"

"Yes, yes! Sorry."

"Okay. Come on over to the chair."

He led me over to a chair in the corner of the apartment. It had a lap belt and straps to bind your wrists and ankles. I became alarmed. "What the hell is this?"

"The restraints help keep you in place during the injections," he said. "If I don't use them, you wiggle all over the place and the whole thing takes forever."

"I thought you said these were three simple shots."

"They are. But I have to inject them deep into your tissue. If you want, I can apply a small amount of local anesthesia to each area. I do it for some of the female patients."

"So this will hurt?"

"It's an ageless life, John. Did you really expect it to be painless?"

I relented and got in the chair. He buckled me in, and I quickly had a vision in my mind of him jumping into his closet and coming back out carrying a cattle prod and wearing a gimp mask. Instead, he wheeled a small cart toward the chair and uncovered the tray on top. There were three huge needles. Hell, they weren't even needles. They looked like railroad spikes. Katy thought you got sixty shots in your armpit. My dad heard a rumor that it was administered via a balloon enema. I would have preferred either option. I handle normal shots just fine. These were elephant shots.

"I do this fast. You'll feel pressure, and it'll sting. Badly. Here, hold this."

He handed me a stress doll, one of those rubber ones with eyes and ears that bulge out if you squeeze it. "I don't think I—"

"Trust me. You'll want it."

I held on. He plunged the needles into me in rapid succession and in increasing order of excruciating pain: first my shoulder (not bad), then my neck (agony), then my thigh (like reverse childbirth). I squeezed the stupid doll until its ears could practically touch opposite sides of the room. It was horrible, but it was over quickly. He bandaged me up, undid the restraints, and I breathed a sigh of relief.

"That it?"

"That's it," he said. "We're all done. Enjoy the rest of your life."

"Thank you."

He gripped my shoulder and looked me in the eye.

"No, I mean it. Enjoy it. You still never know how much of it you have left."

He patted me on the back and escorted me out. I pushed the elevator button. Again it stalled at the fifth floor. I couldn't have cared less this time. Down to the lobby I went. I stepped out into the flawless morning. I made it a point to find that blonde girl again one day. I now have all the time in the world to do it.

DATE MODIFIED:
6/20/2019, 2:06 P.M.

"You realize you can never retire now, right?"

Even if the cure is a complete hoax (and now that I've gotten it, that outcome is a virtual certainty), I still recommend you get it. The placebo effect is marvelous. I'm not supposed to feel supercharged from getting it, but I do. And if I find out ten years from now that it was all a lie, that's still ten years of tricking myself into feeling downright ebullient. I'll have to get it again after that.

I felt like I could run a marathon when I got out onto the street yesterday. But because I am far too lazy, I instead opted for a leisurely walk back downtown. I also stopped for a donut, because it felt like the right thing to do. As I walked down into the Forties, I could hear the growing sound of a crowd in the distance. After a few more blocks, everything came into relief. I was close to the UN. The pro-cure protesters were standing outside. And if there is a group of people out there even more fanatical than the pro-death supporters, it's the pro-cure supporters. They looked angry. One woman appeared to be shaking with rage as she walked around with a sign that said, LEGALIZE IT. YOU ARE LETTING US DIE. She paced in front of the building, stomping her feet like a T. rex.

I made a turn to go across to Second Avenue, but police had already put up a barricade. Helicopters flew over the scene. My only way out was back up First. I quickly turned around to get away. A small flock of new protesters was coming my way. One of them jammed a flyer into my hand.

"Don't take this shit lying down," he said. On top of the flyer was the headline THE CONSERVATIVE CASE FOR LEGALIZING THE CURE, BY ALLAN ATKINS. I didn't know you could now get Allan Atkins rants in flyer form. I turned to the crowd in front of the headquarters.

Normally, you see protesters demonstrating peacefully, walking in circles and whatnot. But these people were in rows, facing a single direction, pressed as close to the building as the cops would allow them to be. They didn't look content to simply voice their disapproval. They looked like they wanted in. I got back up into the Fifties and went across town and back down as fast as I could.

Once I was in our apartment, I downed some cheap champagne, ate a cold can of Chunky Soup, and watched a news report about what I had just waded through. Apparently, cops fired rubber bullets into the crowd an hour after I left. I'm pretty sure that's the first time they've done that.

Katy was already drunk by the time I got to the bar. I had to catch up.

"Happy cure day!" she screamed.

"Shh!"

"Okay, okay. I'll be quiet. But you have to tell me everything. And you owe me some doctor digits. Pony up, kid."

We retreated to a corner table. I gave her Dr. X's info. I told her everything: the chair, the needles, the protesters, etc. Even the blonde girl.

"She sounds hot."

"She was."

"Well, happy cure day. Cheers."

"Cheers."

"Do you realize that you're now always going to look the way you look at this exact moment? From this day on? This is how you'll look when you die. Do you realize that? It's like I'm looking at your corpse!"

"I didn't think of it that way, no. But thank you."

"You realize you can never retire now, right?"

"What?"

"You can't ever retire now. How are you gonna quit your job at sixty-five if you live for another five hundred years? Did you consider that?"

I had, but I'd placed it squarely in the "things I prefer not to think about" pile. "This just gives me more time to figure out what it is I really want to do," I told her. "I'm not preparing for some sixty-five-year end goal anymore. That rush to save money, or whatever, is all gone now."

"Ooh! I just thought of something else. Do you realize we could live another five hundred years and the Bills still may not win the Super Bowl?"

"Will you shut up about all the terrible stuff already?"

"Okay, okay. You're right. No dark stuff. This is your cure day. And in a few weeks we'll be celebrating mine too. Oh yes we will."

We staggered home at 6:00 A.M. and I took a shower before going to bed. I washed off the night and emerged from behind the curtain looking relatively fresh. I looked at myself in the mirror: brown hair, round face, sloped shoulders, two gentle smile creases bracketing my mouth. A barely noticeable strawberry mark under my eye. Slight stubble that steadfastly refuses to grow into anything resembling a normal beard. I took a photo of myself. This is how I look now. This is how I'll look when I die.

Happy cure day to me, indeed.

DATE MODIFIED:
6/21/2019, 3:45 P.M.

"The Conservative Case for Legalizing the Cure"

My friend Jeff sent me this an hour ago:

> I don't know if you've been watching Allan Atkins on TV lately, but he's becoming increasingly unhinged. I'm not political one way or another—though I think a lot of what he says is perfectly reasonable—but he delivered a diatribe yesterday that was pretty nuts. Here's the transcript:
>
> "I don't know what country this is anymore. How can this administration justify doing what it is doing? How? How is it possible? You tell me where it says in the Constitution that this cure is forbidden. You can't tell me, because it is not in the Constitution. It is *not*. If the class action lawsuit against the government over this ever gets kicked up to the Supreme Court—and it will, I can assure you—we're going to see the true face of this Court and of the administration that put many of its judges there. Because any judge worth his salt would look at this ban and see a *crime*. An outright crime against a country and its citizens. And the only judge that would ban it would be a fascist, activist judge who wishes to impose his or her individual beliefs upon us all.
>
> "See, this ban is liberal thinking at its absolute worst. They don't want to give you the freedom to make your own choices. They want you to *suffer*. They are antihuman. It's not enough for them to merely hate America. No, now they hate the very idea of humanity. *Humans are bad.* 'Oh, you can't live forever! You'll emit too much carbon! You'll throw

away too much garbage! An owl will die!' It's insane. It's this mentality that we, as human beings, are some ugly blight upon this world, that we do not deserve to live here with all the other innocent little animals—animals that *kill* and *rape* each other, just so you know. They believe that every action we take, every building we erect, every road we lay down is somehow a massive affront to their pristine vision of what the earth should look like. They are allergic to progress. This is a sickness. An absolute *sickness*. And now it is literally taking newfound years off our lives forever.

"I am a conservative, and that means that, unlike liberals, I deal with *reality*: with the way humans really behave and the way this world truly is. And that's what makes this war . . . this, this war on the cure, such a complete and utter crock. It has nothing to do with reality and everything to do with some utopian-liberal fever dream that is neither economically nor socially attainable.

"To you liberals out there listening—and I know you are, because our ratings' demographic breakouts make it plain as day—I have a question for you. If Abraham Lincoln were alive today, would you keep the cure from him? If Thomas Edison were alive today, would you keep the cure from him as well? Would you willingly let some of our greatest statesmen and inventors perish from the globe? Do you think you're helping the world if you do that? Or is there some special little Hollywood guest list of people you think deserve it? Not Mr. and Mrs. America, of course. They're far too *dumb*, and too busy polluting the world, to make your cut.

"Never mind the positive impacts of the cure, like the end of senior citizenship and all the Social Security and Medicare costs that go with it. Liberals don't have any time for that. They're too busy dwelling on all the horrible things we naughty humans will be doing with it. So you can't have this cure. Not even in this country, *where it was invented*. Can you believe that? Can you believe the gall? Liberals always say they love science. This is science! This is science! This cure is ours. We shouldn't be banning it; we should be *subsidizing* it. But we're letting other countries take this cure and run with it. Do we hand out our gold and oil reserves to other countries? No.

"That is why I say to you friends out there listening now: Buy a gun. Maybe you believe in taking the cure. Maybe you do not. But tell me if you want to live in a country where the government will let you die like this. Buy a gun. I know they're hard to come by now. I've bought plenty myself in recent months. I know my friends at Smith & Wesson— proud sponsors of the show, mind you—are trying to keep up with the demand. But if you have to drive to another state to do it, do it. Buy a gun. Buy as many as you can and learn to be skilled with them. Because the government is robbing you of your life, your liberty, and your happiness. You tell me what they're going to rob you of next. And you tell me what we should do if the Russians decide to visit our shores with an army of twenty million ageless soldiers, because you know they'd like nothing more. Buy a gun. Buy a damn gun! If you love America and what it stands for, *buy a gun*. Because right now I don't know if the country I live in is fit to be called the United States of America. And I'm willing to fight to get it back.

"Are you?"

Jesus.

DATE MODIFIED:
6/24/2019, 11:49 A.M.

"They're all getting divorced"

I've been at work all week, ever since getting the cure. This was lousy planning on my part. I should have booked a vacation in Aruba to coincide with it, so I could sit back, relax, have a fruity drink, smoke a joint, and bask in my own foreverness. And now Katy says I can't ever retire. That was all I could think about this week, as I got loaded with files: You will be doing this forever and ever and ever and ever. I'll always need money, I imagine. But I'm not quite sure what I'm doing here now. I have no life goal anymore. There are no golden years I have to stockpile for, and the idea of trying to save for some thousand-year retirement makes my head explode. I can't worry about the future, because now it's not finite. I can only worry about what's right in front of me at this very moment. It's kind of liberating, when I think about it. I could go be a bartender in Denmark if I wanted. I don't think I want to, but it's a nice option to have.

I said nothing to any of my coworkers about getting the cure. But yesterday, while I was doing research for some eight-thousand-page brief, a colleague pulled me aside. Well, not a colleague. One of my boss's colleagues. Someone far more senior than I am. He asked if I had a few minutes. This terrified me, because I thought I had fucked something up. Then he brought me to his office.

"Do you know anything about divorce law?" he asked.

"A bit."

"You need to learn it all. I know you're buried right now, but I'm organizing a special divorce seminar, and you need to attend."

"Why?"

"Because they're all getting divorced. All of them. Every banker and hedge fund guy in this town is looking for a way out right now. And if they aren't looking for a way out, their wives are. We have three guys here who are good with divorce statutes. That's not enough. We're gonna have to double or triple the load. We're talking about cases that could go on for ages. They haven't even defined the law on most of this stuff yet. Big, big moneymaker. It's where you're going to want to be. You don't want to stay in estate law. It'll be extinct within two decades."

"Jesus."

He then told me a story that had been relayed from one of the divorce partners at some other firm. One day some big swinging dick showed up at the firm, flew past the receptionist, and stormed into the lawyer's office.

"I want an annulment," shouted the big swinging dick.

The lawyer was nonplussed. "What?"

"You heard me! I want an annulment, and I want it done quickly."

"You can't get an annulment," the lawyer told him. "You've been married to your wife for twenty years."

"It was under false pretenses."

"What false pretenses?"

"She got the cure, and so did I. Completely changes the parameters of our original arrangement."

"Yes, but the cure didn't exist twenty years ago. For there to be false pretenses, it would have had to exist back when you signed the marriage license. And even then, I'm not sure how it would count."

"Listen, I'm a traditional man. I believe when you take that vow at the altar, you should abide by it. I vowed to stay with that woman all the days of my life. But I figured that was seventy or eighty years, tops. Now I'm supposed to spend the next thousand years with her? That's insane."

"I think what you want is a divorce."

"Why? So she can take everything I own? That woman has been spending every weekend with her personal trainer for six years. And then I have sex five times with a brand manager and *I'm* the asshole? You tell me how that makes sense. No, I want an annulment. Our marriage never would have existed if this cure had been around."

"I can't issue you an annulment under those circumstances. It's a binding marriage. It lasts forever."

"But no one told me forever would be this long!" the big swinging dick screamed. "I know I swore to be with her till death, but that was under a different definition of death, was it not?"

The lawyer stammered, "Well, that's a bit of a gray area right now."

"Well, ungray it. Make it black or make it white. I don't care which. I'll pay you five million if you can get it annulled. Five million. And if you can't, you get me my divorce. Then you charge me one hundred million in legal fees. That way I'm technically broke and she can't touch the cash. But I only pay you five million, and you ignore the rest of the debt."

"That's illegal in about thirty-seven different ways."

"I don't care! I want my money, and I want a clean break from that woman. Give her the town house if you need a negotiating tool. Between the dog hair and that glass sofa she bought, she's made the place all but unlivable anyway. And I want it done by fall. I have a two-week vacation in Majorca with our former nanny, and I don't want to cancel it. Get it done or I'll find a *real* lawyer."

And with that, the big swinging dick stormed right back out. Two hours later, his wife walked into the exact same lawyer's office, demanding the town house, the Hamptons estate, and "alimony for the rest of his miserable existence, regardless of length."

I'm definitely attending that seminar.

DATE MODIFIED:
6/26/2019, 10:10 P.M.

"I never thought I had the luxury of time—now it's all I'm gonna have"

Katy demanded I go with her to her cure consultation. I explained to her that there was no waiting room in Dr. X's apartment, and that I thought he probably preferred that everyone come alone. I made a compromise of walking her to the building, waiting outside, and grabbing some drinks with her after she got her blood drawn. "You'll get drunk even faster, since you'll have less blood in your system," I explained. She liked the idea.

When we got off the subway and walked east, we could hear the protesters outside the UN. Their numbers have continued to swell. I'm not sure they even take bathroom breaks anymore. The avenue has been barricaded much farther uptown than when I was last caught in the middle of it, as if there's a permanent weekend street fair. I was tempted to see if any vendors had set up shop among the throng, selling paper platefuls of greasy pad thai for two bucks. I resisted.

We stopped at a bagel shop and grabbed a quick lunch before her appointment. Again Katy brought up every cure-related scenario that came to her mind, both the good and the horrific. Mostly the horrific. She let her guard down a bit as we ate. My best friend is not the world's most introspective person. But she took a moment to stop being so damn bubbly.

"I don't know what I'm going to do after this," she said. "Suddenly, I'm all worried about the future."

"That's what Dr. X said. No one he sees thinks about it until they get it done."

"Am I doing the right thing? My grandma's got pancreatic cancer. Is it fair that she has to go through that and I get to side-step it?"

"You could still get cancer. You think your grandma would wish it on you?"

"No, I guess not. I don't know. I never really thought about my life before. I knew it was short, and that I should have a good time before it's over. That's about it. I never thought I had the luxury of time—now it's all I'm gonna have. I feel like I should probably do something more substantial with it."

"You've always had the luxury of time. You're twenty-seven. Cure or no cure, that's still plenty of time up ahead. It's yours to do with as you please. You're not obligated to be Mother Teresa now. This just means you have more time to do what you enjoy, or find what you enjoy, I guess."

"Well, you know what I enjoy."

"I do indeed."

She grew alarmed. "What if we run out of booze three hundred years from now?

"Oh, I think measures will be taken to prevent that sort of thing. We don't need glaciers. But vodka? They won't let the vodka dry up."

"Thank God."

We got up to leave and approached the doctor's building. We got to the southwest corner of the intersection on First. The building was across the avenue, on the southeast corner. The light turned for us to cross. Out of my peripheral vision I saw, on the northwest corner, a tall figure outside a candy shop. Blonde. An impossible body. She didn't have to turn for me to instantly recognize her. In fact, I had memorized the back of her quite capably. I stopped and held Katy back.

"That's the blonde! That's the blonde!"

Katy looked at her. "Oh, she *is* hot."

"I have to go talk to her. I'll meet you out front when you're finished."

I broke from Katy to cross the street. Katy hurried into the doctor's building. As I got to the opposite corner, the blonde turned and looked in my direction. I gave a tentative wave, trying to ascertain if she recognized me or not. She appeared unnerved, turned away from me, and began walking up the avenue. I crossed the street in hopes that she was simply walking away and not walking away from me. She gave another look back, saw me approaching, and quickened her gait. I took the hint and stopped outside the candy store, dejected. She blazed down the avenue, only pausing once to look back at the doctor's apartment building. I turned to do the same.

And that's when the doctor's apartment blew up.

Before I could notice anything, I heard a gigantic BOOM! Then a quarter of an instant later, the corner of the eighth floor blew out onto First Avenue in a single lash of flame. Right where the doctor's office once was. A makeshift hailstorm of pulverized white brick pummeled the traffic below. Hot black smoke began quickly scaling the outside of the building. A Friedrich air-conditioning unit—one of those heavy, old-school units—crashed into the sidewalk below. If anyone had been underneath it, it would have destroyed them.

Everything, everyone, everywhere froze to turn. *What the fuck just happened?* I looked to the doorway but couldn't see Katy. She was in there. She was on her way to the eighth floor, or she was there already. I didn't move. I stood still and hoped everything would suddenly reset and be put back in its proper place, because nothing about this felt possible. It felt absurd, like some kind of prank. The building was on fire, and I knew I needed to run in, but at the moment I didn't know how to run or speak or breathe. Horrible thoughts about Katy dying circled around my consciousness, like strange footsteps you hear outside your window in the dead of night. I heard the sirens blasting and growing louder and more intense, as if they were meant to echo the cries of those suffering inside.

My body finally unlocked, and I began running to the building as the fire truck pulled up alongside it. When I was in the middle of the intersection, I looked down the street and saw two more towers of smoke climbing up and up at points to the west, toward the Hudson—one less than half a block away, another much farther across town.

An elderly woman came running out of the building. She carried a small black Scottie with her and wore a gypsy's head wrap. I stepped in front of her to get her to stop. She stared at me, confused by it all.

"What just happened?" she asked.

I pointed inside. "Did you see anyone else on your way out?"

"No."

"Are you certain? I'm looking for a brunette woman. In her twenties. You saw her. Tell me you saw her coming out."

I held her shoulders tight, begging her for a response.

"I didn't see anything!"

She wrested herself away from my grip and fled. A small number of tenants came out of the emergency stairwell and ran up First. I held the door open for them, let them pass, and then began flying up the stairs. The flow of tenants petered out as I climbed higher. I got to the eighth floor and came out into a lightly smoky hallway. There was a door to a freight elevator room at the end of the hall and beyond that a door to a second hallway where the doctor's apartment was. I ran to the end of the corridor and saw the door of the freight elevator room open. I hoped to see Katy and the doctor hand in hand, making their way out safely. It was a fireman. He stopped me and turned me around.

"My friend is in there!" I screamed.

"I can't let you go. You have to get downstairs right now. Go. Go!"

"Is anyone alive? I'm looking for Katy Johannson."

"Get the fuck out of here!"

I relented and walked back to the stairwell. The fireman turned and reentered the freight elevator room, and I immediately doubled back to go find Katy. The fireman was still on the other side of the door when I opened it, now clearly angry I had defied him. He raised a fist and sent me back where I came from. I heard a huge crash, like a ceiling caving in, and I pictured my best friend pressed and flattened and desperate for air. The door to the stairwell opened and a wave of firemen filed by at top speed and pushed me to the side. Heavier smoke began to fill the hallway and I began to swoon and feel as if the walls and floors were molten and elastic. I retreated to the stairwell like a pathetic child and listened to the firemen shouting orders at one another from the other side of the door. I sat there trying to absorb every sound and sight because it was all I could do. I wasn't remotely qualified to take any sort of bold action. All I could seize was proximity. I felt the urge to run to the doctor's apartment and sit down in the blaze. I kept hoping for Katy to pass by or call me, but instead there was a big, deafening nothing. So I sat on the gray concrete steps, in the sickly fluorescent lighting, waiting. I don't know how long I was there. No one passed by. Eventually, another fireman opened the door and ordered me to go down to ground level.

I walked down the stairs and out into the street. I smelled my sleeves and they reeked of smoke, of things burned that should never be burned. Up First, I could see yet another plume of smoke. Down First, I heard the swarm of protesters yelling and screaming. People were running up the avenue, some to the bridge, instinctively, as a sort of automatic 9/11-type gut response. Many seemed to have the palpable urge to get off the island, to get as far away from the center of the imaginary bull's-eye as humanly possible.

I stayed where I was, as close to Katy as the FDNY would allow. I checked my phone and saw the EXPLOSIONS ROCKING MANHATTAN headline. The cops and firefighters continued shuttling in and out, saying nothing to me because saying nothing is what they have to do. I checked Katy's status updates. There was nothing since the one she posted just before the explosion. She must have posted it while she was in the elevator.

DrinksOnKatyJ: u folks better get used to the idea of ME sticking around here a long, long time! 12:13 p.m.

That was the last thought going through her mind. She was ready to welcome another thousand years of joy and happiness, and I had promised it to her. I had brought her to this place. I had planted that thought in her mind. I could've stayed strong and never told her a goddamn thing, but I barely put up a fight. Deep down, I wanted her to know it all. I wanted the cheap thrill of being her little cure matchmaker.

And now she's gone. No hospital admitted her. No one saw her leave. There's nothing left of her. All the extra plans and hopes and dreams she had for herself will remain just that, forever.

I can't move.

DATE MODIFIED:
7/3/2019, 4:08 P.M.

At the Protests

Our apartment is uncomfortably spacious now. I see the wine stains on the couch, and I hear Katy's manic giggling like she's still present. I don't ever recall seeing her moody or displeased, which makes her abrupt and violent end all the more unbearable. All I can do is keep drinking and banter with her in my mind.

A pro-cure blogger named Ladyhawke posted another account of what happened yesterday, as witnessed from outside the UN. Apparently, she was one of the protesters.

How Many Have to Die?

We were facing the UN and screaming our heads off when the explosion drowned us out for a millisecond. But no one knew what the hell was going on. One person in the crowd screamed, "They're trying to kill us!" and that was enough to set people fleeing in every direction. One guy pushed me to the ground so he could run past me. I was lucky; I saw another guy, who couldn't have been older than seventeen, fall and get his head stepped on. I have no clue if he ever got back up. I got up and immediately began running up First Avenue. I assumed it was a terrorist attack. I mean, it *was* a terrorist attack. But I thought it was, you know, a *terrorist* terrorist attack. Someone from Saudi Arabia or something. My run up the avenue was complicated by the fact that everyone was staring at their damn phones and tablets, and not at the road ahead of them. So I got bumped into from behind and from the side, as if someone had released a stampede of blind bulls onto the street. I got kicked in the back of the leg. Now I have a black welt there the size of a lemon.

Needless to say, now that we know what really happened, that these doctors had been systematically targeted—I'd argue they were assassinated—we are pissed. We're already gathering outside the UN and the Capitol right now. We will number in the tens of thousands by morning, I can promise you that. How many more doctors will the president allow to be blown to pieces before he finally realizes he's made a huge mistake? We've been protesting peacefully for months, but these pro-death people—who *got what they wanted*, by the way—are free to just randomly kill innocent people? These are doctors who treasure life enough to bestow more of it upon the rest of us. We're through being nice about this. We're not taking no for an answer this time around.

—LADYHAWKE

I don't know where any of this is going, and I don't know which side will come out on top, or which side even deserves to. All I know is that I feel an increasing urge to get the hell away from it all.

DATE MODIFIED:
7/4/2019, 8:47 P.M.

"A little bit of bloodshed now or a lot later on"

Katy's family is making funeral arrangements. All the organized grieving happens at light speed, as if it must be done before you realize what you're grieving over. I miss Katy desperately. The bomb goes off in my mind every five minutes, and I'm left no less shaken by it each time. I have fevered daydreams of a blonde running from me and taking out a phone, pushing the secret code number that kills my best friend. I told the police about her. Every detail of her face and figure. I could have sculpted it from clay. They had a crude sketch drawn and posted. No one has responded. I'm not terribly optimistic.

I've spent most of my time reading everything I can about the bombings. The same articles over and over again. I don't know why I keep reading them—perhaps to help drive the reality of it home. They just released a partial list of the doctors killed. Their count (minus bystanders like Katy) appears to have settled at nine: Charles Bane III; Sofia Gonzalez; Gim Lau; Jocelyn McManus; Vishal Mehta; Frederick Polycronis, DDS; Ian Rosenhaus; Pameer Sanji; and Ameet Thakkar. I know Dr. X wasn't a woman, nor was he Indian or Asian (unless he was very, very good at keeping his identity hidden, which it seems now he was not). That leaves three possibilities from this list: Bane, Polycronis, and Rosenhaus. At some point, they're going to release his picture. I don't know if I can stand to find out which one is him. I gave him seven thousand bucks in cash to keep me young for the rest of my life. And now he'll never get to use it. The fact that he gave himself the cure only makes the finality of his death harder to take. Who the hell knows how many lifetimes were just robbed from him.

I should have seen something like this coming. What

happened in Oregon should have prepared me for it. But the truth is that I didn't pay much heed to what took place in Oregon. It happened all the way across the country, so I guess even news about murder suffers from East Coast bias. There's the added fact that I live in Manhattan. When you live here, you can pretend the rest of the world doesn't exist.

I can't do that anymore. What happened yesterday and what happened in Oregon are now so strongly bonded that it feels like Eugene is located right across the Hudson. A reporter named Mike Dermott wrote a huge piece about Oregon last week. I never bothered to read it before now. But I've read it a dozen times in the past couple of hours. I can nearly recite it from memory. Copied from *Slate*:

The Man Who Conquered Death

By Mike Dermott

Graham Otto never set out to conquer death. He was just hoping to help out the redheads of the world.

"I'm a redhead," he noted in his private journal, to which I was granted exclusive access by the Otto family. "I've yet to meet a redheaded guy who enjoys being a redhead." The name of the gene is MCR1. It's located on chromosome 16. And according to the complete map of the human genome, it's the gene that causes red hair (along with a rare condition called brittle cornea syndrome). Working with a team of fellow geneticists, Otto targeted this gene in hopes of finding a way to color hair through gene therapy. "It wasn't the most noble of genetic experiments," he wrote. "It was the sort of thing a wealthy university like U. Oregon does from time to time, when it feels like playing around."

"He was excited about the potential business aspect of it. We all were," recalls his wife, Sarah. "Frankly, I was just thrilled at the prospect of never having to pay three hundred dollars for highlights ever again."

He didn't fit the traditional scientist mold. Otto had attended Oregon on a partial scholarship for track and placed as high as eighth in the two-mile event at the 2000 Prefontaine Classic. He was an outgoing man, who always preferred company while working in the lab and who was always able to talk about his work in ways that laymen found not only accessible but downright fascinating.

"I think that's what made him such a great teacher," says UO president Raymond Lack. "He was passionate about his work but not to the point where he became insular. You never felt like he was talking over your head about any of this stuff. He made it sound interesting, even entertaining. And trust me, that's not a commonplace trait among his peers. His communication skills were a rare gift for anyone, in any profession."

In terms of changing hair color through gene therapy, Otto was a miserable failure. The problem wasn't extracting the redhead protein from the gene. That proved easy for Otto and his self-described team of "Hair Bears." The problem was replacing the color. "If you take away a person's genetically predisposed color, you essentially give them colorless hair—albino hair," he wrote. "You have to eliminate that protein in the gene *and* you have to find a way to add the color of your preference, and that's where the engineering becomes close to a technical impossibility." Otto experimented with altering proteins found elsewhere in the DNA helix of fruit flies (who can have red eyes that are triggered by the same gene), trying to activate a different color. "We tried blue. We tried brown. We tried green. Nothing worked."

Exasperated one night in the lab, Otto became careless. In the midst of deadening the red protein in that day's batch of flies, he removed an extra protein from the gene as well. "I knew exactly what I had done," he wrote. "But it was late, and I didn't feel like starting over. Every good scientist knows that if you contaminate the original sample, you toss it. But I didn't. I figured it wouldn't make a difference in the end, so I went ahead and injected the vector. It was pure sloppiness." When Otto returned the following morning, nothing unusual had occurred. He tried to introduce a new color protein into the flies' DNA, but it again failed. He placed the batch of flies aside and began taking on a new group of test subjects.

But then something odd happened to that tainted sample of flies. "They wouldn't die. A fruit fly usually lives for less than two months. And even then, within twenty-four hours or so, you begin seeing a handful of them drop. But none of the flies I injected with the vector dropped. Ever. They just kept flying around."

Up until Otto's serendipitous mistake, it was assumed that biological aging was controlled by hundreds, if not thousands, of separate genetic proteins found in the body— proteins that worked in concert to determine the rate of aging across various parts of an individual. "We always assumed that a thousand different internal mechanisms and external factors worked together to trigger the aging process," says Dr. Phillip Frank, head of genetics at the National Institutes of Health. "When you think about it, you begin aging from the second you're born. Our studies showed that specific proteins in your body activated all the different physiological processes and free radicals that go into both growing up and growing old. There was no master switch."

Until Graham Otto came around.

The tainted fruit flies carried on living for weeks and weeks, with an apparently limitless supply of energy. The only dead fruit flies Otto found in the container were their offspring (the altered genes, Otto discovered, weren't passed on), the offspring of their offspring, and the offspring of their offspring's offspring. The original flies remained alive and fluttering about indefinitely. Otto acted quickly, retracing his footsteps from that late night in the lab, finding the supposedly unimportant protein he had mistakenly altered, and replicating the experiment again, without altering the original protein in the gene. Again, the flies had a seemingly indefinite lifespan.

The supposedly innocuous portion of the gene Otto had messed with turned out to be much more important than he had ever envisioned. He rushed to form his own independent biotech firm and called a lawyer to draft a patent for the protein. "Normally, this is something you do over the course of years," he told Lack in an e-mail. "But we're doing it in a week, because if we can replicate it across species, maybe there's something there." And replicate it he did, across mice, rats, guinea pigs, and others, including his own aging golden retriever, Buggle. In all instances, the altered animals appeared ageless when compared to their respective control groups, never growing old past the day the vector was introduced into their system. And all of them remain alive and well today, in tourist displays set up by the university—except for Buggle, who remains comfortably in the Otto household.

Despite his extroverted nature, Otto wasn't known as a cocky, presumptuous man. The only careless thing he did in his life was to mistakenly alter the wrong gene in those fruit flies. So when he published his findings, he insisted only on reporting what he had found, and didn't speculate on the potentially enormous worldwide impact of his research. Nevertheless, many in his field declared it junk science. "It just seemed like too easy of an answer," says Dr. Frank. Still, while many questioned Otto's findings, they didn't hesitate to recreate his experiments. And they soon found that his discovery was everything he said it was. Far more than that, actually. "He understated the results because he didn't want to sound like some kook. He refused to call it a cure for aging," says Sarah Otto. "But that's what it was, and the follow-up research proved it."

To see if the same gene therapy worked in humans, Otto solicited an unlikely test group: patients with early-onset Alzheimer's disease. "A disease like Alzheimer's is triggered specifically by the advance of age," Otto wrote in a subsequent e-mail to Lack. "So if we administer the cure to people who are just developing the disease, we can do two things. One, we can potentially prevent further damage to their brains. Two, we can see within a shorter period of time if the cure takes hold. Normally, when you do a CAT scan of an Alzheimer's patient, you see changes—sometimes rather drastic changes—to the brain over a short period. You can see the dark spots, the 'cobwebs,' as it were."

The ten initial test subjects received monthly CAT scans after being administered the cure. "In every case, the cobwebs stopped growing," noted Otto in his second published report. "The dark spots on their brains remained dark but never expanded, which is unheard of in Alzheimer's patients. We studied them for over a year and not one of them saw the disease advance past the early stages. Their brains remained perfectly, blessedly intact." Two of the patients have since died from unrelated causes; the other eight are still alive and well.

By the time Otto had published these subsequent findings, the biotech community was busy stress-testing the cure in every conceivable way. Not once were they able to poke a hole in what Otto had discovered. So miraculous were the cure's effects that many doctors began to confess on the party circuit that they had injected themselves with the vector. According to urban legend in the community, one such doctor, David Spitz, accidentally let spill to a prominent socialite at a charity gala in Seattle that he had given himself the cure. The socialite demanded the cure for herself, eventually wearing Spitz down with offers of cash and signing secretly prepared documents that absolved him of all legal liability. Thus the black market for the cure was born, well before it had even crossed the FDA's desk.

To the very end, Otto remained ambivalent about his discovery and its rapid spread. "I was overjoyed when we did the Alzheimer's study and found what we found," he wrote in his journal. "The idea that we could cure this disease that has ravaged so many families, the idea that we could prevent people's memories from being erased—that was wonderful. And certainly I was excited at the financial prospect of the cure, the kind of money it could generate for the university, as well as for me and my family. I'm not immune to that part of it. That was all very exciting. But when I heard about David Spitz, and what he had done with it, I realized that we had triggered a kind of frenzy we were totally unprepared to deal with. You know, science is usually agony. You conduct millions of experiments just to move the world forward a millimeter. But in a way, that's a good thing. Science gives us time to adjust. But the cure hasn't been like that. I discovered it too quickly, odd as that may sound. That's why, from the outset, I agreed with the president's decision to ban it. I was glad someone was willing to step back and declare that we needed to know everything about this treatment before we unleashed it upon every citizen. Obviously, that didn't stop it from spreading. But I'm glad someone stood up and took that stance. It needed to be done. A lot of the world fell in line quickly after that. And that's good. Just because I benefited from sloppy handiwork doesn't mean the rest of us will. Because we still don't know what future effects this cure will have. Think about how many treatments have been fast-tracked for approval by the FDA that eventually needed to be recalled. This cure could end up not working. And that might be the very-best-case scenario! Heaven help us all if it really does work."

Graham Otto would never get to find out.

It was another late night in the lab. Despite his astonishing success, Otto had yet to realize any of the potential financial gain from his breakthrough. He dedicated himself to making sure the cure was 100 percent bullet-proof, so that it might one day gain legitimate FDA approval and prompt the president to overturn the ban—that is, to overturn it at the right time, not when people found it most convenient or profitable. Otto was monitoring over a half-dozen species that night, comparing their statuses against control groups, trying to detect the slightest sign of aging. The Hair Bears were with him: Dr. Peter Madden, Dr. Brian Lo, Dr. Sidney Brown, and three PhD candidates (Candace Malkin, Dinesh Ganji, and Michael Duggan) in his now-growing department.

The University of Oregon has a security infrastructure that is the envy of most other colleges. Every building requires hologram identification worn on a lanyard. Every entrance is covered by surveillance cameras. The campus is extremely well lit, and hundreds of emergency phones dot the area, for easy access by any students or staff who feel immediately threatened.

But the Hair Bears' lab was no longer located on the Oregon campus. Due to the success of Otto's program, the university had agreed to build a new lab for him and his cohorts—a facility they hoped would rival any genetics lab in America. But while it was being built, the team, which had already outgrown its old quarters, was forced to work out of a makeshift lab in a nearby office park.

The Shelby Office Park looks very much like any other office park in the nation. It's located on Shelby Circle, right near a strip of chain restaurants and home-improvement stores. It's a poorly lit complex—even now, after what happened. A walk from the Shelby parking lot to one of the main buildings in the dead of night is enough to jangle even the toughest nerves. A card-key is needed to enter any of the buildings on the park's campus. But the parking lot has no such requirement. Parking is free, and there's no gate to check into. Anyone can drive up to the main buildings. And on the night of August 7, 2012, someone did.

An unmarked van pulled up to the curb in front of Building D, where the Hair Bears made their temporary home. The team typically finished up work at the same time, but Otto was known to tell everyone to go home and get their rest, while staying on alone in the lab—sometimes for a little while, sometimes for hours. (Although he enjoyed the company of his coworkers, Otto claimed to focus better when undisturbed.) From what police have been able to reconstruct, it seems that night he bade his colleagues goodbye and stayed in the lab for a scant ten extra minutes. After he closed up shop, he grabbed his briefcase and made his way down to the lobby.

As he exited the building, he saw the van. He likely also noticed that there were still four bikes parked in the rack next to the building entrance. Many of the team members used bikes, instead of cars, to get around town. The rack should have been empty. In the time it took Otto to recognize that something was amiss, three men had exited the van and accosted him.

They wore black from head to toe, with black hoods covering their heads. They had guns. They forced Otto to the ground and bound his legs, arms, and mouth with duct tape.

They dragged Otto to the van and opened the back. There Otto saw, to his horror, all six of his colleagues, similarly bound and piled on top of each other—a writhing tangle of bodies. They threw Otto in with the rest, doused them and the van with gasoline, and set it on fire. The three assailants then fled the scene as the van burst into flames. Only one of them, Casey Jarrett of Tacoma, has been identified and charged. Jarrett, who belongs to a pro-death evangelical sect known as Terminal Earth, defended his actions only by saying, "A little bit of bloodshed now or a lot later on." Otto, Madden, Lo, Brown, Malkin, Ganji, and Duggan all perished in the blaze. Just hours later, David Spitz was gunned down outside his home in Seattle.

President Lack still has trouble accepting that his friend and colleague died in such a horrifying manner. "It's inconceivable to me," he says. "If there was anyone you wanted to invent this cure, it was Graham. He wasn't some power-mad scientist hell-bent on destroying the world. He had real integrity, and he rarely acted without considering all the consequences of his behavior. The cure was safe in his hands. I don't think he even gave it to himself. That someone would stalk him down and murder him and six other bright, wonderful minds like that is just . . . It takes away my faith in humanity, a faith that people like Graham instilled in me. He's not here to guide us through this anymore, and we're so much poorer for it."

Two floors above the site where the van burned and burned, a window from Otto's lab looks out over the parking lot. Perched on the windowsill is a very small glass case containing five fruit flies—five very special fruit flies that turned Graham Otto from a desperate redhead into perhaps the most important scientist in human history. They were the first creatures on earth to be cured of death by Otto, and they were among the last creatures on earth to see him alive.

DATE MODIFIED:
7/5/2019, 9:17 P.M.

"How could you be so dumb?"

I had to get out of Manhattan. Katy merrily haunts me in this place, which I more than deserve. I see visions of her all around: in the kitchen, by the television, lunging out the window. Soon there are so many ghosts of her crowding me that I feel engulfed. Sound reason told me that to stay around much longer was to risk insanity. I had to go see my sister.

I have the good fortune of not having to deal with Penn Station on a daily basis. I'm amazed that current events have managed to create an environment in which dealing with Penn Station is somehow even worse than before. I didn't know it could get worse. It already seemed to operate at maximum awfulness. Oh, but I was wrong.

This was an exodus. There was a line just to get in the station. I'd never seen that before. A fire marshal was stationed outside every entrance, holding back travelers until a certain number had exited. They let a handful of people in, then held the line again. It was like trying to get into a nightclub—which is perfect in its symmetry. My goal was the six-thirty train. They ran every half hour, so I figured if I missed the six thirty, I could just hop on the seven with a tall boy of Budweiser, and off I'd go. I just barely made the ten-thirty train.

It was around midnight when I pulled in. My sister was waiting for me. She looked tired, but she has two kids, so I think she looks the same way at midnight as she does at all other hours of the day. Polly exists in a perpetual daze, run down by the burdens of motherhood and falling further and further behind in rest, never again to reach complete wakefulness. I had specifically asked my dad not to tell her what I had done, because I knew she'd make me feel bad about it. I had already suffered through four hours at Penn Station and a train ride so tightly packed you couldn't have slipped a dime between the bodies. But then, seeing her, I figured that I may as well get all the pain out of the way immediately. She drove me back to her house and poured me a drink.

I confessed almost immediately. "I got the cure."

She snapped awake (she can only be alert in short bursts). "What? When?"

"Three weeks ago. That's not all of it. My roommate and the doctor who gave it to me were killed in the July 3 attacks."

"Oh my Jesus. Katy? Was that her name? Are you joking?"

"No. I referred her to my cure doctor, and when she went to get her blood drawn, the office was bombed."

"Oh my God. Are you okay?"

"Not particularly. I . . . I was so excited for her to get it. I didn't think this could happen, and I still don't know how it did. And now she's dead, and I feel like I deserve the same fate."

"Why did you get the cure? How could you be so dumb? You have to swear right now that you won't tell Mark that you did it. He's been talking about it and talking about it. The last thing I want is for you to egg him on."

"Please don't castigate me for this."

"But didn't you realize the danger you put your roommate in? The danger you put yourself in? These crazy people didn't just start killing doctors a couple of days ago, John. And you don't even know if the thing works. I just can't believe you'd go to some back-alley Guatemalan Dr. Nick to get your life fixed."

"He wasn't some quack," I said defensively. "He was a legitimate doctor with a well-known practice."

"Yet he chose to engage in some shady side business. Why is that?"

"It was just some ego thing."

"And that doesn't bother you, even now? I saw the doctor Mark wanted to visit to get it done. His name was Frankie, and he looked like he stole furniture out of trucks. I've heard that some of the people offering to do it aren't even real doctors. They're like chiropractors times ten. I'm not judging you for getting it. I'm just worried about you. That's all."

"I'm grateful for that, P. I really am. But I'm fine. Mentally, I'm a disaster. But physically I feel fine. Great, as odd as that sounds."

She grew a touch curious. "So you think it really works, then."

"We won't know for a while. I've been taking a photo of my face every day just to see if there are any changes over time I don't readily notice."

"And you're not worried about, you know, hogging all the food and stuff?"

"I promise I won't eat all the Nilla Wafers in the house, like last time."

"You know that's not what I mean. There's a reason people are fighting so fiercely to keep this cure out of people's hands. You don't have kids. I do. I think about this stuff. I think about what'll be left for them."

"So you're never going to get it? And you'll never let Mark get it?"

She let out a low groan. "I have no idea. I really don't. I'm guessing there will be a point when it's legal and everyone has it and I feel obligated to get it too. I was like that with cell phones. I was easily the last of my friends to get one. Everyone else had one. And there I was, outside school at some disgusting pay phone that didn't even work. Now, of course, I have one and I'll never go back. That's how I am. I usually have to be dragged into things. I know it's probably inevitable that I'll get the cure and that we'll all get it. It's just gonna be something you do. But it opens up all sorts of odd questions that I don't want to deal with right now. I mean, what happens to Mark and me?"

"Are you guys having problems?"

"No! Not at all. But it's a whole weird thing, to think you'll be with someone for that long. I love him, and I'm willing to do it. It's just . . . daunting. And the kids . . . Jesus. You become a parent, and your whole life becomes about worrying. You just worry constantly whether they'll be okay. And the idea that I'll be worried forever about them and what they do . . . I almost have a panic attack when I think about it. I'm worried, and I'm worried about having to worry so goddamn much."

I told her about all the bankers getting divorced.

"Oh, Christ," she said. "Don't tell me that."

"Sorry."

"See, that completely freaks me out. One day we'll get it, and Mark's friends will all say, 'Hey, what are you still doing with that old bag?'"

"But you won't be old."

"But I'm old already. I have two kids. That makes you old. So then I have *that* to worry about. Do I have the ability to keep my husband happy for centuries upon centuries? Do I need to get lipo so that I can look like some perky goddamn cheerleader? I have no earthly idea, and I don't like the idea of having to confront all those issues somewhere down the road. Right now my whole life is plagued with decisions that have to be made: what to get for dinner, which school the kids should go to, which kid's birthday party we should go to this weekend. It's just decision after decision after decision, from trivial crap to really important things. By the end of the day, I'm mush. I don't even eat dinner because I don't want to choose what to have. I have cereal and call it a day. And now there's this. Big, *huge* decision alert. Every question I ask myself about it begets a dozen more. It's giving me a migraine right now, and I haven't even done anything."

"It has to be better than the alternative, though."

"Does it? I don't know."

"Well, you say you're already old. How does growing old feel so far?"

She sighed. "It *sucks*."

"Well, now I feel somewhat better about my decision."

We changed the subject. Polly handed me a plate of cold roast beef and corn off the cob. We talked, and I ate, and for the first time, Katy's death moved to the back of my consciousness, if only for a moment. This is bereavement: the slow, eventual reassertion of your own meaningless preoccupations. As I ate, the look in Polly's eyes made it clear she was still thinking about the cure. She had tried for so long to stem the tide, to avoid being overwhelmed by it. But there I was: the tsunami at her doorstep.

DATE MODIFIED:
7/17/2019, 5:09 P.M.

DC Apparently Stands for "Don't Come"

I have a friend in DC who e-mailed me this in response to reports about the expanded security perimeters to accommodate protesters in Midtown:

> Dude, the security bullshit you have to deal with up there is nothing compared to what's going on down here. The entirety of Northwest DC below M Street has been cordoned off since that girl was beaten to death for her DieStrong bracelet and the riots in Germany started. You can't drive anywhere downtown. I'm talking about miles the hell away from the White House. And when you come up out of the Metro, there are National Guard members with loaded rifles, and their fingers on the trigger, ready to pull you aside if you look like a threat. They increased the restricted airspace above town by nearly twentyfold. If you come down on a shuttle from Boston to National, you practically have to go through Ohio. It's insane.
>
> Downtown DC around the Wizards' arena is essentially a pedestrian thoroughfare now. I have no issue with this, since people in DC can't drive for *shit*, except that Metro stops can be goddamn light years away from each other. That scene you described at Penn Station? That's every Metro station, except here the station escalators never work, so you have to haul ass up four thousand stairs before you get to emerge above ground. And the buses aren't running. All the protesters have been forced to demonstrate on the other side of the Potomac, along the bike trail in Arlington. I saw a bunch of them trying to swim across the

Potomac to get to the Mall, only to have cops pick them up in a riverboat and haul their sorry asses out of the water. One of them almost drowned in the rip currents.

I have a friend who works on the Hill who says the Supreme Court judges will be moved to an undisclosed location to argue the California case. Lots of bomb threats.

Fucking crazy, man. Fucking crazy.

—MK

DATE MODIFIED:
7/18/2019, 11:07 A.M.

A Blonde Everywhere I Turn

I was walking down Third Avenue today when I spotted a woman across the street with a remarkable body and blonde hair that broke just past her shoulder blades. I turned electric. I saw a gap in traffic and sprinted across the avenue. A cab rounding from Forty-third blithely took the corner and nearly plowed into me. I kept my focus on the blonde as the driver honked three hundred times in the space of four seconds. She didn't turn her head and kept bouncing down Third, with me trailing behind her and trying to figure out a plan before quickening my pace to identify her. I kept thirty yards behind, dodging dog walkers, tourists, and meandering hordes of the unemployed. I took out my phone and queued up the number for the police, without hitting Send, so I would have it at the ready. I took her picture so I could post it to my feed if need be. If this blonde was *the* blonde, I'd call the police and alert them to her presence, then follow her until they arrived to detain her.

I made the decision to pass. I sprint-walked closer and closer, until we were side by side, then I feigned interest in the window of a Hot & Crusty on the other side of her, and caught a quick glimpse of her face. It wasn't her. It wasn't even close.

This sort of wild-goose chase has now taken up firm residence in my daily routine. Spy blonde. Suspect blonde. Chase blonde. Realize I've misidentified blonde. Think of my friend bursting into flames sixteen days ago while I remained outside, like a dumb dog that no one bothered to train. Doomed to follow every pointless distraction that crosses my path.

DATE MODIFIED:
7/19/2019, 9:34 P.M.

The Worst Since Kent State

From the *Washington Post* website:

Developing: Four Dead in Concord Cure Protest

By Luke Spiller and Candace English

Four pro-cure demonstrators were shot dead today by National Guardsmen in the New Hampshire state capital of Concord after a massive protest turned into the most violent cure-related conflict since two students were shot dead in a Berlin riot three weeks ago.

After a widespread report was released yesterday accusing the United States military of offering the so-called cure for death to its own soldiers in exchange for extended pension benefits, protesters here in the Granite State marched on the Capitol. Many were incensed.

"They were trying to force their way inside the building. They wanted to take it over," said lawyer Jim Watley, who works in the Capitol. "I don't know what they would have done if they had gotten in, but that was their aim."

A small group of National Guardsmen charged with protecting the Capitol tried to keep protesters at bay with shields and threats of tear gas. But witnesses say a crazed protestor threw a lit Molotov cocktail at the guardsmen, which prompted two of them to open fire into the crowd, causing protesters to flee in mass panic. Four people are now confirmed dead. An unspecified number of people

were injured, including Jackie Frost of Nashua, NH, who
was shot in the leg.

"They were supposed to use rubber bullets!" she cried.
"No one else was armed! Why didn't they use rubber
bullets?"

The number of people killed in today's incident is the
same as those killed in the 1970 shootings at Kent State
University in Kent, Ohio.

Further details forthcoming.

I looked out my window just now and saw a man running down
the middle of the avenue, screaming his head off as cars threatened to sideswipe him from both directions. He wasn't saying
anything. He was just unleashing the most primal noise he could
possibly make. And he was holding up a sign that said GIVE IT TO
US NOW.

On the TV right now, they're showing protesters lined up
against the barricades in DC. They look like a mob of shoppers
waiting to get into a department store at 7:00 A.M. on the day after
Thanksgiving. The president is due to speak at 8:00 P.M.

DATE MODIFIED:
8/14/2019, 3:20 P.M.

"One infinite generation"

Here's the full text of the president's speech, copied from CNN:

My fellow Americans:

This is a very tense time. The world has been confronted
with a medical innovation that represents a seismic change
in the very nature of who we are and how we interact. I am
not an enemy of science, nor do I ever wish to be someone
who stands in the way of progress. Three years ago, when I
first issued the executive order banning the black market sale
of the cure for aging, it was never with the intention that
the ban would be permanent. Like many of you, I marvel at
the possibilities opened by this cure. It means the potential
to have a very long, very wonderful life surrounded by those
we love for perhaps thousands of years or more.

But we must consider the impact that kind of longevity
will have, both on our fellow men and women and on the
large yet delicate planet we call home. For the past 243
years, we have existed as a country united by a single goal:
liberty for all. We believe in freedom because we believe it
is not only the right of every man, woman, and child but
also because freedom serves as the catalyst for our very
highest ambitions.

It is this idea—the idea that freedom can make the world
a better place—upon which we have built our nation. It is an
idea that so many brave young Americans have fought and
died for. At Valley Forge. At Gettysburg. In Normandy and
Iwo Jima. In Korea, Vietnam, Iraq, and Afghanistan. Our
men and women fought not only for their fellow countrymen

but for future generations—generations they knew they'd never live to meet face-to-face.

But there aren't going to be future generations anymore. Not after this. There will only be us. One infinite generation, forever growing and reaching an unknown and incomprehensible size. And so now we are charged once again with the task of sacrificing for the sake of our nation's future—a future in which we will all serve a much larger role than we ever dreamed possible. Because while we may now have a virtually unlimited lifespan, our natural resources almost certainly do not. Gas. Clean water. Land. Mother Nature has blessed us with only a finite amount of each of these things.

We have known, long before this cure was discovered, that we have been consuming resources at an unsustainable pace—a pace that will now quicken at an unimaginable rate. We are a nation of strong, hardworking people. But it is, I'm afraid, part of human nature that we adapt only when forced to. We are told that there is only so much crude oil left in the earth. Yet we can still buy gas at the station on the corner, and for a relatively decent price. We haven't changed our ways, because we don't feel we have to.

It is only in the face of grim reality that we are able to dig down and discover just what we are made of. And that reality is coming, hurtling toward us faster and faster every day now. I cannot tell you when it will come—perhaps long after I've left office. But it will come. And the question we must all ask ourselves is, are we ready for that reality?

I banned this cure three years ago because I wanted us to have as much time as possible to be ready when that day comes, to be prepared for all the responsibilities this cure demands of us.

But the time has come for me to stop prolonging the inevitable.

One hour ago I signed an executive order reversing the original ban on the sale of the cure for aging. The cure will be submitted for FDA approval and, pending all relevant testing, people will be free to purchase it from their physician as they please. However, I again remind us all that we must think about what is fair. As part of my executive order, citizens who get the cure will no longer be eligible for Social Security or Medicare benefits, regardless of how long they live. Furthermore, in accordance with the recommendation of doctors across the country, no citizen under the age of twenty-six will be allowed to purchase the cure. Doctors who violate this edict will have their licenses revoked and be subject to swift prosecution. I also take this moment to again condemn the attacks on doctors administering the cure in New York and Oregon. Anyone found to be coordinating terrorist attacks against doctors offering the cure will be subject to federal prosecution and the death penalty.

This has been a tragic, awful day in our history. Four of our own were killed in New Hampshire. Our hearts go out to them and their families. We grieve and pray with them, and we promise to take all possible measures to prevent deaths like theirs from ever occurring again. They were four young people, passionate in the cause of retaining their youth, of seeing what they could make of a life extended indefinitely by a miracle of technology. They were willing to fight for what they believed in, for their personal liberty, and that makes them Americans to the very core. We will not forget them, nor shall we let them die in vain.

The nation that adapts to the effects of this cure and masters a world changed by postmortality is the nation that will lead the world into the next century and well beyond. Today I declare my faith that we can and will be that nation. So many have given for the future of this country, and now that future fully belongs to us all. We are ready. We have no other choice.

God bless us all, and God bless the United States of America.

I heard cheers burst from the street as the president gave his closing remarks. I looked out the window and saw protesters hugging
and raising their fists in victory. They sang songs and drank from
open containers. I could see the excitement in their faces, the
pure delirium over all the new and wonderful (and legal) possibilities. They had the same look on their faces that Katy had just
as we were walking to the doctor's office.

DATE MODIFIED:
8/14/2019, 9:11 P.M.

"The floodgates are wide open"

I've tried to pull together as many responses to the president's speech as I could find. Here's what I've gathered so far:

The Atlantic:

Proof once again that we Americans can get what we want if we simply stomp and scream for something, like the immature schoolchildren that we are. Those protesters in New Hampshire weren't, as the president implied, banging on the Capitol doors for some grand, noble cause. The idea that they sacrificed themselves like the soldiers at Iwo Jima is farcical and an insult to our intelligence. They did it for themselves and no one else. They weren't sacrificing for the future. They were trying to hog it. This generation hasn't had to sacrifice one bit, and its reward for such callousness is now eternal life. It's the classic American scenario of people wanting everything *right now* without caring a lick about the long-term. You could excuse it by saying, "Well, that's just the way we are." Well, the way we are is going to cost us everything.

* * *

Bob Mandel's feed:

It's like eating a sausage pizza. You know it's gonna kill you. But it's not going to kill you *now*, so who gives a shit? Let's eat.

* * *

My dad:

Well, now I kind of want to get it. Just to see how all this plays out.

* * *

Allan Atkins:

He's the most gutless president we have ever had. He is a liar, a fraud, a terrorist appeaser, and a criminal. If that *Times* report about the soldiers taking the cure never came out, you never would have seen last night's speech. I guarantee you that. People had to *die* for this man to finally listen to me. Troops had to flagrantly disobey their superiors for this man to listen to me. And then, when he finally does listen to me, he legalizes the cure in the clumsiest, most insincere manner possible. It's disgusting. I am disgusted, and you should be too.

That said, I'm glad he finally legalized it. And now I can finally tell you all: I got it, baby! You're *never* gonna get rid of me now!

* * *

Choosedeath.org:

You have no idea what you've just done.

* * *

My sister:

He legalized it? Oh, Christ. I think I'm gonna pass out. Am I the last person to know this? I am, aren't I?

* * *

Joe Weis (NBC):

In the end the president had no choice but to legalize the cure. Those who would criticize him for his handling of the entire situation need to step back for a moment and consider the issue this president was facing. This is a problem unlike anything any leader of any kind has ever faced. Did we really expect this man to handle the issue of the cure perfectly when it stands poised to tip the entire planet on its axis? His first instinct—the correct instinct— was to be cautious with it for as long as possible. Well, turns out three years was as long as possible. He bravely admitted it was a mistake on his part to stall, but he didn't need to apologize for it. Those three years of waiting allowed him time to decide how to best regulate the cure in a sensible manner. The president spoke of a grim reality that will soon descend upon us all. Well, it seems he is one of the few people out there who has tried to envision what that reality will look like and how we will deal with it. His words were hopeful last night, but the concern in his eyes was unmistakable. He is bracing himself for what's ahead, and he wants us to do likewise. Because the floodgates are open now. The floodgates are wide open.

After the president's speech last night, I took a long walk uptown. The barricades had been taken down and the protesters had dissipated. The entire city seemed to breathe again. Everyone was smiling. Happy. Possibly drunk. The honeymoon was in full swing.

I walked by the UN building: no longer besieged. I walked by the posters on First Avenue. There were no anti-cure messages there this time. Just a bunch of Pepsi ads. I walked by the doctor's apartment building and the Fifty-ninth Street Bridge. Everything felt normal. Everything felt the way it should be. The world was functional again.

But deep in my marrow, I know it won't stay that way.

DATE MODIFIED:
8/15/2019, 10:21 A.M.

II

SPREAD:
JUNE 2029

(TEN YEARS LATER)

Photo No. 3,650

I took my picture again this morning. Still the same. The nose. The eyes. The brow. The chin. Nothing has sagged. No creases have formed. I scrolled through the "Face" folder in my library to compare it with the other pictures. There's no real variation, except when I get a haircut. That's the only time there's any noticeable difference. My hair gets a little bit longer and a little bit longer; then I get it cut and the image resets, like one of those antique typewriters that slides back into place whenever you hit the carriage return. Though the hair gets longer, not a whisper of it gets grayer.

One day I drew a star on my cheek, just to mix things up. You can see it fade over the course of a week or so. Everyone at work looked at me like I was an unruly toddler after I did that. I've tried to keep the same expression throughout the photos, as a control mechanism. But there are some photos where I couldn't hide my mood. The ones where I'm hungover are fairly easy to detect. I don't look happy to have my picture taken, even though I'm the pushy fella who's insisting it be done.

So there are some slight differences there, but the fundamental aspects of my face are identical from each day to the next. If you made a flip-book of it, it would be the most boring film imaginable. The only exciting part is when the star pops up. I haven't changed. I haven't grown. The supposed character that aging features provide has not been bestowed upon me. You wouldn't know that I've lived ten years between the first photo and the last. All 3,650 pictures could—if not for my hair—have been taken on the same day. The time span is invisible. It's as if I haven't lived at all.

I have a friend who struggles with his weight from time to time. He'll reach a certain weight and then grow completely intolerant of what he's become. He'll start running and eating nothing but grilled chicken and asparagus and baked potato chips. Then he'll get down to a fairly acceptable weight, get a girlfriend, eat her cooking, and gain all the weight back. And once he's reached his personal critical mass again, he'll do it all over. If you took *his* picture every day for a decade, it would be far more interesting. It would be like watching someone try to inflate a balloon without bothering to pinch the end between breaths. You'd see the history. You would get at least some semblance of the life he's led and what's he's been dealing with. But you can't see that with me. There's no story. You can't tell a damn thing.

Happy tenth cure day to me.

DATE MODIFIED:
6/20/2029, 12:14 P.M.

"You said you'd love me forever"

Sonia wanted to get married. The issue had come up in the past, but I had managed to stave it off for as long as I possibly could. I have found, though, that once a woman introduces the idea of something to you, she'll never let it go until you finally relent. I don't mean this as a criticism of women. They're all so admirably tenacious, whereas I am the exact opposite. I'll let go of anything if holding on to it comes to require too much effort.

She broke one of the long silences that tended to overpopulate our most serious arguments. "I don't understand what you're so afraid of."

"I'm not afraid of anything," I told her.

"Yes, you are."

"You're not going to get me to marry you simply by challenging my manhood. I already know I don't stack up to most men. The Cap'n Crunch boxes in the kitchen are proof alone of that."

"This isn't funny, John. I've invested four years of my life in this. There comes a point when it's fair for a woman to ask what a man's intentions are. Don't you think that's fair?"

"I do. And I am committed to you. I've never cheated. I've always been there to support you."

"And you say you love me, right?"

"I do. I love the hell out of you."

"You said you'd love me forever."

"I did. And I meant it."

Sonia sat down. She didn't look upset. She looked as if she was trying to solve a math proof whose solution eluded her. That's what I always liked about her. She was never unreasonable. If she had an argument with anything, it was backed up by sound logic and analysis. Not everyone I know acts in a similar manner. I know I don't.

"Then I don't understand," she said. "You know I'm not a needy person. I can take care of myself. But the reason I'm talking to you about this is because I want to spend the rest of my life with you. I want to build something with you. And I don't want to have this conversation with you every four months. I want this settled."

"I understand all that. But look out there. Do you see anyone getting married? At all?"

"What does that have to do with us? Are you telling me it's peer pressure that's holding you back?"

"No."

"Because I know what's going on these days. A man in my office got engaged three months ago, and all the other men laughed at him. They laughed right in his face. Every guy is supposed to be some macho, shit-kicking eternal bachelor now."

I sat next to her on the couch. She had a glass of wine on the coffee table, but she hadn't bothered to touch it.

"It's not just a guy thing," I said. "I'm going to be as honest as I possibly can about this, because you deserve the unvarnished truth. I don't have the capacity to commit to something—anything—for five hundred years or however long we're likely to live. I don't have the knowledge and foresight to say to you, 'Yes. I will stick with you no matter what occurs from now until the end of time.'"

"But you could commit to me if you hadn't taken the cure? That makes no sense."

"Yes it does. I could commit to you if we knew our lives were definite. But they aren't. I have no earthly idea what's coming next, and I can't promise that from now until the end of time I'll always be by your side. Because I don't know. And you can't promise that either, because you don't know."

"But that's what marriage is. It's two people saying that we don't know what's going to happen but we promise we'll get through it together. Being married means there's one thing you can always count on."

"I don't know if I want that. I'm sorry. People got married before because they knew, deep down, that there would come a time in their lives when they would become too old, too ugly, and too infirm to have anyone care about them except their spouse. You needed someone to change your bedpan and help tie your shoes and all that. That's all gone now, Sonia. All that fear is gone. And whatever urge there is for people to find a lifetime companion . . . I don't have that anymore. Every guy I know feels the same way. You want something concrete from me? I love you, but I don't want to get married, and I don't know if I ever will. I'm pretty sure I won't."

Her eyes tightened, like she was about to swing at a baseball. "I'm pregnant."

"What?"

"I'm pregnant."

"How long?"

"Ten weeks. I just found out this morning."

"You spring this on me now?"

"I'm not afraid to raise our child alone, John. I'm not. I'm a strong woman and I know I can do that. But I'd like you to be there. I'd like to raise him with you, as your wife. It wouldn't be a chore. It would be wonderful. Indelible. It would be fifty times more rewarding than spending the next three decades getting blasted and watching football with your friends or whatever."

"I don't know. I like football quite a bit."

"Don't be a wiseass. Not now."

"I'm not being a wiseass. This is just . . . more seriousness than I want. This is more responsibility than I want."

"Don't you think it's time you grew up?"

"No. See, that's what I dislike. I dislike that just because I reach a certain age, I'm supposed to hunker down and stop enjoying my life. That I'm supposed to leave all the fun to the younger generation. I'm not buying into that anymore, and no one else I know is either. This is liberation, Sonia. Honestly, why have this child now?

Don't you want to enjoy your life a little bit more before you weigh yourself down with all this?"

"It's not a weight. It's something I want. I'm not having this child as some sort of self-punishment. Just because I can have a child a hundred years from now doesn't mean I want to wait that long. I'm still a woman. I still have the urge to be a mother and to be a wife. I still have that drive. You're telling me about liberation. I *am* free. I don't have to worry about growing old and never finding a man, like every goddamn magazine used to tell me. I have the freedom now to marry whom I want when I want, and to have children when I want. And I want this child *today*, and I want to raise it with you. Not because I'm some wet blanket. But because I know life is going to be better with the three of us together. I want something in my life that means something. Don't you see that? It's not some invisible cultural force driving all this, John. It's just me, telling you that I love you very much and want to be with you. You tell me that isn't what you want. But is that really true? Are you really so scared that you'll miss out on partying and hooking up with other women down the line? Why have you gone out with me for this long if that's what you really want?"

"Because I love you."

"Then tell me how tomorrow will be any different."

I had no answer. Three weeks ago I helped our firm devise a lucrative new type of prenuptial agreement between a banker and his fiancée. It's a forty-year marriage. Set in stone. No divorcing allowed without significant penalties. The couple agrees to be together for forty years, with the marriage automatically dissolving at the end of that period and the assets divided at a previously agreed-upon percentage. The couple could then pick up an additional forty-year option if they wished. My boss has even coined a new term for it: "cycle marriage." He says it could help raise marriage rates back up to where they were a few years ago. The reason clients like it is because it precludes the acrimony that usually accompanies divorce. You're less likely to claw at each other's throats if you know there's already an end set in place. A couple marries, raises a family, then they go their separate ways to enjoy single life once more after the children are grown and well-adjusted. It's a win-win situation, particularly if you're the lawyer brokering the deal.

"What about a cycle marriage?" I asked her.

"That forty-year thing you do for asshole bankers? Are you being serious? That's moronic."

"That's all I can offer you."

She stood up and straightened her skirt. "So this is it. You really don't want this?"

"I don't. There's too much left in front of me. I love you. But I don't have the certainty that you have. I'm not ready."

"I'm sorry you feel that way. I'm sorry all this has changed your ability to love someone. I can't stay here." On went her jacket. "Will you help me raise him? Will you support us?"

"I will. I promise you that I will be the best father I can be."

"Then I guess that's the best I can hope for."

I watched her collect her things and move to the door. She turned to me. She wasn't crying. But I could see the disappointment. She'd had plans for us. She had envisioned an entire life for us that she thought was going to become reality one day, and she was so very much looking forward to it. She thought I would feel the same way. She felt assured of it. She believed in me. But now that she knew the truth, she saw me as a different man—one I don't think she liked very much.

"I'll let you know when the first ultrasound is," she said. "I'll pack up my things when you're at work this week."

"I'm sorry, Sonia. I'm sorry I failed you."

"Goodbye, John."

And she left.

DATE MODIFIED:
10/31/2029, 5:33 A.M.

I Seek the Grail

I have a friend who's going to have a cure party next week in Las Vegas. He's really doing it up too. He booked a suite at the Fountain of Youth, so our trip is guaranteed to be either cheesy in a fascinating, outstanding way or cheesy in a horrible, soul-sucking way. There's no in-between when you go to Vegas, particularly if you're committed to staying at that monstrosity. Before the trip, my friend had a request.

"You've had the cure, right?" he asked me.

"Yep."

"Do you have a grail?"

"No. That's idiotic."

"You have to get one. We're all gonna buy grails and bring them. You have to do it. Prerequisite."

"Oh, come on. Really? I have to buy one of those stupid things?"

"We're staying at the Fountain of Youth. We have to go all the way with this. I'll even pay for yours. I can't have a half-assed cure party."

"Can't I buy it when we're out there?"

"No, because we're gonna drink out of them on the plane. Hell, I'm looking forward to the plane ride more than any other part of the trip."

So I had to get a grail. Derrick's Grail Shop is located on Christopher Street between a gay sex shop and a head shop. Derrick's is also a head shop, but it seems to do such good business selling grails right now that the bongs have been pushed to a small section on the side. I wondered when the head-shop owner next door would wise up to that fact.

I walked in and took a look. They had thousands of the things. I remember a scene in one of the Indiana Jones movies where Indy walks into the grail room and sees all these shiny, golden chalices. But the real Holy Grail was a crudely made cup sitting meekly on the lowest shelf. All the nice-looking grails in the movie killed you instantly. Well, Derrick's had no crude grails—no *real* grails. They were all like the fakes the bad Nazi guys drank from, designed to tempt you and then suck all the life right out of you.

That said, they were all quite pretty. Some were knockoff versions of the kind you can get in the Diamond District, with the fake gold and the giant phony gemstones lining the rims. But there were some cool ones too. I saw one made of stitched leather with fake gold inlay. Oxo made a couple of stainless-steel ones with comfortable rubber grips—the practical grail, if you will. There were also Goth ones, including a grail that had a curled-up dragon for a stem. If I had a van, I would definitely paint that grail on the side of my van. They had grails made of elaborately carved oak, for the environmentally friendly postmortal. None of them looked all that Jesus-appropriate. But, hey, they were still nice grails.

I saw one in a Lucite box. It was made of crystal, with an engraved pattern of infinity symbols. I looked at the clerk behind the glass counter and pointed to the box.

"What's that one?"

"That's the DX3490," he said. "Designed by the Swift himself. It's the same one he drinks from on tour. You can even send away to have him sign it." He pointed to a poster on the wall. Sure enough, there was the Swift, wearing a white suit and drinking purple drank out of the very same grail. Spiffy.

"Do you think I could pull off rocking the same grail as the Swift?"

"Truthfully? No."

He also showed me a room in the back where you could design your own. They had thick stylebooks you could flip through, like choosing wedding invitations. You could pick the pattern, the font, everything. They even had suggested sayings you could have embossed on your grail. You could paint your own clay grail and then have them fire it in a kiln. I saw a couple up on the shelf waiting to be picked up. One said BETTY'S GRAIL. I have no clue why that made me laugh, but I nearly soiled myself when I saw it. They had matching grail-and-bong sets, which I found highly tempting, though God help you if you ever confuse the two at five in the morning.

In the end I chose a simple gold one. I wanted a grail that made me feel like a knight who had just finished a long day's pillaging. The kind you hold in one hand while you eat a turkey drumstick with the other. The kind that makes you feel compelled to talk like a town crier while holding it. That's the kind of grail I wanted, and that's the kind I ended up getting. Twenty bucks. Not bad for the cup of Christ.

I brought it home, mixed a rum and Coke in it, and gave my usual cheers to Katy. I have to say, the Swift was on to something with this trend. Drinks taste way better when you're drinking them out of a grail.

DATE MODIFIED:
11/7/2029, 8:51 P.M.

Field Trip:
The Fountain of Youth

I hadn't flown to Las Vegas since they opened Fountain of Youth Resort and Casino last year. I already knew it was the biggest hotel on earth, but I wasn't prepared for the view from the airplane. There are familiar sights you see as you approach McCarran at night: the Luxor's pyramid, New York–New York's skyline, the Shanghai, etc. But the Fountain now dwarfs all of them. An old lady on the right side of the plane was the first to spot it. She screamed out in joy when she saw it edging into view through her little porthole.

Everyone spontaneously broke into applause and chugged the contents of their respective grails (three steakheads from Long Island had DX3490s; I'm relieved I didn't spring for one). I swear the jet spray shooting up from the center of the oval fountain could have tickled our landing gear if we were flying directly above it. I read that the fountain continually pumps four million gallons of water a minute. Seeing it in person, that estimate now feels low. I assume when they first turned on the fountain, the guy throwing the switch thrust his hips for maximum effect.

After deplaning we circumvented the cabstand (the line stretched so far they had to move the security checkpoints for the entire airport) and took the shuttle bus down to the Strip. The last time I was in Vegas, the ride took twenty minutes. This time it took so much longer that I asked the driver if there were multiple conventions going on. There were not.

He dropped us off at the main entrance, and we walked into chaos. The hotel has over twelve thousand rooms, and this evening it appeared all its occupants had decided to hang out in the lobby. We stood in the check-in line in shifts; half of us waited while the other half went to get drinks, and then we switched. When it was my turn to help fetch alcohol, I walked out into the main atrium and stared at the fountain, a gigantic edifice of water that defies all reason. It's as if the hotel is trying to put out a fire on the surface of the moon. Colored lights illuminate the mighty geyser in a painstakingly choreographed arrangement. Surrounding the base of the fountain are the cure stations: small platforms with a doctor and a single chair that each soon-to-be postmortal sits in to get their shots. Like in Dr. X's apartment, each chair has straps and belts to hold you down while you are injected. Unlike in Dr. X's apartment, each chair is a specially designed throne. You get to choose the theme for your chair. There's your basic emperor's chair (made of gold; it matched my grail!). There's also the Poseidon: Lord of the Sea chair, which is actually a large, chair-shaped fish tank, with miniature sharks and all kinds of other imported marine life swimming under your backside. There's a Space chair, which is shaped like a giant egg and has two hot girls with big fake tits dressed as green aliens on either side of it. And there's a Viking chair, which features a giant serpent erupting out from between your legs when you sit in it. Those are the four I remember off the top of my head. There were hundreds of the things, no two alike.

I was in awe. I turned to my friend Scott.

"I almost want to get my shots again."

"You can do that here," he said. "They'll throw you a cure party even if you've had it done already. They just shoot you up with something besides the vector."

"What do they shoot you up with?"

"I don't know. Gin?"

They've perfected the process at the Fountain. You get your blood drawn when you check in (separate, even longer line for that), and they have the vector ready for you three days later. In between, you presumably lose all your money, and then spend the next thousand years trying to make it back. It's incredible. After getting their shots, all new postmortals jump from the platform into the pool at the base of the fountain. Fully clothed, of course. I looked out at the pool and saw a horde of people frolicking in the water, all in soaking-wet dresses, suits, and tuxedoes, all drunk beyond comprehension. Baptized into the sweet life.

On the way back to the check-in line, I noticed a small exhibit called *Ponce de León and the Fountain of Youth*. It looked like a pointless waste of time, which intrigued me.

"Hey, let's go in that."

Scott wasn't as enthused. "That? That's for kiddies."

"We go in there, we finish our drinks, we get another round, and then we head back to the line without anyone noticing. That line isn't moving at all."

"Oh, all right."

So we went into the exhibit, which was sparsely crowded due to the late hour and the fact that it was stupid. We walked through a dark corridor for about twenty yards, then found ourselves in front of an enormous scrolling diorama. A life-sized puppet of Ponce de León was sitting in an exact replica of King Ferdinand of Spain's royal court. A voice-over narrated as we watched the puppet hop onto a ship and sail across a miniaturized version of the Atlantic Ocean (with real wind and water!):

In the year 1513, King Ferdinand of Spain commissioned explorer Juan Ponce de León to sail across the seas and find the fabled fountain of youth. It was a dangerous journey, as Ponce de León and his men battled scurvy, hurricanes, and pirates!

At this point, three pirate puppets popped up from the water and dueled with the Ponce de León puppet, who then cut off their heads. I drank to his victory. The Ponce de León puppet made landfall as we kept walking.

Arriving in an exotic new land, which we now call Florida, Ponce de León rewarded his men with newfound riches of gold, sugarcane, delicious citrus fruits, and beautiful Native American women!

One of Ponce de León's puppet crew then started making out with a buxom female Indian puppet. I should have been offended, but I was too busy being turned on. The Ponce de León puppet soon came upon a giant fountain, which disappeared down into the ground.

Ponce de León's quest for the elusive mythical fountain proved fruitless, and the legendary explorer died while trying to find it.

The Ponce de León puppet then shouted out, "Nooooo!" and keeled over.

But now Ponce de León's dream has finally been realized!

The Ponce de León puppet's corpse was airlifted by his strings across a fake U.S. landscape to a miniature model of the hotel we were standing in.

Here, at Daniel Benjamin's Fountain of Youth Resort and Casino! Do all the things Ponce de León always dreamed of doing! Dine alfresco at Fukuku Oh! See Cirque du Soleil in our exclusive new show, *Eternia*! Or try your hand at Texas hold 'em! It's all here, along with over five hundred board-certified geneticists ready to give you the cure for death! Only at Daniel Benjamin's Fountain of Youth Resort and Casino! Eternal life has never been so luxurious! Right, Ponce?

The Ponce de León puppet then sat up, looked at us, and said, "Sí." We walked out.

"I don't think that presentation was historically accurate," Scott said.

"Well, sometimes you have to take dramatic license."

The rest of the weekend was spent in a drunken fog, each hour as pointlessly hazy as the last. For his cure ceremony, our friend chose the Velvet Dream chair, a throne nine feet high and made of a purple fabric that purported to be velvet but was almost certainly some kind of space-age, sweat-wicking microfiber polymer. It was a practical choice. If you're going to be stabbed by three giant fire pokers, you're gonna want to feel as relaxed as humanly possible. Afterward, we visited the Spearmint Rhino IV club. Every girl inside had a long, lucrative career in front of her. I'm not terribly comfortable in these places, which I find reassuring in a way.

Next to the casino floor at the Fountain of Youth is a stadium-sized mall that houses nothing but shops selling cure-related merchandise. You can get your pick of commemorative T-shirts (I'M HOT . . . AND I'M STAYING THAT WAY is a popular choice), steel cookware with a lifetime warranty, go-tox clinics for older post-mortals, safes, laser vision correction, and thirty-year tattoos. There are no wedding parlors, and I didn't see a single bachelor party the entire weekend. Just one cure party after another.

On our last day, there was a bomb threat in our section of the hotel. They evacuated our rooms and made us wait outside, on the Strip. It was the only time during our trip that I was reminded of 7/3/19, and it unnerved me. The manager assured us that they deal with these threats all the time, which only served to worry me more. As we waited on the Strip, I saw a group of men pass by on the opposite side of the street. They stopped, looked at the hotel, whispered some things to one another, and then kept walking. As they did, I saw one of them wave to the building, as if to say goodbye. I ran to alert a nearby officer, who seemed unconcerned. The men turned the corner. One of them saw me talking to the cop and smirked. He held up his hands and gave me the death symbol: a cupped left hand pressed against his straight right hand, forming a crude *D*.

After that, I didn't relax until we were on the plane heading back to LaGuardia. The flight was delayed for three hours due to traffic on the runway.

DATE MODIFIED:
11/15/2029, 3:02 P.M.

A Day in the Life of a Terra Troll

After my experience outside the Fountain of Youth, I came across this anonymous blog posting by someone who claimed to work at the resort.

> Contrary to what hotel officials say publicly, the FOY has been attacked by trolls on numerous occasions. These aren't just simple bomb threats, designed to keep us running around in circles. One troll sneaked into the fountain area, saw a fresh postmortal walking out of her cure ceremony, and threw lye right in her eyes, blinding her. The entire time security personnel were wrangling him and making him eat pavement, he was giggling like a madman.
>
> It's not the pro-death insurgents we fear while working here. We have tight enough security to make sure guns and bombs are kept out. It's the trolls that are the big problem. Because they aren't looking to kill people. They just want to ruin lives. If you stay here, you always have to keep your eyes out for them. Or else, boom! A handful of lye.
>
> —DanBenjaminsACheapskate

I'm glad I read that after I finished my stay, or else I'd have fled from the hotel like a terrified schoolboy. Then there's this profile of a troll that P. J. Matson wrote last month for *New York*. I needed to take a shower after reading it.

Under the Terra Troll Bridge

By P. J. Matson

XMN doesn't like people.

"I mostly keep to myself, because other people are annoying." He tells me this as we sit together in a burrito shop near his home in San Jose, California. The crowd at the shop is relatively sparse this afternoon, but XMN's mannerisms indicate that he feels anxious, even a bit claustrophobic. His eyes dart back and forth. He never once looks at our waitress while ordering. He scratches his face constantly, though he doesn't appear to have any bites or scrapes that would need relief.

"When I found out about the cure being legalized, I was crushed. Because the idea that there would be more people walking around, sucking in air like a bunch of fucking mouth breathers . . . I couldn't handle the idea. I always subscribed to the theory that hell is other people. Well, here come *more* other people! I get sick just thinking about it."

I ask XMN why he dislikes people so much. "Because none of them have ever been nice to me," he says.

At the time of legalization, XMN (pronounced "examine") was part of a large online subculture of people known as "trolls," cyberanarchists who enjoy wreaking as much havoc online as they possibly can—on message boards, blogs, feeds, everywhere. XMN claims to have once hacked into the e-mail account of a famous politician and deleted its entire contents. "The news was never made public, but in the days after you could see it in his eyes. He looked like he hadn't slept for seventy-two hours," the troll boasts. XMN also cites multiple occasions when he found the ping feeds of family members of the doctors killed in the New York and Oregon bombings and sent them hateful messages, some in the voice of their deceased loved ones. "I sent one to Sarah Otto. It said, 'Hey, honey. I can't talk right now. Some kids are roasting marshmallows over my burning carcass. Love, Graham.' I laughed for days."

But soon XMN grew to find simple online trolling unfulfilling. "You have to put out a lot of bait just to catch one fish," he tells me. "And each day it's harder and harder to shock and offend people, even if I send out a photo of a boy being castrated or something like that. They've seen it all before, or they know not to click. It's easy to become desensitized to that kind of stuff online. But it's nowhere near as easy to ignore it if happens to you for real."

So on the message board he calls home, an enormous trolling site called SiPhallus, XMN exchanged private messages with a group of fellow trolls and decided it would be more fun to wreak their havoc live and in person. He refuses to go into exact details about what he has done, fearing it will lead to his arrest. He suggests that I try to guess.

Vandalism? "Yes."

Bomb threats? "Yes."

Blinding people? "Just once, but I'd like to do more."

Keying cars? "Yes."

Killing pets? "Yes. Or blinding them."

Arson? "No, but only because it's hard to get away with."

Draining bank accounts? "Yes."

I ask XMN why he doesn't choose to cross the line into full pro-death fanaticism and kill people outright. "I'm not a nutjob. I'm not a terrorist," he protests. "I'm not going to go around killing people. I just think that if people are going to live in this world, why do they deserve to be happier than me? They should have to go through every day feeling as lousy as I feel. And then, maybe, they'll stop walking around like they own the place. Maybe they'll have some respect for other people, like me."

XMN admits to coming from a broken home. His mother died when he was young, and he says his father physically abused him and sexually abused his sister. Ridiculed at school for his gawky appearance, XMN walled off the people around him and took refuge in the online community on SiPhallus. "They're people like me. They understand that this whole society thing is a bunch of bullshit."

But doesn't he ever crave real contact with people? "Not really. I'm very private. I don't like being touched. I don't like it when people are friendly to me. It's like, 'Who are you? What the hell do you have to be so sunny about?'"

I ask XMN how many other "terra trolls" are now out there, planning to wreak havoc. His eyes twinkle. It's the first time all day that I've seen him express genuine excitement. "There are a lot more of us than people think. And more people are joining every day." It's hard to know if he's telling the truth or simply playing another one of his games. Studies of terra trolling are nonexistent, and laws against it are just now coming into shape. There's no data for terra troll crimes committed as of yet.

I ask XMN if perhaps this is not the best way to spend one's time. I ask if it might be a symptom of a much deeper personal problem that he has failed to address. He thinks for a moment. "Yeah, I'm sure that's part of it. Then again, I don't know if the problems I have can ever be fixed. I don't know how you go about being reborn into a family that loves you. I think I'm damaged permanently. And if that's the case, everyone else deserves the same fate."

He finishes his burrito and tells me a story of the time he broke into a woman's house and stole her cat. He drove the cat fifty miles south and released it out into the wild. "That way," he says, "she'll never know what happened to it. It's a double whammy."

I ask XMN why he did it.

"Because it's funny," he says. "It's so funny to me. It makes me laugh." He does not laugh when he says this.

He leaves the shop early, as I pay the tab. When I walk out to my car, I see a small sticky note attached to my front right tire. I grab it.

"I could have stabbed your tire, but I didn't," the note says. "Just this once, I'll be a nice person."

DATE MODIFIED:
11/16/2029, 10:19 A.M.

Afternoon Link Roundup

❯ A South African freighter had to be rescued by an American destroyer after it became immobilized in the Great Pacific Garbage Patch. (*Mail & Gaurdian*)

❯ Russia's population climbs above two hundred million for the first time as its government makes getting the cure mandatory for all military personnel under the age of thirty. (*The Times*)

❯ Casey Jarrett's mother speaks out for the first time about watching her son be executed. I think it's possible to feel sympathy for her while having absolutely no sympathy for her son. (ABC)

❯ The date of the consumer gas ban has been pushed back to March 1, 2037. (FNN)

❯ Leighton Astor was convicted of killing her billionaire father in an attempt to prematurely claim his estate. Her father had a cure age of sixty-two. The night of the murder, one witness heard her screaming, "I WANT WHAT IS RIGHTFULLY MINE." (*The New York Times*)

❯ New studies show that postmortals are 59 percent more likely to develop cirrhosis of the liver within the next ten years than their true organic counterparts. (DanBlog)

❯ The West Antarctic Ice Sheet may be gone by the end of the decade. (BBC)

▶ The staunchly anti-cure town of Soda Springs, Idaho (home to the Mormon sect known as the Deliverance Church of Jesus Christ of Latter Day Saints, or DLDS), has built a wall around itself and quietly seceded from the United States. Town mayor Thomas Maskin explains why: "The concept of America has outlived its usefulness. Why should we pay 30 percent of our salaries to help keep some crack addict in Detroit on welfare for the next thousand years? Why should we care about people in California? Or Florida? Or New York? Why should we share anything with them? They're not our people. They're not our family. They're as foreign to me as Arabs. They all want to live forever and don't have the faintest clue how they're gonna eat a hundred years from now. Well, they're going to find out soon that their country ain't gonna help them. They're gonna find out every man is his own country now." (*The New Yorker*)

▶ Annual sales of cigarettes have reached an all-time low. My friend Walsh now accounts for the majority of all Parliaments sold in the United States. (NYist)

▶ The producers of the *Saved by the Bell* reboot petitioned the governor of California to allow them to administer the cure to the show's teenage stars, so that their characters wouldn't have to graduate in the show. The governor denied the request. (*Variety*)

DATE MODIFIED:
11/17/2029, 4:44 P.M.

"I've made a terrible mistake"

That's my dad talking. He was grumpy all day long on Thanks-giving, even during the football game.

"I never should have gotten the cure," he said.

"Why not?"

"You know I got laughed at the other day? I was walking to the supermarket and there was a group of kids outside the store. They couldn't have been more than twelve. And they just sat there and laughed at me, calling me 'old man' and all that garbage."

"So what?" I said. "They're just kids."

"Yeah, and they didn't let me forget it. They were more than happy to let me know that I don't belong in this world anymore. I feel like I'm stuck outside a ballroom window, watching a great party everyone but me got invited to."

"I thought you were happy. I thought all your buddies got it."

"They did. Ted Maxwell got it and then had his face done. They pulled his cheeks damn near behind his ears. He looks like a moron. I knew I shouldn't have gotten this done. I knew it!" The tightly upholstered armrests of his dining chair had become worn and frayed. He angrily picked at the loose threads.

"Why are you suddenly so upset about this?" I asked.

"Because I did what everyone else was doing instead of doing what I truly wanted to do. It was such a dumb thing, and now I can't undo it. I'm old, and I'm tired, and I hate waking up to that reality every day."

"But that's just life, Dad. That doesn't change if you don't get the cure. It gets worse because you keep getting older."

"And that much closer to your mother. I could have joined her in a better place."

I rolled my eyes. "Oh, come on. That whole thing about being in a better place is a crock. It's just something to comfort people in the face of dying or in the face of losing someone they love. You don't need that. You don't have to worry about trying to cover up your fears anymore."

He slammed his beer down on the table and grabbed my arm. "Oh, so it's supposed to comfort me to know there isn't a better place after this? Is it really supposed to make me feel better to know that your mom has evaporated completely? That she never had a soul? That her love for me died with her? Is that supposed to make me feel all happy inside, John?"

I retreated as fast as I could. Sometimes I'm far too casual in how I speak to my father. "I didn't mean it like that."

"I don't like the idea of sitting here forever."

"Then don't," I said. "Get up. Get out there."

"I've done that already. Don't you get it? I spent my entire life trying to find the place I liked best. *This* is that place. I don't want to leave here and go touring India or anything like that. This is where I'm most comfortable. This is where my life is. But I don't know what to do with myself anymore. Before all this, I was content. I knew exactly what the plan was. And now . . . now I haven't got a clue. I'm an old person, John. You know old people hate change. This is a *big* change. Your mother bought us a new toaster oven twenty years ago, and I still miss the one we had before that. And that was just a goddamn toaster oven! Everything is upside down. I don't have a job. I don't have enough money to live here for as long as I please, to buy food and pay property tax. It'll run out."

"I'll support you."

"Forever? You have a kid on the way. You have no clue how much those things cost. You'll use every goddamn penny life gives you, mark my words. I don't want you subsidizing my life."

"We'll work something out. I promise you."

"Yeah, yeah. Either way, it was the wrong decision. I've made a terrible mistake. And I'm not happy about it." He held up the gravy boat. "And we're out of gravy. That's what the next two hundred years of my life are going to be like. Just one Thanksgiving after another, without enough goddamn gravy."

DATE MODIFIED:
11/30/2029, 2:03 P.M.

The Truth about China

Chan is a Chinese foreign national who spent a year at our firm as part of an exchange program they set up about nine years ago. The firm was looking into a major expansion in Beijing, setting up a merger over there with another firm. Obviously, after China went back into its shell, that merger never took place. I kept in touch with Chan from time to time via e-mail—that is, before the government blocked his access. After that, I assumed I'd never hear from him again.

But I did. He e-mailed me this week through the account of some American in Beijing. Apparently, he spotted the American typing away on her tablet at an ice cream store. Since the American had an unregulated e-mail work account, he begged her to let him use her account to contact me. This is what he wrote:

To: John Farrell
Re: Chan in China (URGENT)

My wife and I had a child three days ago. It is our first child, a boy. Everything appeared to be fine during the labor and delivery. My wife had to push for two hours, which was quite harrowing. But our son emerged healthy and with all his fingers and toes. They even let me cut the cord, which is much harder than one might think.

My wife had some tearing during the delivery, so the doctors had to give her stitches. I had been by her side the whole time, but now she was knocked out by the anesthetic and had let go of my hand. Rather than stay with her, I followed the nurses as they wheeled our son to the nursery so I could give him a bath. They handed me a warm washcloth, and I swabbed the blood and waxy white vernix off his body while he lay in the clear plastic bassinet, which they had placed under a heat lamp. It was a wonderful moment because I could still feel the heat on his skin from being inside my wife's body. I can't describe it in a way that would justify it, but it was something I won't soon forget.

I was still washing behind his ears, when a doctor came in and began wheeling my son's bassinet away, which startled me.

"What are you doing?" I asked.

"We have to take him," he told me.

"But I'm not finished bathing him," I explained. I held up the bloody washcloth in my hand to show him that I was still using it.

"You can finish bathing him later. We have to take him now." He was very brusque, and I didn't understand why. I know that doctors can be arrogant, but he struck me as particularly pushy.

"What are you going to do to him?"

"Routine shots and blood tests."

"Can I come?"

"No, you can't. We'll bring him back to you in an hour or so."

I wanted to insist on joining my son. But this man was a doctor, so I presumed that he knew best. I didn't wish to ruin the moment with an argument. So I let them take him away and rejoined my wife, who was now in the recovery room, asleep.

After about an hour, they transferred us to the maternity ward on the floor above us. As we exited the elevator, we noticed armed policemen standing in the center of each hallway, which is unusual inside a hospital, let alone a maternity ward. All around the floor, from nearly every room, we heard screaming and crying, as if we were still in the labor ward. I asked the nurse if they also delivered babies on this floor. (This is China, after all. It wouldn't have surprised me in the least if they needed more room.) The nurse turned away from me and said no.

They wheeled my wife into an empty room, with one bed. Again, this was unusual. You don't get a recovery room to yourself normally. At this point I became very anxious to see my son again. I asked the nurse where he was, so that I could be with him and bring him to my wife. She assured me that he would be coming shortly.

But he didn't arrive shortly. My wife and I were forced to stay in the empty room for nearly four hours. She had lost a great deal of blood during the delivery, and now her blood pressure began to drop. I became irritable, constantly yelling at the nurses that they had assured me our son would be back by now. After one nurse worked to bring my wife's pressure back up and she regained her strength, I ventured out into the hallway and asked anyone I could find where the blood tests were being conducted. No official would answer me. I heard more screams from inside the other rooms. I went to a receptionist and demanded to know what was going on. One of the policemen saw me getting angry and approached me.

"You have to calm down here, sir," he said. "It's not wise for you to yell."

"But no one will tell me what is going on or where my son is."

"Your son will be returned to you."

And he was correct. The main doors opened behind me, and I saw a nurse wheeling in my son. I went to him immediately and grabbed him, kissing him all over. I was so relieved—I can't even begin to tell you. Pure joy.

They had him swaddled in a hospital blanket. I didn't want to unwrap him, lest he become cold. So I held him tight to my chest as the nurse and policeman both inspected my hospital wristband to make sure I was the baby's parent.

As I held my son close to me, I noticed something through the opening of the blanket. His left hand was sticking out a bit, so I went to tuck it back in. That's when I saw it.

Just below his hand, about five centimeters up his wrist, was writing. I pulled his arm out to look. It was his birth date, written on the inside of his arm.

"Why would you write on his arm?" I asked, annoyed. "His birth date is already on his ankle bracelet." I used the blanket to try and rub off the numbers, but they wouldn't smudge. I quickly realized that they hadn't written his birth date on his arm. They had tattooed it. While my wife and I were waiting for our son to get "routine shots and blood tests," they had branded him. I looked at the nurses and the policeman, who looked back at me with deep sympathy.

"We're sorry," the policeman said. "This policy was just instituted by the Department of Containment."

"The Department of Containment?" I asked. "What is that?"

"We don't know."

"Why are they doing this?"

"We don't know."

I heard more screams coming from inside the other rooms and immediately became aware that I was just the latest parent to receive this news about their child.

I stared down the hall, in the direction of my wife's room. She was still unaware of what had happened. I felt so awful. There she was, so desperate to see her son. Yet there wasn't going to be any relief once I brought him through the door. She was going to see what they had done to him, and she would begin screaming, as all the other new mothers were doing. I began to cry. I clutched my son tightly to my chest and told him that he would be all right. It was just his birthday they had etched onto him, and nothing more unfortunate than that.

I brought him to my wife's room and walked through the door. She could tell by my eyes that something was terribly wrong, and she began crying. I think she assumed our son had a birth defect, or that he had been injured during the delivery. I handed him to her and unveiled the spot where they had branded them.

I'll never forget the look on her face. She was so shocked, so horrified, so baffled. She didn't understand. She began sobbing and screaming. I held her tight.

"Why? *Why* did they do this?" she asked.

"I don't know," I said.

As she cried, two more doctors and two more nurses entered the room. I was again aggravated, because all I wanted after this was to have some privacy with my wife. I asked for more time.

"We have to move her to a group room," one of the nurses said. "This room is only for people to absorb the news. Another patient is scheduled to be in here."

One of the doctors took my arm. "We need to see you for a moment, sir." I resisted. The policeman showed up at our door, giving me a look that said I needed to go with him. What choice did I have? I went with the doctor and the policeman as they led me to another empty room. I thought they were going to arrest me for yelling, for being upset in the lobby.

"Do you have any identification?" the doctor asked. I produced some. Then he said, "I need you to roll up your sleeve."

I panicked. I jumped to leave the room, but the policeman blocked the way and threw me to the floor. The doctor joined him in holding me down.

"You must not resist!" the doctor screamed.

"Why are you doing this?"

"It is the law now! We all must have it!" The doctor rolled up his sleeve and showed me his tattoo. The policeman did likewise. I stared at their arms for a few moments. I couldn't believe it. They both nodded at me. I had no choice but to relent. The doctor sat me on the table and asked me to confirm the birth date on my identification. I did so. "You look pretty young for a forty-year-old," he said to me.

I never told you this, John, but when I worked at your firm I got the cure. My wife too. We knew China had outlawed both giving it and getting it. And we had heard stories of doctors being killed—far worse stories than even what happened to Dr. Otto back in your country. We thought we were going to live in the States permanently, so we had it done. Then China isolated itself soon after we returned, and our dream of living in America was dashed. But we cannot undo the cure now. Our youth has damned us.

I lied to the doctor as best I could. They didn't know I had lived in America. If they had, they almost certainly would have detained me. I think my receding hairline was enough to convince them that I probably hadn't taken it. Can you believe that? All these years I have cursed my hairline. Now it's the only thing keeping me out of prison. They strapped my arm down, and the doctor branded me with my birth date. I could see the ink spreading under my raw skin, seeping into the dermis and staying there forever.

When I was brought to my wife's group room, I found that they had inscribed her arm as well. To my horror, she was no longer sobbing and crying like the other mothers around her. She simply lay on the bed, staring at the ceiling with her eyes bulging, not saying a word. Our son was crying next to her. I touched her shoulder to see if she was okay. She gave me a look of helplessness and turned back to the ceiling, dead silent—like a torture victim who falls into catatonic shock.

When they discharged us the following day, I saw the hordes of police rounding people up. By this time word had spilled out across the city. Some of them were going quietly, with the attitude that they had nothing to hide. Others were fleeing in terror. My neighbor emptied his apartment and said he was going to drive north until he couldn't drive anymore.

I have no idea what to do, John. We must leave the country now, or else they'll almost certainly figure out that my wife and I had our ages frozen. I do not expect you to be able to help me personally. In fact, I ask that you do not. Any attempt to try to help us leave the country will be seen as an attempt to defect. All I ask is that you send this to others, to let people know what is going on here right now. We have been branded. And I fear greatly that we will be killed.

Your friend,
Chan

One of the superiors at my firm deals with higher-ups in the Chinese government all the time. You can still get out of the country if you know the right people. When my superior asked his contact about the prospect of bringing Chan back to the States, the official said he would make a phone call. This was a trustworthy contact, someone who had helped extricate many Chinese on behalf of American economic interests. He called my superior back, telling him Chan and his wife had already been arrested. Chan sent me this e-mail twenty-four hours ago, a free man. Now, we have no clue where he and his wife are or where his son is. The Chinese official said it would be folly to divulge Chan's real name publicly in hopes of exerting pressure, and that it would likely hasten Chan's death rather than his freedom.

I'm sorry, Chan. I'm so terribly sorry.

DATE MODIFIED:
5/9/2030, 6:17 P.M.

The Back of the Ambulance

I had a nightmare last night about my son's impending birth. I was in an ambulance with Sonia. Only, she didn't look like Sonia. She looked like a blonde woman with an impossible body, the kind that pops up in my subconscious on a near-monthly basis. In the dream I thought of her as Sonia, and she spoke with Sonia's voice. She was lying on a gurney at the front of the ambulance, and I was at the back, some twenty yards away. I was pressed against the back door by a group of policemen wearing blast shields, obscuring their eyes. Three or four more policemen were holding blonde Sonia down on the gurney as she writhed in pain. One of them had a branding iron with her name on it and was advancing toward her. I tried to scream, but my fear was such that my motor function had ceased and my brain couldn't relay the signal for my mouth to open. I wanted so badly to scream at the top of my lungs to get them to stop. I felt that if I could just get the words out, they'd put the iron down. I tried again to shout, but my jaw remained bolted in place. I struggled against the phantom lock. And just as the policeman began to press the glowing red iron into her shoulder, I woke up, fists clenched, my mouth finally opening. Only, I didn't say "Sonia." I just let out a weird nonword: "Swaahhh!" I quickly regained my bearings and shook it off.

The Chinese official our firm knows has told us it's unlikely that he'll ever be able to ascertain where Chan and his wife and son are. I'm powerless to help. Yet, sitting here, I still feel as if I'm complicit in allowing their disappearance to happen.

DATE MODIFIED:
5/13/2030, 8:12 A.M.

Afternoon Link Roundup

▶ In British Columbia, three doctors were killed after a pro-death insurgent with dynamite strapped to his chest ran up to them during a hotel conference. (CBC)

▶ Sales of adult incontinence undergarments (you know them as Depends) have fallen 46 percent since 2016. (ConsumerBulletin)

▶ The mayor has raised tolls at all Hudson River crossings to an even twenty dollars to help pay for the new levee system. (*The New York Observer*)

▶ Some good news from the Middle East. Suicide bombings are down nearly 70 percent over the past decade. The problem is that nonsuicide bombings are up 220 percent in the same time frame. (Al-Ihiri)

▶ In an interview, Russian president Boris Solovyev vigorously denied numerous reports of police excuting any Russian citizen over the cure age of fifty. (Chris Manning's feed)

▶ The family of the last living Alzheimer's patient to be "cured" by Dr. Graham Otto is suing his estate for $100 million. (AP)

▶ On Ryan Wexler's five hundredth home run: "It's clear now that, barring amputation, he should break the all-time record sometime next decade. Of course, he'll hold that record for about three seconds, because teammates Frank Mitchell and Odalis Concepción are right behind him. And so are about fifty other players in

the American League alone. I have no problem with players taking the cure and breaking records and all that. They're just
records. In the end you're supposed to enjoy the game itself, and
not the long-term compiling of numbers. And the never-ending
influx of long-lasting talent (thanks to the cure) will make the
game better than ever. But one thing that does concern me is how
we're going to quantify success from this day forward. Naturally,
Ryan Wexler will break the record, but we all know it isn't
because he is a better player than his predecessors. It's not a
tragedy. It's just the cure forcing us to redefine the notion of
excellence. This isn't just a baseball thing. This is an issue across
the entire culture now. How can you be a success or have a legacy
if your career—nay, your entire life—has no definitive story arc?"
(BaseballNut's Feed)

▶ Utah finally declares cycle-marriage contracts illegal. That was
fast. (*Deseret News*)

DATE MODIFIED:
5/13/2030, 4:53 P.M.

Confessions of a Nonstockpiler

I know everyone's into stockpiling right now. I haven't taken any kind of action on this front. I'm the antistockpiler. I can't get rid of my crap fast enough. I looked in the fridge the other day and found three items, two of which had gone bad. The mustard is still good, if I ever buy anything to put it on. Closet space is at a premium in my apartment. If I buy a sweatshirt, it better be the greatest sweatshirt ever invented to justify the space it takes up.

I have at least two friends who have rented out storage facilities in New Jersey at prices that would make you wince. They haven't put anything in them yet. One of them is still haggling with his wife over what should be included in the cache. But they're amateurs next to this one client I met with a week ago.

This guy was originally from Texas but now maintains a giant compound out in eastern Pennsylvania. I drove out there with my boss. The estate was completely walled, on all sides, and there was a watchtower with a guard on duty twenty-four hours a day. The only thing missing were those little slit windows for archers to shoot out of.

"What do you think?" he asked me.

"I think it looks very . . . safe."

"The best part about it is that my daughter can't sneak out at night anymore to go to parties. In fact, that's damn near the only reason why we have the walls and the guard and all this superficial bullshit. It's not about keepin' people out. It's about keepin' that wild child in. Because unless I got a goddamn chopper in the sky watching her every move, she weasels out and is raisin' hell first chance she gets."

"She sounds cool."

"That's what all the boys say. Like I said, this is just window dressing. Let me show you the real state-of-the-art shit."

He took us out of the main house and across his campus to a very small stainless-steel shack. It didn't appear to have any door. He punched a code into a smooth keypad etched on one side of the structure. A panel opened next to it, with a small glass plank extending out toward us. Then the Texan took a small Q-tip out of his pocket, swabbed the inside of his cheek, and smeared it on the glass. The plank retracted into the panel, and a hidden door materialized on the adjacent side.

"Genetic identification," he said. "When they first set it up, it would take a drop of my blood. But I got sick a havin' my finger poked every time I wanted to show this puppy off, so they engineered one that uses Mr. Q-Tip here."

We walked through the hidden door, which turned out to belong to some kind of elevator. The Texan pushed a button, the door closed, and down we went. Dropping. Dropping. Dropping. I began sweating. The floor finally stopped giving way beneath us, and the doors opened to reveal a vast luxury apartment. I let out a sigh of relief. There may have been four billion tons of dirt and rock above us, but the lavishness of our surroundings served to diminish that fact considerably. It was a fallout shelter. But it was a really *nice* one. We could have been at the top of the Dakota, if the Dakota had somehow been inverted or sunken down into the earth's surface. A low-sink high-rise, if you will. There were marble floors, UDTVs, pieces of furniture that probably cost as much as my apartment, and more. Fresh, cool oxygen permeated the air, as if I were back on the Fountain of Youth casino floor, fighting to stay awake at 5:00 A.M. The Texan poured us a drink and guided us through.

"How did you get all this stuff down here?" I asked him.

"All through that little elevator shaft. Can you believe it? Took 'em two years to build the space and another two years to furnish it. Y'all New Yorkers think you're so smart and tough. But it takes a real Texan to know how to fend for hisself. Don't let all this fancy shit fool you. This space is 100 percent self-sustainable. You see this water?" He turned on the tap. "It's tapped from the groundwater above our heads. Completely independent piping system. I never told the county about it. Matter of fact, I didn't tell the county jack shit about this place. All they see is a steel shit-house. See these air vents?" He pointed to the air vents. "That's a central air system that pipes in oxygen from up on that mountain y'all drove over to get here. There's a filter midway through the system that takes out any impurities, plus a Geiger counter. If the radiation goes over a certain level, the system automatically seals itself off and we go on oxygen reserve. I have a twenty-year stock-pile of it. Same with the water. And the whiskey'll last me *thirty*! Ha!"

"Jesus."

"Oh, he's here too." He pointed to a velvet painting of Jesus behind the wet bar. "I told Jesus that if the water and whiskey run out, I promise to start believin' in him again. He's my backup backup. I'm not a wine guy otherwise. Let me show you the pantry."

He took us into a miniwarehouse with shelf after shelf of packaged goods, condensed milk, and booze. At the end was a walk-in freezer that extended back some thirty-odd yards. Entire sides of beef were vacuum-packed and stacked on large metal shelving units inside.

"I can probably make this last ten years," the Texan said. "Long as I don't get greedy."

There was more to show us. There was a control room with seismic detectors that could create a digital image of the ground above us, presumably to defend against anyone trying to burrow into the shelter and steal all the ground chuck. The command center monitoring this activity was manned at all times. The Texan told us he hired miners for the job, since they were so used to working underground. There was a gaming room. And a walk-in humidor. He also showed us his arsenal. Then he showed us his other arsenal. Then his third arsenal. He showed us a giant wall toward the back of the bunker that was made entirely of vulcanized rubber. Behind the rubber was another steel wall, then more rubber, and then a forty-thousand-barrel oil reserve. He also had a room dedicated solely to his toy train set. I thought that was a nice touch. I pictured him wearing a big engineer's cap and yelling out "choo-choo!" while the world burned above him.

When the tour was over, he turned to me. "You start stockpiling yet?"

I felt inadequate. My lifetime assets could have fit in his liquor cabinet. "Not really," I said. "I do keep an extra stick of deodorant in the closet, just in case."

"Well then, you're wayyyy behind! Hell, I don't really plan on ever living in this stupid place. But at least I know I have a secure area to house my supplies. You best do it sooner rather than later. I'm tellin' you. Just like the guidelines in Marty Frost's book say, you need a couple years' worth of water; a couple years of canned beans, tuna, and vegetables; a couple years of powdered milk . . . What about guns? You got guns?"

"No."

"Good God! That's damn near irresponsible! Most valuable commodity we have right now. Didn't you say you had a baby boy on the way? You need a gun. Here." He opened up the inside pocket of his hunting jacket, took out a small automatic, removed the clip, and handed the gun and clip to me. "Take this."

"Oh, I couldn't."

"Take it! I've fallen out of love with this one anyway. I can't promise you an invite down into this lovely abode when the shit hits the fan. This is the least I can do. Take it."

"All right." I took the gun. There's something about holding a gun. It feels so comfortable in your hand, as if the grip has been molded just for you. It's always inviting you to squeeze it.

"That's right," he said. "You take that gun and you learn to fire it at a movin' target. And start stocking up. Even if you don't end up needing it, there might be some poor soul out there willing to pay you handsomely for it. Now let me show you the septic system."

He showed us the septic system, which he said could treat two hundred pounds of raw sewage a week. At the end of the tour, he took us up in the elevator and back out into the glare of raw daylight. I took in the air, which tasted stale compared to the oxygen buried a thousand feet below in the Texan's nuclear-holocaust condo. On the ride back to the city, I offered the gun to my boss.

"I don't want it," he said.

"What the hell do I do with it?"

"I dunno. Sell it or something."

When we got back, I stopped at the grocery store to pick up dinner. I stared at the bottled water on the lowest shelf. I thought about grabbing a bunch of cases. But I didn't have an airplane hangar buried in the earth's lower mantle to house them. So I grabbed a frozen pizza and a Coke instead. At my apartment I took the gun and clip and stashed them both away in my closet. There's a police station fifteen blocks away that will give you a seventy-five-dollar gift certificate for groceries if you trade in your gun. I'm taking advantage of the offer, because I need all the canned beans I can get.

DATE MODIFIED:
5/15/2030, 12:34 P.M.

What Do We Do with Baby Emilia?

Transcribed from Cara Forlani's piece on CBS's website:

Forlani: Her mother calls her the perfect baby. And by outward appearances, little Emilia Burkhart is exactly that: a beautiful eight-month-old baby girl, with huge brown eyes, a shock of auburn hair, and a half-moon smile that is downright infectious to all around her. Little Emilia rarely cries. She sleeps through the night and can light up any house with the sound of her laughter. She is perfect—and this is the disturbing story of what her mother did to keep her that way.

Mia Burkhart: I love my daughter. I love her. I know people have called me a monster, but I'm not. I look at her and what I see is a happy child. She laughs all the time. She smiles all the time. She's purer of heart than anyone you or I know.

Forlani (narrating): Mia Burkhart is Emilia's mother. She's forty-four years old, with a cure age of thirty-five. Divorced with two grown children, Mia decided three years ago she wanted to become a mother again—this time on her own. With no boyfriend or husband to help her conceive, Mia decided to contact a local sperm bank, secure sperm from an anonymous donor, and receive in vitro fertilization.

Mia: They asked me what sex I wanted the child to be and I said, "A girl! A girl!" I remember shouting it out at the top of my lungs in the doctor's office.

Forlani: You were done having boys.

Mia: Oh yes. Done! When you have two boys, you don't need a third. No, I definitely wanted a girl. And when they showed me the rendering at twenty weeks, I knew she was going to be special. I just sat there and stared at the screen, crying. I knew she was going to be the most beautiful baby in the whole wide world. It was like watching all your hopes in life turn into this little person.

Forlani (narrating): Twenty weeks after that ultrarendering, little Emilia Sugar Burkhart was born in a relatively easy and uneventful delivery. After just a day in the hospital, Mia was discharged and brought her new daughter home with her. For the next eight months, Mia dedicated herself to raising Emilia full-time, having successfully petitioned her employer to let her work at home. She fed Emilia, took her for walks, and practiced cosleeping with her.

Debra Cousin: I thought they were both cute as buttons.

Forlani (narrating): Debra Cousin is Mia Burkhart's former neighbor.

Cousin: They would come strolling down the street and stop to chat nearly every day. And of course, I'm a grandmother, so any baby that comes near me . . . Well, I'm helpless to resist.

Forlani (narrating): But after a year and a half of seeing Mia push baby Emilia around the block, Cousin noticed something unusual.

Cousin: She wasn't getting any bigger.

Forlani: You mean Emilia.

Cousin: Right. The baby. But it's one of those things you can never be sure about. Every child grows differently. I had four children of my own, and they change so slightly from day to day that you don't notice how much they've grown until you take a look at some of the older pictures and say, "My goodness! They have grown!" It's like staring at the hour hand of a clock. You don't see it moving even though it is. So it was very difficult to tell with Emilia. But I never saw her walk. I never heard her talk. She was just always in her stroller, kicking her little feet.

Forlani: Did you suspect then that Mia had given her daughter the cure?

Cousin: No. No, I thought the child, frankly, had some sort of developmental problem. The kind of thing you never, ever bring up. That's what I thought. It didn't occur to me that someone would give an eight-month-old baby the cure.

Forlani (narrating): But that's exactly what Mia Burkhart had done. Around the time Emilia turned eight months old, Mia decided that she didn't want her perfect little baby to grow up at all.

Mia: One day I looked at her, and I asked her if she was happy the way she was. And she said yes to me.

Forlani: But she couldn't talk.

Mia: She didn't have to. I saw it in her eyes.

Forlani (narrating): After deciding to give her daughter the cure, Mia visited an online directory of back-alley curists—curists who are not licensed geneticists and offer the cure to desperate customers at a reduced sum, some for as low as a thousand dollars. Many back-alley curists are scam artists, often injecting their victims with a harmless saline solution, the kind you find in IV drips. Unfortunately for baby Emilia, the back-alley curist her mother hired was legitimate.

Mia: I knew that this was what she wanted, that this was going to give her a lifetime of happiness.

Forlani: But didn't you want to watch her grow? Isn't that the joy of having children? To see them grow and develop into their own people?

Mia: I've seen my children grow before. I don't think much good came of it. They die every year, you know. They turn one and they never wear a onesie again. They turn two and they never use a sippy cup again. The child they used to be dies, and that child doesn't come back. They're born to be ruined. One of my sons is in jail now. The other one is addicted to drugs. He'll disappear for months at a time, then show up at my door demanding money. I've seen my kids grow. I've seen them leave. I've seen them become unhappy people with lives they don't want. That will never happen to Emilia. She'll never be forced to lose her innocence before it's time. The world will always be a wonderful, magical place for her.

Forlani: But you're in jail now. Doesn't that hurt her? Don't you think she misses her mother?

Mia: Well, if they would simply let me out of here to be a mother to my child, that wouldn't be a problem.

Forlani (narrating): Debra Cousin may not have sensed that baby Emilia had gotten the cure. But others did, including Mia's own sister, Wendy Malek.

Wendy Malek: I knew something was wrong with the child, but I was very careful about bringing it up around Mia. I'd always phrase things in the most polite way possible. Just a simple "how is she?" Things like that. And then, one night, I was watching the news. And I saw a report about what was going on in Thailand, how there were young girls over there who had been given the cure and sold as prostitutes. And that's when it hit me.

Forlani: You knew.

Malek: I knew. I knew, and I was horrified.

Forlani (narrating): According to police reports, one evening Wendy decided to confront Mia about her suspicions. Mia then confessed to giving Emilia the cure, begging her sister not to tell anyone. Four days later, Wendy Malek called the police, to tell them what her sister had done.

Forlani: How did it feel, having to make that call?

Malek (crying): It was agony. This baby . . . She's always going to be a baby. I thought maybe the best thing to do was leave it alone. Otherwise, who's going to care for the child? Mia was the only one willing to do it. So I thought about not calling the police, but I knew in my heart I couldn't live with that. Mia has always had her problems. She's been troubled. But I never expected her to do something like this.

Forlani (narrating): Federal officials say that so-called Peter Pan cases, like that of Emilia Burkhart, remain relatively rare, accounting for roughly one-tenth of a percent of people who receive the cure here in the United States. For the time being, Emilia is staying with Wendy Malek and her husband and their four children. But Wendy worries constantly about the future.

Malek: We've all gotten the cure, but I don't know how we handle this kind of burden. Emilia will be a baby for as long as she lives. And I know I have to care for her that whole time. But to think that I'll never see her grow into a woman? That's more than I can stand. It makes me sick to think about it. And the guilt . . . There are days when I don't want to care for her, and that kills me. I feel terrible because I know Emilia's powerless to do anything about it. What if something happens to me? What if something happens to Mia when she gets out of jail? Who's going to care for this child then? Who's going to want that responsibility?

Forlani: Do you still feel you did the right thing in calling the police?

Malek: I don't know. And I don't know that I ever will.

Forlani (narrating): While Hennepin County prosecutors pursue aggravated-assault charges against her, Mia Burkhart remains in the county jail, eagerly awaiting the day when she can rejoin her little girl and spend the rest of their postmortal lives together. Emilia is now twenty-seven months old. There is no telling how old she will be when she sees her mother again. But if she does, she'll still have an irreversible cure age of just eight months.

Forlani: Do you hate your sister for notifying the police?

Mia: I do. I think she was jealous. I think she knew this was the prettiest baby in the world, and I think she wanted Emilia for herself.

Forlani: After what's happened to you, do you regret giving Emilia the cure?

Mia: No.

Forlani: But you're in jail. You may never see her again.

Mia: I know that we'll be reunited someday. They can't keep me in here forever. And when they let me go, I'll have Emilia back. She's going to see me, and those big eyes are going to light up. She'll be so happy. She's going to love me forever. And she'll always love me more than she loves anyone else in the world. It'll be so blissful.

Forlani: You don't think this will hurt her? Cause her emotional pain?

Mia: Well, babies are resilient. That's why I got her the cure to begin with. There's so much ugliness in the world, and it only seems to get uglier by the day. But she'll never have to worry about any of those things. She'll still be a perfect little baby. She'll never know. Ever.

Forlani: Do you plan on having more kids?

Mia (smiling): No.

Forlani: I don't think I believe you.

Mia: Well, I don't let others judge me. I know what kind of mother I am. And so does Emilia.

I already saw that *Sky News* is branding this lady the Freezer Mom. There's a report on Mike O'Grady's feed that she already has a publicist and is shopping a TV show.

DATE MODIFIED:
5/20/2030, 9:07 P.M.

"He looks just like you"

Sonia had another ultrasound yesterday morning because the baby's amniotic fluid was low. I was at work when she called me from the doctor's office.

"The baby has a low heart rate," she said. "I have to go to the hospital and be induced."

"Right now?"

"Right now."

"Holy shit."

I hung up and flew out of the office. When I got to the hospital, Sonia was still on her way. I tried to sit and wait, but I was far too restless for that. I felt the need to be productive, even though I had nothing to do. So I got up and—I don't know—dawdled. I spent two solid hours being a great annoyance to myself.

Eventually, Sonia came sauntering through the door with Nate, her fiancé. She looked relaxed, as if she was going for a pedicure. Her hair was a different color. She was a blonde now.

"Are you okay? Are you okay? Are you okay?"

"John, relax. I'm not in labor. I have to check in, and then they give me the Pitocin. We'll be here awhile. Just mellow out. You're here for the long haul."

I exhaled. "Your hair looks different," I said.

"I had it done. I found a new geneticist, Dr. Neil. He's great. Like the blonde?"

"Sure. Absolutely."

She checked in and we were escorted to a delivery room. They stripped Sonia down, put her in a gown, squirted a tablespoonful of transparent goo onto her stomach, and strapped a heart monitor onto her. For the next twelve hours, we sat watching the contraction monitor, staring at the peaks and valleys. At some point the contractions were supposed to become more intense and frequent. But as far as I could tell, the peaks on the screen stayed the same—or even worse, the peaks would diminish a bit. After a while I stopped staring and turned my attention elsewhere. I even had a couple of not-too-awkward conversations with Nate. Then we turned on sitcom reruns. No one tells you just how dull waiting for a new life can be. Eventually, around midnight, Sonia rolled to one side and felt around in her bed, underneath her backside. The gauze pad separating her from the fitted hospital sheet was drenched with diluted plasma.

"I think my water broke."

I assumed this was a huge deal and that it meant the baby was forthcoming. I was wrong. It's just a thing that happens along the way. More waiting. More staring. Four hours later the doctor came in and told Sonia it was time to push. Nate and I each held one of Sonia's legs and lifted them up to her ear for ten seconds at a time while she tried to get the baby out. We did this for two hours. Sonia looked at ease with the entire thing (the epidural helped, no doubt). I, meanwhile, was about to collapse to the ground in crippling pain. But I wasn't the one passing a child out of my body. No sympathy for me.

I pressed on until the doctor told Sonia to stop pushing and ordered an emergency C-section because the baby's heart rate was too low. They made us pack up all our things and escorted us to the operating room, where a team of masked doctors awaited her with long scalpels and pads to soak up the blood, as if they were preparing to disembowel her. I sat behind the curtain and held Sonia's hand; Nate sat opposite me and grabbed her other one. I thought this would be strange. In fact, it was quite the opposite. We made a good team, Nate and I. Whenever I started to wear down, he'd pick up the slack, and vice versa. I highly recommend that any woman giving birth pack two men for the trip.

Thirty minutes later one of the doctors reached over the curtain. "And here's your baby," he said casually.

Our son was screaming, soaked in blood, announcing himself. The umbilical cord extended out from him, shiny like an
old-fashioned twisty phone cord, the kind my grandma used to
have. They quickly took the baby over to a corner of the OR to
wipe him off, check his vitals, and weigh him. They cut the cord
without first asking me if I would have liked to do it, which
aggravated me. They asked Nate and me to stay in our seats while
they did all this. Sonia passed out as they massaged her uterus
back into place and stitched her back up. The nurse came back
with the baby swaddled in blankets, bits of blood still caked in
the crevices of his ears and entangled in little clumps of his hair.

The nurse looked at us. "Who do I give him to?" she asked.

Nate nodded toward me. "Him."

"Here you go."

She presented the baby to me. I stared at him. I held him close
to Sonia's face to show him to her, even though she was knocked
out. I ran my hand over his head, which was still bruised and
misshapen from being stuck in utero. I checked his hands. They
were pruny from spending months and months bathed in amniotic fluid. They were wrinkled and puffy—like an old man's hands.
And like an old man, there were stray bits of skin peeling on different areas of his body. The nurse assured me that this was normal. You'll grow younger, boy. Yes, you will.

I handed him to Nate. He counted all of the baby's fingers and
toes. Then he examined its face, studying its eyes and nose and
little ruby mouth. "He looks just like you," he said.

He was right. He hadn't taken definitive shape yet, but I could
tell from the creases around the eyes. He looked like me. He *was*
me. He's the part of me I'll leave behind whenever I exit this plane
of existence. I looked at his face, and it was as if he existed both
inside and outside of my body. I turned to Nate. He had a look of
envy about him. Nothing malicious. No jealousy. Just a look of
wonder, a desire to feel what I was feeling at that moment. I gave
a small nod and smiled at him. He smiled back warmly.

Soon I felt an envy of my own—for Nate. I thought I'd feel freer
without marrying Sonia. But at that moment I didn't feel that way

at all. I knew it was Nate who was going to go home with Sonia and my son, while I would be trapped in a world just outside of theirs. I didn't love Sonia anymore. But she had been right. I wanted to be part of something that meant something. I just never knew it. And nothing could be done now to get back in. I kissed my son on the head and held him tight to my chest. Forty-five minutes later, in the recovery room, Sonia woke up. I handed our son to her, and the past nineteen hours were jettisoned in her wake, like so much useless flotsam on the ocean. She was reborn.

After I gave the baby his first bath in the nursery, they took him and Sonia to a new recovery room in the maternity ward. It was Sonia's own room. No other new mothers around. An hour later a nurse came in and asked to take the baby away for some "routine blood tests." On instinct, I leapt for him and cried out, "No!" clutching his arm tightly in mine. I heard phantom screams come from behind other doors. Everyone looked at me like I was crazed.

"I'm sorry," I said, "I had a friend in China."

The nurse looked offended. "We don't brand babies in this country, sir."

"I know. Can I come with you? That's what I meant to say."

"Of course you can. Has he had any genetic work done or is he organic?"

"Just the Parkinson's. Otherwise, he's organic."

"Wonderful. Come with me, sir."

And so I did. They took his blood and pricked the heel of his foot, and he came back safe and sound. No branding. No Freezer-Mommying. It was all routine. Just like they said it would be. He weighed eight pounds, four ounces. He's gonna be a big boy. He's gonna be a load.

DATE MODIFIED:
6/1/2030, 11:58 P.M.

The Man Who Will Live Everywhere

I was out at a restaurant last night and sitting at the bar, waiting for a date to arrive. We had an eight o'clock reservation, but I like to show up for these things early so I can have a drink and stuff myself with free mixed nuts. Another guy occupied the stool next to me. He was a tall man, as I am. He had intensely bright blond hair, almost white, along with a deep tan complexion. He was striking both in his looks and his mannerisms. His personality—warm, gregarious—radiated out of his body without him having to utter a word. I took a gamble and chatted him up. Turned out he was an Australian. Of course he was. Every Australian I've ever met possesses that exact same effusive quality. His name was Keith.

"What are you doing here in the city?" I asked him.

"Aw, this is the first stop of my American year."

"Your American year? Is that some sort of work thing?"

"Work? Nah, I don't work. This is my year in America. I'm spending one year in every country on earth. January 1 to January 1. When the year is over, I pack up my kit and move on. I started in Canada, last year. Figured I'd get the easy countries out of the way first."

"So, why are you staying in every country for a year?"

"Why not? I got the cure. I'll be around for a bit. Why not take advantage?"

"But don't you miss home?"

"Home? Nah, mate. Why would I miss home? It's always there. Frankly, home is a bit of a crutch. It's just so easy to stick around and keep doing all the same shit, isn't it? What's the point of that, especially now? I can go back home a hundred years from today, and it'll all be the same. My friends will be the same. My wife will be the same."

"Your wife? You're doing this entire trip without your wife?"

"Sure, why not? She'll be around. If I'm going to live 1,000 years, I'm not gonna spend 999 of them in Wahroonga. Anchor yourself to one spot, my friend, and you'll eventually grow contemptuous of it. I'm doing North America and Central America first. Then South America. Then Africa. Then Europe. Then Asia. Then Oceania. A rough circumnavigation. Should take just under two hundred years. If I'm lucky, Russia will invade Ukraine and I can kill two birds with one stone. Maybe bring back a Russian bride to show off to the missus." He laughed at the notion.

"She'd be okay with that?"

"Why not? I'm not gonna spend a year in a country without sampling the 'culture,' if you get my drift."

"What about her?"

"Oh, she can have sex with anyone she damn well pleases," he said. "Fine by me. She's an attractive woman. No sense in saving herself for me all that time. She shacks up with my mate Kevin every now and again. I think they have a good time together. It's great. Don't want her getting rusty—figuratively or literally."

"Holy shit."

"You know, it's amazing to me how tight-assed you Americans still are, even after all this. I don't care about what people think of me or my relationships. Let my morals be some other idiot's concern. You know what I care about? Indelibility. That's what gets me hard. I have a chance to experience everything on earth with this cure, and you can bet your ass I'm gonna do it. Why would I do anything else? You stay in one place, and you forget your day the second it's over. Everyone and every place and every thing get old if you do them enough. Even the best things. I'm not gonna forget a single day of the next two hundred years. I'm gonna camp out with bushmen. I'm gonna swim in the Amazon. I'm gonna machine-gun a dead cow in Cambodia. I'm gonna do all that. And when it's over, I'll be able to tell every story I've ever wanted to tell. I'll be the richest man on earth. I promise you I won't be a bore when someone decides to chat me up in a bar."

"I think you're already a raging success on that front."

"Just you wait. Just you wait until you talk to me in 2230."

My date arrived. I asked Keith to join us. She got up and left halfway through the meal. I barely noticed. Most enjoyable three hours I ever spent. As he rambled on and quaffed glass after glass of wine, I began envisioning Keith traversing the entire earth. I saw him among the hordes in China. I saw him hiking up mountains in New Zealand. Such was his enthusiasm for his prospects that I felt I was already on the trip with him. I was living vicariously through him, though I had the exact same freedom he did, just not the balls to carry it out. After we ate, we walked outside. He took out a cigarette case, one of those old-fashioned ones. He tapped a cig against it, lit it up, and basked in the idea of his present and future life.

"I'll say this, though. I can't wait for my year here to be up. Next country I go to is gonna be one that lets me smoke a fag."

DATE MODIFIED:
9/13/2030, 7:15 A.M.

"Warmest greetings from the Church of Man!"

I was walking on the Upper West Side yesterday, after a dentist's appointment, when I passed by a huge building under construction. Since scaffolding covered its entire facade, I was forced to walk through one of those makeshift corridors they always set up where there's a work zone. I hate those things. They're always half the width of a normal sidewalk, and I usually have to plaster myself against the wall every twenty feet to make way for some giant robostroller. As I made my way, I saw a group of people in the center of the walkway, handing out fliers to passersby. I kept my head down and tried to wriggle past them. One of them jammed a flyer in my face. I took it just to be rid of him and kept on walking. He walked with me, beaming one of those creepy frozen-in-place smiles that's always a telltale mark of the deluded.

"Warmest greetings from the Church of Man!" he said.

"Yeah, not interested."

"Did you know that when this building is completed it will be the largest Church of Man in the world?"

"Not interested, thanks."

I kept on walking and eventually the Church of Man guy gave up and walked back to his little congregation. I was privately shocked that there was a twenty-story building going up dedicated entirely to the Church of Man. I mean, I know a couple of celebs are big on the church. But I didn't think real people actually cared. I kept the flyer and read it. Here it is:

THE DAWN OF THE
NEW YORK CHURCH OF MAN!

On January 1, 2031, the new Manhattan headquarters of the
Church of Man will have its grand opening. We'd like to offer you,
fellow Men and Women, this *exclusive* invitation to join us that
day at 10:00 A.M. sharp for our inaugural service. There will be
singing, dancing, and free nibbles for anyone who attends.

If you're new to our church, we hope the following FAQ will
help clear up any misconceptions you may have about the faith.

Q: Do I need to pay money to join the Church of Man?
A: No. All Church of Man services are free and open to anyone
who wishes to attend. Like any other church, we do ask that
regular attendees give when we make our collection. However,
this is never mandatory.

Q: What is the mission of the Church of Man?
A: The Church of Man is a nondenominational faith that promotes
the worship of Man (and Woman!) on earth. We do not believe in
traditional Christian, Jewish, or Muslim theologies. We do not
believe there is some dark and omnipresent God above us trying
to manipulate our world based on unexplained whims. We
believe that the greatest faith we can have is faith in *one another.*
We believe that too often people are intolerant of one another
because they fail to recognize the transcendent power of their
fellow Man. We are the creators of this world. Every great
advance in our civilization has come not because God bestowed
it upon us, but because we made it so. Our Bible is a history
book. Our apostles are the likes of Einstein, Lincoln, and Aristotle.
We believe that true happiness and peace lie in learning to
appreciate the incredible power that we have as a species.

Q: How can you be a religion if you don't worship a god?
A: The Church of Man believes that God and Man are one and the
same. We believe that we can become better people if we

recognize that the forces of good in this world—kindness, forgiveness, generosity, love—are inherently within us, within our control. The old religious dogmas have outlived their usefulness in a world where people can live hundreds and thousands of years. This has been borne out in recent studies showing the radical decline of church attendance across every known traditional faith. Membership in the Church of Man, on the other hand, has grown an astonishing 400 percent every year since its inception. We do not believe in preparing for an afterlife. We believe this life *is* the afterlife. We believe that earth *is* heaven. And we strive to make this the best world we possibly can. That's a message people need to hear in 2030.

Q: Isn't it arrogant to worship at the altar of Man?

A: This is the most common misconception about the Church of Man. We do not believe in the worship of the self. Nor do we promote the idea that Man is somehow superior to all other animals and life on earth. Rather, the Church of Man believes in the idea of collective divinity: that the powers that control human destiny lie within us as a group. History proves this is true. We believe in praising and loving *all* people, of all races and lifestyles, together. We believe in the higher power that is the product of a miraculous dynamic between us.

Q: What can I expect to see at a typical Church of Man service?

A: Joy! Joy and a shared spirit of unity. Our daily services usually last a grand total of forty-five minutes. We have morning, afternoon, and evening services. We have reverends (yes, they get to marry) who preside over each service, offering readings from select historical texts, along with daily sermons on how best to love your fellow Man, particularly those less fortunate! We believe in a service that creates a shared moment of peace and reflection, and in respect for what we have accomplished as a species. Think of it as a giant group hug.

Q: Does the Church of Man ban the consumption of alcohol or drugs?
A: We do not label such actions as "sins" per se. But we believe such controlled substances damage the purity of our spirit and hamper our shared goals. However, we do offer free drug and alcohol counseling to those in need.

Q: Does the Church of Man ban fatty foods?
A: We do not have an expressed ban on any kind of food. But we firmly believe that our own holy vessels should not be polluted with toxic processed foods.

Q: What do I call your religion—"manism"?
A: We prefer "collectivism," but you are free to make up your own word for it and ping it to our feed.

Q: Is smoking allowed in the Church of Man?
A: In accordance with city ordinances, smoking is not allowed on the premises.

Q: Is it true that I'll be kicked out of the church if I'm ever seen hitting or kicking someone?
A: All excommunications are handled on a case-by-case basis. But we do believe violence against your fellow Man is the most serious sin any Man can commit.

Q: What nibbles can I expect at the grand opening of the Church of Man?
A: There will be assorted crudités and fruit, along with Mrs. Karsten's homemade kelp brownies. Attendees are encouraged to bring their own goodies and to respect the bodies of their fellow Men and Women when they consider what to bring. Organic food only, please!

See you in January! And remember:

TOGETHER WE ARE THE PATH TO SALVATION!

I showed the flyer to my friend Scott. "Oh, man," he said. "Collectivists. Those people are losers. I once dated a girl who was into this. She took me to a service. Everyone held hands and ran in circles, like it was *The Sound of Music* or something. And they make you hug people all the time. It's creepy as hell. And you have to confess to your sins against your fellow man—like cutting him off in traffic. They consider that a sin. I'm surprised they're opening a church here. It's the most anti–New Yorker set of policies on earth. You ever see the top of one of their churches?"

"Yeah, it's got a big capital *T* on it."

"Did you know it stands for 'teamwork'?"

"No, it doesn't."

"Swear to God. It's a goddamn hippie day camp. Those people are nuts."

DATE MODIFIED:
9/21/2030, 11:31 A.M.

"We'll see you again"

Last night I was out at a restaurant bar with Callie, a friend from work, to celebrate her positive pregnancy test. She brought twelve female friends with her. They were all jumping and screaming and crying and poking her in the stomach and asking her if she was throwing up yet. I drifted away from the pre-baby shower and sat alone, happily absorbed in drinking my drink and pleased that, unlike Callie, I was medically cleared to have as many as I wished.

I tried to chat up the bartender, but he was the only one on duty that night, and the crowd was three or four deep. I'm convinced that fancy new bars are understaffed on purpose. An establishment isn't truly trendy unless it pisses you off. My barstool became a little island. People swarmed around me without paying me much heed, leaving me to survey the bar and people-watch with impunity. I could stare at other people for minutes at a time and not be noticed because so many bodies were obscuring me. I could watch the first date unfold at a nearby table in real time and all its spectacular, awkward splendor. I could also check out good-looking women if I wanted to, even though I would creep myself out when I stared for too long.

In the middle of this mess, I spied a girl quietly walking in with a friend and waiting for a table. I knew this girl. Her name was Alison. I knew her because twenty-seven years ago I loved her more than I've loved anything, anywhere, ever.

She was a classmate of mine in middle school, and she looked then like she did now. Tall, with long arms. Simple brown hair. You could even call her gawky, though I'd never dare. It was as if she was somewhat embarrassed by her natural beauty and did what she could to not call attention to it. This only made her more attractive. I remember in school she wore very plain clothes, and she was still the best-looking girl I'd ever seen. Occasionally, an event would come along where she'd have to dress up—an eighth-grade dance or something like that. And she'd dress up just a touch, just a little bit better than she usually did, and then she was not only the best-looking girl I'd ever seen but the best-looking girl I'd ever seen by an overwhelming margin.

I was no one in eighth grade. I was terrible at sports, and I was already tall, which only accentuated my glaring lack of athleticism. I wasn't unpopular, I guess. I had some friends. But I occupied the periphery of the school's social structure. I was just another forgettable kid who was trying to get by, the kind of kid who never turns up in any of the candid yearbook photos.

I made friends with Alison in Spanish class. She was nice to me. She was nice to everyone. Sometimes I got to sit next to her, which was both ecstasy and agony. I'd get to see her in full, and smell her. If she was wearing a skirt, I'd get to see that little crease running up the side of her thigh that made every neuron in my body flare. It took everything in my power to not grab her in the middle of class and consume her entirely. This is the problem with eighth-grade boys.

As the year went on, I began calling her at home and having the occasional half-hour chat, which is pretty much all I lived for back then. I was her friend, and I assumed this was the best way to become something more. Hindsight makes it clear that this was the wrong angle to take. I stayed friends with her even as she dated the captain of the hockey team (who was a bastard) and even went so far as to give her relationship advice, despite having no relationships of any kind on my résumé, and despite internally rooting for her relationships with other men to fail miserably.

Whenever Alison was without a boyfriend, I'd pull her aside at a dance and ask her to go out with me. On more than one occasion I told her I loved her. She'd reject me, but such was her kindness and good nature that she could never reject me entirely. She'd give me a hug after turning me down, which was torture. And any time

I asked if I'd ever have a chance with her, she'd tell me that things can always change, that she couldn't predict the future. It was her way of easing my pain, but it was ten times crueler because I always imagined that fortunate turn of events would soon be on the horizon.

I began envisioning all the ways in which she could be mine. I daydreamed of a nuclear attack that left us the only two people alive. I daydreamed of rescuing her from being raped by an overaggressive suitor. I daydreamed of mastering the guitar, becoming a rock star, and having her fall in love with me after spotting her in the audience and playing my greatest song for her and her alone, our eyes locked the entire time. I even took guitar lessons to see if that fantasy could be realized. I'm a fucking train wreck with that instrument.

My daydreams soared far beyond initial courtship. I dreamed of her growing to love me with equal intensity. I pictured going off to war, fighting in the Middle East, and returning home to her to make love on the staircase. You name an insane fantasy, and I indulged in it with her. Alien invasions, riots, earthquakes, floods, hurricanes, rogue dinosaur cyborgs—all of it. I spent every waking moment thinking of her in alternate dimensions, well past the point of mere pitiful obsession. I even abstained from full-blown sexual fantasies about her because I viewed her as too virtuous for them. Again, this is the problem with eighth-grade boys.

We moved from Buffalo when I was in tenth grade. I begged my parents to let me stay behind and live with a friend so that I could still go to the same school. So that I could see Alison. I was that hell-bent on torturing myself. My parents refused, we left, and life went on. I grew. I somehow managed to kiss other girls, even have sex with them. The pain of that extreme and sad crush eventually went away, worn down by generous helpings of time.

Then I saw her again last night, and a feeling that had lain dormant for so long burst up through me in an instant. I assumed I was too old for raging-hormone teenage love, but I was wrong. And that screwed with my head, because if I couldn't chalk up that love to teenage hormones, it meant I was still vulnerable to it. I was still weak.

I wasn't going to make the same mistakes I made before. I'm older and presumably wiser. I hatched a plan. I'd stalked this poor girl for three solid years. I wasn't going to do that again. Instead, I finished my drink, ordered another, and headed back Callie's way. When Callie is at a bar, you notice her. All I had to do was stand in her general vicinity, do a shot with her (lemonade for the pregnant gal), and Alison would easily notice me *not* noticing her.

It worked. I am a genius. Alison quickly spotted me.

"John?" she said. "John Farrell?"

"Jennifer?" I did that on purpose.

"You don't remember me?"

"Wait. Alison? Oh man, of course! Alison. How are you? It's great to see you!"

I gave her a cursory kiss on the cheek. I could smell her hair, same as it was the first time I caught a whiff of it. I nearly died on the spot.

"What's the occasion?" she asked.

"Friend of mine got herself pregnant. Throwing a little party."

"Are you the father?"

"No, no. Thankfully not."

"Are all these girls your friends?"

"Not particularly. In fact, I've dated a couple of them, so if you could perhaps save me from this little coven . . ."

"Well, we were just stopping in for drinks and maybe some appetizers. You're free to join us."

And I did. I ordered wine. I feigned having as much interest in Alison's friend as I did in Alison. I told stories. I made Alison laugh, to the point where she playfully punched me in the shoulder. She never did that in school. As we talked, the thirteen-year-old boy still very much alive within me tried to crawl out of my body and expose himself in all his stupid, awkward glory. I violently beat him back with equal parts courage and scotch. The friend got up to use the bathroom. Alison took a sip of her drink and began digging deeper.

"So . . . Married?"

"Me? No," I said. "Almost was."

"But you backed out of it."

"No no. We never got engaged. But we had a son, see."

"Ah. Does he live here?"

"He does. He lives with his mother and his mother's fiancé."

"Oof. Is that awkward?"

"Not as much as you'd think. What about you? Married?"

"Divorced."

"I'm sorry to hear that."

"Don't be," she said. "He was a jerk. Don't tell me you're a jerk now too."

"Little bit, I'm afraid. I'm a divorce lawyer. Tends to coarsen a man."

At this point the conversation paused. When I was younger, a moment of silence with a woman would cause me to panic, and I'd desperately attempt to fill the vacuum by saying anything. Usually something pointless. Something dumb. I didn't do that this time. I let the moment breathe.

She circled the rim of her glass with her finger. "So, this woman you had the baby with. Would you have married her if you hadn't gotten the cure?"

"Yeah. Yeah, I would have. But I didn't. So there you have it."

"What's your cure age?"

"Twenty-nine. You?"

"Ah, you beat me. Thirty-one."

"Sorry."

"I can't believe I'm two years older than you now. That's unfair."

"Well, you don't look a day over thirty, if that's any consolation."

"Oh, stop." She surveyed the bar. "This ever get old for you?"

"Does what ever get old?" I asked.

"This. This whole process. Going to the bar. Wedging yourself between people for a drink. You ever get tired of this?"

"Every week."

"This is what I had in my head when I went to the curist. This is what I was looking forward to, all this carousing and shit. I thought it would always be a good time, and then I got married and this scene got old, and then I got divorced and this scene got *really* old. But I still do it anyway. I think I lack imagination. No one should find themselves bored in this town. At this age. But here I am."

"I made friends with a guy who is going to live in every country for a year, for two hundred years."

"That's crazy."

"That's what I thought. Turns out he made perfect sense."

"Would you do it?"

"If I ever had the stones. Or maybe the right company. Seems foolish to have roots anywhere anymore. I feel like I'm supposed to go on a journey—one I'm continually putting off. I always have an excuse handy: money, work, some other bullshit. I don't know. The longer I delay, the more daunting it seems. I look at my kid and sometimes I feel like we're the same age."

"Except you don't wear diapers."

"Not that you know of."

She gave me a look. I'm old enough now to know when a woman likes me and when she doesn't. It's one of those skills you pick up later in life and wish you had had back in school when you desperately needed it. It's a sense that grows even sharper if you're in a committed relationship, where it's virtually useless to you. But here I was. Free. Unencumbered. She was looking at me. Leering at me. I was a different man now. Older. Better looking. Postmortal. Things can always change. Always.

"You look good, John."

"Thanks." I purposely held out on returning the compliment. "Listen, I have to go meet a friend for dinner." (Note: this was a lie.) "But this was fun. If you feel like grabbing another drink sometime, a few weeks from now or whatever . . ." If I asked Alison in eighth grade if I could take her somewhere, she'd immediately ask if she could bring forty other people with her. But not this time.

"Absolutely," she said.

I gave her a kiss on the cheek goodbye and excused myself. I could feel her eyes trailing me as I walked out the door and waved a quick goodbye to Callie at the bar. As I passed over the threshold and stepped out onto the avenue, out of her line of vision, my face turned beet red, and I let the thirteen-year-old boy out to play for a split second. I walked ten blocks and found myself in need of a place to calm down and stuff the boy back inside my psyche. There was bar nearby, tucked away on the street, and I made a beeline for it. I called a friend and invited him to join me there to get properly drunk.

At 3:00 A.M. I stumbled out of the bar alone (my friend had left an hour earlier, and I stayed to keep drinking for reasons that escape me) and walked back toward the avenue. A bright light from a storefront hit me, and I turned to see what it was. I was in front of Derrick's Grail Shop, which was—remarkably—still open. I had no need for a grail at 3:00 A.M., but I was drunk and unreasonable, so I moseyed inside to check out the wares for three seconds. The Swift has a new DX model. It's made of pure imitation jade. Very classy.

When I came out of the shop, I crossed to the dark side of the street and turned to walk to the avenue. But something was off. I felt eyes on my body, like when Alison was looking at me—and nothing like when Alison was looking at me. I turned around, my back to the avenue, and there they were.

They were three men. Short. Bald. Dressed entirely in black— shoes, socks, pants, belt, and long-sleeved tunics that made it look like they were wearing sports jackets backward. Their heads were painted bright green, like the Wicked Witch of the West. Halloween wasn't for another two days. When I saw them, they grinned at me. Maniacally. It was as if they had been waiting for me this whole time. I would have preferred they do anything but grin at me. Frown, grimace, anything. Their sickening grins made me feel like there was something they wanted to do to me that they were very much looking forward to. I froze in terror.

One of them spoke. "What's your birthday, buddy?"

I turned and ran. I made it three steps in my stupor before they dragged me down. There was an alley between two town houses, used to store garbage cans. They pulled me into it, laughing the whole time. One of them held a knife to my throat.

"Pull up his sleeve," the head troll said. He was the only one of them to speak.

Another one of them sat me up and pushed the sleeve of my shirt up over my shoulder.

"Take my wallet," I pleaded. "You can have my phone and my tablet too."

"I don't want your wallet. I want your birthday."

"It's October 1, 2000."

His smile dissolved. The green on his face grew a shade darker, and his entire head swelled with anger. He pressed his nightmare face into mine. He grimaced. He had long, thin, nasty teeth. The kind that could bite cleanly through an eyeball.

"I said, *what is your fucking birthday*?"

"Please don't do this. Take anything you want."

He pressed the knife into my upper arm.

"If you don't tell us your real birthday," he said, "we'll write the whole alphabet on your body."

I succumbed. "October 1, 1990."

The head troll began cutting. I started to scream, but they covered my mouth.

"Stop squirming. Don't make us cross it out and start over."

I stopped resisting. My system went limp and shock took over as they carved the numbers and slash marks into me. I closed my eyes and tried not to think about the blade digging into my arm just below the shoulder. Another knife was coolly introduced to my neck.

"Open your eyes. Look at us."

I did as I was told. Three hideous green faces were staring at me, still grinning, imprinting themselves into both my flesh and my memory. I was helpless to stop them. I thought about my apartment. I thought about the Texan's gun I never bothered to donate to the police. I thought about it sitting inconveniently under a pile of shirts on the top shelf of my closet. Useless. Impotent.

"Having fun yet?" the troll asked me. They finished and let me fall to the cracked pavement. "We'll see you again."

I saw them turn tail and run west, screaming with high-pitched laughter, the backs of their green heads swimming downstream in a river of darkness. I looked at my shoulder and saw blood gushing out. I tried to scream, but my mouth wouldn't open. A handful of people saw me but assumed I was a homeless person and kept walking right on by. At last I summoned a low groan that was miserable enough to persuade one of them to approach me ever so slightly. They saw the blood, and that was all they needed to know. An hour later I was in the hospital being stitched up. A policeman was asking me to describe my assailants in detail. He told me the trolls who attacked me are part of a larger sect called Bridge606, or "Greenies." He said there are hundreds of them attacking people in the dead of night. He told me he'd call if they ever arrested some of them. Given the current state of the NYPD, I was less than optimistic.

I'm looking at my arm in the mirror now. The stitches only serve to accentuate the trolls' good knifesmanship:

$$10/1/1990$$

That's my birthday, all right. My real birthday. I used to celebrate that date when I was a kid. Now three monsters will forever mock me with it.

DATE MODIFIED:
10/30/2030, 11:45 P.M.

XMN Was Right

At night, when I get up to take a leak, I stand at the toilet and can't help but imagine three green lunatics stationed right outside my bathroom door, ready with smiles and knives for me when I open it back up. I've taken to leaving all the doors in my apartment open, and I sing to myself if I ever get too freaked out. But it's never long before the trolls rush back to the forefront of my mind, laughing and burrowing under my skin.

In bed I hold my bladder for as long as I can stand it, until the agony of holding it in forces me to confront them again and again and again. I take Vicodin and I drink, because it's all I can do to try to ignore the fear. And the worst part is that I don't know when this all goes away. I don't know when this will stop causing me to wake up in an icy sweat, the pillow flattened by my soaking hair. The fear itself becomes this tangible thing that terrifies me, and on and on it goes. I forget about the butchery on my arm until a chance look in the wrong direction reminds me. Then my heart shrieks. The stitches are supposed to come out next week. After that I'll see a plastic surgeon, though I doubt he can erase the scar entirely. There'll always be a reminder.

For an hour I tried sleeping with the Texan's gun under my pillow. But I'm a restless sleeper, so I spent that hour scared that I'd shoot myself in the head. I get up every hour and turn the TV on and leave it on, to give myself the illusion of safe company. Or I sit here and type. But never without looking over my shoulder. They're always there before I turn, blades at the ready.

DATE MODIFIED:
11/2/2030, 5:22 A.M.

"Does it hurt?"

They took the stitches out yesterday. I ran my fingers across the numerals on my arm. They were raised, the date now embossed on my skin, like what you would see on a fancy business card. I showed Alison when we got back to my place after dinner.

"Oh Jesus, John."

"Yeah. Not so pretty."

She ran her fingers over the cuts. I half expected the scars to disappear the moment she grazed my skin.

"Does it hurt?" she asked.

"Depends on who's touching it."

"Does it hurt right now?"

"No. Right now it feels pretty great actually."

"Are you flexing your bicep?"

"No."

"You are!"

"I swear to God, I'm not."

"You are, a little bit."

She kept rubbing the scar, as if it were her own. "I can't believe this happened to you right after I saw you. I feel terrible. I feel as if I'm bad luck."

"You're not bad luck."

"Oh, but I am." I watched her face grow dark as she began rummaging through her saddest memories. "My father left my mother a month after I was born. Did I ever tell you that?"

"You did."

"And the week after I married my ex-husband, he got into a car accident. It shattered five of his vertebrae. He was in pain twenty-four hours a day after that. No drug helped. He couldn't sleep. He couldn't walk ten steps without collapsing in pain. The pain left him angry all the time. Angry at me. Angry at God. Angry at everything. I know it's irrational that I feel responsible for that. But the way he would look at me as he writhed around on the bed . . . He needed to blame someone, and I was the one who was there. I got that look enough times to start believing I was the one who'd done it to him. And, justified or not, I haven't shaken that belief. I'm bad luck, John. I'm terrible, rotten luck."

"You're not. I found you again, and I found you when I was ready for you and not a moment sooner, and that is *not* bad luck. Quite the opposite."

She squeezed my arm. I took her opposite arm and leaned in. Every atom in my body split in two. There was no hiding the fact that I loved her again. She smelled it on me.

"Have you thought about me this whole time?"

"No," I said. "Wouldn't have done me any good."

She drew closer. The thirteen-year-old boy in me curled into a squash ball as I awaited her. "Are you thinking about me now?"

"I'm not thinking."

For twenty-seven years, I had waited. I didn't wait a second longer. For the first night in a very long time, no green men with knives were waiting outside my door.

DATE MODIFIED:
11/14/2030, 2:43 P.M.

"Yeah, that's one of them"

Yesterday morning I received a call from a police precinct in Midtown. I initially assumed they were calling to see if I could donate to their benevolent association, which they do about once a week. You can be rude to every telemarketer and feed spammer in the world, except the ones working for the NYPD. They know this. It's very sneaky on their part.

"I told you last week," I said. "I love you guys but I'm not interested."

"Sir, I'm not calling to solicit donations. You were attacked in the West Village on the night of October 29, correct?"

I stared at my arm. "Yes."

"We've arrested a Greenie here in Midtown, on an unrelated charge, and we want to know if he's one of your assailants. Would you be willing to try to identify him in a lineup?"

"Yes, I would."

I got out of bed, put on my clothes, and hustled out of the apartment. I left the Texan's gun at home, to avoid setting off the metal detector. At some point I should stop referring to it as the Texan's gun. It's my gun now. I bring it almost everywhere I go. I only refer to it as his because it makes me feel like a less-aggressive person.

I got down to the precinct, which was as crowded as Penn Station. The temperature inside was, by my estimation, a balmy ninety-five degrees, and about as humid as the bottom of a tar pit. Everything in the station looked like it was made in 1977 and left that way, right down to the coffee mugs and mustaches. Herds of homeless people were being corralled through the halls and into holding pens. Desk cops with too much to do scurried about trying to put out administrative fires. The blotter feed scrolled along at light speed on a monitor above us. I checked in at the main desk.

"I'm here to see a lineup."

The clerk didn't even look up. She just pointed to a bench over on the side, which was fully occupied by ten homeless men and a man in a suit with a broken arm. I stood. I took out my tablet and diddled. Two hours later, they called me in.

An older officer took me through the bowels of the precinct, which looked modest on the outside but magically grew into the size of the Pentagon once I entered. He escorted me into a tiny black slot of a room. Two other officers were waiting for me, standing in front of a shaded window.

"Are you ready, Mr. Farrell?" one of them asked me.

"Yes."

"Before we begin, please note that your assailant may not be among the men we show you today."

"Okay."

He threw a switch and the shade opened. Five men stood before me. Only one of them was a Greenie. Second from the left. He was small. Bald. His entire head was painted green. He had short, Chiclet teeth. I didn't recognize him at all. None of my trolls were in the lineup.

"Sir, do you recognize any of these men?"

The Greenie smiled in our general direction. He wasn't one of the guys who cut me. I didn't care. The fact that he smiled was enough. I turned to the officer and lied.

"Yeah, that's one of them. The Greenie. He's one of the guys that knifed me."

They let me go, and I walked home. I regret nothing.

DATE MODIFIED:
12/6/2030, 3:41 P.M.

"Did you know that cigarettes have almond oil in them?"

I didn't tell my dad about the attack. Not a single detail of it—the scar, the lineup, nothing. Thanks to the chilly weather, long sleeves have made the birth brand relatively easy to hide. I didn't want to distress him. He's living out the rest of his life in peace and quiet. I didn't want that tranquility marred with visions of his son being accosted and left for dead in an alley. Since David was born, I've known that feeling of worry Dad has always talked about. It doesn't matter where your child is in life or how he's doing. You always worry about him. I didn't want it to consume my dad, so I was determined to leave the incident unmentioned. Turns out it hardly mattered. When I got to his house, he told me the news.

"I have cancer," he said.

"What? Where?"

"In my pancreas. Worst of the worst."

"Jesus. Does Polly know?"

"I told her last week when she visited."

"When did this happen?"

"I got the diagnosis last month."

"Why didn't you say anything?"

"I wanted to tell you in person. This is the only time we were going to be together."

"How bad is it?"

"Well, they also found it in my lymph nodes. So it's spread, which is obviously not good."

I had kept a positive attitude during the entirety of my mother's illness, right up until the day she passed away. I vowed to do the same again. "Okay, so what now? How can I help? What's the treatment?"

"There is no treatment."

"No chemo? No radiation? They didn't offer you anything?"

"Eh. They offered chemo. I don't want it."

"Why?"

"Because I don't want it."

"But you could beat this. At the very least, you could buy more time."

"Why would I want that? I saw your mom go through it. I'll pass." He took my hand. "This is good, John. This is good. I want this. Hell, I even planned it. For the past three months, I've had a slab of bacon and a pint of chocolate ice cream for dinner. I even tried taking up smoking, which is disgusting, by the way. Did you know that cigarettes have almond oil in them? I think that's just bizarre. You'd think you were puffing on a macaroon."

"You're killing yourself?"

"I'm not killing myself. This doesn't count as suicide. Suicide is when you stick a gun to your head. I'd never dream of doing that. You have to understand: I made a mistake getting this cure. I don't want it. It's not that I want to die. It's that I'm at peace with the idea of it. It doesn't bother me. I've had a good life. I saw my children grow. I saw my grandchildren born, including your son. That's all I've ever wanted. And then some! For God's sake, they found a cure for aging! Isn't that stunning? I can't believe I lived to see it. There's just no way the world is gonna progress much further than that. This is the top, as far as I'm concerned. No, I've had a good life, and I've had more than my fair share of it. I'm not some depressed old man trying to hang himself. I'm just looking for a gracious exit. A way back to your mom. And here it is. A tumor. A big, fat, lovely tumor. I could kiss the damn thing."

I sat staring at him. I didn't know whether to hug him or punch him in the eye or raise a toast. He saw that I was at a loss.

"I'm sorry," he said. "I don't mean to be flip."

"It's okay. I get it."

"This is not a tragedy, John. It really isn't. Death shouldn't be some big tragedy anymore. I lived plenty, and everyone else is going to get to do the same now. Life is just right like this."

"How long do you have?"

"A year, at most. I'm hoping it doesn't play out that long. I'm going to throw away all the Christmas decorations after this year. I never want to string lights on a goddamn tree ever again." He pointed to the tree. "All they have are these LED lights now. They're awful. It's like the tree was trimmed by an office lighting company."

"Yes, but the tree can live forever now."

"Who wants a tree that lasts forever?"

"Well, it makes oxygen."

"Then I bequeath it to you. You may have my Forevergreen and all its precious oxygen. What do I give a shit?"

He poured a drink, and we settled into a night of conversation that was miraculous in its normalcy. I was alarmed at how quickly I was becoming comfortable with the notion of him being gone. He had convinced me so entirely, and it was clear that he didn't want me moping about it. So I fell in line. I joined him in embracing the idea, perhaps as an easy way to avoid dealing with my own eventual grief. Like with my mom, I kept a positive outlook. The only thing different here was the desired outcome. I stared out the living room window. In the moonlight the trees were mere silhouettes, the outlines of the hundreds of branches flat and appearing to form the world's most intricate transit map—one with a zillion destinations, all unmarked.

"You mind if I stay here an extra day or two?" I asked.

"What about that new girlfriend of yours? Don't you have to get back to her?"

"She can wait."

"Don't make her wait too long. Not for my sake."

"I won't. I promise."

I raised a glass.

DATE MODIFIED:
12/28/2030, 8:12 A.M.

When They Tell You Not to Mess with Texas, They Mean It

If this law ends up applying to terra trolls, I'm 100 percent in favor of it. From WUSA via Spencer Hall's feed:

Convicted Rapist Maclin Executed

By Lindsay Reardon

LUBBOCK, TX—This morning convicted rapist Jerome Maclin became the first person to be executed in the state of Texas this century, despite never having taken the life of another person. Maclin was executed via lethal injection and died twelve minutes after the drugs took effect. He was forty-three (cure age thirty-six).

In 2028 Maclin was found guilty of over thirteen separate counts of rape and sexual assault. He confessed to assaulting seven different women in the greater Lubbock area, making him the worst serial rapist in the city's history. The judge, Robert Matheson, used the recently enacted Darian's Law to hand down the state's first nonmurder death sentence.

Darian's Law, which passed the state legislature by an overwhelming margin in 2027, expanded death-penalty offenses beyond murder to include violent crimes such as rape, arson, child abuse, and capital assault (assault resulting in either paralysis or deformity), as well as large-scale drug trafficking. Maclin was the first Texas prisoner ever sentenced to death under the law, which was named after Darian Ruiz, a twelve-year-old girl who was severely burned and suffered brain damage when she was attacked by her father, Carlos Ruiz. Mr. Ruiz was sentenced to life in prison at a cure age of thirty-two.

State lawmakers praised Maclin's execution as a sign of Darian's Law finally taking hold. "Today, we saw justice served for seven brave and wonderful women," said state senator Kay Lorring (D). "They never have to fear this man again, nor do they have to fear him getting out of jail hundreds of years down the line to commit similar atrocities. What you saw today was Texas stepping to the forefront of innovation in law enforcement in the postmortal world."

But not everyone shares Lorring's outlook. This morning hundreds of protesters stood outside the county prison to demonstrate against Maclin's execution, including members of the ACLU, some of whom decried the execution as the beginning of "systematic African American genocide." Most notable among the crowd was Keisha Dunn, who was one of the seven women assaulted by Maclin three years ago.

"I believe in forgiveness, and I do not believe in this case that the punishment fits the crime," said Dunn, age twenty-four. "I believe Jerome Maclin was a bad man, and that what he did to me is one of the worst sins anyone can commit. But I do not believe that justifies killing, particularly those who have not killed others. That is not the Christian way of doing things. I believe Mr. Maclin belonged in jail for the rest of his life, however long that may have been."

But state legislators argue that isn't a financially viable option for taxpayers anymore. Since the advent of the cure for aging, the state's prison population has increased nearly 25 percent, and the growth shows no sign of abating—all while the state faces a massive deficit.

State prosecutor Alberto Vizquel says, "There are only two fiscally smart things to do with some of these prisoners: kill them or let them go. In the case of Jerome Maclin, you're talking about a serial rapist who almost certainly would have carried on assaulting women if he had ever been released from jail. But how can you possibly imprison someone for three hundred years, or however long it takes them to die of a heart attack or what have you? How are we supposed to deal with criminals who have an indefinite lifespan? I admit this may not constitute equal justice. But we have to be pragmatic. We have to think seriously about who deserves to remain on this planet and who does not."

ACLU chapter president Niles McCormick vehemently disagrees. "The state of Texas has just created a complete mess. I may have been against the death penalty before this, but I thought at least it made a modicum of sense: If you kill a person in cold blood, you pay for it with your life. What this execution has done is blur that line completely. Now, who the heck knows what merits death as a punishment? Do you deserve to die if you blind someone? If you take their arm off? Does intent matter? And we're not even talking about people who have been wrongfully convicted. These are impossible ambiguities. It's not a can of worms they've just opened. It's an entire barrel of them."

Already many states have adjusted their sentencing guidelines to prevent the indefinite housing of prisoners. Some states, like California, have instituted a one-hundred-year-maximum collective sentence, despite fiery opposition from victims' rights groups. Maine is now tinkering with the idea of a permanent island prison, which is not expected to get financing approval. And officials in Oklahoma have considered implementing a delayed death sentence, which would mandate the execution of any state prisoner over the true age of eighty-five, regardless of cure age. The ACLU has already decried that measure as inhumane.

Maclin's death was witnessed by his aunt, prison officials, and members of the victims' families, though none of the victims themselves chose to attend. Maclin was given a last meal of barbecued chicken, corn on the cob, and chocolate pudding; escorted to the execution chamber; and allowed to read a statement to the families and state officials. That statement consisted of just four words: "This is some bulls——t." Fifteen minutes later, his heart stopped beating.

DATE MODIFIED:
1/4/2031, 10:09 P.M.

"I'm not even sure this is a marriage anymore"

My sister never comes into the city. She doesn't want to deal with traffic or parking or even taking the train, even if it's a relatively short trip. When I spotted her at Ocean Bar, she had ordered a bottle of wine for herself and had already drunk half of it. She looked exceptionally fragile.

"You heard about Dad?" she asked.

"Yeah. Of course."

"He give you that whole spiel about how great his illness is?"

"Yes, and I have to say he was rather convincing. I take it you aren't so giddy about it."

"Eh, it's not that. In a way I'm relieved. You know I'm a worrier, obviously."

"Me too now."

"Right. And he's getting up in age. I know he had the cure, but even so. It had started to weigh on me, what his fate was gonna be. And it's just another goddamn thing. At least now there's some measure of certainty. And he seems okay with it. So I guess that makes it easier." She took a piece of bread from the basket, tore it, and left one half on the bare white tablecloth while she gnawed on the other. I did likewise.

"Mom helped prepare me for this," she said. "I mean, *nothing* will throw me off more than when she was dying. Having dealt with that makes it easier, in an odd way. I know what's coming. I know how I'm going to feel. It's almost like planning a birthday party. I can forget all about the emotional aspects of the event and get bogged down strictly in the coordinating. That's the best way to grieve, you know. To become mired in logistics."

"He talk to you about what he wants done with his body?"

"Yeah. He wants the same thing as Mom. Donate his body, throw his ashes in the ocean when we get them back. And thank goodness for that. I heard it costs twenty thousand dollars a year to keep someone buried in a cemetery now—which is just insane. You'd think they were teaching philosophy to the corpses."

"Well, whatever happens we'll get through it. If you need anything . . ."

She took a drink of wine and began weeping.

I tried reassuring her. "Polly, it's gonna be okay."

"It's not that," she said. "It's Mark. He wants to convert to a cycle marriage. He wants to leave me ten years from now."

"Oh no."

"It's awful. He hasn't cheated or anything. He's helped with the kids and been supportive of me—the night classes, the master's degree, and all that. He's never been anything but wonderful. And now this."

"You don't want it?"

She looked at me like I was a fool for asking. "Of course I don't want it. He's my husband, and I always want him to be my husband. That's why I married him. I don't care that we all got the cure. That's not a factor for me. I love him. I was excited at the idea of seeing the kids fully grown and then having some real time with him. Traveling. Walking. All the stuff Mom and Dad did. I liked that idea. We could have even had another group of kids somewhere down the line. That's what I loved thinking about. Now all I see is this ticking clock. It's like he's already left. I see him notice women on the street. He tries to hide it, but I know. It never bothered me before, because I knew he was just looking and nothing more. But now? Now it's like seeing a dog trapped in a cage. I know he's looking forward to life without me. I'm not even sure this is a marriage anymore."

"What do the kids say about it?"

"We haven't told them. They probably wouldn't even hear me. They'd just go back to their tablets. You know they don't want to finish high school? Jay walked right up to me the other day and told me he wanted to go to New Zealand next year. I asked for how long. And he said, oh, maybe a decade. A *decade*! He's just casually tossing out the idea of a ten-year pit stop. I don't even think he knows where New Zealand is. He just wants to go somewhere new to spend twenty hours a day pinging friends. I bet he could be there for ten years without noticing the sheep."

"Well, that's a big thing now," I said. "I read about how all the college enrollments are way down and kids are putting everything off."

"Exactly, and who ends up screwed in the process? Parents like me. Because now I have an extra fifty years to fret over these kids getting a proper education. I'm telling you, John, it's a train wreck. And now I've got my husband asking to be single again. I'm not ready for that. I'm not ready to be a postmarried person. It's . . . it's fucking *weird*."

"Then fight for him. Tell him you want him to stay. I know when you tell me to do something, I listen."

"It's not so easy when every jackass at Mark's work is negotiating cycle marriages. I'm not blaming you for that, mind you. If your bosses hadn't invented it, someone else would have. These men are going completely bonkers over it. Last week we were invited to a divorce party. Again, *weird*."

"Did you go?"

"God no! I had to shower for forty minutes after looking at the invite. I know the woman getting the divorce: Karen Welsh. She did *not* want that divorce to happen. So the idea that she's going to be forced to sit there with some bullshit smile on her face, pretending it's Independence Day? Yuck. I'd feel more comfortable at a key party."

"See, I would have gone. At least it's not some boring regular cocktail party. At least there's some sort of interesting, awkward dynamic to it."

"But these are people's lives being ruined, John. Do you really find it so amusing? What will you say when I have to invite you to my divorce party?"

I stared down at the crumbs and little stains around my place setting. "I'm sorry. I didn't mean it that way."

"It's not funny. Ten years from now, I won't have a family anymore. I'll be forced to start over. At fifty-four."

"But your cure age will be thirty-five."

"Oh, like that'll help. You watch. Thirty-five-year-olds are about to become the new senior citizens. I'll be the youngest old maid on earth."

"Don't talk that way."

"I want the family I already have. Yes, they annoy the hell out of me sometimes, and sometimes I'd like to be airlifted out of my house and flown to Italy for a month alone, with some beefy guy named Gianni hand-feeding me grapes. But that's what you sign up for when you have a family. That's part of the whole package. I don't mind that kind of angst. It's better than starting some new, weird family every time the century turns. I don't want that, John. I want everything I had before all this began."

"So, what do you do?"

She finished the bottle. "I don't know. That's the worst part of it."

DATE MODIFIED:
1/6/2031, 11:34 A.M.

"I don't know if anyone will ever get married again"

Alison turned to me in bed. I gently pressed my nose against hers, so her face occupied my entire field of vision. I stared at her intently, trying to take in as much of her as I could. I studied her eyes and her cheeks and her pores, as if I were looking through the porthole of a wrecked ship at the bottom of the ocean. I wanted to see into her.

"Do you ever regret not marrying Sonia?" she asked.

I kissed her. "No. Not really. She's happy with Nate. Our son is happy. Everything seems to have worked out."

"Would you ever get married?"

"Is that something you'd like?"

"No, I think I've had enough of marriage for a little while. I don't know if anyone will ever get married again."

"I'd marry you."

She laughed. "I'm not talking about one of those forty-year things."

"No, I mean it. Real marriage. The whole thing. Forever and ever. Death do us part. No sleeping with other people, blah-blah-blah. I'd do it."

"Why are you so certain about getting married now, when you weren't back then?"

"Different people. I love you more than I ever loved Sonia."

"Ah, but how do you know you won't find someone after me who is even *more* appealing? How do you know that I'm the apex of what you're looking for? That you can't love anyone out there more than you love me?"

"Because I know. There's no one else out there but you. I know it." I sat up. "Is this some sort of test?"

"No," she said. "I'm genuinely curious about this. You loved Sonia, but you were afraid that at some point you'd stop loving her. You wanted a chance to find someone even *better*, particularly given your pleasant looks and your ability to remain ageless, right?"

"I guess. But I don't think I thought it out as articulately as you have. I just didn't want to marry her."

"But why? You loved her."

"I guess I knew I'd stop loving her at some point."

"How can you really love someone if you know it's got an expiration date?"

"Because most things fade," I told her. "I'm old enough now to know that sometimes I go really gaga over someone or something but that eventually the euphoria wears off."

"That's what I'm curious about. I'm wondering if now the euphoria's always going to wear off. I had a friend once whose parents were genuinely in love. I mean, wild about each other. Even when they were fifty, they were still kissing in public and giggling and doing all those things. It was disgusting, but it gave me hope. It made me think, yes, this whole big love ideal is really out there. It can really happen to people."

"What happened to them?"

"They divorced a year ago. No warning. Just over, like that. It all came apart so easily. It made me think, Jesus, everyone's gonna grow bored of each other now, and everyone *knows* it. That's so odd. Because here we are, in bed. We're happy, right? Are you happy?"

"Oh, I'm ecstatic."

"Me too. But I can't seem to settle in the moment right now. There's always that strange new vanishing point on the horizon. I can't get it out of my mind. I can't stop worrying that . . . that love is bullshit now."

"You're not going all mopey on me, are you?"

"No. I just want to be able to believe in something."

She ran her hand over my scar. The plastic surgeon said the procedure would wipe out the birth brand entirely. But I can still see it there, barely discernible in a little speed bump. No one will ever notice, except for me, which makes it doubly haunting. It's a thin bubble of tissue, a membrane that appears to be in constant danger of bursting wide open. The doctor said the slight swelling would reduce over time. I almost want the trolls' handiwork back.

Alison glided her fingertips along the bubble. She looked up at me. The thing that had never changed about her, in all this time, was her genuineness. Cynicism was still something completely alien to her. She wasn't asking me these questions because she was growing bitter. It was because she was fearful. She wanted to see good things in the distance.

"Love is not bullshit," I said.

"You can't know that. No one can. There are things that will happen that you can't possibly expect. Maybe love could survive them when the end of your of life was only decades away. But not now. Not with centuries ahead. Not when everything is so fucked up."

"But everything's always been fucked up. Since the dawn of time. That's why people find each other. For comfort. For shelter. They find their own little crevice in the world, shielded from all the horror. We can do that, Alison. When I got cured, I didn't know why I was doing it. I just knew I wanted it. But now I know. I know precisely why I want to live forever. It's you. Things may be fucked up and may get even more fucked up. But it never has to touch us. Ever. We can find our little niche, and we can hide there. We can find our own little perfect slice of eternity. We can. That's everything. The rest doesn't matter."

"It doesn't work that way. You can try to avoid the world for as long as you can, but it will find you." She tapped my scar. "The world will come for us."

"Then let it. Love is not dead, Alison. Not in this room. People have been getting married for a very long time. Even before the cure, a lifetime was still a hell of a commitment to make. And that was back when you knew the person you loved would grow old and ugly and sick. That won't ever happen to us, Alison. We don't ever have to fear that."

"But how do you know that isn't why people love each other to begin with?"

I climbed on top of her. "It's not that I don't know. It's that I don't care. Because right now I'm enjoying myself way too much to give a damn."

DATE MODIFIED:
3/4/2031, 8:06 A.M.

Afternoon Link Roundup

▶ The U.S. Army desertion rate has increased over 104 percent in the past year alone. (*The New Yorker*)

▶ Detailed analysis of why Russia finally invaded Ukraine yesterday. (*Lisbian*)

▶ Users in tiny Santa Claus, Indiana, are finally getting a Wi-Fi signal, giving the National Satellite Wi-Fi Initiative 100 percent coverage. (*IndyStar*)

▶ Betty Hathaway, star of the latest *Guys and Dolls* revival, was murdered by her understudy, who was apparently not interested in an eternal apprenticeship. (Dora Smith's feed)

▶ Senator Conrad Kenny (D-MA) has proposed reducing the number of allowable dependent-child tax credits from two to zero. (C-SPAN)

▶ A census study found that only around thirty-five million true organics remain in the United States, many of them sick or elderly. (USA.gov)

▶ Oil prices soared over $1,200 a barrel after a leaked memo from an Exxon executive divulged that only 1.2 billion barrels of oil remain in the recently tapped Arctic National Wildlife Refuge. I thought that sounded like a fair amount. I was incorrect. (*Washington Post*)

❱ Newly coastal McComb, Mississippi, was recently named the best new party town in the nation. Expect Jackson to hold the title a decade from now. (*Maxim*)

❱ Tap-water fees at city restaurants are now regularly hitting the five-dollar mark. (Bruno Ili's feed)

❱ Another day, another homeless person preying on someone I know. My friend Jeff had a burrito snatched right out of his hand as he was walking down Eighth Avenue. I'm told the contents of the burrito included carnitas. (Jeff's feed)

❱ City orphanages are now waiving all adoption fees in hopes of getting more people to adopt abandoned children. Maybe if that tax credit is still around . . . (also from Bruno Ili's feed)

❱ My friend Juri's cousin had his Jerusalem cheese shop bombed yesterday. He didn't seem to care. This is what he told Juri: "Two thousand years from now, we'll still all be here in the Middle East. I promise you. We'll still be fighting, of course. We'll still be killing each other. But this is what we do, you see? We're very good at fighting and killing each other. We know how to do this without going overboard. The cure changes nothing. They'll make more Arabs, and we'll make more Jews. They can kill as many of us as they please. We'll never die completely. Now if you'll excuse me, I have to go clean Gorgonzola off the toilet." (Juri's feed)

DATE MODIFIED:
4/12/2031, 4:04 P.M.

"This is good"

Dad was slipping away faster than I had anticipated. Three weeks ago we had to arrange 24-7 nurse care. I came up all three week-ends to help, despite pro-death extremist threats against the trains. Two days ago one of the nurses called and told me that my sister and I needed to come and stand round-the-clock vigil, to wait for the end. Alison and I rented a plug-in, went to Sonia's apartment, grabbed little David, and drove up as fast as we could.

As we pulled into the driveway, I saw the nurse through the big kitchen window. She was a slender black woman named Toni. It used to be that I'd arrive home and Dad would have food and drinks ready and waiting. That isn't ever going to happen again. But Toni, who over the past few weeks had proven adept at making us feel comfortable in the face of unrelentingly grim circumstances, had put a small bowl of Goldfish and two glasses of water on the kitchen counter for us. I hugged her for that. Toni is quite used to being hugged by people.

She led us over to Mom and Dad's room, which is on the house's main level. I say "Mom and Dad's room" because it still very much feels that way. After my mom died, my dad preserved their room exactly as it was. He left her toiletries by the sink, sometimes replacing them if they started to look old or rusty. He cleaned the room on Tuesday mornings, just as she did. He kept the numerous throw pillows on the bed, even though he spent the majority of my mom's life bitching about them. And he still slept on the left side of the bed, leaving her spot unoccupied. He said he tried sleeping spread-eagle once, but it just wasn't comfortable.

That was the driving force behind his upkeep of the room. It wasn't to keep Mom's spirit alive, though that was an unwitting side effect. It was because that's what made him most comfortable: to live the same way he lived when she was still breathing. He liked the room that way and had no intention of ever changing it.

Alison and I came into the room. Toni went to Dad's bedside to awaken him. He had to get up for a moment to take his pain medication. I had seen him just a week ago, yet the change was drastic.

He was on his side. A thin, blue waffle blanket stretched over his body from the neck down. He was curled up, his back hunched into a crescent and his legs bent at the knee, turning his entire body into the shape of a question mark. His torso looked slight, as if the lump under the blanket had been caused by a fold and nothing more substantial. His legs, once sturdy, had dissolved into the kind of spindly appendages you'd see on a newborn foal. Under the blanket, they gradually faded down to nothing. You couldn't even make out his feet. It was like he was slowly being erased from the bottom up.

Toni patted his shoulder, and he stirred. He smacked his lips. Little flecks of dried yellow mucus surrounded his mouth. Toni took a damp cloth and wiped some of them away. She turned to me.

"He's not producing a lot of saliva now," she said, "so we have to keep his mouth moist." She took out a small squirt bottle filled with water and drizzled some into his mouth. He recoiled, like a toddler tasting spinach for the first time. "His gums and sinuses are inflamed, so the water causes lots of irritation."

He looked up at Alison, David, and me. His face was noticeably thinner, making him look oddly younger—like a sickly person twenty years his junior. He tried to reach for his glasses, but he was too weak. Toni took them off the nightstand and gently slipped them on for him. He looked at Alison. His voice was very faint.

"That's a pretty lady," he said.

"Thank you," Alison replied. She barely whispered the words to him, fearing anything louder would cause him to shatter into a thousand pieces.

I took Dad's hand. "We're thinking about getting married," I told him.

"Good. That's good. Where is your sister?"

"She's an hour behind us. She'll be here soon."

"Okay. I can wait."

"Are you comfortable?"

"Yes."

"Are you happy?"

He licked his lips. "Oh yes. This is good, John."

I placed David at the edge of the bed. The baby stared at Dad as if he were a new stuffed animal that he didn't quite know if he liked or not. Dad said hello to him. David said "baaaaaaa" and looked up at me.

He's going to turn one soon. When I picture David, I can only see him as he is. I can't summon an image of how he looked two months ago without consulting a photo. The memory of what he was is replaced all too easily by what's directly in front of my face.

I turned to Dad. I saw him as he was now: gaunt, frail, dying. I tried to envision his face four months earlier, a face so familiar to me that it may as well have been a monument. But I couldn't picture it. I could only see the atrophying man before me. The cancer had wiped the old him—the *real* him—away entirely.

Polly arrived. Alison took her boys and David out for pizza while we stayed at Dad's bedside with Toni.

My sister patted Dad on the shoulder delicately. "I'm here, Dad."

"Good."

"Can we get you anything?"

"No. I'm fine. You're all here. That's plenty."

He let out an exhalation that lasted a minute, blowing his spirit out of his body. His fate was his own now. His eyes opened wide, the whites now a yolky color. He took both our hands and spit out his last words. "Thank you. This is good. This is good."

He lay back and let go.

That was it. I sat there with Polly for forty minutes, still as the body in Dad's bed. It's a funny thing when someone you love dies. You spend all your time with them, caring for them. Then they die, and you're left with nothing to do. Your obligation to them is fulfilled. There's no more consoling or hand-holding to do. There's just this gigantic, yawning space of free time, which feels at once liberating and unnatural.

We heard the front door of the house open and Alison and the boys stepping back inside.

Polly rushed to tell the kids. I went out into the family room and looked at Alison. David was sitting on the floor, chewing on a board book. She could tell from my eyes. She ran to me and buried her head in my chest. When we'd talked about marriage a few weeks back, I'd told her I was certain I could stay married to her forever. Yet there remained, deep in the back of my mind, the tiniest shred of doubt. It was that eternal male instinct recoiling from the idea of anything other than total sexual liberation. I had waited for Alison all this time. I had dreamed beyond my wildest hopes of the day that she would be mine. And now she was. She was mine. All mine. No one else's. Forever, if I chose. Yet the little animal in my brain was dissatisfied even with that, still yearning for blondes with impossible bodies and unknown motives. I wondered then if it would ever go away.

It did. As Alison embraced me and my dad lay dead down the hall, that last vestige of irrational boyhood was extinguished. Gone. There was no doubt anymore. Everything I wanted was clear.

Toni opened a bottle of wine and offered me a glass. I took it and sat down on the sofa in front of the TV. She picked up David.

"You mind if I play with him?" she asked.

"Not at all."

She wiped David's mouth clean and pushed his nose in. He let out a joyous wail. He looked around at his surroundings and pushed off of her chest. He wanted to get down and explore everything. Grab everything. Stick it all in his little mouth to get a better feel. He turned and stared at me as only a baby can. Everything is a puzzle they're trying to solve. Hope and terror are the same emotion.

"He looks just like you," she said.

"Like his grandpa too."

"Well, he's a cutie. Yes you *are*."

I gestured to my wine. "Would you like a glass?"

"No no. I don't drink. I've got grandkids waiting for me at home."

"Shut up. You're a grandmother?"

"I have three grandkids. And I'm due again at the end of January."

"That's amazing. You are the youngest-looking grandma I've ever seen."

"And I'll be the best-looking great-great-grandma you've ever seen. If there's one thing I know how to do, it's produce children that have children. The more the merrier, as far as I'm concerned. God gave me the energy to do it, so I'm gonna take advantage. I'm gonna make a family so big that it's gonna need its own government. I told my husband I don't want a family tree; I want a family rain forest. I've watched my kids raise their kids, and I'll watch their kids raise their kids, and their kids raise their kids, and on and on and on. That's the miracle."

"That sounds pretty solid."

I looked at Alison. David bounced on Toni's knee and let out a squeal.

DATE MODIFIED:
5/24/2031, 3:08 A.M.

Home Cure?

This just broke on Pharmawire:

Home Cure Ready Soon

By Cady Rourke

Test results for a "home version" of the cure for aging produced by pharmaceuticals giant Pfizer have been "massively successful," according to an internal company memo. A single-injection version of the vector could be ready for the general public as soon as next year, possibly for under three hundred dollars.

Until now the cure has been administered as an outpatient procedure that requires drawing blood, followed two weeks later by three painful injections. Pfizer's drug, tested under the name Vectril, produced similar results with just one injection, with no prior blood work required.

"This means you can now get a prescription, pick the vector up at the pharmacy, and do it yourself at home," said an anonymous director at the company. "In the future, this is how everyone will get the cure."

Pfizer's stock tripled this morning when news of the successful testing was confirmed.

DATE MODIFIED:
5/27/2031, 2:16 P.M.

"Look at me"

Alison took me out for beer and pizza after David's birthday party, and it was the first time since Dad died that I'd found myself in a convivial mood. With enough beer poured straight down my gullet, I was able to actually interact with everything around me. I noticed the copper tops on the restaurant tables and the gruff Italian waitress (who was clearly either the owner of the joint or at least married to the owner) barking orders at the Mexican cooks in the back. I saw two other kids who were also having birthday parties. This was at nine at night. As a father, I did not approve.

I ordered a bourbon. "I always used to do this," I told Alison.

"Drink bourbon? I don't remember you stopping at any point."

"No, I always used to order it at the tail end of a meal. My dad would sometimes come into town and buy me dinner. Whenever he did, I'd order a bourbon at the end of the meal, and he'd roll his eyes because he thought I was being Mr. Fancy Pants. Then the drink would come and he'd say, 'What bourbon is that? I better have a taste.' Then he'd drink half the glass. He'd never order one for himself. He always preferred to have the pleasure of drinking half of mine and giving me crap for ordering it. He was a devious old man."

"Well, now I have to drink half of yours when it arrives."

We lingered there for a bit while we shared the drink. I felt that gratifying warm burn in my throat after the last sip. I got up, took Alison's hand, and escorted her out of the restaurant and back onto the street. We crossed over to East End Avenue and loitered a little bit more, along the railing overlooking the river.

A handful of night joggers and drunken prep schoolers passed behind us. I was drunk myself and spent our moment there happily not giving a shit about anything. We turned and began walking back to First Avenue. The area had cleared. No one was around—a rare occurrence.

I noticed a solitary figure walking down the street with his back to us. He was bald. As we got closer, I could make out his green scalp.

"It's a Greenie," I said.

"Let's just turn around."

I refused. The beer had made me rambunctious. "HEY, ASSHOLE!"

The Greenie turned and saw me. He wasn't a random one. If I had picked him out of a lineup, I wouldn't have been lying. He pulled up the corners of his mouth and flashed his big shark whites. "How you doing, birthday boy?"

Since the attack, I'd always slip the Texan's gun into the back of my waistband whenever I'd leave the apartment at night, careful to hide it from Alison. She helped keep my fear partially shrouded, but the feel of the Texan's gun served to eliminate it entirely. It replaced fear with a compulsive desire for correction. Sometimes when I was walking on the street at night, I'd reach back and clandestinely wrap my hands around it. Grasp it, squeeze it, daydream about having the chance to take it out and exact a toll on those who would fuck with me. It was a joyful kind of paranoia, in which you believe they're coming to get you, and you very much look forward to them trying.

The Greenie flashed a knife. I took out the Texan's gun. It was the first time Alison was made aware of its existence. "John, don't."

The troll shifted his eyes to her. "She got a birthday too?"

I broke. Immediately, I burst into a full sprint after him. He turned tail and ran away from me. Alison tried to keep up with me, to hold me back. I felt the grip of the pistol sweetly nuzzle against my fingers as I drew it upward. The Greenie turned into a small alley between two houses, stumbled on an uneven slab of pavement, and fell sharply to the ground, the knife flying out of his hand and hopscotching well out of reach.

I pounced, jumping on the troll and pressing his bald head into the little raised pebbles in the asphalt. I pressed the gun to his temple. "How's this? Is this funny to you?"

"You don't have the balls," he said.

"Look at me. *Look at me!*"

He turned his head and faced me fully, still smiling. I hated that smile. Hated it, hated it, hated it. So I decided to destroy it. I turned the gun in my hand and brought the butt down right through his big, stupid veneers. They shattered on impact, like china falling out of a cabinet. He recoiled in pain, blood gushing from the corners of his mouth. I grabbed his jaw and twisted his face back in my direction, bringing the butt down again and again, breaking every last tooth I could find inside his hideous mouth. I broke and I bashed. I unleashed every hateful whirlwind that had ever gusted up inside my being. Whip, whip, whip. In no time his smile was gone. I grinned at him, his blood spattered across my face and oozing between my fingers. I kept grinning, trying to impress on him the absolute drunken joy I felt in crushing his face.

"If I ever see you again," I told him, "I'll cut out your eyes and shoot off your fucking ears."

He fell unconscious. I let his head roll back on its side, cheek to cheek with the ground. I turned to Alison. I had forgotten to stop smiling. She saw it. She saw the demented joy. She stepped back away from me. And back. And back.

"Alison."

Another step back. Then another. I tried to get closer to her. She kept backing away, in a daze. She backed to the end of the sidewalk, farther and farther out of my reach.

"Alison, please. Alison."

The gap between us grew ever larger. She didn't hear the truck coming down the street. She never saw it in her periphery as she stepped down from the curb and into its speeding path. She never turned to look as it plowed decisively through her in a single effortless sweep. It all happened in a blinding shot, as if meticulously choreographed.

I ran to her and cradled her body. She was a loose bag of bones, like holding my son when he was first born. I could feel assorted parts inside her, but I couldn't feel any structure to them. I turned her head so we could be face-to-face, but it was too late for any kind of touching goodbye. She was gone. My heart made a fist. I looked to the alleyway. The gun lay there. The troll was gone. I looked down the street and saw his head disappearing again into the darkness, slowly shrinking like the blip of an old television set when it's been turned off.

The sirens cruised into my skull and bounced around dreamily, like a conversation you overhear when you're half-asleep. I saw paramedics rushing toward us. They tried to pry Alison from my arms, but I instinctively refused to surrender her. I had waited so long for her to be in my grasp. I pressed against her, trying to absorb her. They took her away. The best part of my life is now over. A wisp of beautiful reality that I'll spend the rest of eternity desperately trying to hold on to, as it floats away like a speck of dust in time's ever-expanding black chasm. All that's left of her is the feeling—the memory of finding her again and telling her I loved her and hearing, at long last, her tender reciprocation. I love you. I'll love until there's nothing left. That was the moment I should have perished, and not one second thereafter. All was right then. Nothing ever will be again.

While the police questioned me, I realized that what I'd done to the troll would be considered a death-penalty offense in Texas. I wish I were a Texan. I have become unhinged. I have to leave here. I have to get away from the world I've made for myself, lest it engulf me. I need to get away now, so that all that remains is a quickly dissipating apparition and nothing more.

DATE MODIFIED:
6/23/2031, 3:07 A.M.

III

SATURATION:

MARCH 2059

(TWENTY-EIGHT YEARS LATER)

"The cure for the cure"

The address on the slip of paper led me to a garage door that was painted green. It was one of several garages littering the B side of the street—the alley that runs behind the storefronts. At first I thought I had the wrong address, since most of the garages were plug-in body shops. I double-checked the number on the scrap paper.

> JonesPlus End Specialists, Inc.
> 206-B W. Martinson St.
> Falls Church, VA

I knocked on the door. No one answered. I took out my WEPS and punched in the number I was given. After half a ring, some-one answered.

"Yeah?"

"Yes, is this Matt?"

"Yeah."

"My name is John Farrell. We have an appointment."

"Well, where are you?"

"I'm outside your door."

"Why haven't you come in yet?"

"Because no one answered the door when I knocked."

The door opened. Standing before me was, presumably, Matt. He had orange hair mussed atop a big round head. He had an orange goatee. He had a bright-orange shirt and orange clogs on. He looked like a goddamn orange. He was tall, yet somehow still managed to appear schlubby. He peered at me over his orange-framed glasses. "Dude, I don't have time to be answering the door all day long. Get in here."

I walked into the space. In place of cars and auto lifts was an open bullpen with three mismatched dining room tables lined up on each side. Odds and ends littered the tables and shelves: old Coke machines, ancient stereo equipment, very large red-painted springs, woodblock carvings, and the occasional dusty toy. Four people were using the tables as work spaces, typing and iFacing. No two of the work chairs were alike. A pair of very small dogs immediately rushed at me and began licking my knees. Matt snapped at them, "Pepe! Daisy! Knock it off!" They retreated. Matt yelled to everyone in the room, "Everyone! This is John Farrell."

No one said anything. Matt beckoned and started in the direction of a small room attached to the back of the garage. On the way we passed—smack-dab in the middle of the office—a bright orange boat.

"What's with the boat?" I asked.

"Ugh. That goddamn thing. You wanna buy it?"

"No."

"Someone's gonna say yes to that question one day. I have to get rid of that thing by next month, when the new boat comes in. Where the hell is Bruce?"

A quiet man with a stubbly beard raised his hand from one of the stations. "I'm right here."

"Well, come on! Let's do this!"

I followed Matt to the back room. There were two couches. Both old. One of them had visible dog-urine stains. Matt lounged across that one. Bruce opted for a modest straight-back chair over in the corner. I sunk down into the other couch, my ass now three inches from the ground.

"So," Matt said, "you're the guy Jim recommended, right?"

"Right."

The power went out for two minutes. Matt cursed. The lights came back on. "Goddamn grid. How do you know Jim?"

"Through an old work friend."

"Did Jim say anything about what we need you for?"

"No."

"Hang on. Lemme look at your résumé again. You haven't worked in nearly thirty years. These goddamn résumés, Bruce. Every single one has some giant gap in it. Everyone's gotta have their hobo period now. So, you were a lawyer?"

"Yep. Divorce and cycle marriage."

"Ha. Cycle marriage. I tried that. Twice! What a load. Never made it past ten years either time. You should have seen the second woman I tried it with. Came from a family of the biggest Arkansas rednecks you will ever see. I mean, we're talking people who play the fiddle with their goddamn teeth. Why did you quit?"

"Because I didn't want to do it anymore. I didn't like what I was helping facilitate."

"So you cashed out."

"Yeah. I took the money and I spent some time just . . . out there."

"So why start work now?"

"Well, I got tired of drinking. And I ran out of money."

"Yes, I'm sure you did. I mean, why start *this* job? Why do this? I mean, this is a weird job. You know that, right? We're end specialists here. That means you're basically half angel of death, half event planner. What about that appeals to you? And don't say the event-planning part, because no one likes the event-planning part. That part is *shit*."

I answered him carefully. "I've had people in my life who got to die on their own terms. And I've had people in my life who didn't have any say in the matter. I don't want anyone to have to go out that way if they don't want to. I want to help."

He cocked his head. I thought, for a brief moment, that he took me for being full of shit. "Jesus, that's a good answer. Ninety-nine percent of the time when I ask that question, the answer I get is 'Durrrrrr, I just like killin' folk'—which is *fucked*! It's good to know you aren't a complete chucklehead. Besides, that's not the role Bruce and I have sketched out for you. Let me ask you this: Do you have any military experience?"

"No."

"Do you have any police experience?"

"No."

"Do you have any experience working in surveillance?"

"No."

"Do you have any experience working in medicine?"

"No."

"Do you have any experience working in journalism?"

"No."

"Good. Have you ever killed anyone?"

"No."

"Do you own a gun?"

"Yes."

"Have you ever used it?"

"Yes. The butt end, anyway. I've never shot it at anyone. I've had to pull it on gangs from time to time."

"Ugh. We get gangs once in a blue moon around here. That's the real reason I don't answer the door. If you ever see some shady homeless nutjob busting into this garage, use that." He gestured toward an ancient-looking shotgun on the wall. I was surprised he spoke of it as if it were still functional. "I'm not losing my life just because some jackass needs a sip of water and won't take no for an answer. Anyway, keep your gun. You're gonna want to have it on you at all times. If you need ammo, we have plenty here in the garage. We're gonna be sending you to dangerous places every now and then. Don't get me wrong—most of the time you're gonna be servicing the chronically old or losers with depression or something like that. But sometimes you'll have to go to the slums or to some creepy walled-off town in Bumfuck, Egypt. Really hairy places. The other thing you need to know about are the collectivists. Sometimes they throw false leads our way in order to sucker us. Two years ago, when we first started this business, one of our guys was kidnapped by them, and we never heard from him again. So be aware. I don't want them shooting you in the foot, and then dancing some dipshit prayer circle around you."

"Okay." Minutes in, and I already liked Matt immensely.

"Now, the most important part of this job involves three

things. First, *verification*. We don't treat anyone whose cure age is unverifiable. When you field a call from a client, you get their full name and driver's license number if they have one. If they don't have a license or address, you get their mother's maiden name. You send that to me with your WEPS, and I can get it instantly verified in the government cure database."

"There's a cure database? What about doctor-patient confidentiality? Isn't it illegal for the government to do that?"

"Oh my God! You're right! I can't believe I didn't realize that! Hey, Bruce, go alert the feeds! The government is doing illegal shit! Of course there's a database. Only those backward idiots in China would brand a kid physically when you can do it digitally. Now, the second-most-important part of this thing is estate planning. Jim says you did a lot of that when you were Mr. Big Shot Lawyer, correct?"

"Yes. Before I went into divorce law."

"Good. Perfect. Every client needs to have a will. If they don't have one, your job is to produce one for them. Most of them have nothing to pass down, so it shouldn't be hard. Use our template if you need to. Last part of the job: exit interviews. This is going to be your biggest thing. All exit interviews must be conducted in person and alone. No one else present except you and the client, and Ernie over there."

Matt gestured toward a muscular bald fellow with a black goatee, who was eating from a giant plastic container filled with nothing but chickpeas. He smiled and waved back at us. That was Ernie.

"One time," Matt continued, "we let the brother of a deaf guy stay in the room to do sign-language interpretation for him. Well, it turned out the brother was translating everything wrong on purpose. Goddamn deaf kid thought it was an ear-implant consult. The brother was schtupping the deaf guy's lady and wanted him out of the picture. So do *not* allow anyone else in the room. Witnesses can come in when it's done. And when you conduct the interviews, you use this app to record and stream. The conversation will be transcribed in real time on our server. I upload it directly to Containment, and you can get approval right on the spot. We do not perform an end specialization without that clearance. *Ever.* Containment assumes all legal liability once they've approved the interview, and it becomes a matter of public record right away. After that, you can get paid and Ernie will perform the end specialization. He's the closer. Don't do it yourself. Ernie's the one with a nursing degree, which means he's the only one allowed by law to perform it. Then you upload an end report, get the signed waivers from the witnesses, and call our boy Mosko to pick up the body. Then the relatives get their precious little tax rebate and insurance kickback, and the whole thing is over."

His WEPS rang. He took the call and went off for thirty minutes, leaving me to sit there and do nothing. He came back and acted as if no time had passed at all.

I had questions. "What do I ask people in the interviews?"

"Oh, the standard crap. 'Hey, buddy, why you wanna die?' That usually does the trick. Bruce and I have a list of sample questions you can use."

"What does Ernie use to perform the end specialization?"

"Eh. It depends on what they want. Everyone usually asks for the quickest, most painless route, in which case we always suggest this." He held up a very small, torpedo-shaped plastic tube with a lance on the end. "This is sodium fluoroacetate. Highly diluted. Stick and squeeze, and we're done. No muss, no fuss. I would suggest you steer everyone toward this option. Don't let some idiot talk you into having Ernie shoot him in the head."

Ernie spoke without looking up. "I don't like shooting people in the head."

"See? He doesn't like shooting people in the head. Besides, violent end specializations are bad for our brand image. We want to be perceived as the warm and friendly end specialists. Like Saint Peter. Another thing: Please, under no circumstances try to talk a client out of it. That's not your job. Your job is to prove that they are making a sober, rational decision that's entirely their own. If during the course of the interview they decide, 'Whoa, hey! I don't wanna do this!' that's fine. Whatever. But do *not* try to be Mr. Nice Guy and rescue them."

"Why not?" I asked.

"Because *screw them*—that's why. That's lost revenue, lost time, and another mouth breather walking around, not fully appreciating what's left of *our* water, and eating what's left of *our* bacon. Now, I can't have you go out on any client visits until you pay me two hundred bucks so I can enroll you in Containment's end specialization course. Then you have to take the certification test. After that you're certified."

"What if I fail?"

"Don't worry. I take the test for you. Just give me the money, and you'll be a certified end specialization consultant five minutes from now."

I handed him the money.

"Excellent," he said. "Now, do you know what soft end specialization is?"

"Yes. Soft end specialization is voluntary. Hard end specialization is not."

"That's right. And hard end specialization is, as you know, not legal as of yet. Everyone here knows that will change at some point. However, Bruce and I made the decision when we started this business that we would always deal in soft end specialization. So, are you okay with never having a chance to do hard end specialization? Or do you get your nut off being Mr. Bounty Hunter?"

"No. I'm fine with soft. This is good."

"Goddamn! You are the only person who hasn't bitched about that. I can't believe it. Jim must have given you the answers in advance."

Matt got up and went to eat a donut. It appeared our conversation was over.

"Does this mean I'm hired?"

"Well, I'm gonna send you out on a call with Ernie and see how you do. If you're fine, then we'll give you more work. If you suck, then it's back to drifterland with you." He walked back, mouth full of crumbs. "Now, one last thing: You were a lawyer. I'm told you were very good. Right?"

"Yes."

"Good. That means you know when people are bullshitting you. That's why Bruce and I brought you in. If you're out on a call with Ernie and sense that anything is weird, follow your instincts and bail. Got it?"

"Got it."

"Okay. First place you're going to go is the car graveyard in Bowie. Some hippie jackass filed an RFE. Do you have a plug-in?"

"Yes."

"Where's it parked?"

"About a mile away."

"That's pretty good. You live in it?"

"No, I'm staying with a friend. Maybe for good."

"Okay. Ernie'll be ready to go with you in fifteen minutes. Always wear this hat when you go out on a call."

He threw me a big orange baseball hat emblazoned with the company motto:

JONESPLUS END SPECIALISTS.

PROVIDING THE CURE FOR THE CURE SINCE 2057

"It's good for branding," he said. "Get back in time and we'll order dinner for you. You have any questions?"

"Yeah. Do I get a house discount?"

He let out a mighty chuckle. "Are you kidding? If you're any good at this, I'll *never* let you croak."

DATE MODIFIED:
3/2/2059, 9:08 P.M.

The Hippie in the Graveyard

The biggest car graveyard I ever saw was along I-76 in Nebraska. People came from as far as Florida and the Texas coast to live there. They had no money, no home, and nowhere else to turn. And every day they showed up, in increasing numbers, to settle down in a formerly barren stretch of the Nebraska plains, now a dead sea of old cars that lined the road.

That place used to be drive-through country. Motorists on their way to Denver or the West Coast—or anywhere more interesting than Nebraska—could drive through that expanse for hours and hours and see nothing. Spotting a cow counted as a legitimate event. But when I showed up, it was clear that a giant migration was unfolding. It was as if the whole country was in a massive inward retreat. Along the shoulder you saw a washed-out kaleidoscope of people, tents, windscreens, bonfires, and clotheslines.

And cars. From the road to the horizon, on both sides, stretched an enormous, undulating metallic quilt—a mix of vapor greens, galaxy whites, Icelandic blues, and thousands of other colors found nowhere in nature. The old limos were dubbed McMansions by the people living there. And the campers and Winnebagos were like forty-four-acre estates. It was the world's largest used car lot, petrified in amber and transformed into one of the more unpleasant cities you will ever visit. The Nebraska car yard is supposedly where the D36 gang began. It formed well after I left, but apparently some of the vagrants decided the best way to survive was to join together and start pillaging the hell out of everything. Then the drug dealers joined in, and the whole area became a giant black tumor on the landscape.

The Bowie car yard was nothing like that. When Ernie and I showed up in the plug-in, we got out of the car (Ernie grabbed a duffel bag with two shotguns and his closing equipment) and surveyed the landscape. It was a fairly small car yard, maybe a thousand vehicles total, with various cheesy rock songs blasting out from each one. Prince George's County made from concentrate. Steakheads wore wifebeaters and drank cheap vodka while trying to hook up with any chick in sight. I saw at least two touch-football games going on. It was a perpetual tailgate party without any real game to play, which I found to be a solid concept.

Matt told us to look for the microbus. It was the only one of its kind in the lot, once white and now the color of a quail's egg. We spotted it in short order and advanced. We knocked on the door. A soundboard recording from an MMJ show blasted from inside. The whole thing reeked of hydro. We knocked again. Someone inside turned the music down a bit, then a voice said, "Hello?"

"Someone ordered an ES?" Ernie asked.

"Dude, if this van's a rockin', don't . . . uh . . . like, don't come in."

"Your van isn't rocking."

"It isn't?"

"Nope."

"Damn. Feels like it is. Crap." The door slid open. Out popped a skinny, pale fellow with long, stringy red hair. He was shirtless, with dirty white jeans, dirty white sneakers, and patches of bright-red eczema all over his chest. He beckoned us in. "I'm Chuck. Get in the van. Everyone steals my hydro whenever I come out."

We stepped in. The bottom of the van was cut out, and my foot sank into the soft earth below. The entire inside of the van reeked of sewage.

Ernie looked at his feet. "What am I stepping in?"

"Mud. I swear, muchacho. I use the Lincoln five cars over to do my dirty work. When it gets hot, you can smell the seepage. Shit's not so bad today though, right?"

He offered us gummy bears, which we politely declined. He signed the paperwork and filled out a will form. I fired up the recorder on the WEPS, and off we went. Chuck rattled off a list of reasons why he'd called: He was bored, he had nowhere to go, everyone at the car yard was trying to bogart his hydro, etc.

"Why not move away from here?" I asked.

"Move? What's the point? Anywhere I move, there's someone else there, man. This is my little space, and that's about all I can get, brother. One time I went down to Bonnaroo for three days. I smoked all the shit that was lit. I drank every cup that was filled. I sucked all the acid that was printed. It was *wild*, man. Wild. But after three days, shit's over, man. That's what makes a party a party. It's a special occasion. That third day, it isn't so special anymore. You get that itchy ass. That's what I feel like now. I feel like I'm trapped at the show. I need to experience something way beyond that now. *Way* beyond. That's why I called you."

"How do you want this done?"

"All right. Good. Are you ready for this shit? Cause I'm about to blow your nuts off. Come on, back door." He opened the opposite side of the van and escorted us out. He led us, through the mud, all the way to a scrap heap near the back of the yard. I made out lots of old circus equipment. There were faded red tent canvases, trapeze swings that were tough to recognize at first glance because they weren't taut, and old trampoline springs. Then Chuck maneuvered around the pile and showed us a giant metal pipe painted with red, white, and blue bunting. He nudged me.

"Huh? Huh?"

"I don't get it," I said.

"Human. Cannonball."

"You want to be shot out of a cannon?"

"Just like Hunter S., amigo."

"Okay, Hunter S. Thompson shot himself, then was cremated, then had his *ashes* fired out of a cannon. He wasn't blasted out of a cannon while still living."

Chuck thought about it, then had a revelation. "Then I got him beat!"

"You'd need a team of engineers to figure out how to do something like this. Now, I know there are a lot of ex-NASA people out there with nothing to do, but I don't know them personally."

"Just WEPS it, brother! Find one to 'face with. Can't be that hard."

Ernie cut in. "Custom specializations incur additional fees."

"That's fine. I got a little bit of money. This is my last splurge. And I want this shit posted."

"Endcasts are an extra hundred dollars."

"That's cool! It's cool, dude! I can scrounge it!"

Ernie and I excused ourselves for a moment to discuss the situation. We brought Matt up on the WEPS, and I told him that Chuck wanted us blow him out of a cannon.

"Does he have the money for it?"

"Yeah," I said.

"Then blow his ass out of a cannon."

"How?"

"I don't know. Figure it out. That's your job. Now go away. I'm winning an auction for a new hood ornament."

He signed out. I looked to Ernie, befuddled. He patted me on the shoulder. "The thing you're gonna learn about Matt," he told me, "is that he likes to spend lots of time buying shit he doesn't need. Also, he's a fucking psychopath. But that's why he's fun to work for." Ernie led me back to the van, opened his duffel, reached in, and took out an explosive charge. "I'm told this has a blast radius of twenty feet."

"You always keep that on you?"

He shrugged. "Sometimes you find yourself in situations where you gotta blow some shit up."

I had to draw up additional contracts and liability waivers. While I tended to the grunt work, Chuck came back to the van and took out a small red blanket, which he then tied around his neck as a daredevil's cape. He also had an old motorcycle helmet that he'd scavenged from the heap. As a final touch, he donned an old pair of red plastic women's sunglasses. I estimate he spent at least five whole minutes planning this extravaganza. When he was finished getting in costume, he stepped out the front door of the microbus to address the crowd.

"Who wants to watch me blow up? Anyone who helps gets the last of my hydro!"

Instantly, dozens of steakheads and tramps descended upon us, ready to pitch in. We led them to the heap where the old cannon lay prone on the ground. It was upright and pointing northwest within seconds. If douchebags are useful for anything, it's performing brainless displays of strength to impress everyone else around.

Someone brought in a ladder from the campground. Ernie wired the charge and dropped it in the bottom of the tube. After that, Chuck reemerged from the van to thunderous applause. He put on his helmet and advanced toward the human-missile silo. He turned to Ernie and me.

"This is gonna work, right?" he asked.

"Absolutely," Ernie lied. "That thing'll shoot you right to the heavens, kid."

"Sweet. What happens if it doesn't go the way I want it to?"

"Well, you could ask for a refund, but you'll probably be too dead to claim it."

"Right."

Chuck began scaling the ladder. Ernie turned to me and shrugged. He had no real clue whether the charge would have the desired effect. At the top of the cannon, Chuck took a last hit of hydro, which was met with more clapping and hooting. He jumped into the barrel and slid down to the ground. I made everyone sign a waiver. Ernie asked Chuck if he was ready.

"Let's fly, muchacho!"

Everyone took cover behind a row of cars fifty yards away. Ernie set his WEPS on the hood of an old truck and began streaming a shot of the cannon. He grabbed the charge remote and leapt behind our row. He opened the switch. Suddenly, the entire vibrant mood of the scene flicked off, an aura of unease and tension taking its place. But Ernie didn't allow it to linger for more than a split second. He plunged the button down, and the bottom of the cannon made a loud sneeze. A few stray bits of Chuck flew out of the top and landed on some of the surrounding windshields. The top of the cannon began to smoke, like a novelty-sized Marlboro. We rushed to the cannon, fire extinguishers in hand, borrowed from a nearby camper. I wrapped a rag around my fist and knocked on the side of the cannon.

"Chuck?"

There was no answer. Three steakheads pushed on the side of the cannon until it fell back to the ground. We looked in the opening at the bottom. Some of Chuck remained. The rest was ash, never even close to touching the sky.

DATE MODIFIED:
3/3/2059, 3:08 A.M.

What They're Saying about
End Specialization

There have been times over the years when I didn't feel all that much like living anymore. When Keith and I spent 2047 in Guatemala, I'd stay up every night and stare at the Texan's gun, daring myself to use it, before I eventually passed out drunk. I've never had the guts to put my money where my mouth is. When I was a kid, I was always told that suicide was the coward's way out of life. I don't feel that way anymore. I feel the exact opposite. Chuck may have been a burnout and a hippie living in a van, but at least he had the balls to think of an exit and see it through without hesitation. I don't have that inherent bravery, chemically enhanced or otherwise. I'm not courageous enough to die now, nor have I ever been. I just keep on hanging around.

The first week of the job went according to Matt's description. Mostly older people, many disabled and in pain. There were a couple of exceptions. There was an alcoholic woman with a cure age of only thirty or so. Very attractive. But she had been in and out of AA for three decades. She hated it. Called it a rest home. She didn't want to live without drinking, but she knew she couldn't stay alive if she stayed on the bottle. She chose the third option. Ernie gave her the shot while she downed one of her own. Then there was a gamer who asked for us because he had grown despondent over the fact that Omni-Warrior: Dhuria had become too overpopulated for his tastes. None of these clients wavered in their decision making. All of them appeared to be at peace—a peace that has eluded me for so long that I'm not sure I would even recognize it if it came around again.

So that's how I justify this new gig to myself, I suppose. I know other people don't particularly agree. I went around the cloud and found plenty of disparate voices ready to sound off on the issue.

Bob Maclin:

We're no better than Russia now. End specialization is the single most unethical American enterprise since slavery. I am all for population control, but what is unacceptable to me is how this government can endorse subsidized suicide. It's downright ghoulish. We are preying on the weakest members of our society—the elderly, addicts, people with mental illness—then handing them a loaded gun and saying, "Go ahead. Pull the trigger."

* * *

Shepard Anson:

This is the least evil solution to a situation that has nothing but evil solutions. There are 720 million people in this country right now. We're a third-world nation, and we have been for quite some time. If we don't get a firm handle on our population, which is spinning wildly out of control, nature will be more than happy to assume command for us.

* * *

Paolo Estes:

I understand the need for end specialization. But this whole Patriots Program where they enshrine suicide victims like they're opera donors? That's creepy. I'm sorry. That's really, really messed up.

* * *

Kensi Patton:

My brother had an end specialization performed three months ago. He was thirty. That wasn't his cure age. That was his real age. Thirty with a cure age of twenty-six. And when he decided to end his life, the state was more than happy to send two people over to assist him.

I can't help but think he died not only because he wanted to, but because everyone else wanted him to. That's what this is really about. We spend forty minutes waiting in line at the charging station, we spend an hour looking to park, we share a one-room apartment with three other people, and we're wishing everyone else would just get out of our way.

And now we've agreed, as a society, to implement a program that performs assisted suicides without any consideration of whether someone has been here thirty years or a hundred years. Aren't there some people out there worth saving? Karl Olmert tried to commit suicide as a teenager, and now he's one of the finest architects on earth. Now that wouldn't happen. Should we simply let people like him vanish because we aren't willing to share?

I heard a rumor recently about a fire department dispatcher in a town in Massachusetts. Sometime last year the dispatcher got a call in the middle of the night. It was a relay from a 911 operator. There was a fire in a housing project. One of the really bad ones—drugs, gang members, all of it. When the operator told the dispatcher about the fire, he refused to send a truck to put it out. "Spontaneous end specialization," he said. Then he hung up and went back to playing solitaire on his WEPS while the firemen slept upstairs. They just let the thing burn. No one ever reported the fire on their feed. No one ever figured out how many people perished or how the fire began. No one cared. That's how cheap life is now. We get a surplus, and we burn it off.

I wonder if those firemen would have rescued my brother. Clearly, no one else wanted to bother.

DATE MODIFIED:
3/8/2059, 4:09 P.M.

A Few Minutes with the Worst Domestic Terrorist in American History

Randall Baines is still ranked number one on the FBI's list of most-wanted fugitives. He's been implicated in the July 3 bombings, so I know all about him. I see his face and I find myself again chased out of that hallway by the FDNY, forced to sit in a cold, gray stairwell while my best friend burns alive.

An anonymous journo who uses the pseudonym Flywheel was able to score an iFace interview with the guy. Everything about the video appears to be real. Here's a section of the transcript:

Flywheel: You're sick?

Baines: I am. I'm very sick.

Flywheel: Cancer?

Baines: I'm not going to go into details. But suffice it to say that my time here is nearing an end, which is as it should be. As you can see, I'm quite old.

Flywheel: You never got the cure.

Baines: No how, no way. True organic to the core.

Flywheel: Never tempted?

Baines: No. The people who have gotten it are fearful and weak. The average man—and I mean the truly average-in-every-way man—is led by a set of profound, animalistic urges that forever enslave him. And the cure has amplified those urges. That's why you're seeing the secessions. That's why more and more walls are going up around homes and towns. That's why the D36 gangs are raping and looting all over the place and why kooky Texans are shooting at trespassers with their bows and arrows. This is an epidemic of living.

Flywheel: What about you? What about the lives you've taken?

Baines: Everything I have done for this cause has been motivated by a single goal: saving lives. That's what people fail to understand. Without death, we don't learn a goddamn thing about life. I'm trying to *help* us here.

Flywheel: Explain how killing over five hundred people helps.

Baines: Because the people I have helped kill are facilitators of spreading the human virus across this planet. They are reckless people who are endangering the lives of everyone alive just so that the so-called luckiest generation can go around eating and drinking and having sex for an extra millennium.

Flywheel: Well, wait a second. Wait a moment. Let's get more specific about the people you have killed. In 2035 you helped orchestrate the bombing of a Vectril processing plant, an attack that killed over seventy-five people.

Baines: That's correct.

Flywheel: Of those seventy-five people, fourteen were children who were attending a day care center in the plant. And the rest of the victims were plant workers and administrators who were simply trying to earn a living.

Baines: Let me ask you a question. When we were in Afghanistan, did we kill civilians? Did we kill children?

Flywheel: Yes. But that's war.

Baines: So is this! This is a war! This is the *only* war! In your so-called useful war, strategic targets, such as enemy arms stockpiles, are taken out. If there's a kid killed in the blast, what does the army say? Well, that's too bad. We're sooooo sorry. But this was something we had to do in order to protect ourselves. Same logic here. Every doctor that prescribes Vectril and every store that sells it is a weapons stockpile.

Flywheel: So is that how you justify having, in 2045, one of your colleagues walk into a CVS store in Chicago wrapped in C4, blowing it up and killing two dozen people?

Baines: Yes. It's justified because it helps contain the damage the cure is causing. I know much of this insurgency is powered by evangelicals and more extreme religious groups. But that's not why I've taken up this cause. I have pragmatic reasons for trying to end postmortality in this country and the world at large. We've already seen the devastating effects of it, haven't we?

Flywheel: But how does killing hundreds of people change the situation? Isn't it simply a drop in the bucket? You haven't stopped the cure from spreading, and you aren't going to. So why not face reality and look for solutions that don't include shooting up a medical school or planting a pipe bomb in a testing facility?

Baines: Excuse me, you're saying *I* should face reality? Me? I am practically the *only* person in this nation who has any grasp on reality. I could have told you forty years ago that this cure would turn the Congo into a permanent slave state. I could have told you that it would deplete, entirely, the world's supply of fish. I could have told you that it would cause India to instantly revert to abject poverty and despair. Look at that nation. It was on the brink of becoming one of this century's great powers. Now it has two billion people and no possible way of accommodating them. That's reality, and no one out there seems to give a shit because they're too busy jumping around all excited and saying, "Whee! I get to live forever!" That's why this cure is so insidious. People are endangering the entire planet simply by sitting there and *being*. What I am doing is providing the only jolt of reality left. Everyone thinks that they can't die now. Well, they can. And they will.

Flywheel: But now you're going to die.

Baines: I am.

Flywheel: Don't you fear that the cause dies with you? I've seen your face on the shirts. You're the spiritual leader of this movement.

Baines: That's a load. I'm nothing. I am insignificant. The insurgency lives on with or without me. That's the beauty of it—how decentralized it is. I didn't plan the killing of Graham Otto. I didn't plan the T. J. Maxx massacre in Houston. Those were all independently conceived and executed. And that's why this insurgency will succeed. It needs no leader. The cause itself is strong enough to attract followers on its own. That's why you're seeing more people take it up, including those too poor now to afford the cure. You can't kill the insurgency simply by killing one person or even a thousand. You can't kill an idea.

Flywheel: Will you kill again before you die?

Baines: Yes.

Flywheel: Would you kill me if I were sitting directly across from you?

Baines: Did you get the cure?

Flywheel: I did. I got it twenty years ago.

Baines: Yes, I'd kill you. I wouldn't even think twice about it.

DATE MODIFIED:
3/12/2059, 7:12 P.M.

Exit Interview:
Edgar DuChamp

Matt called me into the back room. I passed the giant orange boat and sunk down into the pit of couch cushions. I noticed a giant stuffed rooster in the middle of the coffee table. This was a decidedly new feature. The pictures on the wall had also been rearranged. Ernie says Matt does this at least six times a month.

I pointed to the rooster. "What is this?"

"It's a rooster. I found it in a dumpster. The little auction house down the street was gonna toss it. You believe that?"

"Yes. I do."

"Listen, we're going full-time freelance with you."

"Isn't that a contradiction in terms?"

"Look, do you want the job or not? You've done just fine with the alkies and the old cripples. Time to take you off the bunny slopes."

"Are you sending me to a compound?"

His eyes sparked. "Yes. I am. Prepare yourself for the very mysterious, extremely dangerous slum known as Potomac, Maryland! You may never get out *alive*."

Ernie and I got into the plug-in, sat on the Beltway for ninety minutes, crossed over the American Legion Bridge, and soon found ourselves in Potomac, a slice of lily-whiteness that remains unaffected by the general lunacy of the rest of the DC area. It doesn't matter what happens in the future—wars, epidemics, whatever. I'm all but certain there will still remain these little bucolic footholds dotted across the land. Flawlessly landscaped country roads featuring one oversized house after another, all occupied by people who possess inexplicable amounts of free capital to spend as they please. Protected by walls and by the inherent charm of their existence.

I stared at the houses and compounds and considered an alternate version of my past that would have brought me to a place like this. A life where I had never stopped being a lawyer, where I married the mother of my child and settled down in a pristine burg, sealed cozily in a life of mild content. Each house we passed felt like a reflection of the finality of my own choices. I will never live in a place like this, and I have no clue if that's a tragedy or not.

We cruised along one of the back roads at a crawl and came upon a white gravel driveway leading into a flat, wide crest of land that overlooked the far-stretching county below. The entrance to the compound was blocked by an enormous gate supported by a giant, whitewashed brick arch. At the top of the arch was a coat of arms featuring Mercury's winged shoes. The gate itself was a set of huge cast-iron doors. No bars. Impenetrable as the darkness in a windowless room. We pulled onto the lip of the driveway.

Ernie stared at the crest. "I've seen this gate before. Like on TV. That coat of arms."

"It's the RideSwift logo," I said.

"RideSwift?"

"Yup."

RideSwift. The record label. The clothing label. The boutique mescal label. I once bought RideSwift sheets at Daffy's. It was not a wise purchase.

I looked at our case file on the WEPS. The name was Edgar DuChamp. I hadn't even bothered to glance at our client's name before we left. But there it was: Edgar DuChamp, the Swift. Ordering himself a deathgram.

We pushed the button on the intercom in the archway. A stern voice immediately asked us what we were doing in the driveway. We told the voice who we were and where we were from. The voice angrily dismissed us and told us to leave. But just as it was finishing berating us, another voice in the background started yelling at the first voice. "Charles! *Charles!* Those are the guys! Those are the guys he asked for!"

The intercom went dead and the gate opened. Two very large men were standing behind it. Both had guns. They approached our plug-in, dressed in black suits with orange bow ties. Official uniform of the black collectivist movement. I know very little about the Church of the Black Man, only that I have never been invited to any of its functions. The two men flanked the car and knocked on our windows. Ernie rolled his down. One of them leaned into the plug-in and pointed ahead. "Drive to the end of the road," he said. "There's a parking circle in front of the house. Park at exactly nine o'clock on the circle—that's nine o'clock if the front door is at twelve. Do *not* park right in front of the door. It messes with the aesthetic. And leave your keys with Terry, at the door, in case he needs to move your car or go out for snacks."

We did as instructed and got out of the plug-in. The wall of the compound ran along the driveway and down the hill like a giant white zipper. Another man in a COBM uniform walked our way and immediately escorted us through the huge wooden portico and into the house. I expected to be blinded with opulence upon entering the Swift's home: framed movie posters, gold banisters, stripper poles in the kitchen—every cliché fast money can purchase. It was nothing like that. Instead we entered a deluxe log cabin. Stacks of notched tamarack trunks lined the walls and met in cog joints at every corner. Thick log rafters strutted end-to-end across the tops of the stacks. Fleecy blankets were draped over every handrail and easy chair. Big, soft, smushy sectionals dominated the vast main space that lay below the foyer. A butcher-block island the size of Manhattan was all that separated the open kitchen from the main room. Hanging overhead was a chandelier made entirely of reindeer antlers. It was the kind of house the Texan's gun felt at home in.

The two uniformed men led us down the steps into the main room and handed us a couple of bottles of water. Then they took us down a pine hallway lined with photos of the Swift and every famous person you or I have ever seen on a screen or heard through a pair of headphones. At the end of the hallway another small flight of stairs led us to a thick, sealed studio door. One of the men pushed it open, and it made that whoosh sound you hear when you open a new jar of peanuts. Inside was a very small Asian engineer, sitting at a control panel, fiddling with the thousands of knobs at his disposal. Next to him, in carpenter jeans and a plain brown T-shirt, was Edgar. Out of his flashier garb, the Swift cut an even more striking figure. Light from the recesses above shined brilliantly off the cut of his jawline. He was lean— compact like a boxer. He didn't bother to acknowledge us as we entered the room. He was far too busy scratching his goatee.

The engineer leaned back in his chair and swiveled around to face the Swift. "What do you think?" he asked.

"I don't know," said the Swift.

"I think it sounds like stock."

"You think everything sounds like goddamn stock. You're Pippi Longstocking, for shit's sake."

"Should I play it again?"

"No, that only makes it more confusing." He looked my way. "You listen to a lot of hip-hop?"

"Not particularly," I said.

"Good. Listen to this and tell me what you think." He gestured to the engineer, and suddenly the room flooded with a staccato beat that rumbled through my core, treating my body like the tine of a tuning fork. Each measure was punctuated by a blast of horns and a single brash guitar chord mashed together. I thought about nodding along to the rhythm like any white person would, then thought better of it. The Swift cut the music. "So? What do you think?"

"I like it. It sounded like rock."

At that, his eyes lit up. He snapped his fingers. "That's right. Rock and roll. That's exactly right. You see? A lot of people think hip-hop is a kind of music. It's not. Hip-hop is *all* music. It is a population of music. And that's why it'll never die. That's why it's still here, even though most white folks thought it would be good and gone fifty years ago."

"This is for your new album?"

"My *last* album. My final statement. No comebacks this time. That's why it's taken nine goddamn years to put it together. Listen to this." He had the engineer queue up another take. Again my insides quivered. "That sound any different to you?"

"Yeah, there was a cymbal smash in with the horns."

"You like that better or worse?" He scanned me for advance signs of my answer.

"I don't know."

"Well, then shit. You're fired as my music director." He slumped back in his swivel chair, grabbed a handful of pistachios from a nearby dish (food was everywhere), and started cracking them open. "This is a hell of a process, man. A hell of a process. I've been doing this my whole life, and it never gets any easier. You're building a whole something out of nothing, with a trillion choices at your fingertips, like the one I just presented to you. I could work on it for *years* more, and I still wouldn't know if it was worth a shit until the rest of the world heard it and gave me the validation I need. I mean, I have no clue. I could love it and think it's the greatest song in the world, but that doesn't mean it'll make anyone else's ass move. Do you two remember 'Fun Dip'?"

"I loved that song," Ernie said.

"Well, you know how long it took to write, record, and mix that song? Twenty goddamn minutes. Jason here found the beat, I laid down the vocals, and that was that. We'd been working fifteen days straight on another track before we stumbled on 'Fun Dip.' The other track was the one I thought would blow up. Instead, four months later everyone's going around singing, 'I got yo fuuuun dip, come on and have a lick.' The other song didn't even make the record. Now you tell me how that's fair. You tell me that isn't bullshit. Come with me."

He stood, waved off the guards, and brought us down a second hallway that led deeper into the bowels of his wooden fortress. This time the walls were lined with drawings, marvelously detailed in richly colored ink, of superheroes of unknown origin. Bulging muscles and everything. Biceps on top of biceps. Triceps on top of triceps. The occasional octocep.

"Are these yours?" I asked.

"Yep. Drew them when I was sixteen. All the white kids at school got cars. I got a set of pens. This was how the whole Swift persona came to be. It all started on paper."

He stopped at one of the drawings: a young black man in a blue jumpsuit who bore more than a passing resemblance to Edgar. His fists were clenched and his teeth bared. There was a giant rift at the center of his body, with an intense white light, like a halogen lamp, bursting out of it. "This is the Supernova," he said. "Any time he gets worked up, his body bursts into white-hot light that disintegrates anything around him. That's how I felt when I was growing up. Everything I had inside of me, I just wanted to turn loose. Felt like my heart had a nuclear reactor melting down inside of it. That's how you feel when you're young and you want everything."

He continued down the hallway. I pointed to a drawing of a man made entirely of purple crystal.

"What about this guy?"

"That's Eterno. Another superhero. His power was that he could live forever. Not so super these days, is he?"

At the end of the hall was a conference room with thirty-foot-high ceilings and a wooden table in the center. It was a slab cut from a cross section of what must have been the largest tree that ever lived. Such was its heft and diameter that you could have built a twenty-story building on top of it. He sat down and beckoned us to do likewise.

"You boys want something to eat?" he asked.

I politely waved him off. "We're fine."

"You sure? We've got red-list fish here. A piece of halibut tastes even better when you know it cost a thousand bucks."

"We're okay. Let's just proceed with the interview."

He tossed his license my way and started talking. I hit Record.

"This is really simple. I want this album to be my biggest. I want to become a legend for real. The GOAT. But I can't be remembered as the greatest of all time unless . . . you know. I wanna be canonized, lionized, and immortalized."

I gave his license back to him. "Why not just release it and see what happens?"

"Because no one gives a shit until you're gone." He put his elbows on the table and clasped his hands. "I'm no fool. I see where my career is now. The last album was downloaded by fifty thousand people. That's it. I used to be able to move fifty thousand in an hour. I used to be able to get hundreds of thousands on their feet simply by walking out onto the stage. That's over now. I know that. People out there are either indifferent, or they're flat broke. Poor people in this country used to have some money, you know? And anyway, people lose the love. They get tired of your face on those records. And on the grails."

"I almost bought one of your grails once."

"The DX3490?"

"Yup."

"Those things were made of shit. Like I said, people move on. Only one way to get that love back: Check out. Remind them of what they missed."

"But you seem happy. You seem like you have everything."

"Everything'll be gone soon. Everything you see in this house is rented. From the furniture to the brothers manning the gate. It'll all be gone. I don't wanna be around for that. Hell, I wasn't supposed to make it this far anyway. I'm playin' with the house money. You gentlemen are my ticket into history. Okay? That's the deal. I need you two to welcome me to the pantheon." He made a gun with his hand and pointed it at his temple. "Know what I mean?"

"You want us to shoot you?"

"Assassinate me. For maximum impact. It's how the top dogs go out. Any other way is for suckers."

Ernie didn't like shooting people. "John and I don't do weird stuff like that," he said. "We can give you the dose, and then you can arrange things as you see fit."

"Not a chance. I don't go for that SoFlo crap. There's gotta be some blood. There's gotta be some production value in this. Blood is a flourish. I'll pay extra. I don't care."

"How exactly would this assassination take place?" I asked.

"Look, I'm not gonna have you drive up to my car and blast through the windshield. This is really simple. I'll be asleep here tonight. You folks just camp outside for a bit. You'll see me in my bed through the window. Just aim a rifle at my head, do what you have to do, and get the hell out."

"That won't work," Ernie said. "Your interview is already public record. It's sanctioned. We're recording this and streaming it to the office."

"Oh, please. I already talked to your boss about this. What was his name? Matt? Didn't he tell you any of this?"

"Matt never tells us anything," I said.

"He said he could do this off the cloud. Come on. It's not that big of a deal, right? Your job is to help me, so help me! Help make the Swift number one again." He took out a wad of hundred-dollar bills. "This is easy money. Come on now. I'll be too drugged up to even move. Couple of shots and you're good to go. Do it. Make me the Supernova one last time."

I stopped the recording and excused myself. I got Matt on the WEPS and didn't bother hiding my agitation. "You tell this guy we could do his ES off the cloud?"

"Yep," Matt said. "I haven't patched Containment in on this."

"Why didn't you tell us this beforehand?"

"I told you, John. You're off the bunny slopes. Now piss off. I'm bidding on a boat lift and I'm winning."

Four hours later we were perched outside the Swift's bedroom, on a patch of grass near the lowest part of the compound wall. Our car was parked outside the gate, to provide us with a clean getaway. Ernie held the rifle in his hands. I shook as if the music in the studio had never been turned off. One of the black collectivist guards drew open the curtains and gave us a nod. Ernie brought the rifle up and offered me a look through the scope. I saw the Swift lying flat on his stomach, drooling away on a cotton pillowcase that cost more than my plug-in.

"Ernie, why did this guy hire *us* to do this?"

"I don't know. Everything about this is skeevy."

"The whole point of retaining an end specialist is so that everything is a matter of public record. So you get the tax rebate and all that crap. Without certification, they may as well get anyone to do this. It's not like there's a shortage of armed men inside that house. This is all wrong. We never should have agreed."

Ernie took the rifle and looked. "I'll tell you what's even stranger. That's not Edgar."

"What?" I grabbed the rifle and looked through the scope. The man in the bed was lean, ropy. He had a goatee. I moved the rifle away from my eye to wipe away the sweat that was dripping down from my brow. I looked again. Moonlight reflected off the man's drooping face. It wasn't the Swift. It wasn't the Swift at all. "You're right. It's not him. It's not him!"

"Keep your scope trained on him," Ernie said. "Don't make it look like you're hesitating." I opened my left eye and could see Ernie surveying every window and shrub in the compound. His eyes darted around manically, looking for a scope trained back on us. He whispered to me, "Do you see the small shrub by the air conditioner, at eleven o'clock?"

I looked with my left eye. I saw the shrub but nothing obscured by it. "I see it."

"On three, turn and fire at it. One shot. Then we run. Ready?"

"No."

He gave me a second. "Are you ready now? Fire it."

I turned and fired wildly at the bush. I heard someone shout an obscenity above the rustle. A countering shot rang out from the general vicinity. The man in the bedroom never moved. We booked it for the wall and scaled it with relative ease. I heard another shot, but we were already over and making for the plug-in. We saw the massive cast-iron gate begin to swing open behind us, and we drove like hell. Soon we found ourselves stuck in a blissful midnight traffic jam, close to the center of town. I've cursed the fast-spreading crowds for the longest time. I won't be doing that for a while.

We got back to Falls Church and told Matt that our client tried to steal death. He didn't care much about that. "You got his money, right?"

Ernie threw the wad of hundreds on the glass table.

"Perfect," Matt said. "And our little newbie here smelled the rat? That's excellent. That's just why we brought you in, Johnny Boy. Congratulations. You get to pick up Chinese for us."

He promised us no more off-the-cloud killing, but today still felt more like the beginning of something unwanted, not the end of it.

DATE MODIFIED:
4/1/2059, 4:23 A.M.

"You look just like me"

I hadn't seen David in person since he was one. I'd seen him on the WEPS. Spoken to him. I remember seeing his face on my screen when he was three or four. Kids that age, they have this thing where, when they see something they really like, they open up this wide smile that employs the maximum effort from all their facial muscles. You get the feeling that if they could stretch the corners of their mouth from the West Coast to the East, they would. They're so purely happy that their faces can't even accommodate an expression bright enough to convey it. This usually happens in the presence of ice cream. I know no adult who can smile like that. I remember David used to be excited to see my face, regardless of the time of day or year. But gradually he grew up and his world expanded, and seeing my face beaming in from Ecuador, or wherever I was, proved more of a waste of his time than a special treat.

I followed his high school basketball career religiously (he was twice the player I was). That was my way of staying close to him—through his team's status updates and game wraps. I didn't see him so much as I covered him, obsessively. I happily barged in on his feed from time to time to give unsolicited advice about women or how to properly tip bartenders. Sometimes he'd reply, and the fact that he did would make my hair stand on end. Other times he'd brush it off and carry on. That's how he was. I never resented him for it.

Sonia asked if I wanted to see him for his birthday. I hadn't spoken to him in more than seven years—a time span in which he had become, according to his mother, an extremely devout collectivist and Church of Man emissary. This was the first such invitation I'd been extended since returning to the States. (I didn't want to come back and barge in on David with no invite. I preferred to let it breathe). I happily took up the offer.

I remember when David was a baby and he'd sleep in the room adjacent to mine in my old apartment. There was a laminated construction-paper cutout of a bear on his door, with his name written on it. Whenever I walked by that door while he was asleep, I'd always stop for a moment and look at the bear. I felt like I was outside the dressing room of a rock star when I did that. I was such a fan of his. Standing outside his door felt like standing outside the door of someone I was desperately eager to meet. *The kid in all the pictures is behind that door!* That feeling never waned, especially as he grew up and we fell out of contact.

And so, preparing to meet David once more after so long took on the feeling of getting backstage passes to an Elvis concert. I felt that same sort of giddy terror. I rehearsed everything I wanted to say to him. I imagined every possible retort he could make, kind or cruel. I laid out my clothes for the day and waffled about what I'd wear. I never do that. I was not myself.

Nate and Sonia had moved to Morningside Heights after Hurricane Jasmine destroyed downtown. The BoltBus took twelve hours to get to Port Authority, but the WEPS kept me occupied throughout. I sent David a few pings about my impending arrival, but he didn't reply. I nursed a small flask of scotch to help speed up the clock. When the bus finally arrived, I stepped down into a dense thicket of bodies in which I found myself in constant danger of being snagged. I hadn't been back to Manhattan since it was made entirely pedestrian, and the difference was jarring. Nothing felt familiar when I stepped out of the station. I felt like I was in a city that had been airlifted in from China. Everyone around me moved as fast and true as bullets. There was no knocking them off course, and I repeatedly found myself in their oncoming path. The bikers blew up and down the avenues as if on rails. I spotted a subway entrance and began negotiating my way through the throng to get to it. Years on the road with Keith have calloused my nerves. Bodies may bump against me. So long as they aren't penetrating me, I'm fine and dandy. I get the hang of things.

I squished myself into the third train that arrived and emerged in Morningside Heights to find relatively calmer waters as I made my way to the address. Sonia opened the door. She had a baby bump.

"Holy shit!" I said.

"Come in quickly." She was alone. David was out with his half sister and Nate, having a slice of pizza.

"How far along are you?"

"Five months."

"So you're going 2G. That's great. I couldn't be happier for you."

She slumped onto the couch and put her hand to her forehead.

"Are you all right?" I asked. "Did I do something wrong?"

"It's getting harder each day to hide it, John. I'm running out of empire-waisted clothing. I tried wearing a sari the other day and I looked like I was going to a toga party. I knew when Nate and I decided to do this that it wouldn't be easy. But these next four months, these are gonna be rough. I can't say I'm looking forward to it. I've already gotten a few looks."

"It's New York. People give you dirty looks just for breathing."

"That's the problem. I can feel their eyes on my gut. I can hear their minds working: 'Oh, Christ. Another mouth to feed.' You know they killed another pregnant woman in Queens a week ago? A big horde of scumbags just ran right through her."

I patted her on the thigh. She gave me a look of gratitude. Long ago, all the signs of affection Sonia and I displayed for each other had become unmistakably fraternal. "You'll be okay."

"You don't know that," she said.

"What matters is that you have people around you to help you feel secure, even if you can't truly live inside some big force field or something."

"I need a force field. I may not leave the apartment for a good long while. I may even deliver the baby here. I just expand the

WEPS and project a mountain range on the wall, and then I don't get cabin fever."

"How does David feel about all this?"

"Protective. Like you. He wants the baby to be baptized in the COM, of course."

"Did you agree?"

"Oh, sure. Nate and I have gone to some church stuff with him. It's not so bad. It's all perfectly normal. I know the sects get all the attention, but the church proper is pretty harmless. The baptism is no big deal. There's cake. Cake is good."

I went to the kitchen and grabbed her a glass of water and some dried apricots. I heard the lock being turned from outside the apartment. I gripped Sonia's water glass tightly, to keep from spilling it at the sight of David. The door opened, and the three of them walked in. There he was. Right there. Right in front of me. I stared at him. I couldn't help it.

"Jesus," I said. "You look just like me."

He shifted uncomfortably at the remark. I had seen him on screen for virtually all his life. The ads always tell you that using WEPS is like never leaving home or whatever. But there's no substitute for real, live presence. In front of me, he existed in two separate states: as the man before me and as a living memory of the screaming infant I saw pulled from his mother's body ages ago. I felt small. I rushed to fill the vacuum. "Would you guys like some water?"

"Sure," David answered. Just hearing one word out of him felt surreal. I wanted to capture it and put it in a jar.

I ran back to the kitchen to fill the water glasses. He looked like me, only slightly bigger. More muscular. Like an improved version of the original product. I certainly didn't feel like his father. I felt like his mere shadow. I had no sense of paternal authority over him whatsoever, as my dad had had over me. A colossal feeling of immaturity pulsed through me. He was twenty-nine now. I was twenty-nine now. I felt like I was five. The realization of twenty-eight years of neglect collapsed on me like a rotting building. I saw in my mind the ghost of a child suffocated in his own crib. The permanence of it all lay bare in my psyche, inescapable. The burden of finality. I wanted to shrink down to nothing.

I came back. Nate, Sonia, and Ella dove into the conversation, to keep things feeling natural. I chimed in from time to time, but everything that came out of my mouth felt wrong when I said it, like on a terrible first date. I pined for alcohol. I wasted no time. It was worth risking David's judgment to dilute the awkwardness. "David, would you be interested in getting a drink?"

He deliberated for a moment that seemed to forever elongate. Finally, he said a small okay, and we were riding silently down in the elevator. There was an Irish pub nearby. We were early enough to avoid the 2:00 p.m. drinking rush. He sat at a table while I ordered the drinks. He asked for a mineral water since he didn't drink alcohol. There's that moment, any time you're about to sit down at a bar with someone you've been looking forward to seeing, when you rush to the bar to grab the drinks to prolong engaging with them, because you're still a touch nervous for whatever reason. Half my beer was finished by the time I sat back down. David wore plain khakis and a denim shirt emblazoned with a COM crest.

"You're living in Virginia now," he said.

"Yep."

"Mom says you're an end specialist."

"Technically, no. I'm the consultant who tags along. I handle the paperwork and the interviews. Another guy handles the actual specialization."

"So you kill people."

"I'm only trying to help."

More awkward silence. I scanned the menu for food to busy myself. I had no plans to order anything. The horrible thought occurred to me that had it been up to me to decide twenty-nine years ago, he wouldn't be sitting with me at all. My guts ached.

"You don't seem comfortable around me."

"It's not you," I said. "I don't feel comfortable around myself. And sitting here now, across from you, I feel unnatural. I *am* unnatural. All I can think about is how sorry I am and how little my regret helps you."

"You don't have to apologize. That's all understood and digested."

"That's far too generous of you."

"It's okay. It's what the church teaches us. It teaches us that the goodness and selflessness of man will always rise to the surface. Man is gifted in that way. I knew we'd have this conversation at some point, and I knew it would be fine. I knew it was only a matter of time. Every man eventually aims to redeem himself." The conversation began to turn. A low warmth. He took my hand. "I'm fine, John. I'm just fine. You may find this hard to believe, but you've *helped* me. It's true. I was thinking about this just before you arrived. I realized I was destined to become a messenger of man because of you. I grew up without my father, and yet I have a father. I have Nate, who is a wonderful man. I have a wonderful mother and sister. I have another beautiful sister on the way. I have a girlfriend I love very much and will marry one day. And I have the church. I have so much. I have a support system with endless backups. And it'll never go away. Ever. Because the church will never die. I have a heart, but it's not inside my body." He gestured outside. "It's out there. You've proven that. You made yourself superfluous to my life, and yet here I am. At peace. Happy. Able to sit with you without rancor. That's a miracle, John. That's a miracle this church performs every day." He squeezed my hand fervently and looked me over with great curiosity. "You should join us. You look . . . You look lonely. Disconnected. Are you lonely?"

"I don't know. I don't really think about it."

"Our northern Virginia parish is the second largest in the entire nation. Reverend Swanson's church seats over five thousand people, and yet they have an overflow at virtually every service. Think of that. Think of what it would be like to know all those people are by your side. Thousands of unseen forces that you never even knew were there, guiding you through the world. Billions perhaps."

"I'm not sure I need quite that many."

"I'd say you need some. They could give you a job. A proper job. You wouldn't have to be an end specialist anymore. You wouldn't have to help kill people and live in that grimness. I can see it in your eyes, and you've only looked at me three times. I can see . . . resignation. You have skills that could serve the church in a much more productive way. There is an insurgency out there *murdering* people. Trolls that are maiming and disfiguring people. Acts of evil. Acts of extreme cruelty to other men and women. Violations of the holy vessel. The church has proclaimed a mission to put an end to this, and you could be part of it. Tell me that doesn't appeal to you more than what you do right now." David noticed the speed-bump scar peeking out from under my shirtsleeve. He let go of my hand and brushed it gingerly. "You could fight with us."

I wanted to say yes, but the truth was that his recruitment made me terrifically uneasy. I grew up believing that religion was a cover people used, and I've never been able to shake that. Even now, though David was being so open and kind, I instinctively resisted. He was talking to me more like a customer than a blood relative. "This is a wound I avenged a very long time ago," I told him. "Much to my detriment and yours. More than you know. I want to join you, David. But I can't. I'm not a lost soul. I didn't stumble into my new job. I chose it. I saw my father—your grand-father—get the cure and regret it. Deeply. I saw him welcome the ravaging of his insides by cancer because it was the only solution he felt he had. I don't wish that on anyone. And his curing was *my* doing. I goaded him into it. I never told you that before, but it's true. There are people who feel as if they have led a complete life and need no more of it, and if I can be the one who brings their existence to a proper and fitting conclusion, then I relish that opportunity. I work for those who have the good fortune of knowing their exact destiny. Maybe by serving them I can finally figure out what mine is."

"You feel incomplete?"

"Every second. Given my track record as a father, I may walk this earth a very, very long time before feeling otherwise."

He looked disappointed but not deterred. "Go to a service. Just one. Go without prejudice and see the church. If it's not what you want, fine. I won't begrudge you that. But I ask you to go just once. So that you see where I'm coming from. Is that fair?"

I nodded my head. "Of course."

He got up. "There will come a time when you will need the church. I know you think that's bullshit, but it's true. It has precisely what you're looking for. And when that time comes, I'll be there to welcome you. I promise. The church is the future of all men." He held out his hand, and I shook it. "I wish you nothing but serenity."

He walked out and my body loosened. I took a sip of beer and felt more like myself again. Relaxed. I felt eager to return home to Virginia as soon as possible.

DATE MODIFIED:
6/3/2059, 4:35 A.M.

Alison on Stage

I had another dream about Alison. Every time I dream about her, I never see the fully grown woman who learned to love me right before she died. I always see the one from eighth grade, the version of her that turned me away no matter how desperately I tried to curry her favor. Tonight I saw her in an empty playhouse. We were just outside the main auditorium, in one of those red-velvet-lined, ramped hallways with periodic entrances to the theater rows. Such was my excitement at seeing Alison in the dream that I ran to embrace her and accidentally knocked her down to the floor. When I went to give her a lift, she remained stuck there, fastened to the ground. No matter how hard I tried, she stayed glued in that position. She began speaking to me, but everything she said was barely audible. When I leaned in to try to make out what she was saying, she disappeared. I could see through a door that she had teleported over to the main stage and was warming up with an orchestra, a cello in her hand (she played no instrument in real life, as far as I know). I tried to get in to see her but was rebuffed by the usher for not having a ticket. A throng of concertgoers rushed in front of me and quickly erased her from my view, sweeping me back farther and farther until I was standing in a pond somewhere. Another country. Water up to my knees. Alison gone.

It's not just my subconscious that delights in torturing me about her, even after all this time. It's been long enough now that my brain has started to wonder, independent of my own commands, what our relationship would be like if she were still alive. Sometimes I wonder if we would have grown bored of each other. Sometimes I think the fact that she died is the reason I'll never stop loving her. She wasn't around long enough for me to grow tired of her personality or her appearance. Every relationship seems to lead to that end. She said it herself. She left me just as my mind had perfected her. The prime condition of love. A simple glance from her was enough to send my body into a frenzied state. There was never enough time for that feeling to go away. Sometimes I wonder if that's a good thing. I despise myself for thinking that.

DATE MODIFIED:
6/8/2059, 2:31 A.M.

"You get six shots"

One of the drawbacks to conducting exit interviews is that the subjects are often all too eager to participate. These things are, after all, a matter of public record. There's some measure of posterity involved. And so people will talk. And talk. And talk some more. From the beginning, Matt urged me to never let the conversation slip away from my control. There's a certain skill to cutting subjects off and steering them back on topic. Mastering it is not unlike learning to be a good TV anchor. That way you don't waste time or money. Matt dislikes it when we waste time or money. As the head of the company, he's free to do it all he likes— and he does. I've never seen him actively engage in business at the office. Most of the time, he's either trying to buy an old car part or to sell one. You can do things like that when you own the joint.

Matt also has a more compassionate reason for demanding that exit interviews remain as brief as humanly possible: He doesn't want Ernie and me to get stuck somewhere far away after dark. Until yesterday we had been successful at this. We hadn't had many appointments slip past dusk. Not in bad areas, at least. By dark we were either back home, at the office, or in the plug-in in a safe neighborhood. The only time we ever failed was on a call in Great Falls, Virginia. The interview went well past 10:00 P.M. But that's Great Falls. Not much fear of D36 there. We slept in the plug-in, inside the town gate.

Four days ago we had a call at a housing tenement in Southeast DC. The subject was a man with a bad back and a cure age of seventy-eight. He'd had several operations on his lumbar region and was more than happy to discuss the finer aspects of each and every one of them. I tried to get a word in edgewise, but I had slept poorly the night before, and I was still mentally discombobulated from seeing my son a week earlier. I wasn't sharp. Nothing I could say was going to stop this man from talking about his sciatica. I saw the last vestiges of sunlight collapse outside the window. I tried to give every visual cue I could to get the guy to wrap things up. I yawned. I looked at my watch. Ernie grew impatient and took out the dose before the man had even signed anything. Still he prattled on, nightfall becoming ever more pronounced outside. Once the clock struck nine, the look on Ernie's face turned from annoyance to fear. My mood followed suit. Southeast is not Great Falls. Finally, I told him we needed to stop.

"What?"

"We need to stop, sir. We can come back tomorrow." Ernie kicked me. "But we must go now."

"But I was ready for this to be done tonight," he said.

"I'm sorry, sir. We simply don't have time left to finish."

"Well, then I'm gonna call DES. Maybe they'll be able to get this done."

"If that's what you think is best, then we're happy to turn over your case to th—"

Ernie stood up. "Shut up. Both of you."

We heard commotion coming from outside. Down the street, a woman screamed. Ernie had the WEPS expanded up on the wall. He opened a population-monitor app on the screen. It mapped a 3-D layout of the boulevard down below. Two parallel streets ran along either side of the building and past the abandoned warehouse on the opposite block. On either side of the warehouse, I could see two thick red masses slowly advancing in our direction.

Ernie grimaced. "Shit." Then he lunged for his duffel bag. He looked up at the old man. "What kind of security system does this building have?"

"Security system?"

"Double shit. Well, Thomas, today is your lucky day. You

won't be needing to call DES to finish you off. The folks coming toward us will be more than happy to take care of the job for you."

"Should we call the police?" the old man asked.

"In Southeast? That's a joke, right? You're joking." Ernie turned to me. "We need to reach the ground right now. We can't be stuck up here, or else we're dead. Go. *Go!*"

I grabbed the Texan's gun from the back of my pants and flew out of the old man's apartment. The door was situated directly in front of one of the building's two massive stairwells. We saw people poking their heads out of their doors as we began to descend the stairs using that brisk stutter step everyone employs when they feel the urgent need to reach the bottom of a staircase. We jumped over a handful of vagrants who were sleeping on the steps. A black woman in a bathrobe met us at the third floor. She demanded to know what was going on.

Ernie answered her without breaking stride. "They're coming. Get out. Everyone get out!"

News traveled up the stairwell instantly. Every apartment door above and below swung wide open, and bodies began pushing into the stairwell like an emptying arena. Ernie and I got held up in a tangle of people just as we reached the bottom. Ernie began nodding and turned to me. "This is good," he said. "Lotta people. Big crowd to handle them. Are you a good shot with that handgun?"

"I don't know."

"For our purposes, that counts as a no. Put it away. Take this instead." He handed me a shotgun from the duffel. "You said you've fended off these jokers before?"

"Groups of two or three. One look at the gun and they scattered. Nothing like this."

"Okay, then here's the deal. That's pump action, that shotgun. You get six shots. Five pumps. Count each shot. One. Two. Three. Four. Five. Six. By the time you've gotten off that sixth shot, you better have cleared a path for yourself out of their way."

"Fire directly at them?"

"Yes."

"I can't do that."

"Why not?"

"Because I can't."

He looked into my eyes (the only part of my body not shaking at the time) and knew instantly that I had never shot and killed anyone. Even outside the Swift's house, I deliberately aimed too high. Ernie patted my shoulder. "Brother, trust me. When a bunch of these jokers start coming at you, trying to claw off your face, you'll be able to do it. I promise you. I'll have the WEPS up in front of us as we go. Just run where it isn't red."

"What if they're armed?" I asked.

"Some of them will be. Just shoot and don't get shot."

We reached the glass doors at the main entrance and burst onto the street. The center of the boulevard quickly filled with tenants, many of them armed. Otherwise everything was quiet. The side streets, where the rovers were displayed on the WEPS, showed no trace of them. The plug-in was parked twelve blocks to the west, on the twenty-seventh level of a garage. We immediately booked it in that direction. A handful of tenants followed us. We reached the cross street and I looked to the right, down the side of the block. I saw a massive crowd of homeless people walking in our direction. When I was a kid, my father told me to never establish eye contact with a bum on the street. Once they have you engaged, he said, they target you. Same thing here. We all looked squarely at the mob, which was the wrong thing to do. Immediately, a bunch of them quickened their stride and made for us. A wine bottle came hurtling in our general direction and picked off a slender man running beside me. He dropped straight to the asphalt. Ernie and I kept running up the boulevard. I heard a shot ring out behind me and I reflexively ducked my head as I sprinted. I felt my hands curl around the shotgun in an industrial vise grip. I was hanging on to the thing more for moral support than protection.

As we approached the next street, another group of them came around the corner. Now we had them in front of us and behind us. We crisscrossed the boulevard, and they followed suit. I yelled over my shoulder to Ernie, "Where do I shoot?"

Ernie extended the WEPS as we ran. I could barely make out the details on the screen. Everything in my line of vision had become shaky and blurry with panic. Then a speck of dust got in my right eye and I had to shut it violently.

"Forward!" Ernie shouted. "Shoot *through* them! Aim at the center!"

Our little group fell into a makeshift shoulder-to-shoulder formation. I saw the drunk and angry mob in front of me prepare for us—a gaunt collection of mostly grown men, dirty and unkempt. There may have been a hundred. Maybe two hundred. I'm bad with head counts. The only clean spots on them were the gleaming steel blades a handful of them gripped in anticipation of our arrival. Ernie fired the first shot toward the scrum. I followed suit but lost my nerve again and fired over their heads.

One.

Another shot rang out from behind us, and I saw a tenant slip down to the ground, as if a trapdoor had opened underneath him. Ernie fired again. We were now ten yards away. I saw a small path clear in the middle, in our line of fire. We began to funnel toward it, right into the center of the mob. Two other tenants fired at the same spot, clearing more room. The pack lost some of its density as those on the periphery began to look for less-feisty action. My shoulders retracted into my torso as I grew terrified of coming into direct contact. Ernie fired again. Now they were on either side of us. One of them grabbed my arm, but I wrested it back, firing in the grabber's direction.

Two.

I saw my target fall immediately. I couldn't help but stop to make him out. It looked like a younger one. He was still alive. He may have been in his twenties, but who the hell knows how old he really was. My hesitancy cost me. I was grabbed from behind and pulled down onto my back. A monstrous three-hundred-pound man sat right down on my gut and began pressing his fingertips into my sternum. I saw blood caked on his moustache, forming a dried trail down the center of his gnarled beard. I wore the horror right on my face, which seemed to delight him. He flashed his brown teeth at me, his mouth like an open wound.

"I'M GONNA FEED YOUR HEART TO MINE."

He pressed deeper into my chest, and I began to feel the skin break. Then I heard a shot and saw his face explode like a pumpkin shot from a catapult. He fell on me like a lead blanket, and I wriggled out from beneath him, his stench attaching to me as I got up and saw Ernie standing there, fourth shot freshly discharged. The thugs and tenants were now completely intermingled. I saw another man being held down and knifed by a group of them and I fired at the group out of principle.

Three.

Ernie grabbed me and steered us back in the direction of the garage. "Don't waste shots. Make a path."

None of the killers seemed interested in touching us, as we were the most heavily armed members of the group. Instead they focused their appetites on people who couldn't help themselves: women, children, the elderly. Ernie and I both fired again to fully clear the way in front of us. I could make out the WEPS screen better now, and saw a thick black opening in the red mass. I kept running forward. The crowd thinned toward the end of the block.

Ernie told me not to look back, but I had to. I glanced over my shoulder and saw heaps of filthy street guerillas bringing down people in their pajamas and nightshirts. I saw them rushing into the old man's building to claim whatever food and water was inside. I saw a five-year-old kid being tackled, the thug sinking his teeth into his leg. I turned and ran for the kid. "Get off of him!"

I unloaded.

Four five six.

The man fled, untouched by the buckshot. I rushed to the boy and helped him up. When I turned back to run up the boulevard, the path in front of me was blocked once more. I pumped the shotgun, even though the chamber was empty now. They began to disperse. Ernie fired at them from behind and suddenly I had a way out again. Six shots for me. Six shots for Ernie. We had nothing left. I carried the boy as we ran west, away from the melee. I could hear more random gunfire and people yelling. With each block, the chaos began to fade away out of earshot. We heard helicopters arriving. Once we reached the garage entrance, the sound of the riot was gone, a world away now. We pushed the elevator button. It failed to light up. I began the slow, brutal ascent of every floor with the kid on my back. The stairwell was dead empty, which only made the experience more rattling. Ernie and I took turns carrying the boy, switching at every fifth floor. At last we reached twenty-seven, chugging air with every step. I breathed a sigh of relief and rested for ten minutes, slumped against the ice-cold cinder-block wall.

Ernie opened the door to the garage. We walked out. A gang member jumped in front of us and came at Ernie with a knife, wild violence blazing across his face. With one move, Ernie reached into his pocket, grabbed the dose he had never gotten to give the chatty old man, and stuck it right in the thug's breast. He died as quickly as he had appeared.

I stood there, barely able to process any of it. "Jesus."

We drove the kid to a hospital close to Matt's garage and checked him in. I've tried to sleep since then, but I can't. The giant man's ghastly odor has leached into my body through my pores, so that my very insides feel like they've been dragged through a field of manure and left to ferment. I reek like a piece of raw hamburger left out of the fridge for too long. I feel infected, as if a real zombie has bitten me and turned me into a walking, decaying cadaver. Every time I close my eyes, there's a large, smelly man parked on my stomach, trying to claw his way into my heart. We're never going back to Southeast.

DATE MODIFIED:
6/13/2059, 5:12 A.M.

A Field Trip to the McLean Community Friends Church of Man

I made a promise to David to go to a collectivist service and to do so with an open mind. Last night I tried sleeping but could only hear the phantom whispers of oncoming vagrants outside my window. I leapt to the sill a handful of times, gun in hand, and saw nothing. My body settled into a locked state of unease. My visit to a religious congregation couldn't have come at a better time.

I drove the plug-in from my apartment down Old Dominion Road until I saw the stretch of Church of Man congregation houses that served the various ethnic needs of the town—the Korean COM, the Chinese COM, the Spanish COM. Each had a welcoming sign posted outside the fortified double walls of its compound (I learned later on that a series of underground tunnels connects them all). At the end of this de facto Collectivist Alley was the town's Community Friends church, which offers services in English. It was the closest English-speaking COM, so it was the one I picked. I arrived early, to beat the morning rush, but there was still a line to get in, all waiting plug-ins redirected by a traffic cop to the shoulder of Old Dominion. I waited a scant twenty minutes before reaching the gate and being greeted warmly by a church volunteer, a smiley fellow named Jack, who wore basic khakis and a denim shirt and asked for my church ID.

"I don't have one," I explained. "This is my first visit."

He was unfazed. "Oh, no problem! I can register you. All I need is your name and an e-mail or feed address."

"Can I just give you my name? I'd rather not disclose the other stuff."

He smiled the way restaurant hostesses do when they tell you all members of your party need to be present for you to be seated. Somehow the smiling makes it more aggravating. "Unfortunately, we *do* need an e-mail or feed address." I gave him Matt's. He stole my lunch out of the fridge last week, so I owed him one.

"And what is your occupation?" Jack asked.

"I'm a solutions consultant."

"That sounds interesting!"

"It isn't."

"Okay! Go right on in. Please do not park on levels P1 to P5. Those are reserved for our Superfriend donors. May the world of man bless and keep you!"

I drove through the gate and was confronted by a large California-style villa. White stucco. Red adobe-tile roof. The church was arranged as a quad, with buildings at each corner and open walkways between them. In the center of the quad was a pristine green lawn, not a single blade of grass touching another. I saw families eating breakfast on blankets and circles of young (looking) people reading intently. It looked like Stanford. I've never been to Stanford. I just assume that's what it looks like.

I went down into the garage and parked at level P8. I got into the elevator, and a short, bald gentleman wearing khaki pants and a denim shirt rushed in behind me. He wore a bracelet that said JESUS IS US. The doors closed behind us, and as the elevator stopped at each successive level, more and more church members mashed into the car, pushing me and my original companion to the back. Some of them were clad in the same khakis-and-denim-shirt ensemble. All of them—women, men, kids—made a point of greeting the man next to me as they entered the car. They addressed him as "Reverend." He seemed to be important. At one point during the ascent, he took notice of me.

"You look unfamiliar," he said. "I deliberately park on the lower levels, to see if any new people pull in alongside me."

"I am new. My son asked me to attend a service, so I figured today was as good a day as any."

"Well, that's lovely. My name is Carl Derron, I'm the reverend of this congregation."

"John Farrell." We shook hands. "Carl, may I ask you a question? Or is it Reverend Derron?"

"Carl is fine. Ask me lots of questions."

"My son wears the same outfit you have on now. Is there a certain meaning behind it?"

He shut his eyes and nodded his head rapidly. "Very good question, very good. John, church members are allowed to wear anything they wish. That's fine with us. We accept each other any way we choose to present ourselves. But it is the belief of some, including myself, that ostentatious clothing and tattoos and piercings and all those other things tend to dilute a person's purity and the connection they have with those around them. These clothes are, frankly, boring. And they're that way because I don't want them distracting people from who I am—from the essence of me. That's why you see the COM nudist colonies from time to time. That's taking it a bit too far for my tastes. Then people get distracted for a whole other reason."

"Do you wear this all the time?"

"Not when the Skins play, my friend. Not when the Skins play."

The doors opened and we walked out into the main chapel, which looked like the giant study of some very rich man's house. Books lined the walls on all sides, stacked to the rafters. Dozens of library ladders were placed on a rolling track around the stacks, with many congregants using them for makeshift seating. Stained-glass windows depicted various historical events: Ben Franklin flying a kite with a key attached in a thunderstorm, D-day in Normandy, Neil Armstrong on the moon, Graham Otto with his fruit flies, etc. A handful of folding chairs were placed at the front of the room for the perma-elderly and handicapped. Everyone else stood. It was like a giant cocktail party. Everyone was busy talking to everyone else, and the din rose to the ceiling and bounced harshly back down. People came en masse to introduce themselves to me, but I couldn't hear anything they were saying. I just smiled and shouted out my personal details as best I could.

I saw Derron make his way through the crowd, shaking hands and giving babies raspberries on their tummies before finally making his way to a small stage. All I could see was the sheen off his bare scalp. I could make out part of a band sitting behind the reverend. He raised his hand, and the band began playing. They played "With a Little Help from My Friends." The Joe Cocker arrangement. Half the crowd danced, while the others just kept shouting over the party. I was passed a stapled printout listing the day's readings and songs. I flipped through it to make an educated guess about how long the service would last. The song finished; then Derron raised his hand once more and began speaking to the now morgue-quiet room.

"Good morning," he said.

The entire congregation replied in unison. "Good morning!"

"I was going to speak to you today about my usual boring stuff, like being good to your fellow man and knowing your COM history book inside and out. But instead I want to talk to you about . . . flying."

The crowd tittered.

"I was looking into flights to go see my granddaughter in Nevada this fall. I don't know why I looked, given that I already knew I couldn't afford the ticket. But I looked anyway, just for sport. The total round-trip ticket—not including baggage fees, of course—was $12,230."

The crowd let out a proper gasp at the figure.

"Now, I knew I couldn't pay for that ticket unless I were the sort to be rather loose with church collection. So I was despondent, because I knew I'd have to make that endless drive in the plug-in. Then I saw something that made me even more despondent. It was an article—I'm sure you saw it as well—about the plane that crashed earlier this week. This airplane was a long-awaited prototype. The first battery-powered electric passenger jet: the VoltAir 717. And it crashed on its maiden voyage, killing two people: the pilot, named Wyatt Embry, and the company CEO, named Sir David Paul Furniss. Now the article said that one year earlier Furniss's beta version of the prototype had successfully lifted off the ground and remained airborne for fifteen minutes. But the new version was said to be able to fly on electric power for a full hour, good enough for a short regional commute. So Furniss assembled a press conference and declared the VA717 'ready for takeoff.' He even had a nickname picked out for the plane: the *Crimson Wasp*, which is very catchy. And the plane had all kinds of fancy features inside—interior designed by Layla DiGiorno, panoramic Lucite windows, showers, and a buffet restaurant in the main cabin. The whole shebang. So this was a big deal. And what happened was this: Embry and Furniss climbed into the plane and taxied down the runway in front of a grandstand containing what was said to be more than three hundred family members, company employees, and spectators. Next—let me just read from the article: 'Witnesses report that the plane lifted off the ground and began sinking back to the ground shortly afterward, crashing into a nearby orchard.' Now, this is tragic on a number of levels. Obviously, two men died and their loved ones have been left bereft. And our hopes for a more eco-friendly and cheaper form of air travel, one that would presumably one day make the trip to see my granddaughter more affordable, were delivered a big setback. I think, despite our quibbles with the flying process, most of us would give anything to be able to fly regularly again. Do we all agree?"

Everyone nodded.

"So I was sad, because I hate to see progress derailed. But the more I thought about it, the more I thought there was a lesson to be learned in all this. A wonderful lesson. Here we have two men, Furniss and Embry, who gave their lives to an idea that would, in turn, better the lives of each and every one of us in the postmortal world. They gave everything for the chance to help us. Why? Money? Well, sure. The desire to be known as aviation pioneers? Of course. Ambition plays a role. But that ambition is a gift—something inherent in man that drives him to help society and technology evolve in ways that are *always* better than what came before. Don't you see how amazing this is? This is a blessing *all* of us have. So even though this news is tragic, I am uplifted. They interviewed a man named Juan Ozuma, VoltAir's vice president. And this is what Ozuma said in the wake of the crash: 'I assure you that we remain determined to see the mission of this company through.' Is his company going to give up because these two men died? No! They're going to keep going. They're going to fight in the face of tragedy to realize the dream of electric air travel. And you know what? I bet they'll succeed. Maybe not now. Definitely not now. But somewhere down the line, someone will figure it out. Because someone always does. History proves this time and time again. Discoveries are made. Walls are torn down."

I listened intently, and everything Derron said seemed rational. But then I saw his scalp crinkle, the tops of his eyebrows bobbing up and down over the head of the blond fellow standing in front of me, and the sermon took a turn.

"This is divinity, people. This is what we talk about when we talk about the collective—this massive, unstoppable life force that is the progress of man. This is the blessing we have bestowed upon the earth. Other congregations may tiptoe around this idea, but I do not. We are the gods of this world. Make no mistake. An ant—a little, tiny ant walking on the ground—that ant looks up at you or me, and what does he see? A titan. A higher power he cannot even begin to comprehend. One that has absolute control over his destiny. We are fate. And the death of these two wonderful, innovative men does not change that a lick. When you go home today, I want you to think about your ambition and the awesome power you have over this earth and the creatures that reside upon it. For they are yours. I want you to—"

Just then, a heckler began shouting from somewhere in the crowd. I couldn't see his face, but I could hear him screaming at Derron from the center of the chapel floor. "You are a fucking abomination!" he said. "You are a fucking abomination, Reverend Carl Derron! This whole fucking church is going to crash and burn soon, and I will see to it! RIGHT FUCKING NOW!"

The entire crowd gasped, and I found myself in the midst of a struggle as panicked churchgoers fled for the exits. Through the escaping bodies, I saw a team of men holding down the heckler, and just the quickest glint of metal somewhere in the heap. A knife, a gun, a cane—I don't know. All I saw was the shine. I quickly turned and headed for the doors, as security officers in riot gear stormed through. Derron's voice reassured the crowd that the heckler had been subdued. I felt no such reassurance and quickly left the Church of Man, mind closed shut.

While waiting to leave the garage, I pinged David to tell him about the service. I described the creepy way Derron had concluded his preaching and what the presumed assassin had done. He said I'd simply picked the wrong church. He implored me to seek out a different congregation and try again. I promised nothing.

DATE MODIFIED:
6/14/2059, 12:03 A.M.

"We're going to take what we need to survive—and then maybe we'll take a little more"

This is transcribed from Joe Mascis's CBSNN report yesterday on RMUs:

Mascis: Petr Dmitrov has served in the Russian army for nearly two decades. During his time in service, he has participated in Russian invasions of Georgia, the Ukraine, Latvia, Lithuania, Kazakhstan, and parts of northern Mongolia. In addition, he claims to have participated in secret, small-scale invasions of Finland, Romania, and eastern Poland—invasions the Russian government refuses to acknowledge. It has been an era of relatively unchecked military expansion for Russia, thanks in large part to the firm grip that President Boris Solovyev has on his army of over 140 million soldiers. But that grip may be starting to loosen. And soldiers like Dmitrov are the reason why.

Mascis (narrating): We found Dmitrov and his entire army unit here, in an undisclosed town near Dubrovnik in Croatia. They were not sent here by the Russian government. They were supposed to be stationed outside of Odessa. Instead, three months ago Dmitrov, who is the leader of this unit, decided to bring them here in act of collective desertion.

Dmitrov: Our last mission, before we decided to defect, was to infiltrate a small Romanian border town, the name of which escapes me at the moment. I think I've managed to forget it out of sheer will.

Mascis: What were your orders?

Dmitrov (sighing): We had gotten to the point where we didn't need to receive explicit orders to know what we were supposed to do. They simply named the next target and we went.

Mascis: What were the unspoken instructions?

Dmitrov: Scout the town, ascertain resources in it that would be of value to the cause, and then devise a plan for resource collection.

Mascis: You call it "resource collection." But really it was pillaging, right?

Dmitrov: That's exactly right.

Mascis: What resources were you asked to collect?

Dmitrov: Food, fuel, water, and men. And not necessarily in that order of priority. Most of the towns we scouted were located on bodies of water: lakes, rivers, creeks. Wherever there was freshwater.

Mascis: You said "men" on your list of things that needed to be collected. Kidnapping?

Dmitrov: That's correct. Women were also on the list, but for far more temporary use.

Mascis: What happened to the men that were kidnapped?

Dmitrov: They were sent to the farms.

Mascis (narrating): "Farms," which could accurately be described as slave-labor camps. The Russian army is the fastest-growing military entity on earth, and a steady supply of labor is needed to produce food and clothing for every ageless soldier, so the army can continue to pillage, to kidnap *more* men to make more food and clothes in the farms, to help sustain an even larger army. As the army has grown, so have the farms.

Mascis: Did you enjoy your work?

Dmitrov: No. I didn't. But I knew that I had very little choice in the matter. I come from a family that had nothing. Anything we made often had to be turned over to the town *mafiya* or to the police. Really, they're the same thing. It's just a matter of dress. There was a policeman who came to our house one day and took my grandmother. She was sitting at the kitchen table, making bread, and he wouldn't even let her wash the flour off her hands. He just grabbed her, and poof! she was gone. I never saw her again. And I knew, after my grief had settled, that I could not suffer the same fate as her. I knew I had to be on the side that had all the power. So when I got the conscription notice, there was no hesitation.

When you've served in the army for as long as I have, it becomes clear that you are not really serving your country, but that you are serving the very small group of men who control that country. You serve at their pleasure. I knew that to survive I had to do whatever they said, but some of the things they asked of us . . . We were forced to go to some very, very dark places.

Mascis: Killing the elderly?

Dmitrov: Yes. Anyone who was too old or too sick to be of use, particularly if he or she had gotten the cure, was considered a drag on the nation's future. At first we were ordered to shoot them.

Mascis: Did you personally shoot them?

Dmitrov: Some of them, yes.

Mascis: Why?

Dmitrov: Because I would have been shot if I had disobeyed.

Mascis: Wouldn't it have been more noble to refuse and die?

Dmitrov (laughing): Nobility sounds wonderful as a concept. But nobility tends to go out the window when you find yourself forced to choose between life and oblivion.

Mascis: How many people did you shoot?

Dmitrov: Not many.

Mascis: Do you remember their faces?

Dmitrov: Every wrinkle. Every strand of hair on their head. I try not to think about it, because what good does it do me? I'm just relieved that I wasn't forced to shoot more of them. After reports of the shootings began to leak out, Solovyev decided the water purges would be much more effective. He learned about them from Ndiaye in the Congo.

Mascis (narrating): Water purges like the one executed in the small town of Dunsk, which has no water supply of any kind. In 2032 over fifty thousand elderly people were transported to a small, walled-off section of town, then left to die of dehydration.

Mascis: Were you part of herding people to Dunsk?

Dmitrov: Yes, I was.

Mascis: Did that bother you?

Dmitrov: It did, but I was caught up in this bizarre mentality where, as I said before, I was just glad that I didn't have to shoot people directly. Obviously, there's not much difference in shooting someone and leaving them out in the middle of nowhere to die. But somehow it felt less severe. "It's not murder if you're supposed to be dead." That's what our superiors told us, over and over again, whenever we sent the old geezers off to Dunsk. After a while, I took it as gospel.

I remember one time I was going into a house to claim an old woman to get her on one of the trucks, and her family was hanging on me, clawing at me, desperately begging me to let her go. And while they were doing that, all I could think about was my grandmother. She had been taken from us by the police. And now here I was. I was the guy who stole my grandmother now! That was me! (*laughs*)

Mascis: You're laughing.

Dmitrov: Well, how else can you react? Laughter helps to cover it all up. I don't know how else to deal with the memory.

Mascis (narrating): After performing mission after mission, Dmitrov grew weary of his job—of the ugliness of his orders, and of his unit's payoff for successfully carrying those orders out.

Dmitrov: We noticed that our food supply was growing smaller and smaller. Our supply of vodka was growing smaller and smaller. We were continually asked to go and find these resources, and once we found them, they were immediately taken and given to people up the chain of command.

Mascis: You didn't feel like you were getting a good cut.

Dmitrov: We felt like we weren't getting a cut at all. And there we were, doing all this dangerous work, sacrificing our very souls, yet the payoff was less and less. All the water. All the coal. All the women. All of it was going to government officials or the *mafiya*. Just like my childhood. It occurred to me that, while we were sending people off to the farms, we were part of the farms as well. We were servants just like the Latvians or Ukrainians we brought in.

When we were sent to that small Romanian town, our plan was, as usual, to burn the village down and take anything and anyone useful with us. So we began the collection, and right in the center of town was this very small girl. She couldn't have been more than four years old. But she was beautiful. Gorgeous. With the brilliant blue eyes and everything. I saw her, and I knew we would have to claim her. And she was very still as I approached. She had a small wooden train car in her hand, and she sat there calmly, as if she knew what was coming and had accepted it. That's when I knew I couldn't do it anymore. I didn't want to be part of this process where a child who is only four years old has already given up, has already accepted that her life will be thrown away into prostitution or organ harvesting. I went and picked her up, and I ran with her to the west edge of the town, gave her all my food, gave her a pistol, and told her to go. I don't know if you're familiar with Romanian terrain, but the woods there are darker than any woods I've ever seen. The forest doesn't even have a floor. Between the trees, there's just this black void. So when this little girl ran into the forest with my pistol, it was like she had vaporized. Like she never existed. And I thought, better for her that way. To have never existed.

Mascis (narrating): After pillaging that small Romanian town, Dmitrov gathered his men, and together they agreed to defect. They spent the next year, between missions, planning their escape. When they were again sent into the Romanian woods in the winter of 2057, they fled into the forest, disappearing from sight.

Dmitrov: We decided, as a group, that it was worth the risk to defect and go into business for ourselves, so to speak. To be our own bosses.

Mascis: Do you think they'll come after you?

Dmitrov: Well, they have the men to do it, don't they? But no, I think they have a desertion rate that they deem acceptable.

Mascis (narrating): But that desertion rate is growing. The occurrence of RMUs, or rogue military units, is rising in Russia. Long a problem for the U.S. Department of Defense, the Russian military is now feeling the sting of entire battalions going AWOL and becoming armed, unaffiliated gangs.

David Miles: I don't think Solovyev will tolerate the problem for very long.

Mascis (narrating): David Miles, professor of Russian history at Georgetown University Online, estimates that over fifteen hundred Russian RMUs are at large in eastern Europe, China, and the Middle East.

Miles: You have to understand that, while Solovyev is cruel and a dictator, he is also a visionary of sorts. He knew he had to win the so-called bodies race, so he immediately hatched this plan to increase and revamp his country's population. And he knew that in order to control such a massive population, dictatorship was not an option but a necessity. And while he has killed *millions* of people in the process, his nation is growing at a manageable rate. Its military hasn't suffered greatly under the weight of overextension and desertion, as ours has. Violent gangs are a foreign concept within Russia's borders, unlike here and in Mexico. The population is under control. Oppressed, for certain. But under control. Whereas we just throw more and more people on death row, yet crime is worse than ever. Solovyev knew that the cure would lead to mass tragedy, so he had the foresight to engineer that tragedy in his nation's favor. And he's succeeded, which is a terrifying thought.

RMUs are a natural by-product of an army as large as Russia's. But when someone suggests to me that Solovyev will tolerate *any* RMUs in his midst, particularly ones that reveal themselves publicly, I say no. No, he won't abide that. He will seek out threats to unity, and he will crush them.

Dmitrov: If they do decide to come for me, fine. We'll have it out. And if I die, I'll at least know that I died a free man, and not as one of Solovyev's farm crops.

Mascis: Have you killed anyone since deserting?

Dmitrov: It hasn't come to that yet. Many people assume we still have the backing of the Russian army, and so they lay down their guns when they see us.

Mascis: But you're still marauding. You're still taking what isn't yours, by threat of force.

Dmitrov: But that's the world now! You take or you get taken from. That's what we have to do, until the day someone decides to stop us. We're going to take what we need to survive—and then maybe we'll take a little more.

Mascis: How is that a better life than when you were in the army? How is that any more ethical?

Dmitrov: It isn't. But at least what we take will be ours. Mine. I deserve that after all these years. I deserve what I take to be mine and no one else's. That's the very least this world owes me.

DATE MODIFIED:
6/19/2059, 1:34 P.M.

My Cure Day Surprise

I woke up yesterday with my WEPS going nuts. I brought up the screen. Matt appeared before me, his hair shooting out from under his hat like little orange wings. Before he said anything, he belched. "You like that?"

"Wonderful."

"Hey, I heard it's your cure day today," he said. "Bruce told me. What's your cure age again?"

"Twenty-nine."

"Yeah, well, you don't look a day over sixty, fella. Anyway, you have to go to Annandale today. It's your cure day surprise. You get to kill a glampire."

"Christ. One of those vampire poseurs?"

"Oh yes. With the white face paint and dopey satanic rituals and everything. It'll be fun. You guys should pack a lunch."

"Where's the file?"

"I don't know. Don't ask me that. Ernie has all that crap. I have to go to the river and try and sell this Chris-Craft. Do you like Chris-Crafts? This one is gorgeous. I redid the hull myself. Also installed a new electric engine, which *sucks*. But it's in there."

"I live in a room in a town house nowhere near water."

"But it *will* be near water someday. I keep telling you: water is the new land."

"What am I gonna do with a boat?"

"Oh, mope, mope, mope. I could have given you a solid deal. You would have been the boat king of Falls Church. But now you've screwed it up. Go kill the glampire, and then have fun not owning a boat."

Traffic was especially miserable yesterday. At least three

clusters of parked plug-ins had spilled off the shoulder and into the right lane. By the time Ernie and I got to the house, it was two o'clock. That part of Annandale is relatively tranquil, but I didn't want the Southeast incident repeating itself. I chewed my nails during the whole ride out. I ripped off the white parts with my teeth, and my nail beds started bleeding; then I started chewing on the newly uncovered skin, biting and nibbling on small flecks here and there. Ernie looked at me. I tucked my fingertips into the center of my palm, like a poorly made fist.

He tried to calm me down. "It's okay, John. We'll leave while there's still plenty of daylight."

"I had a friend who was attacked by glampires a long time ago," I told him. "He was trying to hook up with some suicide girl, and she dragged him out to this dipshit vampire chanting circle in the middle of a forest. He went with the whole thing, because . . . Whatever. He was looking to get together. Then they passed him a cup with blood in it, and he drank it, and then he turned and saw a dead dog lying a few feet away, out in the woods. He flipped out and tried to run, but then the head vampire grabbed him and took a chunk out of his shoulder."

"They hurt him badly?"

"He ended up getting fifty stitches. I know they're kinda goofy. But still, I don't like being attacked."

"Don't worry. One flash of the shotgun and they'll stop baring those stupid fang implants in a snap. Come on."

We got out of the car and walked up to the house, which was painted black from top to bottom. Ernie knocked on the door. No answer. He twisted the knob, pushed, and the door swung open. We strolled in, leaving the door open to let in air and light. Every room on the main floor of the house was empty and, with the exception of the hardwood floors, painted black. We went into the kitchen—also black. We opened the fridge, which was black. The light inside the fridge was purple, like a hippie's black light. Random two-liter bottles of fluid were scattered in the fridge. Thick, rusty, sludgy liquid filled each about a third to halfway full. Each was marked DOG, CAT, RAT, etc.

I looked at Ernie. "Well, that's disgusting."

"Let me ask you a question," he said. "If you were a pretend vampire, where would you pretend you had to spend most of your day?"

I glanced past Ernie and saw a closed door in the foyer, next to a rickety, incomplete staircase that led to an upstairs that was probably never used. I looked at the door, looked back at Ernie, and nodded. He did likewise. He took the shotgun out of the duffel. I took the Texan's gun from my waistband. We approached the door and slowly opened it. The stairs descended into blackness. I saw a light switch on the wall near the doorframe and flicked it. Nothing. "Shouldn't there be torches on the wall for me to grab?" I asked. "I feel like I'm in a video game."

Ernie took out a flashlight, and we walked down into the basement. It was essentially a massive utility room with an exposed ceiling and wire-strewn rafters looming overhead. In the center of the room, on the speckled black linoleum floor, were two dozen large Styrofoam containers painted to look like stone. They were arranged in rows of six, with just enough room between them to walk single file on any given side, and had small holes poked in the top. We could hear people breathing inside. There were no name tags on the makeshift coffins, which aggravated me.

"How do we know which one is our guy?" I asked Ernie.

"No problem. TYLER MCKINNON!"

Nothing happened. The rhythmic breathing from inside the coffins continued unabated. "They certainly commit to the role, don't they?"

Ernie wasn't as impressed. "Yeah, well, they can wake their asses up." He kicked the lid of one coffin, but with the force needed to dislodge the top of an actual sarcophagus, not the picnic coolers that these things really were. As a result, he accidentally knocked the whole thing on its side. He pried open the top, creating that unmistakable Styrofoam-on-Styrofoam sound that has ripped eardrums asunder for decades. Nothing inside, save for a small ratty blanket.

He pried off a second lid, revealing yet another vacancy at the glampire motel. I knelt beside the adjacent coffin and pressed my ear to it, to see if I could hear any breathing. Nothing. Ernie took to shaking coffins, since they were so light. I did likewise. None of mine, nor his, had any weight. On my third shake, I heard a small rattle come from inside. I lifted the lid.

Inside was a small WEPS speaker, wireless and about the size of a thumbnail. Loud breathing sounds were coming from it.

"This is weird." Just as I said it, Ernie shook a fourth coffin. The second he did, the top flew off like a jack-in-the-box, and out popped a deranged Greenie with a knife. He shrieked, "Hello!" and plunged the knife deep into Ernie's thigh, then let out a laugh that reverberated through the three decades' worth of nightmares piled up in my psyche. A nearby door burst open, and dozens of them filled the crypt like a replicating virus. My brain fired off orders to my body to raise the Texan's gun and point it somewhere, anywhere, and pull the trigger. None of the signals reached my shoulder, arm, or hand. Giant clusters of fear and rage and despair all rushed to the front of my mind and wound up jamming the exit. The Greenies were on me within seconds, and that's when I was finally, stupidly able to physically resist.

"Get off me!" I screamed.

Ernie lay writhing over in the corner. A particularly fat Greenie took out a long blade and pressed the side of it against my left eyelid. "Good eye," he said. "Good eye. Could fetch a decent price. Don't squirm too much. I don't want you breaking a blood vessel in there. And what's this?" One of the others lifted my shirtsleeve and ran his grubby green fingertips over my scar. He jabbed into it roughly with a long pinky nail. A cocaine nail. A small amount of blood began trickling out. "I see we've seen you before."

"Go ahead and carve it again," I told him. "I don't care."

"Please. Carve it again? That's so not as funny as it used to be." I saw another troll whitewash Ernie's face with a soaked rag. "No, we're gonna saw off your hands and feet. That's much more creative. That way you get to spend the rest of your life like Mr. Kitty here." He held up a knit doll of a cat. It had long, simple protrusions for arms and legs, nothing more. "Hello there, Mr. Kitty! You're such a nice little kitty, yes you are!"

"FUCK YOU!"

I felt a hand come from behind my head and mash a white cloth into my face. A harsh vapor hollowed out my sinuses, and I found myself instantly transitioning into a state of astonishingly vivid unconsciousness, unlike any dream I had ever had. I was sliding down a playground slide and landing in a huge pit of recycled-tire mulch. I lay in the mulch while it bounced me up and down, as if I were in the center of a crowded Moon Bounce. Nearby, someone was swinging gaily on a swing. I looked up from my feather bed of old Bridgestones and saw an unmistakable blonde with an impossible body. She said hi in the same husky voice she always had. I said hi back. She smiled. And everything felt okay.

Then the scene shifted, and I was sitting in the window seat of an airplane in the middle of a blizzard. The blonde was next to me, sitting perfectly still as the plane began to land. I looked out my window to see snow pounding the wing and the plane quickly drawing even in altitude with the Manhattan skyline. The plane landed gently on the frigid Hudson River. Hundreds of ferryboats were lined up beside us, their lights illuminating an impromptu runway. I saw the water, blue as the liquid inside an old jar of Barbicide, filling my window like an aquarium. I remained unfazed by this, glued to my seat. I didn't resist. I didn't try to get up. I simply watched the chaos unfold around me.

Then, like someone had blasted my chest with defibrillator paddles, I shot back to life, back into the here and now, on the main floor of the glampire house, black walls all around me, night falling outside. I let out a guttural wail, like I had just come up from being trapped under ice. I brought my wrists up to my eyes.

And there they were. My hands. Both of them, still delightfully attached to the rest of my body. I looked at my legs and saw that my ankles and feet were still married to one another. I counted my fingers, one through ten, as I did with David when he was born. Yep, all there. I looked for Ernie, who was propped up against one of the black walls, two men tending to the hole in his leg. I made out his hands and feet. I felt along my body for wounds or bandages. Nothing. Every muscle in my body slackened in relief.

Three men in jean shirts and pleated khakis stood before me. A trail of scraped blood passed by them and out the door, where similarly dressed men were milling about. The three men looked at me sternly. My mind told me I should be wary, yet I was so relieved that they weren't painted green or carrying knives (as far as I knew) that it didn't matter to me. Also, I still had my hands and feet. All three men had blood spritzed on their clothing, yet they betrayed no trace of having physically exerted themselves. The man in the center held Ernie's duffel in his hands. He appeared to be in his forties, with a flat receding hairline. He had curled the front of his hair back behind his head, creating a bizarre, poofy ridge that accentuated both the hair and the missing patch in front. I couldn't stop staring at it.

He spoke slow and low. "Well, this is a curious intersection indeed."

"Who are you?" I asked.

"I'm the Reverend Steve Swanson. These are my fellow congregants, Jack and Brandon Fordyce." He had one of the twins hand me a bottle of water. "No charge for that."

"Thank you. And thank you for . . . for whatever you did. What did you do? Where are the trolls?"

"The Greenies? Yeah, you won't be hearing from them for a while. That was a nasty little bunch you came across. Very nasty."

"I want to know where they are."

"Shh. Shh. Quiet now." He took out a piece of gum and chewed on it. Slowly. Very slowly. He'd chomp down once, then spend a few seconds letting the piece languish in his mouth before chomping again. I've never seen that before. "Your friend over there is gonna be just fine. But I have a few questions for you, Mr. Farrell. I take it you're not a COM member."

"No. No, sir."

"Uh-huh. And obviously you were lured to this house by the Greenies. But I'm curious as to what the purpose of your visit was. As you understood it to be, of course." He held up Ernie's duffel. "Your friend has quite a few interesting toys in here. Shotguns? Explosives? And what about this?" He took out the dose. "Shot of SoFlo! Not exactly something random people carry around with them, even in this day and age."

A bell rang in my head. "Swanson . . . I know your name."

"Indeed you do. Your son is an extremely hardworking and dedicated young man. You should be very proud of him."

"I wish I could take more credit."

"He told the church what it is you do. Don't be angry with him. Oversight of your . . . industry . . . is an important part of our mission. We aim to reform it, though I'm sure you've gathered that. Just our luck, the worst Greenies in Fairfax County were also eyeing you. Isn't that a happy little coincidence? Your son saved your life here today. The divine goodness inside him compelled him to do so. That shouldn't be lost on you at a time such as this." He stared at me. I envisioned myself being hauled off along the trail of Greenie fluid to a similar unknown doom. "So, an end specialist. How is that working out for you? Is it exciting? Do you get to travel and meet new people, and then kill them?"

"I don't kill anyone," I said. "I'm just a consultant."

"And your friend over there? What's his role? Am I going to find a black hood in this bag if I search a bit more thoroughly? Hmm?"

"What do you want from us, Reverend?"

He knelt down beside me, his face set in sharp relief against the black wall behind him. "Would you agree that my fellow congregants and I have given you a gift today?"

"Yes."

"The men who attacked you are the scum of the earth. They're just as bad as the gangs—in fact even worse, because they work with the organ dealers, who are themselves even worse. They are repeated violators of the holy human vessel. Would you agree with me about that?"

"Did you kill them?"

"We don't kill anyone, Mr. Farrell. We don't kill anyone, and we don't harm anyone. That is a damnable, unholy act. The Greenies caused themselves to bleed, I assure you. Those gentlemen will be dealt with in our own unique way. They'll be reintroduced to the idea of treating their fellow man with dignity and reverence."

I grew angry with him. "They're not yours to keep," I said. "They were going to saw off my hands and feet, and I would like a chance to retort."

"Well, aren't you the brave one, now that we've come to your rescue?"

"I am through being acted upon, Reverend. I don't trust you any more than I trust them. What are you *really* going to do to them? What if they don't buy in? What if they don't want to be collectivists?"

"That's never been a problem," he said. "Do you believe me when I tell you that we deploy methods that will not harm you but that you would never want any part of? Ever?"

"Yes. I absolutely believe that."

"Then I'm going to give you two gifts today. The first is your life back. The second is a chance to reevaluate your life on your own, without our assistance. This is an unusual gift. We aren't usually able to extend this sort of arrangement. Particularly for the likes of you. Because, while the trolls, and the gangs, and the organ thieves are all bad, *you* are worse than all of them. Because you have the government on your side. Because you have the public convinced that what you do is somehow acceptable, even noble."

"And you beg to differ."

"I do. I strongly beg to differ." He drew closer. "I want you to stop killing people. Do you understand? *Stop*."

"I don't have many choices open to me outside of this job."

"Bullshit. Any man who says he has no choice in life is just too lazy to make his own way. How much time do you waste at night justifying who you are to yourself? You don't have to kill people, and you know it. What did you do before you killed people?"

"I was a lawyer."

"What kind of lawyer?"

"A divorce lawyer."

He laughed. "Well, Jesus, don't go back into that either. If you need work, we can always provide it for you."

"Thank you for the offer," I said. "But I'd rather not."

"I don't care what you'd rather do. I'll say it again: Stop killing people."

"I want the Greenies back in our custody."

"Are you thick in the head? You're lucky I didn't drag you out the door with them. Stop killing people. Do you understand? Otherwise we will see you again. And you'll find yourself spending the next decade reading history books in a single room buried twenty stories under my parking space." They began walking out. "Tell your friend. And enjoy the gift."

DATE MODIFIED:
6/21/2059, 11:58 P.M.

"They can't do anything to us"

My boss is a unique individual in the sense that he is so terrifically full of shit. Everything that comes out of Matt's mouth is a gross exaggeration or an outright lie. Yet that's an innate part of his charm. I never really believe anything Matt says, yet I often choose to believe it anyway. He's just so damn enthusiastic about being full of shit. I'd rather buy into what he's saying than accept the harsh reality of it all. You have to experience it firsthand to believe it. How many liars out there are so good at lying that they don't even have to be convincing? It's a maddening characteristic— one that was on full display when I called him after leaving the glampire house.

"Collectivists? Oh, come on," he said. "You're gonna let those hippies scare the bejesus out of you?"

"You weren't there, Matt. You didn't have the guy get right in your face and tell you bad things would happen if we kept doing this."

"They can't do anything to us. We're subcontracted by the government. You're practically a cop. If they assault you, boom! Jail. If they kidnap you, boom! Death penalty. These guys aren't even worth a drop of sweat on your forehead. They literally can't hurt you. It's against their stupid religion."

"Hurting people is against *every* religion, but people do it anyway. Those edicts are written to be disregarded, Matt. They don't even have to hurt me. They can lock my holy vessel away in a cell for years on end. Besides, they saved our lives. Where the hell were you? How could you just send us into that ambush without any support? Without having done any of your goddamn homework?"

"I'm genuinely sorry about that, John. I am. Look, you want to take a vacation? You can take a long one if you want. No restrictions."

"I freelance, you jackass. If I don't work, you don't pay me."

"That's true. I'll tell you what. Take the week. Sit it out. I'll pay you the same as if you were working. You rest, let the shock wear off, and then come see me. Or don't, if that isn't what you want to do. Take the week off. Take my boat, if you want. You want to use the boat for a week? You could rent it."

"I don't want the fucking boat. I want assurances."

The bouncy goofiness left his expression. "You have my assurances," he said. "Call me a blowhard all you like, but I'm telling you that you are supported by government-backed security measures that would shock you if you knew their depth. Even as a freelancer, your license makes you a very important and productive worker for the U.S. government. And what if I were to tell you that there is a very strong likelihood that your responsibilities will expand in the coming years, if not much sooner?"

"What do you mean?"

Ernie clarified. "He means hard end specialization."

"I thought you weren't into that sort of thing, Matt."

"I wasn't, until I saw the incentive program. Besides, I kinda lied to you during your job interview about being averse to the idea. Just a light finessing of the truth."

"I'm stunned that you would be less than forthcoming."

"I had to be nicey-nice with you, otherwise you would have walked away from the job and some chucklehead would have taken it instead. Bruce and I always pictured you as growing into the job."

"I hate you."

"Trust me. You won't hate me when I finally get you a license to blow away every dipshit Greenie that dares cross your path. You've got a lot of demons to exorcise there, kiddo. We'll help you out with that. For now, just take the week."

He signed off. I turned to Ernie, who was slumped in the passenger seat. "Are you gonna keep doing this?" I asked him.

"Well, here's the deal," he said. "Matt's insane. You and I both know that. But he's loyal. And hell, it doesn't matter if I keep doing this or not. Every door I open these days might have someone waiting to kill me behind it. That's the way it goes, brother. This is what I do now. Once life takes you in one direction, that's it. You're pretty much locked in. My father was a cabinetmaker. A craftsman. He taught me that the job didn't matter so long as you took pride and care in it. So that's what I do. And if it turns out that the job entails blowing away a bunch of trolls and insurgents, then all the better. We all need shit to do." He took a swig of water. "Yeah, I'll keep doing it. But I want that paid week off too. In fact, I want two. I'm the joker that got stabbed, you puss."

DATE MODIFIED:
6/22/2059, 3:06 A.M.

"Let it overwhelm me"

I spent the majority of today doing very little, saving my energy for the eventual call to David to explain how his people both saved and threatened me in the course of a single evening. I felt I owed David a measure of gratitude. I was also angry at him, and felt guilty for being angry at him, given that I had abandoned him. The dynamics of all this confuse me at times. I finally called just before dinner. He picked up and knew it was me from the ID: "I figured you were resting," he said. "I didn't want to call."

"They threatened me, David."

"They would never hurt you."

"No, they made it quite clear that they have means other than physical pain."

"Those are idle threats. Nothing more. Reverend Swanson knows precisely how well connected your industry is."

"Why am I being threatened at all?"

"Did you really think being an end specialist would come without scrutiny, John? I was concerned. And I don't mean that in the sense of proselytizing. I know the church isn't for you right now, and that's fine. But I worry about you on a human level. I worry for your safety. I worry for your peace of mind."

"You don't have to worry. I'm fine. It's my job to fret over you."

"Not to be mean, but I think we both know that's not a job you're particularly well suited for."

I let out a deep breath.

"I'm sorry," he said.

"Don't be. I more than earned it."

"What was the last job you did? Before this attack? What was it like? Give me a window. Give me an understanding of all this."

"You mind if I make a drink before I tell you?"

"By all means."

I poured bourbon over ice until the glass tumbler leaked over like a pot of rice left to boil too vigorously. I took a swig and began telling him the story. I told him about a very rich man living in Herndon. His wife had just passed away, and he wanted to pass his money on to his daughter without gift taxes. He grew up in Massachusetts and he wanted to die there. So he paid for Ernie and me to go with him in a private jet that somehow had government clearance to fly. He took us to his giant compound on the shore, and he cooked this enormous feast for lunch and had all his friends and family over. There were lobsters and steamers dunked in butter and beer can chicken. Bottles of good wine all over the place. Everyone drank and talked and looked so content. Just this air of absolute comfort, like the world couldn't touch them. The guests cleared out by three, and that's when he asked Ernie and me to do the job.

He had us drive him to a nearby beach on Cape Cod Bay, in a pickup truck that was all sandy and rusty in the back. The tide had gone out by then, and the entire bay had emptied. You could walk from one side to the other and not get your ankles wet. We walked with him into the basin, and I could see the surface of the earth, drained. I could see the little ridges in the sand, like the surface of a crater on some distant, old planet—a crater that was once a great sea, now dead forever. I could see the little hermit crabs popping up in the tiny streams, skittering down that liquid highway because it was the only road they had left to travel.

It was clear he'd had this plan in mind for years and years. It was meticulously organized. In the flatbed of his pickup were a couple of cinder blocks with manacles attached. He told us we were to fasten the blocks to him, and he would wait for the water to come in. When the water rushes back into the bay and fills in the giant pool at dusk, he explained, you can see the sunlight bounce off the surface and watch as the dead sand gives way to an ocean of gold. Gentle, lapping ripples beckoning you on and on, until you are fully consumed. I'm going to sit here, he told us, and I'm going to wait as the water crawls farther and farther up my body, past my knees, my waist, my torso. I'm going to let it overwhelm me, until there's nothing left. I'm going to float there as it overtakes me, then I'm going to let go and let it sweep me away. The end of my wife. The end of my parents. Like the countless dead unburdened of a future far out of their control. Life is a monument, and mine is finished. I want to leave now before all I once thought indelible is sanded down to nothing. Before I can find nothing inside myself.

Ernie clasped the blocks to him, and we stood with him while the tide lapped in. You couldn't see it rising with your eyes, but every time you turned around the water had gained another inch. The old man didn't flinch. Not once. Ernie waded back to shore, but I stayed there. Swimming in my clothes. Watching him stare at his final sunset. I saw the water reach his chin, then his mouth, then bubbling up into his nostrils. He never thrashed or betrayed any unease. I watched the water go over his eyes, and they never bulged. He looked like he was at home in an easy chair.

I recounted all of this to my son with an air of envy. "There was something . . . romantic about it, David. Affirming. He had something within him that I didn't, and I won't leave here until I find it."

"I know where that feeling can be found," David said.

"I don't share your opinion."

"You will. I'm well on my way to finding the serenity your client discovered. I daresay I'm closer to it than you are. Care to wager on who gets there first?"

I didn't. I knew a losing bet when I saw one.

DATE MODIFIED:
6/22/2059, 8:02 P.M.

"The cure for everything else"

This is transcribed from Micah Resnick's Sky4 report about Steven Otto:

> **Resnick:** Steven Otto was just two years old when his father, Graham, and six of his father's colleagues were murdered by a group of pro-death insurgents outside his temporary lab in Eugene, Oregon. Over four decades have passed since that night. Steven Otto has asked enough questions about what happened, and gotten enough answers, to be able to construct a full, violent, searing memory of it in his mind. He thinks about his father often, and he never discourages people from bringing up the subject. That openness will serve him well in the coming years, as Steven now stands on the cusp of a scientific breakthrough that may exceed even his father's. It's a robovaccine that goes by the code name Skeleton Key. And it's a breakthrough that he says he was ready to throw into the garbage.
>
> **Otto:** If you'll just join me in the lab . . .
>
> **Resnick (narrating):** Otto works here, in an anonymously funded private lab near Portland. To enter this lab, visitors must go through what is known as a "blow shower," a fifty-second release of cold air designed to blast away any stray hair and skin cells. We also had to wear full hazmat suits and helmets to get inside this facility. No open seams are allowed. He led us to a series of glass vials that, to the naked eye, appeared to contain nothing but clear liquid.

Resnick: So there are robots in here?

Otto: Very small ones, yes.

Resnick: And what can they do?

Otto: We're still ironing out the kinks. But ideally Skeleton Key will be able to identify enemy viruses, harmful bacteria, and malignant tissue inside the human body, then destroy them before they ever have a chance to metastasize and do lasting damage.

Resnick: What are we talking about here? Are we talking about curing cancer?

Otto: Preventing it permanently, yes.

Resnick: Heart disease? Clogged arteries?

Otto: Yes.

Resnick: Flu?

Otto: Yes.

Resnick: Can it make you thinner?

Otto: Actually, yes. It can. We program an ideal body mass based upon your genetic blueprint, and Skeleton Key will destroy any fat cells that cause you to exceed that target.

Resnick: Like internal liposuction?

Otto (laughing): See, this always happens. People skip right over the cancer part and go right to the "make me thin" part.

Resnick: So your father invented the cure for aging, and now you've come along with the cure for everything else.

Otto: Well, we have a ways to go yet. But that's the goal: to create a very comprehensive vaccine that remains operational in the bloodstream for the duration of your lifespan, however long that may be. I'm encouraged with what we've been able to engineer thus far. I could easily see, within the next decade, perfecting Skeleton Key and making it available on a mass scale.

Resnick: What made you want to pursue this?

Otto: It's all the dog's fault. We had this dog, Buggle. And Buggle was known to many people for being the first dog to receive the vector. But he got sick nevertheless, and this was after we had owned him for, I dunno, thirty years or so? I didn't want to see him go.

Resnick: You loved him.

Otto: Of course. He was our family dog. And he was my father's dog. So to me Buggle was this remnant of Dad. Something real that I could touch and look in the eye. I didn't want to lose that. I wasn't ready to lose that. You hear all these stories now about people who give their pets the cure and the pets get sick and die, and then the owners end up calling an end specialist because they can't handle their grief. And I understand that to a degree. Anyway, rather than cope with Buggle's sickness like a healthy person, I decided to try to cure cancer instead. So much easier, am I right?

Resnick: Were you also driven, in a way, to top your father's discovery?

Otto: No. That was never my intent. My father's discovery, as far as I'm concerned, remains the greatest scientific discovery in the history of mankind.

Resnick: A discovery that ended up costing him his life.

Otto: Well, no. The discovery didn't kill him. *People* killed my father. Let's not confuse the two. People like Casey Jarrett decided to throw him in that van and burn him to death. The cure itself meant no harm.

Resnick: But he himself was ambivalent about the cure and what would happen once it spread.

Otto: Oh, no doubt about that. If there's no cure, there are no farms in Russia or insurgency or Peter Pan cases or any of those horrible things.

Resnick: In hindsight, do you understand the motives of the people that killed him?

Otto: I understand their viewpoint but not their methodology. The tragedy of my father's murder was that he and the people who killed him weren't in disagreement. They shared the exact same fears. But instead of working with my father to see that the cure was used responsibly, they decided to kill him. And that will never make sense to me. It doesn't make sense to me now. It won't make sense to me one hundred years from now, if I'm lucky enough to still be here.

Resnick: Do you wish he had never discovered the cure?

Otto (pausing): Sometimes. But wishing is a fool's errand, isn't it? There's only one reality, and that's the reality that I have to deal with. I think a lot of people mistakenly hoped the cure would end not only death but also the anguish of processing death, of processing finality. I think people thought they would be able to escape that, and the opposite has proven true. They have to spend much longer dealing with their grief.

Resnick: Are you scared the discovery of Skeleton Key will also give people a false sense of security?

Otto: Yes. And that's why I very nearly threw away the initial prototype.

Resnick: I bet you never thought you'd one day be on the verge of perfecting a cure for cancer, and then wonder if it was a *bad* thing.

Otto: I know. It's insane that we've gotten to this point. But it's a legitimate thing to think about. Is it a good thing to eliminate an illness, or many illnesses, that are devastating on an individual scale but necessary in the grand scheme of nature? And, if we're being honest, why am I trying to develop something that will help all these other people? We now live in a world where I think many people walk around asking themselves, do other people matter? Does the rest of the world mean anything to me, or is all that matters this very small world of friends and family and colleagues that I've constructed for myself? It's easy to navigate that minefield of questions and come to the conclusion that this vaccine is a bad thing.

Resnick: So why didn't you destroy the vaccine?

Otto: Because deep in my heart I know you can't stop progress. Ever. There are plenty of private labs out there working on something similar. You think Michael Ornster doesn't have forty people working on this over at Delvair?

Sooner or later this vaccine *will* be perfected, and it is going to be used, both for good and ill. You can't stop people from doing what they want to do. That's a realization I had a long time ago—one that came back to me when I was standing on a bridge, ready to throw the prototype down onto the rocks below. I remembered when I married my wife . . .

Resnick: Your current wife.

Otto: I've only had one. No cycle marriages for me. Anyway, I remember all the wedding planning we did, and we were scurrying around to bakeries and caterers and God knows where else. And my wife was having panic attacks on the day of the wedding. She'd say to me, "Steve! Do *not* let the guests switch the place cards!" And she'd order the ushers to make sure all the guests signed both the guestbook and some special photo that we had placed on a table in the foyer. Of course, the guests didn't obey any of our little commands. They switched seats and never bothered to sign the picture, and not everyone danced on the dance floor. I think after about six glasses of champagne, my wife finally decided that there was no use in trying to stop it. That she may as well enjoy the day instead of trying to make sure everyone acted exactly as she wished. You can't stop people from doing what they want to do. They're always going to do it. Mankind has a path for itself, a trajectory, and you can never knock it off of that course. All I can do is usher in this vaccine in the most responsible manner I can. After that I have to have faith that people will be as well-intentioned as I am.

Resnick: But hasn't this century been proof positive that they aren't?

Otto: To a degree. But there is still some good out there, Micah. Not everyone took the cure and decided to become a crazed goon. A breakthrough like this will solve the organ theft problem, at the very least. Perhaps *this* is the key to turning everything around. That's what I have to hope for. I have to.

Resnick: Do you wish your father were still alive to see some of the breakthroughs you've made?

Otto (choking up): I wish he were still alive. Period. That's all.

Resnick (narrating): Steven Otto believes Skeleton Key could be ready by 2070. But just today Nobel Prize–winning bioroboticist Lars Anderssen said Otto's timetable is wishful thinking, and that a vaccine with Skeleton Key's abilities may never be possible. Either way, Steven Otto will continue working on his vaccine, to improve upon the cure his father gave the world. For better and for worse. As for Buggle the dog, he died from stomach cancer in September 2042.

DATE MODIFIED:
6/23/2059, 4:31 A.M.

"They don't think this is the end of it"

From Darian Clark at *G9* (and everywhere else):

Breaking: Massive Explosions in China

By Darian Clark

Three massive, nuclear-scale explosions in China were detected by U.S. and Russian satellite imagery just one hour ago. The explosions appear to be centered on the cities of Ürümqi, Harbin, and Linfen. U.S. military operatives say no incoming missiles from outside of China were detected prior to the blasts. The three cities share a combined population of nearly sixty-five million people.

ANBC has some of the satellite images up right now. You can see the caps of the mushroom clouds growing and eclipsing any topographical features of the landscape. I went to check the feeds, but connections are slow all over the place because everyone else is doing the exact same thing. I managed to get through once and see a handful of messages posted.

DerrickOLE32: DUDE, CHINA JUST NUKED ITSELF

MartyBTV: Lookn @ China on the big WEPS right now. HOLY MOLY

SeraFoster: I have a very good friend who lives in Linfen. If anyone has any information, PLEASE POST IT. Can't get onto other feeds Grrrrrr!

2000XiangXiangXiang: I'm in Hong Kong. Everyone's panicking. They don't think this is the end of it. Please post pics if you have them

Farooq: Ürümqi is almost entirely Muslim. If China were going to nuke itself to control its population, that's the first place they'd start. Jesus. Jesus, Jesus, Jesus

HsangDuvoy12: My cousin lives far outside Harbin. He said he saw a flash out his window and then everything went dark. They're in the basement right now. They don't know when they should come out.

DATE MODIFIED:
6/24/2059, 10:34 P.M.

"They just can't help themselves"

I tried to sleep but all I could see in my mind was a tangled day-mare of Greenies and Chinese mushroom clouds and very small robots and stern collectivist reverends and old postmortals drowning in the ocean. Drinking did little to stop the visions. I needed someone to talk to or just to be with. There's only one option for that kind of companionship at three in the morning on a weeknight.

The "friend" listings said Julia was a postmortal blonde escort available for house calls 24-7. Very few of the girls listed were available for house calls, so I pegged her as the best of the bunch. I pinged her and told her to meet me outside the apartment complex, so as not to wake up Scott, my roommate. I smoked a bowl of hydro, grabbed the Texan's gun, shuffled down the stairs, and waited. This will sound pathetic, but I found myself excited to meet her. They have pictures up on those listings, but they never match what you end up getting. I felt like a nervous little kid going through puberty again, in all the good ways. Someone was going to pull up to my door, and I had no idea who. Something was going to happen.

An hour later a ratty-looking plug-in cruised into the lot, and out stepped a girl who barely looked eighteen. She wore jeans and a small white camisole. I took one look at her and felt like a creepy old man. She locked pupils with me and hurried to the door, a small pistol in her hand. I held the door for her. We walked up the stairs and got to the apartment, not a word exchanged between us. I got her a bottle of water from the fridge and escorted her to the bedroom, turning on the light. She began taking off her pants. I stopped her. "Wait, wait."

"What?"

I looked at her face. Outside, she looked like a teenager. Inside, under the lights, her skin looked artificially stretched. It had a blotted, bronze quality to it—the kind of skin you only get from sitting out in the baking sun for years and years without regard for the damage it'll cause. You could see the flattened creases along her jaw, like a pair of chinos that had been poorly ironed. I've seen a lot of girls lately with trophy-wife syndrome. Julia was no different. She was legitimately young and artificially young all at once.

"How are old are you?" I asked.

"I'm eighteen, sweetheart."

"No, I mean how are old are you really?"

"Forty-two."

"Jesus."

I sat down on the bed. She plopped down next to me. "Eighteen's my cure age," she told me. "They paid me ten thousand dollars to get it."

"Who did?"

"Franz Hornbacher."

"The designer?"

"Yep. That's the guy."

"So you were part of that whole Beautiful Town thing?"

"Yeah," she said. "It was so weird. One day I was walking along the street in Adams Morgan, when this really tall guy with a blond wig and red glasses walked up to me with about six people around him. He pointed at me and said, 'She's in. She has the look.' He was eating a banana when he said it. He ate, like, thirty bananas a day. It was all he ate. I think it was for, like, virility."

"So just like that, it happened?"

"Yep. They put me on a plane to some island in the Bahamas with a few other people he'd selected. Then they put us up in some bungalows and just kind of set us free."

"You didn't have to do anything?"

"They gave me the cure and told me to go be beautiful. They had film crews and design teams walking around the island all the time, taking photos of us, telling us to try on certain clothes, asking us if we'd consider sleeping with various other models on the island. Honestly, I spent so much time drinking champagne and snorting coke that I barely remember any of it. I remember Keith Richards visited one day, which blew my mind."

"How'd he look?"

"Not bad. I think that's his secret. Everyone expects him to look like a corpse, so when he shows up and looks somewhat alive, people are really impressed. It was a cool trick. He and Franz drove around the island in this gold golf cart, and Franz would be shouting at us from a megaphone all the time. 'Hey, funboys, doesn't it feel goooood to be beauuutiful?' It was something."

"So, what happened? How come you didn't stay?"

"I couldn't get pregnant. We found out later that that was the real reason Hornbacher brought us all down there. He was experimenting. He was trying to mix and match different people with different looks and to figure out what they'd produce. I think he was looking for some sort of ultimate breeding prize. He expected one of us to pop out some perfect, eternal muse for him to dote on forever. A clotheshorse. That's why we were there. He was looking for a perfect blend of person."

"That's creepy. Like a master race."

"Not quite that, but way creepy all the same. I mean, he wasn't a *white* supremacist. But he was definitely a supremacist of some kind. There were blacks and Latinos and Brazilians and all kinds of people there. He was extremely snobby, and you never knew when he'd cast you off on a whim. One day they came up to me and told me to leave. Franz himself never said goodbye to me, even though we had nice conversations every once in a while. They flew me back to Dulles, gave me a check, and then left me in the terminal. They also never told me that your skin could still get sun damage, even if you got the cure." She waved to her face. "The ten thousand dollars was barely a drop in the bucket compared to the lifting procedures."

"You look good."

"If the lights are dim enough. And you? How old are you, since you got to ask me?"

"I'm sixty-eight. Twenty-nine's my cure age."

"Not bad. You look good. You look your cure age."

I looked out the window. When I was hanging in Mexico with Keith, we'd sleep on the street at night sometimes. And I remember all the houses were set behind these crude concrete walls with shards of broken bottles sticking out at the top. I remember in Cuernavaca that even at 3:00 A.M. night never really became night. There were too many streetlights and too much haze in the air for the lights to reflect off of. Instead of a dark sky, the night there always maintained this bizarre ethereal glow. Phosphorescent—like a bug zapper hanging over your head. Now I could see that same glow out my window. It's been there for a while. Night has become extinct here. The world never fully comes to a rest anywhere I go. I turned to Julia. "I don't feel my cure age, truth to tell. Every morning I look in the mirror and see a body that's a lie. I feel like this skin of mine is just a shell—that if you knocked against it, it would crack and chip. You could peel it away and all you'd see underneath would be a sick, wrinkled old man. This body is just a hiding place."

"At least you're fully formed," she said. "You're a man. What am I? For the past two decades, I've been nothing more than jailbait. No one listens to a word I say because they think I still have the brain of a flighty little teenager. The only men who look my way are creeps looking for some barely legal action. No offense."

"None taken."

"I see the twenty-six- and twenty-seven-year-old women walking around and think, my God, those are *women*. Real women. Women who can wear a business suit and look professional. Women who have careers and cycle husbands and babies and all this shit I'll never have." She leaned in. "Do you know what the worst part of it is? I'm always acting my cure age. I can't help it. I look eighteen, so I feel this urge to play the role or something like that. I get drunk. I act ditzy around boys. I was at a party a while back and this guy asked me a question about China and I pretended not to know anything about China, when I *do*. I know boatloads about China: Chairman Mao, Tiananmen Square, the open period, the return to isolationism. You know anyone in China? Lose anyone in the blasts?"

"Not that I know of."

"Me neither. Still, I know all that stuff. But half the time I feel compelled to act like this stupid little girl."

"It's like your body is dictating to your brain what role you should play."

"That's right! I go read a book or something, and there's this little voice in my head that says, hey, girl, why aren't you out partying? But I got sick of that kind of thing ages ago. I stay in on a Friday night, and the girl in the mirror tells me that's a lame thing to do. But I'm a forty-two-year-old woman. It doesn't make any sense for me to go out raging. It doesn't make any sense for me to wear tube tops—but my drawer is full of the stupid things. I don't know . . . I just wish I had gotten the chance to become who I was meant to become."

She took a sip of water. I gave her space.

"Why are you asking me these questions?" she said. "Don't tell me you're looking for a real girlfriend or something."

"No no. I'm not like that. Honest. It's just . . . I couldn't sleep, and I needed some company. I guess I'm lonely, even though I don't think of myself like that."

"It's okay. I get it." The power went out again. We were left alone, bathed in the manmade glow from the working parts of the grid that seeped in from outside. "I spent two years living at this place called the Honey Ranch in LA," she said. "It was run by some sleazeball porn guy. A real Joe Francis type. And all these actors and athletes used to come around to smoke bowls and get laid in the pool. Anyway, this porn-king guy lived there with his mother. His *mother*! This very dowdy-looking fifty-year-old lady. Maude. That was her name. I think she ran most of the financial aspects of the place. And she'd walk around from time to time while everyone was playing naked pool volleyball and all that. I used to stare at her. I couldn't walk twenty feet through that house without having my ass grabbed. But Maude, no one bothered her. The men ignored her, and I guess that's not always what you want when you're a woman. But still, they left her alone. She had the freedom to walk around. And when guys talked to her, they talked *to* her. They didn't stare at her tits and then whip out their IMDb credits. I thought that was, I don't know—cool. I would have liked to have evolved to the point where I could be treated that way."

"You want to be fifty?"

"Well, maybe not fifty. That's pretty damn old."

"That it is."

"And what is it that you do, given that you know so much about me now?"

"I'm an end specialist."

"Are you? Really?"

"Kind of. I'm the consultant."

"How does it work? How do you kill them?"

"With a shot. It's painless."

"What's it cost?"

"It's based on your income," I told her. "Most of our revenue on lower-income clients comes from government subsidies."

"So if I don't make all that much, you could do me for cheap. Right?"

"Yeah, but you don't want that."

"Says who?"

"It's a whole thing if you want this done. I need an RFE form filled out. I need a will. I need your license for clearance."

"I've got my license, and I don't have jack shit to leave anyone."

"Even if I could, I can't. I'm not the one who administers the dose. My partner is in charge of that, and it's a bit late to get him over here."

"So do it yourself. Come on." She scooted closer. "It'll be fun. We'll bust your cherry."

"I can't do this off the cloud."

"Like hell you can't. I know how you end specialists work. I know how you deal with those freezer babies in the foster houses."

"DES may do that, but my outfit doesn't."

"Do this for me as a favor. I've gotten all the pleasure I can out of this good thing. The lemon's out of juice, darling. You can give my hourly fee to charity or something."

"Look, it's late and I'm high. You should really take a day to think about this."

"No," she insisted. "This is not an impulse purchase. I've thought about it before. I've come across you for a reason. I want it now, and I want you to be the one who gives it to me. No one ever does me favors, so I'd appreciate it if you were the first."

She was intractable. I went to the bathroom and called Matt, who never sleeps. He came on the WEPS from his garage. He was working on an old BMW. Orange, of course. "What's this girl's deal?" he asked. "She's a hooker?"

"Yep."

"What's a hooker doing in your place at 3:00 A.M.?"

"Do you really need me to explain that to you? Look, I'm gonna send her on her way."

"Don't do that. That's free money walking out the door. It's a perfect little transitional assignment for you. Is she sober?"

"I think so."

"You have supplies with you?"

"They're in the plug-in."

"Then get them, scan her license, and get it done. I can get you e-certified to administer the dose. Go for it."

"Are you sure this is the right thing to do?"

"I don't give really give a shit. Listen, there's something you should know before you do this. It's not a warning. It's just a fact."

"What's that?"

"There's a certain emotional strength you need for this, Johnny Boy. That's why it makes sense now to see if you have it. Every one of them you take is gonna take a piece of you with them."

"I already know that."

"Not the way Ernie, Bruce, and I know it. You'll be surprised. So I wish you good luck."

He turned on a blowtorch and waved goodbye. The call cut off, and I went back to Julia and told her to wait while I got the supplies. I came back with a dose, sat down next to her on the bed, and gave her the RFE to fill out, which she did. She handed it back to me. "What now?" she asked.

"I give you the interview," I said, "and then you get the dose."

She looked at me with suspicion. "I think you forgot something in between." She put her hand on my thigh.

"We don't have to do that."

"Oh, but we do. This is where I shine. That's the bitch of it. This is the only time when I get to be convincing. This is the only time when men realize that I'm a woman in full." She slid her hand up. It felt good.

"I was built for this," she said.

"I feel like a scumbag."

"That's okay. Sometimes it feels good to feel like a scumbag. Run with it." She turned and slipped one of the straps of her camisole off her shoulder. She began breathing deeper. I followed suit. "Men know I'm bad for them, John. They always know what's bad for them. But they just can't help themselves. Because it feels so . . . fucking . . . good." She looked over to the dose sitting on my nightstand and whispered in my ear. "I want you to stick me with that when I'm getting off."

"I can't do that."

"You can. You can because I want you to. We don't need an interview. No one will care what I said or what I didn't say. I just I wanna go as I come. Do it. Be my angel."

She started kissing my neck and sliding her hand farther up. I laid back and let her. She started to unzip my fly and peel off my jeans. I returned the favor and turned her around on her knees. I fucked her in a trance until I could hear her barking at me now, Now, NOW. I reached to the nightstand and grabbed the little plastic tube. She strained and moaned as she hit the point of no return, and I jammed the lance into her backside. She looked back at me with a devilish grin and set her head down on the pillow, where it froze in place. Her eyes half-open, as if drunk. Her smile drooped a bit, giving her the look of someone having a good time but certain to forget all of it. I stared at her naked expression. Then I looked over to the empty shot in my hand.

And that's when I had a heart attack.

DATE MODIFIED:
6/29/2059, 4:56 A.M.

"Wait over there"

Scott entered the room and was greeted with the sight of a naked dead girl on my bed and me convulsing in pain beside her. It was like someone had wrapped a swimsuit drawstring around my heart, and then cinched it as tightly as possible. He ran to me. "What the hell?"

I could barely wheeze out any discernible words. "She . . . was a client," I said. "Hospital . . ."

Scott pinged the hospital for an ambulance, and we waited. He covered Julia with a blanket. He held my hand as I locked my back in an arch and turned eggplant. He tried to slip pants on me, but my legs were buckling and he couldn't wrestle my jeans back on. He threw a top sheet over me, and I waited with Julia at my side—two shades of death parked next to each other.

I felt like a very small Greenie was inside my body, trying to crush my heart in one hand while eagerly slicing through my diaphragm with the other. I took in a small amount of air at a time. Each breath seemed to tighten the Greenie's grip, as if he had caught me defying orders. Scott looked at me writhing on the bed and concluded that waiting for the ambulance was a bad idea. He threw my pants in a gym bag and wrapped a belt around the sheet covering me. He cinched it, and now I was in a makeshift toga. He made a move to get me off the bed, but I pushed him away.

"Her . . . first."

"I can come back for her," he said.

"We can't . . . leave her . . . Oh, Jesus Christ!"

A solar flare went off in my chest, and my neck hooked wildly around until my ear was practically grazing my back. I passed out from the pain and woke up in the front seat of Scott's plug-in. Julia lay covered in the back. I could see tangles of her hair poking out from under the blanket.

The roads were packed, bottlenecks every fifty yards because groups of plug-ins huddled together on the shoulder and in the right lane in impromptu car towns. The crushing sensation in my chest periodically subsided during the ride, allowing me to sit up. I glanced back at Julia's body. I didn't want her ignored. I fought against recalling her death and recalling that I was profoundly turned on by the look of ultimate satisfaction on her face. We pulled up to the ER. Scott ran in and left the plug-in idling.

The ER's enormous automatic glass doors were already wide open, with a line of people stretching out of them and hugging the side of the building where the line extended around the corner. Some of them were in wheelchairs. Some were lying on the ground, ailing. Scott sprinted inside the building to find the front of the check-in line. People were packed against all sides of the hospital breezeway, between the two sets of glass doors. Beyond that, I could only see slivers. More bodies. Every time a crack between two people opened as they jostled around, it was filled by another body not that far past. Scott gave up and ran back out.

The ER drop-off was a rotary, with a grassy infield at the center. Scott dragged me over to the infield and let me fall to the ground, where I joined numerous other folks with bullet wounds, hacking coughs, burns, and pretty much anything else you could tick off on a chart. We lay there together in the night's deathly humidity, melting and spreading like lumps of cookie dough thrown in an oven.

"I'm leaving you here," Scott said. "I'm going to drop her off at the morgue with her ES papers, and then I'll come back to check you in. I won't be long."

"Thank you."

My little infield became very crowded, with broken people lying down closer and closer, eventually almost spooning me. Occasionally, one of the spotlights on the roof of the hospital would sweep the infield, the beams blasting straight through my shut eyelids. The pain returned, and I felt like my heart was being flattened by an invisible stone monolith.

Scott got back and saw me still on the ground. Before he tried to pick me up, he looked around to see if any of the other able-bodied folks would offer to assist him. None did. They ignored him as if he were a late-boarding train passenger looking for an empty seat. He wrapped his arms around me from behind and hoisted me up, tightening my chest even further. I felt my rib cage turn to crumpled cellophane.

"Sorry, brother," he said, "but you have to be present at check-in."

He dragged me into the melee and stood in the line. Hours passed. I lay on the ground. When the line advanced, Scott prodded me with his foot to move me forward a bit, like a carry-on bag. I called David to tell him I loved him. He offered to come down, but I insisted he remain in New York. An hour later a very nice collectivist named Ken met us in line and offered to relieve Scott of his duties. Scott accepted and went home to sleep. Ken opened a fanny pack and gave me carrots and diet soda. He brought clean clothing for me (khakis and a denim shirt, of course), and I put it on slowly, while remaining on the ground. He offered to have a church healer come and lay hands on me. I declined. The line ticked forward. A very large, very stern nurse awaited us.

"Name?"

I stood and gave her my name in short, halting breaths.

"Symptoms?"

I told her I was having a heart attack.

"Date of birth?"

I told her October 1, 2030. She gave me a derisive glare.

"A heart attack? At twenty-nine? I don't think so. Wait over there."

She nodded to a giant room labeled POSTMORTAL TRIAGE UNIT. That's where I was sentenced to go, my own heart attack serving as evidence that my heart attack should not be treated right away.

Just as the nurse pointed in our direction, my sister ran frantically into the ER, fresh from Jersey, happily elbowing anyone in her way. She helped Ken drag me over to the PTU and laid me gently on the carpeted floor. She stroked my hair. I grew light-headed, fighting against the urge to pass out a second time but wanting to pass out all the same. So I passed out.

I woke back up. The pain had subsided once more. I could breathe. Not deeply. But at least my chest had regained the ability to expand. I was still in the PTU. A young black man with a gun-shot wound in his shoulder sat with his mother on a bench nearby. He had a towel held up to his wound. The blood on the towel had dried ages ago and was now brown. He saw my eyes opening. "You have a nice nap?" he asked. "Wish I could nap like that."

"We've been here for twenty-six hours," his mother said. "I wasn't in the hospital that long when I gave birth to him."

I looked at Polly and Ken. They were staring up at a flat screen with dispatches from China. All the networks had available to broadcast were still photographs. I saw shadows burned into the ground. Blackened bodies. A lone shoe where a pedestrian once stood, before being blasted into nothingness. I saw stretches of rubble that I assumed were once city blocks. They looked more like extensive gravel driveways. Only a few photos were shown at a time. Mostly, talking heads yammered on about the situation. Snippets of their dialogue piled up in my LifeRecorder:

> "There have been whispers coming from China for ages that something like this might happen, Tom . . ."

> "I don't see why America should take any action other than official denouncement, Taryn. What do you do to a country that nukes itself? Nuke it again?"

> "I'm aghast at just how indifferent the international community has been in the wake of this, David."

> "I think this is only phase one. There are plenty more cities that China would like to 'reset,' to use one of its euphemisms."

◗ "Really, Jill, what else do you expect from a country that tattoos newborns?"

◗ "The people who make Vectril have blood on their hands today, Karen. They have been illegally supplying China with the cure through Russian channels for decades now. There's a stack of evidence a mile high to support it. Is it mere coincidence that this is the same company that helped develop the TEZAC tattoo-removal equipment? They've supported population growth in China to the point where the government felt compelled to do this. *This* is insane! This is insanity!"

I looked away. I tried to block it out of my mind, because I could feel the drawstring tightening again. I could hear other would-be patients in the PTU getting angry and cursing over at the check-in desk. I could see nurses walk by and everyone shouting questions at them as they avoided eye contact at all costs, like a waiter who isn't ready to serve your table. I pictured every doctor in the hospital sequestered behind a series of elaborately constructed vault doors. I shut out all the commotion. A small pamphlet had fallen to the ground beside me. I picked it up and read it over and over. With my WEPS battery in need of recharging, it was the only thing I had to read, the only words I had to stare at to keep me from hearing about the self-inflicted devastation going on half a world away—to prevent my brain from reminding me that I had just euthanized someone. I can now recite the copy verbatim.

NEED A LITTLE MORE BREATHING ROOM?

Try once-a-day Claustrovia

Claustrovia is the first prescription drug ever medically proven to help treat symptoms stemming from overcrowding anxiety disorder (OAD).

Claustrophobia
Germophobia
Sudden increase in heart rate
Irritability
Stress
Paranoia

Ask your doctor if Claustrovia is right for you. Claustrovia
is not recommended for women who are pregnant or nursing.
Children under eight should not take Claustrovia. If you're a
postmortal over the real age of sixty and you have liver
problems, check with your doctor before taking Claustrovia.
Side effects may include drowsiness, dry mouth, and liver
damage.

Polly saw me staring at the brochure. "I don't think that does
anything for a heart attack."

"It might do something for the wait, though," I said.

"It doesn't do anything for anything. I've tried it. Why are
you dressed like a collectivist?"

"I lent him the clothes," Ken told her. "They're mine."

"Why did you need new clothes?" she asked me. "And why
did you have a heart attack?"

"You don't want to know," I said. I steered her off course. "I
didn't know you were on Claustrovia."

"If it comes in pill form, I've tried it."

"Are you depressed?"

"In waves. You know me. It's only when I have time to sit
down and think about things that I realize I'm a bit of a wreck."

"You look good."

"Well, you caught me early in the day. I always look my best
before noon, before the day starts pounding away at me."

"How's the little one?"

"Tony's climbing now," she said. "He climbs up to the top of
everything—stairs, boxes, shelves, desks. It's like he thinks he

just won a gold medal in something. It's very cute. Everything is good. Everything is fine. Dave and Tony are fine. Everyone's happy and healthy, and we can afford water, and that's all I can ask for."

"Ever hear from Mark?"

"I saw him at the store a couple of weeks ago. He had his new kids with him. We did that thing where we spotted each other and gave a friendly wave. That was about it." She paused. "I still feel like he's my husband, you know. I see him with these new kids of his, and my wiring starts smoking and shooting sparks. Something doesn't compute. It's like I've been reincarnated, but God or whoever let me remember every damn thing from my past life. Then I come home to Dave, and I think to myself, wait, did I hire a substitute Mark? And shouldn't this kid I have be my grandchild? Shouldn't I be handing him off to some nice, sensible daughter-in-law somewhere? How many more husband iterations am I going to go through? Two hundred years from now, will I realize I already married my eighth husband five husbands earlier? I go to buy a couple of oranges, and I end up tied in an existential square knot. So that bats my head around the tetherball pole pretty good." She stuck out an open bag of chips. "Dorito?"

Just then a nurse called my name. I sprung up and jumped for her attention, in case she decided to pass me over and send me to the back of the ER's deli line. She waved me forward. I gave Ken a limp hug and thanked him for his help. He left without asking for his clothes to be returned.

They brought Polly and me into the emergency ward and sat me in a lone chair in the center of the hallway. I still wasn't sick enough to merit an actual room. Dozens of patients lined the corridor in wheelchairs and on gurneys. They stripped me, dry-shaved a couple of patches on my chest, hooked me up to a WEPS screen, got an EKG reading, and left Polly and me there for another three hours. We passed away the time betting on whether nurses passing through the corridor would trip and eat the floor. I said nothing about Julia.

I noticed, as we gambled, one patient being escorted down the hall. Unlike every other patient I'd seen in the ward, this one seemed to be getting treated as if his condition were a real emergency. There were nurses *and* doctors surrounding him. I hadn't seen a doctor all night and day. It was like catching a glimpse of a movie star walking along a red carpet. *There he is!* And they moved with alacrity, as if they were genuinely interested in saving his life. Again, not a common occurrence in hospitals these days.

The man looked older, perhaps in his fifties. He lay on his back, head turned to me as they wheeled him by. I could see mottling on his skin, particularly on his face. Dark violet spiderwebs had spread over his cheek and down his neck to the opening of his shirt. Copper-colored fluid drizzled out the side of his mouth, like tainted maple syrup. He hacked and wheezed violently, a disturbing half retch. It was enough for everyone lining the hall to sit up and take notice. They hurried him into one of the side rooms. One of the nurses in the battalion tailed off and let the rest go in without her. She grabbed an IV bag and a needle kit from a cart left out in the hall. She took off her latex gloves and began approaching me. She went for my arm. I saw some of the copper fluid dotted along her wrist. I reared back.

"I have directions to give you some fluids," she said.

"Could you wash your hands before you do that?"

She was either mortified or pissed—I couldn't tell which. "Of course." She went back to a hand-sanitizer dispenser, squirted once, and rubbed her hands together. Again, she approached.

Again, I recoiled. "With soap and water?"

Now she was annoyed. She went to the bathroom and came back out, wiping her hands dry on her scrubs. She stuck me with the saline bag and disappeared. Two hours later I was sent for an MRI. Another two hours later, well into the next day, the molded plastic of the chair and my backside now fused together, a doctor casually appeared before me. He wasted no time. I could tell he was already thinking ten patients ahead of me.

"Your EKG looks steady, Mr. Farrell," he said. "But the MRI shows a 95 percent blockage of one of your arteries. I think it's clear that you suffered a mild heart attack. As long as the artery is blocked, you're going to occasionally feel that tight discomfort."

"Can you clear the artery?" I asked.

"No insurance will cover the cost of that. Not at your age. Can you afford to pay for this yourself? I can probably book you for something in December."

"December? Jesus. I don't know."

"Well, you don't have to decide now. Go home and talk it over with your wife."

"That's my sister."

"Talk it over with your family. But don't wait too long. You don't want this spilling into 2060."

"What do I do in the meantime?"

"Just don't do things that will make your heart uncomfortable."

"Can you be more specific than that?"

"Not really. Just try to take it as easy as possible. And take this." He gave me a prescription for meds and left. Polly walked me out of the hospital to her plug-in. Thirty-six hours at the hospital, and nothing in my body had been fixed. Polly took out her bag of chips and started eating. I reached for the bag, then remembered the withered muscle beating meekly in my chest and drew back. A small pleasure, now surgically removed. Polly stopped eating out of sympathy. She studied me, not bothering to press the ignition. She didn't want to start it up until she saw in my eyes that I was ready to go on.

I dropped my veneer of patience and began to seethe. The hospital seemed more like a mirage than a resource for medical treatment. They didn't give a shit. They just let everyone loll around suffering. I thought back to Julia and saw her dying in ecstasy. I treated her better than any doctor would have. I helped. I went out of my way to give her what she needed.

I let the constraints of my conscience go for a moment and basked in the fulfillment of having given her a proper send-off. I embraced the memory. And suddenly everything shifted. I didn't feel hopeless or helpless anymore. I felt charged. I felt eager to go back to work *now*, this very instant. Matt was right. I didn't know this job the way the others did. But I do now. I get it.

Polly patted my shoulder and gave me a fresh bottle of water. "It's gonna be okay, John." She still thought I was afraid and despondent.

I sat up and addressed her, as if in perfect health. "I know that. I know precisely how I'm gonna deal with this."

"You do?"

"You can turn on the car. I'm ready."

DATE MODIFIED:
6/30/2059, 12:02 P.M.

"You're a real end specialist now"

I got back home to the apartment and stripped the sheets. I called Matt. He was busy eating an Italian sub.

"Where the hell have you been?" he said. "The suspense has been making me eat."

"I had a heart attack after finishing the ES."

"Holy shit." He finished his sandwich, then picked up a second one that was just like the first and began eating it. "Why didn't you call me?"

"Because I was having a *fucking heart attack*. I went to the hospital."

"A hospital? Oh Jesus. Those things are roach motels. You know that. You should have called me."

"There's a huge blockage in my arteries, and I need it fixed, and I want you to pay for it."

"Fine. Fine. We have a guy. No hospitals. It's our own network with the government. You won't have to deal with that crap again."

"Good," I said. "Put it in writing. I want to be covered, I want to do what Ernie does, and I want more pay."

"Well, look at you! Little puppy wants his own bone now. This is good, Johnny Boy. I'm glad you found the ES part to your satisfaction. You are officially broken in. You're a real end specialist now, kid. Now we can start the real work. I'm telling you, John—you'll be glad you didn't croak from that heart attack. Business is about to boom. I can feel it. You made the right decision. You're good at this. You're good at death."

DATE MODIFIED:
6/30/2059, 5:03 P.M.

That Was My Hospital

This just came up on the DC8 feed:

Thirty-Five Dead in Hospital Outbreak

By Ken Weary

Officials at Inova Fairfax Hospital confirmed that thirty-five people—including seven hospital employees—have died here since yesterday as the result of an outbreak of an unknown illness in the building.

"We do not know what this illness is or how it is spreading," said hospital spokesperson Mary Cartwright. "But we are doing all we can to keep it contained."

The Centers for Disease Control has sealed off the building at all points of entry. Patients and employees inside the hospital are said to be undergoing rigorous testing before being allowed back outside. Anyone with symptoms of the illness will remain sequestered at Inova Fairfax until further notice. Cartwright asked all people needing immediate medical care to go to the Virginia Hospital Center in Arlington in the interim.

DATE MODIFIED:
7/1/2059, 3:10 P.M.

There Is Nothing Left to Lose

I spent the day preparing to go back to work and looking at more footage from China. Aerial shots showed entire sections of land blasted clear and clean. It all seemed so futile—empty swaths just waiting to be restocked by the fresh, burgeoning masses of humanity immediately surrounding the blast areas. They zoomed in on sections of Harbin, showing terraced palaces that had collapsed down flat, as if they had been made of cardboard. They showed the remains of recently built glass towers that had been crushed and scattered about the rest of the city like shards of ice. You could click an option alongside the KBNR feed to see some of the casualties. I never took a look.

On the WEPS I watched a story—another one—about a postmortal ambushed and killed by an involuntary organic, one of those poor old folks who somehow couldn't access or afford the cure. I watched a story about the U.S. destroyer that got sunk in the Arctic Ocean by a Russian sub. I clicked over to music and sat around, taking up space. I longed to put my new purpose to good use.

The doorbell rang. No one ever comes to our door, but I suspected it was a hospital or police official looking to finish the paperwork for Julia's ES. I opened up the door and saw Ken, the nice collectivist David sent to help me at the hospital. Denim shirt. Khakis. All that.

He had a look of deep concern on his face. "I wanted to check on you, to see how you were coping."

"Oh, it's a blocked artery," I said. "But I'm working on getting it fixed. It's terribly nice of you to stop by like this."

"I wasn't talking about your heart."

I paused. "Is this a sales call?"

He cocked his head and opened his eyes in surprise. "You don't know what's happened."

"I guess I don't. Why?" I grew alarmed. "What's happened?"

"Can I come in?"

"Of course." I let Ken in. He walked past me and stopped, with his back to me for a brief moment. He turned around.

"Something happened with David," he said.

"What's happened? What the fuck is going on?"

Ken took out his WEPS and enlarged the screen. I saw a picture taken of the outside of a church. I could tell from the little symbol of a man with outstretched arms in a circle that it was a COM congregation. Half of the church was on fire, shrouded by a mountainous plume of thick, oily, black smoke. Ambulances and fire trucks were crisscrossed haphazardly in front, as if they had been parked there by the blind. Paramedics and congregants in casual clothing were running out of the church carrying stretchers. I made out a pregnant female victim on one of the stretchers. She had blotches of blood all over her white shirt, like red sunspots. She held her hand to her head. I couldn't tell if she was dead or unconscious or just in a state of shock so severe that she couldn't stand to open her eyes, to be reminded that what was happening wasn't a fabrication. It was Sonia. To the left of the photo was a reverend wearing pleated chinos and a white shirt, trying to go back into the church but unable to because a firefighter was restraining him. People were still in that church. People he desperately had to find. But the picture told me nothing of his fate, or the fate of whatever people inside he was trying to rescue. He was frozen, agonized. Below the picture was a link to a feed report with this headline, posted thirty minutes earlier:

SEVENTY PRESUMED DEAD IN
MANHATTAN CHURCH OF MAN BOMBING

I looked to Ken. "David?"

"Yes."

"Nate?"

"Yes."

I pointed to the woman in the picture. I knew the answer before I asked the question. "Sonia? Ella? The baby?"

"They're all gone," he said.

My blood cooled and my skin turned to a thick, coarse armor. "Who? Who did this?"

"We don't know. Could be Terminal Earth. Could be any number of insurgent groups. We get threats every day. I want to assure you that we will get to the bottom of it."

"Who the hell are you to get to the bottom of it? My son is dead. What the fuck did you people do to protect him? You just let anyone walk into that church because you think every person on earth is so fucking perfect and beautiful. And now David is gone and Sonia is gone and Nate is gone, and they're all dead forever. Because of *you*."

"You're lashing out, John. You're taking out your grief on—"

"Fuck you," I hissed. "What will you do if you catch the people who did this? Huh? Stick them in a room until they're ready to take my son's place in your congregation?"

"Just because we don't believe in violence doesn't mean we don't believe in justice."

"Bullshit. You don't have a fucking clue. You don't have anything that resembles a useful solution for this. These people are a fucking mold. Not every goddamn person you come across is so precious. Some of them aren't worth the stink off my shit. And they need to be destroyed."

"I understand your grief. We have groups that can—"

"Get out."

"John, this is not the right way to deal with—".

"OUT."

He left. I stood and tried in vain to remember all I could about David and Sonia and Nate. Their hair and eyes and hands and ears. Sonia speaking low and calmly during arguments. Nate holding my hand during David's birth. David as an infant, chewing on his own lower lip. I tried to gather it all up, like a spilled drink racing to the edge of a table. I tried to paint their commemorative portraits in my mind, but I found their memories etched in sand, quickly wiped away. All I could see was a red, spiked flame—a righteous hate that gave me the life force of both the living and the dead. At last, clarity.

The WEPS buzzed. I picked up the call. On the other end was Matt. He was holding a glass of champagne. He paused when he saw my face. "You don't look yourself," he said.

"I never have."

"I have good news if you want to hear it."

"Okay."

"We're cleared for hard ES's. We can get started with paramilitary training right away. Bad. Ass."

"Good. Good. That's just in time. Almost divine in its timing. I'll be right over."

"Would you like to see the first person the tracking agency is trying to locate for us? I can send it to you."

"Do it."

I ended the call. Two seconds later, a ping came in. I opened the message to find a picture of a remarkably attractive blonde woman with an impossible body. Unmistakable in her ravishing beauty. I saw her name listed in the header: Solara Beck. That's the one. That's the blonde I've been looking for all this time. The girl on the corner. The girl from Dr. X's office. The one I see in crowds even though she's never there. The red flame burned hotter. I grabbed my gun and walked out the door. I'm ready to work. I'm ready to work right now. I have my purpose. I am the correction.

DATE MODIFIED:
7/1/2059, 9:47 P.M.

IV

**CORRECTION:
JUNE 2079**

(TWENTY YEARS LATER)

"We weren't afraid to love her like our own"

From Bruce's feed:

Mrs. O'Neill's Sheep

By Dara Hughes, iWire

Frederica was thirty-five years old when Abby O'Neill began to notice something was wrong.

"She didn't look like herself," says O'Neill. "You know a sheep for that long and you can tell when they aren't right."

O'Neill bought Freddie from a neighboring farm back in 2023, when she was just a lamb. After she grew to full adulthood, O'Neill sent her to a livestock biochemist near her family's farm in Goshen, Connecticut, so that she could receive the cure for aging.

"This was the original vector," says O'Neill. "Pre-Vectril days. So they had to strap Freddie down on a table and give her the three big injections. Being in there with her was a more emotional experience than I had anticipated. That's the paradox about us farmers. I spend all day around these animals. I milk the cows. I feed the chickens. I soothe the horses when they whinny. I've killed my share of livestock, but that doesn't mean it's easy for me. I care about all the animals we raise here. When you touch them and look them in the eyes, you feel like you have an understanding with them. They're not just a tray of meat you buy at a market."

Abby took Freddie home that night, and soon Freddie became a mainstay of the O'Neill household, providing an average of thirteen pounds of fresh wool every May, in shearing season—a good five pounds more than the average American sheep.

"We used it for everything—clothes, oven mitts, butter-dish cozies," says O'Neill. "I used to open my kid's closets and joke that these were the closets Freddie built. We used to let Freddie into the house. We never did that with any other sheep."

Together with her "husband," Wally, Freddie also gave the O'Neill family a continuous supply of fresh lambs, giving birth to a new one at least once a year, sometimes twice. Two years after buying Freddie, the O'Neill family purchased two more ewes and had them injected with the vector. The family also paid to have three "master" cows and a dozen chickens given the cure, to provide the household with a seemingly endless stock of fresh veal, milk, chicken, and eggs all year long.

In addition to receiving the vector, every animal on the O'Neill farm was given vaccinations for a range of potential illnesses, including tetanus, enterotoxemia types C and D, rabies, and foot rot. Two of the vaccines given to Freddie and the rest of the flock were influenza vaccines.

"We thought nothing of it," says O'Neill. "It was just standard operating procedure to get the vaccinations."

For the next three decades and beyond, Freddie and the animals on the O'Neill farm lived, by outward appearances, healthy lives. The farm continued to thrive, even as the surrounding area grew more crowded with urban transplants. But as the years progressed, unforeseen consequences of the vaccinations were preparing to manifest themselves.

"It's impossible to know exactly how long the sheep flu strain incubated in Freddie's body," says biochemist Arlen Maxwell in a ping exchange. "My theory is that the strain took years to develop. The flu virus probably attacked Freddie's body multiple times, only to be rebuffed by her

immune system. But nature has an unlimited power to
adapt to its environs to suit its needs—to sustain itself. It's
not unlike a group of robbers trying to get into a bank vault.
They may fail the first dozen times they attempt to break in.
But they're constantly scheming, constantly trying to find a
way in. As long as they go unnoticed, it's only a matter of
time before they succeed."

And succeed they did. In early 2059 O'Neill let Freddie
into the house and noticed a deep yellowing in the sheep's
eyes. She drove Freddie to a Goshen veterinarian named
David Millet, who had worked with the family's animals for
years. Unable to properly diagnose Freddie, Millet
suggested that O'Neill leave the sheep with him for further
observation.

"And I almost didn't do it," O'Neill recalls. "I mean, this
was Freddie. We'd had her for years, and there was no
reason to think she wouldn't be around forever. That was
the nice thing about her getting the cure. That's why we let
her in the house. We weren't afraid to grow attached. We
weren't afraid to love her like our own. My kids could nuzzle
in bed with her, and I never had that horrible vision of
having to sit down and explain to them, 'Well, Freddie had
to go to sheep heaven.' That was the blessing of the cure to
me. It wasn't about the wool or the food. It was that you
never had to worry about love ending."

At Millet's insistence, O'Neill left Freddie for the evening
and returned home to her family. When she returned to the
doctor's the next morning, an ambulance and a police car
sat outside his home. O'Neill remembers that a local police
officer came out of Millet's house to tell her that Freddie,
Millet, and Millet's wife had all suddenly passed away in the
middle of the night, and that the paramedic on site had
ordered the area sealed off.

"I didn't know what was going on," says O'Neill, "and
the officer didn't have a good explanation to offer me. I
asked if anything violent had occurred, and he said no. He

said that they appeared to have died from some extreme sickness he'd never seen before. He talked about purple lines on their faces. I just sat there, dumbfounded. I didn't even have time to be shocked."

What the officer had seen, of course, were the first outward symptoms of sheep flu in the United States. Three days ago, working from his home compound, Maxwell sent a ping to the scientific community pinpointing Abby O'Neill's farm as the precise origin of the outbreak that has now killed over one hundred million Americans and five hundred million people worldwide.

"Now that Skeleton Key is widely available, I was able to go out to the O'Neill farm and dig up the contaminated soil," Maxwell explains, "and find traces of remains from the animals the family had to destroy. We now know that those remains contain fragments of the S36 virus. We also know, anecdotally, that the northeastern portion of the country, and more specifically the Berkshire region, is where this outbreak was first reported on the feeds. And medical reports concerning David Millet are, from my search of the indices, the earliest to describe the symptoms, even if the medical personnel reporting on them had no idea what they were looking at. One of the few nice things about sheep flu is that its symptoms are so unmistakable."

For her part, Abby O'Neill has no idea why she and her family were able to avoid contracting the lethal virus. After being ordered to destroy all their livestock, the family moved north, to a very small farm in Northern Ontario. They have no animals; grow only fruits, herbs, and vegetables; and regularly defend their compound from stray Russian RMUs and bandits. Abby has kept every article of clothing ever made from Freddie's fleece, even the items that no longer fit her or her children.

"I don't know why she was the one, of all the animals out there, to start this outbreak. I know we didn't do anything wrong. So when someone tells me that this innocent animal I adored, who was part of our family for so long . . . When someone tells me she was at fault for killing all those people . . . Millions upon millions of men and women and kids and animals . . ."

She holds up a pair of blue mittens and kisses them.

"Well, that's not fair. It's not fair to saddle all that blame on a single living being. We were just trying to live our lives. We didn't want to bother anyone. Freddie never meant any harm."

DATE MODIFIED:
6/3/2079, 3:11 A.M.

Today's Insurgent

A request came in from Containment to handle the file of one DeFors Lewis of Tysons Corner. I took the file and stared at his picture. He was short and squat, with a thick frizz of curly black hair that washed down past his shoulders and a small bald spot crowning his head. He had a full beard and all the attributes of a lieutenant in a motorcycle gang. A true organic, he was in his late forties. His current mailing address listed him under the alias Murray Holdman.

Matt bought a new armored plug-in last week, and this was our first chance to use it. It's very big and very orange, with a giant plow attached to the front. It does not get good wattage. I spray-painted HAVE A NICE DAY on the front of the plow. I thought it was a nice touch. We nicknamed the thing Big Bertha.

I opened the doors to the East Falls Church compound, bay number eight, and Ernie drove in. We could hear a handful of people just outside the bay doors. Usually, they go away after a while, but we were pressed for time given the inevitable traffic. Some of them were scratching—looking for a crack in the facade to pull at. I went to the front of Bertha and cranked the hoist on the plow, lifting it off of the ground. Ernie fired the engine. Two town guards stood with us in the bay, rifles at the ready. Ernie gave me the signal. I threw open the latch and leaped into the plug-in. Ernie put it into drive and gunned it. The plow bashed against the stacks of rubber bumpers bolted to the bottom of the bay door, causing it to fly upwards like a loose flap. The door banged back down on Bertha's padded roof as Ernie took her all the way out. A handful of people got knocked back by the force of the impact. Ernie laid off the gas and edged the plug-in through the crowd. The bay door swung back down too quickly and violently for anyone to get inside. One glimpse of the guards inside the bay and most of them scrammed anyway.

A couple of people outside the compound threw themselves at the plug-in while others just stared. The rain was steady, and I saw more than a few people with their heads tilted back and their mouths stretched wider than coffee cans, catching as much rain as they could—baby birds waiting to be fed by God. Everyone stayed clear of the plow. A random man lazed on the hood, staring at us both. He pantomimed for a drink of water. Ernie paid him no mind as he turned on the music and gradually sped up. He even started chatting. "They ran out of gas, you know. The military."

"So I heard," I said.

"Except in the missile silos. That's it. That's the only gas left."

"Uh-huh."

"That's the only thing holding Solovyev back. Can you believe it? That little bit of gas?"

"Dude, I know you're used to driving with people on the hood, but I'm getting distracted."

"Oh, him?" He jerked the plug-in leftward, and the vagrant rolled harmlessly off to the side. "Sorry. It's like forgetting to put on the wipers at this point."

We got onto the main road and joined a morass of makeshift electric tanks—old plug-ins covered with scrap picked up at a car graveyard. Layers upon layers of old sheet metal fused together and piled onto their frames, like a child who decided to put on all his clothing at once. We inched forward. Homeless people lining the shoulder occasionally tried to pry their way into our plug-in, only to give up. I saw one of them successfully weasel into a poorly fortified plug-in up ahead. The driver pulled a gun. And eventually he got back out and left the driver alone, a touch of embarrassment crossing his face.

I tried to ignore the commotion outside as best I could by perusing stories on the WEPS.8 screen. Ernie was right about the gas, of course. Capt. Strong's feed said that most of the gas left on the continent is tucked neatly away in private compounds and forts. Matt has a small reserve of it on hand. He doesn't tell us where it is. Says it's for the boat.

I noticed a hangnail on my thumb and ripped it out with my teeth; blood leaked out onto the ridge of my cuticle and into the small gutters on either side of the nail. I licked away the blood, but the crevices just kept filling up again, unyielding. Blood after blood. I bit down on my index finger and tore off the top layer of the nail, then spat it onto the floor mat. My guns kept me company in the passenger seat.

The address we were given was located off Dolley Madison Boulevard, in an office-park compound in a cul-de-sac. The street was packed with plug-ins—on the grass, double-parked against the sweep of the curb. Ernie drove another mile and found a place to leave the plug-in on the shoulder. I stashed one gun in the back of my waistband and tucked another into my boot. We both put on our riot gear. There was an arepa stand nearby. I bought one, along with an orange soda. As the vendor handed me the soda, a vagrant ran by and intercepted the exchange, running away with the drink. He chugged it immediately. He stared down my arepa. I stuffed it into my mouth as fast as I could, felt the roof of my mouth burn, and spat it back out. The vagrant ran and scooped up the chewed-up food for his own. He saw the rifle in my hand and the license hanging from my lanyard. He didn't care.

We walked through a mess of tents and grills to the main entrance of the compound and waited. The grid shut down, and I saw the stoplight on the boulevard go out, though I don't remember if it was functional to begin with. A man walked out of the gate five minutes later, and we accosted him inside the entrance bay. We didn't need to say anything for him to know what we required. He keyed in the code for the second door, and we were inside the wall.

The office park was a series of somber town-house rows built up ten stories high. All gray, drab on top of drab. The rooms inside were divided down to nothing, like little cubbyholes, each with its own pathetic little window. I checked the address. It was five houses down. Ernie moved along the wall and stayed low. I saw a brown wooden fence, scaled it, and found myself in an empty backyard outside a dentist's office. In front of me was a narrow stretch of green. The dentist, framed in one of the windows, stopped his drilling and stared at me, then went back about his business. I gingerly walked down four houses. A small partition jutted out between them, which made for excellent cover. I saw no one in our target's window. Ernie came up on the WEPS.

"Confirmed?" he asked me.

"Confirmed."

"Okay."

I heard Ernie crash through the front door. No shots were fired. Two seconds later a short, fat, bearded fellow came running out of the back door, armed and barefoot. He saw me and raised his gun—a very big, shiny, chunky handgun. I shot him in the gut, and he lazily somersaulted to the ground, as if tripped by a tree root. He shot the ground as he fell, and a sharp vapor of gunpowder enshrouded him for a moment. The smoke crackled in my teeth. I waited as Ernie came out of the back door and kept his rifle on Mr. Lewis. Mr. Lewis didn't move. The gun smoke cleared, and I advanced on the body, kicking his gun away. It was a Desert Eagle. A show gun. He wouldn't have been able to hit his neighbor's house with it. Mr. Lewis was alive, his doughy torso expanding in and out. I rolled him over. Grass clippings stuck to his bullet wound, and blood rose from the opening like the head of a small animal. The bulb of plasma broke like a bubble and ran down his side in thick streaks, like the legs inside an expensive glass of wine. He tried to spit in my face, but it landed back on his chest and melted into his black T-shirt. I hit Record on the WEPS. Ernie ran back in to secure the house. Neighbors gathered at their windows and stared.

I knelt beside Mr. Lewis. "I need confirmation that you are Mr. DeFors Lewis of Tysons Corner, Virginia."

"Fuck you," he said.

"Do you have a license on you?"

"Fuck you."

"Do you have family members you wish to notify of your death?"

"Fuck you."

"My records indicate that you are the father of Darienne Lewis of 2309 Cribbage Drive in Palo Alto, California. Would you like your soft assets transferred to her? There is no taxable penalty on this transfer."

He thought about it for a second. "Fuck you."

"Dude, it's your kid. If you don't will your things to her right now, the government is allowed to seize them. You don't want that."

He relented. "Fine. You have my approval. Now fuck you."

"We're not done," I told him. "You were tried in absentia for the bombing of a Remo's Tanning Salon in Sterling, Virginia, on May 3, 2077—a blast that injured five people. You were assigned a public defender named Ken Blodgett. Mr. Blodgett presented your case before the Loudoun County district court, defending you to the utmost of his ability. A jury of your peers found you guilty on February 16, 2079. The judge sentenced you to death, and JonesPlus End Specialists, Inc., LLC, was hired to carry out your hard end specialization. This is your final chance to make a public statement. An admission of guilt and remorse will be streamed to Judge Harry Edwards, who sentenced you. Should Judge Edwards be satisfied with your statement, he may see fit to reward your beneficiaries with a one-time $1,800 tax rebate. Would you like to make a public statement of guilt and remorse?"

"I fucking hate you."

"It's your daughter. You have no control over your outcome, but you do have some semblance of control over hers. Your public statement can be just to her, if you like. We can send it to her."

He blew snot out of his nose. "You take your tax rebate, and your little goodbye e-card idea, and you fucking *die*."

"Okay."

I turned off the recording, aimed the rifle at his forehead, and gave the trigger a squeeze. When you fire a gun, the trigger seems difficult to pull, in a physical sense. You have to squeeze it hard, and the second it gives way is when the bang comes, well before you've brought the trigger all the way back. That quick release surprises me every time. I heard a muted thump, like a firecracker set off under a pillow. I watched as the blood and gelatin blew out of Mr. Lewis's cranium in a sudden flare, like flames from a booster rocket. Little pieces of his skull scattered like ocean plastic on the loose grass. Shreds of his scalp ripped open and hung loose. He looked at me, and his eyes were once again those of a newborn. Seeking. Longing to be told everything about everything. All the hate and misplaced righteousness gone.

Ernie came back out with a box of crude PVC pipes and other bomb-making materials. There were also two handguns in his stash. We sealed everything in Ziploc freezer bags and labeled them. I took the official file photos of Lewis's corpse.

"There's nothing else inside," Ernie said. "Just a lot of books. And it's a rental, obviously. No real estate paperwork for you."

"Did you check his fridge?"

"For what? Nitroglycerine?"

"No. Water. I'm thirsty. I'm gonna get a drink and see if he has anything else to eat. Call Mosko for a pickup."

He had bottled water in the fridge, but the setting was so cold that the water had partially crystallized. I took a bottle out anyway and squeezed it until the sides of the plastic hit the iceberg inside. I drank all the liquid in a single gulp. I took the rest for the plug-in.

DATE MODIFIED:
6/23/2079, 6:07 A.M.

The Girl in the Marketplace

The Eden Center compound is accessible from our East Falls Church compound via a network of narrow underground tunnels that can only accommodate foot traffic. It was made hastily by a co-op of Vietnamese store owners who didn't want to lose business from our part of town when it got sealed off. They dug tunnels to us and to compounds all over Arlington and McLean. The tunnels serve as an underground version of Seven Corners.

I like walking down there. The tunnels are little more than giant gopher holes, with halogens strung along the top, and a constant procession of people moving through them like cells in a blood vessel. But the exposed earth is cool to the touch, and I like to stop and press my body against it on days like yesterday, while letting everyone else slip past. It feels like dipping your hand in a spring.

For two decades, Matt has ordered group lunch for the firm, and it's always been a mixed blessing. He constantly asks what we should have for lunch, then shoots down any idea we throw his way. Thus lunch becomes a stalemate that can drag on well past two in the afternoon. I often end up bolting at twelve thirty to get something on my own, because I know damn well that three o'clock can come and go without a morsel in sight.

On Wednesdays the Eden Center plug-in lot becomes home to a market where you can buy fruit and vegetables and dried goods and even some meats. You can get dried fish and shrimp, but they cost a fortune. The Four Sisters restaurant has a booth that sells summer rolls: rice-flour wrappers stuffed with bean curd, mint, noodles, and scallions. These were in my head as I walked through the damp tunnel and up to the surface of the shopping plaza. I had my gun on me and my ES license dangling from my neck.

I walked up the muddy ramp until linoleum emerged beneath my feet and I was in the center's generic atrium. Through glass doors, the market beckoned. I walked through them and found myself outside in the bustling lunch-hour chaos. Workers criss-crossing the pavement, carrying pallets of cabbage on their heads. White-collar workers standing with coffee and sandwiches, look-ing for a place to sit and eat. An abundance of little homemade jewelry booths that couldn't possibly turn a profit. I zeroed in on the Four Sisters booth and got in line for food. I opened the WEPS screen and texted Matt to ask if he wanted anything. He told me to go screw myself.

I clicked off and saw a flash of strawberry on the edge of my vision—a crop of hair that stood out against the mostly Vietnam-ese crowd like a golf umbrella. I turned to it and saw the back of a woman wearing a tight jean skirt and red tank. An impossible body. A slinky gait that begged you to follow in its majestic swag-ger. A sashaying creature that inspired pure want. I abandoned the line and walked behind her, bobbing and weaving through the commingling rush of workers and eaters. I took out the WEPS and got a snapshot for a reverse ID. The proportions were a match. She stopped at a coffee stand one hundred yards away from me and waited patiently for a drink. I walked in a zigzag, flowing with the pedestrians, charging left and right, and slowly getting closer, never moving above three o'clock in her line of sight.

But I fucked up and walked directly into a worker schlepping a box of cantaloupes. They bounced to the ground and broke and gushed on the asphalt. I crouched down and helped the worker scoop up the mess, saying nothing. I kept my eyes on the ground for a moment, that one crucial microsecond when I knew people would turn and look. I let it pass, then looked, and she was gone. I popped up and saw a flash of red sailing to the back of the shop-ping plaza. I broke into a sprint and hurried after her. The Four Sisters restaurant was to the rear left of the plaza, and I saw her rushing for it. I ran through and over and around the masses. A man tried to stop me, and I yelled out "ES! ES! ES!" and the sea parted. She turned and looked at me. Suddenly, we were standing near the Queensboro Bridge, she was blonde, and the eighth floor of 400 East Fifty-seventh Street was being demolished in an instant, my dear friend blown into the atmosphere. Solara Beck gave me the same look she had six decades before: a mix of fear and aggravation I didn't understand then but know every nuance of today. Here she was, the time between now and when I saw her last flattened like a bug that's been stepped on.

I ran into the restaurant after her. The entrance was separated from the main dining hall by an oversized aquarium, and I saw the girl running to the back of the hall through a pristine village of seahorses and clown fish and other inedibles. I wove through the enormous round tables to the back. Lu, one of the four sisters—and the only one who speaks English—waved to me as I passed. I waved back. Solara ran out the emergency exit to the parking lot and grease dumpsters at the back. I ran through the door and into a mess of dented plug-ins. She was nowhere to be found. I took out my gun. The back of the plaza extended to my left, and the outside wall of the restaurant kitchen jutted out on the right. I ran along the outside of the kitchen wall and peered around the corner. I saw the girl forty yards ahead, scaling the center's brick wall. I ran for her. She turned, gun in hand, and fired at me. I hid behind a minivan. She blew out the rear windows and the tires. I looked again and saw that she had made no further progress up the wall. I ran for her, and she threw her gun at me, nailing me in the shoulder. I winced in pain as she got a better hold on the white brick and neared the razor wire on top.

"What are you gonna do when you get up there?" I asked. "That's razor wire."

"I've fought through worse."

"You need to come down. I'm not gonna kill you."

"Fuck you."

I leapt for her and grabbed hold of her ankle, bringing her back down. She fell on top of me, then gave me a swift kick to the head. She kicked my hand to dislodge the gun, but I kept my grip in spite of the agony. She ran for the opposite side of the parking lot. I got up and followed suit.

She was an excellent runner and clearly spent a good amount of time running in marathons and steeplechases and parkour superstar competitions and anything that required a proficiency in bipedal locomotion. I can't say the same for myself. The gap between us widened, and I fired into the air to shock her. She stopped, turned, and then went back to sprinting like an Olympian. She fled around the back of the center and up the covered walkways of the front to the main lobby. Bodies in the way slowed her progress as well as mine. She turned to look back, and I kept my eyes square on her. She went in the lobby and down into the earthen tunnels. Now we were moving single file, with stacks of people in front of and behind us. I rudely cut in front of as many as I could, and I saw her stumble as she tried to do likewise, toppling the man in front of her. Catching up to her, I laid a hand on her shoulder to see if she was okay. She pivoted and punched me in the gut. I grabbed her upper arm violently, like a parent frustrated with a child, and shouldered her into the wall. We held up traffic, and complaints started coming down the line. With my gun barrel now firmly planted in her back, we turned around, and I led her out into daylight in the most uneasy two-hundred-yard walk of my life. We went behind the Eden Center. She turned and slugged me again, just for good measure. I held firm and kept the gun on her.

"Solara, *stop* hitting me."

"You have the wrong person, and I don't know who the fuck you are."

"My name is John Farrell and I am a licensed end specialist. I have your death warrant, Solara."

"My name is Ingrid."

"Yes, I know that's your current alias. Ingrid Malmsteen. You've also gone by Michelle Turin, Liza Harvin, and Jenna Frank. It's all in your file. I have it committed to memory."

"That's great, but I don't have a file. You're looking for some other idiot, somewhere else."

"Do we have to keep doing this? I don't want to have to shoot you just for a positive ID that I already have." I held up the WEPS and showed her Containment's file photo of her.

"Okay. You have my death warrant. So why haven't you shot me?" I hesitated to answer. She assumed the worst, which was halfway correct. "Oh, you gotta be fucking kidding me, fella."

"That's not the reason why," I said.

"Bullshit. I know exactly who you are. You were that creep in Manhattan who was trying to talk me up."

"And then you killed my best friend."

"I didn't kill anyone."

"The file says otherwise."

"The files *lie*. Do you really think every scrap of info you get from the folks at Containment is infallible? Are you that stupid? Is that how you justify going around shooting people?"

"You were found guilty in absentia."

"So is everyone else."

"You were guilty. I saw the way you ran."

"Did it ever occur to you that I ran from you because I didn't feel like being hit on by yet another douchebag that day?"

"I think you're hit on often enough to have a more inventive rejection method than running away."

"Then explain this." She gestured to her own body, which I admittedly lingered on for a fraction of a second longer than was appropriate under the circumstances. "Do I look like I've aged to you since that day? I'm a postmortal. Does that strike you as characteristic of a pro-death terrorist insurgent?"

"No, but you were connected to Randall Baines, and you were spotted at two other bombings within three months of the July 3 attacks. And I don't take that as coincidence. I don't think you just happened to be around, turning away suitors, at those particular moments." I brought down the gun. She didn't move. "Katy Johannson was my best friend," I told her. "She was getting the cure the day I saw you. She was in the doctor's office when the bomb went off. There were no remains of her. They couldn't even find a tooth—nothing they could send to her family to bury in the ground. She was obliterated. I have free rein to kill you, but I just want to know why you ran. That's all. I'm not arrogant enough to believe every woman I approach will throw her arms wide open and leap into my embrace. But you ran away like some-one who had *done* something. And I would like to know what."

Her hair fell in front of her face and she blew it away like it was a rude housefly. She sat down on the hood of a dirty white Nissan and didn't speak for three minutes. Finally, she looked up.

"He was my boyfriend," she said. "Randall. I served as look-out for him three times. At your doctor's office, I was asked to go in for a consult to survey the office. I didn't get the cure then. I was only posing as a patient. But I never planted bombs. I never killed anyone. I just stood there. I was supposed to look out for cops and all that."

"Why'd you help him?"

"Because he was violent. Okay? Violent enough to make me think he was a cloud hovering over the surface of everything. I was chickenshit—I admit it. I'm not proud of it, but I'm not a murderer. I'm sorry he killed your friend."

I was compelled to move closer to her. I had seen this woman in my head for over five decades. The memory of everyone else I knew had grown more distant over that time. My father. My son. Their lives had ended so long ago, they felt like they belonged to another dimension. Sometimes, if I concentrated hard enough, I could remember them perfectly. I could bring their faces and bodies into focus. I could conjure them and spend time with them. Other times, they felt more like vague, wonderful ideas that I couldn't quite fully form. But Solara Beck was different. Her image stayed at the forefront of my memory effortlessly. Immedi-ate, as if she had been walking beside me this whole time. I remembered her exactly as she was, and knew exactly what was different about her now. I knew every hair on her head—from just two glances, fifty-eight years ago. It may as well have been yester-day. She was beautiful and strange and maybe that was the reason why, but there was more to it. There was a sense that I had kept her alive so vividly in my memory because I knew, somehow, that this moment would eventually present itself. Things always change. Perhaps it was raw lust masquerading as a foolhardy sense of destiny. It didn't matter, because I was drawn in regardless. Before this moment, I had assumed I'd shoot her when we met again. Just like anyone else I've shot or stuck with the dose. But now that was the last thing I wanted to do, right or wrong. I didn't feel any anger toward her. I felt charged, like an old V-6 engine ignited after spending decades collecting dust.

"You need to listen to me," I said. "It doesn't matter what hair color you choose or what name you pick for a fake ID. The ES order is binding, and my firm is not the only one contracted to carry out your sentencing. DES is after you as well. You're a discovery many people are eager to make. They won't leave you alone until the order is carried out."

"So, what? I have to go hide in an attic for the rest of my life? Keep a diary?"

"I don't know. Why haven't you explained your situation to the cops or someone?"

"Because Randall would kill me."

"But he's dead."

"But his cause isn't," she said. "They'll kill me. Don't you get that? And there was no point in showing up twenty years ago, when the government found out who I was and had me tried. Because I did it. And they don't give a shit about the why of it. I'm not gonna show up at my own death trap."

Everything about her made me want to act irrationally. "I can help you."

"Why would you help me?"

"Because I was the one who brought Katy to that doctor," I said. "It was my fault. I can't bring her back, but maybe helping you would give me some bullshit illusion that karma has been balanced. Unless you're lying to me."

"I'm not lying."

"Then I can help you." Just telling her I could help her made me feel like a living, breathing person for the first time in a very long time.

"What can you do?" she asked.

"Well, I can kill you. If you catch my loose meaning."

"You mean . . ."

"If I record your exit interview and file your end specialization as completed, that ends the search. We file a certain number of mock end specializations each year, at the request of the government and certain special interests."

"So you stage deaths. The reports are true."

"They are. Old CIA analysts who don't want to be hunted down, witnesses, political donors who have an intolerable number of counts on their rap sheets . . . They go into the database."

She laughed derisively. "You are one twisted business. You know that, right?"

"It's like a messy room. Only the person living in the room sees the order to it."

She looked me over as if I were the only prize left on the shelf to choose from. "All right. How do you do it?"

"I can explain it in the car." I extended my hand to help her up from the plug-in. "You can say no and keep running. I won't shoot you. But I can help because, I dunno . . . It feels like what I'm supposed to do."

She took a few minutes and then tentatively accepted my hand. "All right."

I helped her up. The WEPS buzzed. It was Matt, with an urgent request to sweep an area to the south, near Fredericksburg. Ernie was out on another job. It was all mine. I turned to my new companion. "Come with me. Looks like your demise will have to wait."

DATE MODIFIED:
6/24/2079, 10:09 P.M.

The Sweep

Solara napped in the passenger seat of my plug-in as we sat on I-95 south, traffic moving like food being passed through your guts. Sleeping urchins and families lay on the roadside. Hitchers knocked on the door every ten minutes, their hands swaddled in rags to protect them from germs. Hours passed and the traffic began to thin. Rain pounded down, and I sat on the edge of my seat, trying to see through the glaze on the windshield. We hit forty miles per hour at certain points. I looked over at Solara, who lay curled up under an orange blanket. Her eyes opened and she gazed at the road. She smacked her mouth to get the taste of sleep out. "This is a long drive," she said.

"They all are."

"Where are you taking me?"

"On a sweep," I told her. "Sheep flu victims."

I pulled the plug-in over to the shoulder at a random mile marker. Solara had gotten Skeleton Key, so there was no need for a hazmat. The shoulder was relatively unoccupied, save for a small caravan a couple hundred feet ahead. All I could see was a handful of black people, listening to music and staring at a small grill. They saw us and I mouthed the word to them: "Sheep."

They pantomimed turning a key. They were vaccinated.

We turned toward the woods and could hear sounds of people in the distance. Every distance. Every direction. The woods were full of them, buzzing, the world a giant hive. But no one was immediately discernible. The rain had made the trees wet and black. Thousands of cracked and fallen branches littered the forest floor, the cumulative accomplishment of all those powerful storms piling up on one another, year after year. Litter abounded—wrappers, plastic bottles, e-waste, random car parts. Things once useful, never to be of service again. We cleared through the brush and followed my screen, closing in on a large collection of little white dots. My boots tracked softly atop the large tufts of soaked weeds and old brown pine needles. We passed by four people, naked and fucking. I discreetly whispered a warning to them, and they froze in midcoitus to run, their assorted naked parts flopping around like numb limbs in the thick mugginess.

We came to a redheaded woman slumped against a tree. She knelt by one of the branches, sucking on it like a bone. She saw us. I gave her a warning: "Sheep."

"I saw them," she said. "They're up ahead." She stared at me. She had dull green eyes, like the shards of a bottle thrown into the sea and washed ashore years later. "I know why they're sick. I know why the world got sick. Do you know?" I didn't answer her. She didn't need my approval to go on. "It's the ghosts. It's the ghosts who did this. I hear them. I feel them cozy up to me when I'm asleep on the ground. The ghosts aren't happy with us. They saw us grab more life than they got, and they *raged*. They howled and they shook their chains, and they swore they'd get back at us for being on the right side of history. It's the ghosts who have made this world sick. You don't shortchange the dead. There's a whole lot more of them than there are of us, and there always will be. You watch. They'll claim us all."

I took out a candy bar and gave it to her. She wolfed it down, wrapper and all, and went back to sucking on her wet branch.

We moved forward. A clearing came into view up ahead. We heard moans and rustling. A few steps farther and I could see the muddy tangle of the forest floor give way to pale white and violet webbing. A field of sick. A collection of victims, arranged haphazardly on the ground, faceup and facedown, like a deck of playing cards that had been thrown into the air. Some had already succumbed. But the living and the dead were indistinguishable. I gently nudged each one with my boot, to check for a reflex. Solara stood by a tree on the outskirts and remained fastened in place.

I went to work quickly, sussing out the living from among the human scrap. I tagged their drenched jeans and sweatshirts with a generous swipe of a fat Sharpie. I searched them for identification while I opened the kits and took out the doses. I knelt beside the first victim, a woman in her cure twenties. I gently rocked her shoulder, as if to wake a sleeping child. She opened her eyes. Green gunk slimed her tear ducts. Copper fluid drooled from her mouth and drizzled onto the leaves and needles, leaching death into the soil. I took her license. Her name was Olivia.

She looked at me. "Am I dead?"

"No," I said. "You're very sick. You probably only have about six to eight hours left." The news had no effect on her. I began recording. "I need to know if you have loved ones, Olivia. People you want informed. People you want to leave your belongings to."

She weakly rolled her head over in the direction of a man who was lying faceup in a puddle of standing, fetid water—lounging spread-eagle, eyes open to the sky. Luxuriant in death. You could have put a drink in his hand. He had no Sharpie mark on him.

I asked her if she had any belongings. She took out an old WEPS.4 device. I turned it on and the screen buzzed to life. The battery was still good, but the moisture inside had caused half the screen to turn to randomly colored lines. I sealed it in a bag and marked it for discarding. I presented her with the dose.

"My name is John Farrell and I'm a subcontractor with the U.S. Department of Containment. Containment mandates that all remaining sheep flu victims be swept immediately to prevent further infections. What I have here is one cc of diluted sodium fluoroacetate that will end both your sickness and your life. You will not feel any pain or discomfort, beyond what the flu is causing you right now. Alternately, there is a robovaccine available that will cure you. This robovaccine costs five thousand dollars, and Containment will only accept payment via direct withdrawal through a bank routing number. Do you have the ability to pay for this vaccine?"

She shook her head.

"Then I have to administer the dose."

I rolled up her sleeve. She grabbed my arm. "Wait," she said. "Just . . . one more minute. Please. I'd like one more minute."

I sat back. I looked over to Solara, her eyes never leaving Olivia. The woman looked skyward, through the canopy of harsh, wet branches. Leaves glossy like wrapping paper. The sky gray and flat, as if it had been born that way. Her eyes scanned left to right. Her face was madly perspiring from a broken fever. Big fat raindrops rolled off the leaves above and rinsed the beaded sweat away. She appeared comfortable, if only for a moment. Her irises contracted, as if she'd just been exposed to a flashbulb. Her pupils tightened to snake eyes on a pair of dice. She turned back to me. "This isn't how I planned on it all turning out. I wanted more than this."

"I'm sorry, Olivia."

"It's okay."

She gave me the nod. I turned off the recording and stuck her with the squeeze syringe. Her body quickly deflated, nesting within the compressed underbrush. I went around and finished the sweep. Most of the victims were unable to speak. As I finished, I could feel the ghosts pressing against me. I looked up and envisioned myself at the bottom of a vast ocean floor, white phantasms densely packed above and around me, like swarms of giant jellyfish. I imagined them multiplying by the second, an army of the dead ever growing and compacting in the emptiness. Frenzied. Screaming. Moshing. Coiling around my body and constricting it. Slipping into my mouth with every breath. They were screaming silently at me, as if I were staring at them from a soundproof room. They crammed in tighter and tighter. I held my breath. Solara came up and tapped my shoulder, her red hair matted down by the falling rain.

"Are you all right?" she asked.

"I'm okay," I said. "You?"

"Not at all."

"Come on. There's beer in the backseat."

I unloaded bags of quicklime onto the victims and drew a red circle around them, then nailed the warning sign down into the ground, and that was that. I hurried Solara back to Little Bertha. She got in the passenger seat, and I threw my key fob on the driver's seat and closed the door to walk around. I went to open my door and it was locked. I looked through the window at Solara, who had her right hand on the lock and her left hand on the fob. She looked at me, scouring my face for signs of rage, but I wasn't mad. If I were her, I'd have considered it too. She relented and unlocked the door.

"I'm sorry," she said.

"It's not a problem. I get it." I felt an uncommon comfort in her presence.

"You do those sweeps a lot?"

"Not as often as I used to. They tend to let the outbreaks go unless they come near the DC area. Has PR value—proactive, merciful, whatever."

"It's creepy to be in the center of it. To see it all laid out like that."

I grabbed two beers from the backseat and opened them. I offered one to her. She rebuffed me at first, then thought better of it and grabbed the can.

"My sister died this way," I said. "A call came in one night from her. I got bad vibes from it. Ever have that feeling, where you feel compelled *not* to answer the call, as if you already know something horrible awaits you on the other end?"

"Of course."

"I'm the sort of person who always has to answer the phone. I've tried screening calls before, and I never make it past the third ring."

"I have that problem."

"So I opened the WEPS screen, and all I could see was the leg of Polly's coffee table, with the sofa parked behind it. I could hear labored breathing in the background, and I screamed out for her, but all I could hear back was this unintelligible whisper. Then a hand reached into the frame. There were dark, violet spiderwebs from the fingertips down through the wrist. I remember that hand, that *thing*. It grabbed the WEPS and aimed it upward at the couch. And there was my sister, sideways on the sofa. There was a copper-colored stain beneath her cheek where she'd been drooling on the pillow. And it was all over her ears and hair, like an oil slick. Her eyes were all yellow like old parchment paper. She was hacking and wheezing, and I felt like I was holding on to her hand and she was dangling off a cliff, with gravity slowly loosening my grip."

"Could she talk?"

"Barely. Every sentence seemed to take a year off her life. She had been with me in the hospital a few months earlier, when I had a heart attack. There was an outbreak of sheep flu in that hospital and, I dunno, it must have incubated in her body like they say it can. She and her husband had been quarantined, and she told me DES was coming for her, and I begged her not to do it. I begged her to wait for a cure. I wanted to deny it all. But that was what she wanted. She said she couldn't live with the dread. That there was nothing left but the dread. She said she was relieved that this was the last decision she ever had to make." I turned to get another beer for myself. Solara remained attentive. I felt a need to funnel every crevice of my soul into her brain as quickly as possible. "The thing that killed me was that I couldn't see her. You know? All I had was her image on the WEPS. Everything felt so disconnected. She let the WEPS go, and I saw her kid crawl into the screen, and he was already discolored too. But he knew nothing—you know what I mean? His demeanor was exactly the same as it was before he got sick. He was too young to let anything ever hurt him. I wish I had that power sometimes. I wish I could float blissfully above it all, in the world but not of it. But I can't. Anyway, that was the last I saw of my sister's family."

"And you never got sick?" she asked.

"I thought I would. I thought, '*I* was in that hospital. Matter of time.' But here I am. I'm the last. I'm the leftovers." I finished my beer in three quick gulps. "I'm sorry. I spaced out there."

"It's okay. I had a mother figure I watched go on the WEPS."

"'Mother figure?'"

"My mom committed suicide when I was fourteen."

"I'm sorry. I didn't mean to pick a scab."

"It's okay," she said. "My father was rich, but he abandoned us when I was four and went off to start another family, and they were the lucky generation of his family tree. They were the ones whose existence he acknowledged. My mom, brother, sister, and me he treated like a fungus in the crawl space. So she was left to deal, and it must have been too much, because she turned out bipolar. A manic among manic-depressives. Every conversation with her was like spinning a roulette wheel. One day my brother found her in her room. He never told me exactly what he saw. I had a friend, and her family took us in. Her mom became ours, so to speak. Then ten years ago . . . you know."

"I know."

"I saw her dying on the screen, and I had to fight the urge to turn it off, because it was just so easy to do that and not deal with it—to let her be some distant problem I didn't have to acknowledge. But I left it on for as long as she let me. Then they took her off, and that was that. Another lamb." She held the wet beer can tight. "This is good beer."

"I've kept you too long," I said. "Let's do what we need to do for you."

I fired up the plug-in, and we drove back onto the highway, cutting through the gathering mob of wraiths and specters.

DATE MODIFIED:
6/25/2079, 12:04 A.M.

The Birthday Girl

I booked a hotel room inside the Fredericksburg compound, to avoid driving at night through the freelands around I-95 north. I asked Solara if she wanted a room of her own. She said one with two beds was fine. I checked in alone. Solara waited in the plug-in, and I led her to the room via the fire stairs. I fully expected her to be gone by the morning, but I didn't mind letting her slip out of my grasp. Truthfully, I still hadn't quite figured out how to stage her mock end specialization. You need clearance from Containment to do a mock ES and wipe away the file. And they were unlikely to grant me such permission for a convicted domestic terrorist.

Solara slept in her clothes. I had extra shirts in the plug-in and told her she could have a fresh one for the morning. I'd had too much beer on the drive to the hotel, and I woke up at three since alcohol gives me insomnia. I turned toward Solara and could make out her form in the opposite bed. Still there. She'd toss and turn on occasion, and I would fret that I'd woken her up. But it was nothing. I kept my gun under my pillow.

Being stuck awake in the middle of the night feels like prison. There's nothing to do with yourself, especially when someone else is in the room. I couldn't turn on the WEPS or read a book. I didn't want to get up and leave Solara in the room alone. What's more, I was still horribly tired, and so jealous of Solara for being comfortably ensconced in easy slumber. My eyes didn't want to open, and my body had no wish to rise. But any further rest was out of reach. I could hear families packed into the adjacent rooms, using them as temp housing—babies crying, impossible to soothe. I let my mind go free, and it took me to familiar, unwanted places. My mother and father. My sister. Katy. Alison. David. Sonia. I mouthed their names. I heard myself whispering hello to David as if he were in the room and still an infant. I couldn't make out his face, but I could feel myself pressing against his warm, pink skin. *Hi, little fella! Hi!* I hugged the pillow as if I were greeting my father at the Waterbury train station. I do this sometimes. I try to comfort myself with their imagined company. And then they slip away again.

I thought about the clients and the parade of government-approved bowling pins I had to knock down. The Greenies. The weird secessionists in their little neofeudalist bunkers. The insurgents. The tax cheats. I thought about them, the gorgeous sheen of vengeance long ago scratched away entirely. Then my conscience would toss those nagging little queries back into the hole it had dug just for them. My visions turned sexual, and I had to strangle my mind to keep it from fantasizing about the creature resting ten feet away. Even from my bed, I could smell her. She smelled so good, I wanted to scream. I looked at the glowing red digits of the old-fashioned hotel clock. It was three thirty.

I fell back into a three-quarter sleep at the futile hour of seven thirty in the morning. I got a minuscule dose of rest and woke up to find Solara putting on one of my spare shirts. She was over in the corner, with her back to me. When she spun round, I caught a glimpse of her belly just as the shirt was falling, and I could make out a series of thick scars carved into her abdomen. I opened my eyes wide.

"I didn't mean to wake you," she said. "I wasn't gonna flee."

"It's okay. I know. I saw your scars."

"That's not something I like to discuss."

"No no. You don't understand. The Greenies got me too." I rolled up my T-shirt sleeve and showed her my bump. "It used to be my birthday," I told her, "but I had them fix it. Well, fix it as much as it could be fixed."

"Mine wasn't Greenies. It was Randall."

"Jesus."

"He found out I had gotten the cure. So he had a friend hold me down, and he took a coat hanger and made his little Picasso."

"I'm sorry."

"Don't be. He dumped me after that. If I had known all it took to be free of him was a little branding, I would have let him do it much earlier. He's what I fear. He's what I've always feared. Even now that he's dead. Especially now, because he bequeathed his hate to so many. I don't know what they look like or which one's coming for me. I never know who's gonna be lurking around the corner. The police and the end specialists and the nutjobs out in the freelands, that's all no big deal. But I know Randall's folks have an eye on me. I know there's an hourglass with my name etched on the side."

She raised her shirt. I saw the date hewn in jagged tears, as if it had been done with an old fork.

$$6/27/99$$

"I turn eighty tomorrow," she said. "That's when he said they'd see me again. That's my expiration date. That's when I go bad."

"I can fix this. I can get that removed."

"You aren't the first to offer."

"Yes, but I may be the first in my industry to make the overture." I decided in that second to stage her death myself and file it as if it were a real ES. I didn't give a shit about the consequences. "I can wipe out the scar, and your file, and I can house you in a compound the insurgency wouldn't dare touch. They choose much easier targets. Plus, it's my own place. No roommate. You'll have free run of the joint."

"Why would you do that for me?"

"I already told you why."

"No. That's not all of it." She glanced down at herself. Her shirt (my shirt) was still bunched on the left side. Her skirt rode low on her waist, and I could see the curve of her bare hip, a tiny hipbone poking out amid her tender flesh. I felt cosmic at the sight of her, like I could blow apart into a hundred million suns. She fixed the shirt, and it fell all the way down her body. "Is it?"

She was waiting for me to make an idiot of myself. I resisted. "It is," I told her. "I have very little to hang my hat on, but I do pride myself on having some semblance of professionalism."

"So your thoughts are pure right now?"

"Pure as cotton."

She sighed. "I'm tired of men falling in love with me."

"I don't doubt that for a second. But I have been doing this for two decades. I don't like to mix love and death."

She held her gaze on me, and I gave her the very best poker face I could muster. I loved her the moment I saw her in the market. Maybe I'd loved her for far longer.

But miraculously, she bought it. "All right," she said. "Then I guess it's time for you to kill me."

I showered and packed up. Solara threw up in the toilet. She wasn't really going to die, but she said it made her nervous all the same.

I took out the list of questions for the interview and ran through them with her, asking for fierce hostility in the interview. I showed her the shot of saline that would be playing the part of SoFlo. Then I studied the map on the back door of the hotel room and blocked out our choreography. I hung my license around my neck, took out my gun, placed it against the small of her back, and escorted her out of the room. Families and men in cheap suits flooded the hallway and skittered around like vermin. I led Solara back to the fire stairs and down to the ground floor. We walked down a crowded hallway until I saw an entrance to the hotel lounge's kitchen. I whispered for Solara to go, and she broke free from me, running into the kitchen. I chased after her and tackled her into a hard metal dolly filled with dishwasher racks. Plates and glasses crashed to floor as the cooks stared and backed away. Solara kicked and punched and clawed my face until I fired in the air to make her stop.

"I can either shoot you or you can stop on your own," I told her.

She relented. I moved to begin recording, then turned to the kitchen staff. "I need this area clear!" I shouted. They pushed out the front, and I hit Record. "I am asking for confirmation that you are Solara Beck of Santa Monica, California."

"No," she said.

"Do you have a license on you?"

"Kiss my ass."

"Do you have family members you wish to notify of your death?"

"I don't have to tell you shit."

"My records indicate that you are the aunt of Kitana Beck and Elise Beck of Arlington, Virginia. Would you like your soft assets transferred to them? There is no taxable penalty on this transfer."

"Fuck you!"

"Come on. Give it to the nieces. Do something right for once in your life."

She spat out the agreement, like they all do. "Fine."

"You were tried in absentia for being an accessory to the bombings of nine separate doctor's offices in New York, New York, on July 3, 2019. A public defender named Vincent Scagdiviglio presented your case . . ." And on and on I went. "Would you like to make a public statement of guilt and remorse?"

She looked away, then turned back to the camera defiantly. This was not her first screen test. "Guilt? Remorse? Are you fucking joking? I never did anything wrong. You people chase me for decades, and now you want me to say I'm sorry while you fucking kill me? Why? So you can look good? So you can feel like you did something great for humanity? You people are the most hypocritical piles of shit to ever walk the earth. You're gonna get what's coming to you, I swear to God. And when you do, I'll watch your blood run from heaven's front row. Fuck you."

I left the WEPS on for false posterity, took out the saline tube, and jammed it in her thigh. Her eyes kicked back and closed, and she gave a little snort and held her breath for ten, twenty, thirty, forty . . . I took her pulse, then called in the time of death. When I shut off the WEPS, Solara stayed limp on the ground, just as I asked. I took the file photos of her "corpse," then I took her WEPS from her skirt pocket and smashed it to bits under my boot. A short-order cook walked in as I was about to collect the body. "Get the fuck out of here!" I screamed. He ran away.

I circled behind Solara and cinched my hands just below her breasts. I dragged her out of the kitchen and through the back entrance of the hotel to my plug-in, which was waiting nearby. I threw open the back door and laid her inside. The WEPS started going bonkers as I tossed the blanket on her and closed the door. It was Matt.

"Solara Beck!" he shouted. "Solara Beck! Holy shit, you found the little firecracker!"

"I did."

"You get to pick lunch when you get back. No lie. I'll let you pick anything, and I will go get it personally."

"I'm tired. I'm going home. I'll be back in tomorrow."

"What about the body? Mosko wants a peek at her."

"I already found a guy to deal with it in the Fredericksburg compound. The body's gone. It's all filed and done."

"Really?"

"Yep."

He looked disappointed, like I had failed to invite him to a good party I was throwing. "Okay."

"One more thing," I told him. "No more sweeps. I don't wanna deal with any more flu victims. Give it to the interns. I want a Greenie tomorrow. Or an insurgent. Someone whose teeth I can kick out."

"Well, aren't you bold? Did DES make you an offer just now? Whatever they're offering, I'll match it, provided it isn't that much more than you make right now."

"I'll see you in the morning, Matt." I clicked off and turned to Solara. "How do you feel?"

"Like I'm dead," she said.

"That'll work."

Then I brought Solara to her new home.

DATE MODIFIED:
6/26/2079, 5:17 P.M.

"They wouldn't stop eating"

No gangs swept by on the drive back home. We talked for hours and could have talked for hours more. I brought Solara into the Fairfax compound (the guards at the gate knew me and didn't bother to check the back of the car) and ran over to a drugstore to buy her some basic necessities, including one of those old-fashioned, nongenetic hair-coloring kits. She had been staying with a friend and had little interest in going back to fetch her clothes, so I grabbed a handful of items at the Dress for Less and threw them on top of the cruddy blanket in the backseat. I bought her a new WEPS with a clean IP address and registered it in the name of Katie Baker. When we made it to my place, it was night all over again. I have no concept of days anymore. Just long patches of haze and glow.

My energy was sapped. Solara used my WEPS to erase all of Ingrid Malmsteen's social accounts, as well as the ones the real Solara Beck still kept active. I asked her not to use the new WEPS to search for anything related to her old self, lest the search engines solve her new identity in a matter of frames. I asked her if she felt like watching a movie, and she said yes. So I overcooked a frozen pizza and gave her half as we sat down to watch. She sat on the couch, I on the recliner. Both of us craving distraction.

It was a bad idea to choose *The Coldest War*. I should have chosen a movie I could watch with my mind and body set firmly on autopilot. Instead I chose an Arctic War documentary that on the cloud had elicited the following samples of horror and outrage:

Carl Laing:

Filmmaker David Coggeshall gets great interviews with soldiers and generals who had a hand in the war that killed over ten million people and led to the eventual Russian annexation of Alaska and Canada. But it's his moments with people on the outer edges of the conflict that bring the entire disastrous conflict into sharp relief. One of those moments includes an interview with an Alaskan woman named Sadie Carruthers.

Alaska, as you know, served as the base for American operations during the war. What most Americans don't know is that the state, along with all other countries with landmasses close to the Arctic Ocean, was ravaged by Russian and American RMUs who had deserted the conflict and began pillaging at random. Sadie tells the story of soldiers from an American RMU who infiltrated her home and began eating everything in sight, including the houseplants. These American soldiers were part of an early test program for the Skeleton Key vaccine (Russia had a similar program in simultaneous development). And because the vaccine eliminated weight gain, many of the soldiers, according to the film, gradually increased their food intake to ten thousand calories a day, sometimes higher. Coggeshall found WEPS footage of an unidentified Russian RMU feasting on a live seal, devouring it until nothing but bones were left. Even from a distance, you can see the blood coating the soldiers' faces. It's far more terrifying than any horror film you'll sit through this year.

"We had Russian *and* American RMUs sweep through our home, and they wouldn't stop eating. Ever," Carruthers said. "We'd stored five-pound bags of rice in our basement, and they found them. They opened them up and guzzled them uncooked, as if they were bags of crumbled potato chips. I lived in constant fear that they would return and try to eat me if I had no food around. I know for a fact that a woman outside of Barrow was eaten by AWOL Americans. You've heard stories, I'm sure. We called them LLs: the 'living living.'"

The living living. That's what the Arctic War helped produce.

* * *

Emily Hinton:

Coggeshall interviews army ranger Michael Armstead, a "super warrior" who has served a mind-boggling fifty consecutive tours of duty, which isn't uncommon in the ranks today. Armstead explains that many of the American RMUs are not only converted collectivists and ex-cons but also longtime veterans such as himself. "You're talking about people who have given decades of their lives to fighting on the front lines for our country," says Armstead. "The military isn't simply going to kick them out because they're too shell-shocked to serve anymore. Most of the super warriors with thirty tours or more were given free rein by the army to do as they pleased. I know I was. It was half 'we trust you' and half 'we don't know what else to do with you.' Now, think about what fighting and killing for that long does to a man's psyche. I've been fighting for fifty years, and I'm relatively normal for my group. But there are others who have been fighting forever and can't imagine living day-to-day without experiencing bloodshed. And they're still physically able to make that happen. Those are the men who went pillaging in Alaska and Scandinavia. Those are the ones who became their own armies."

* * *

Evan Bruni:

You see satellite photos showing the rapid expansion of the number of ships and rigs in the Arctic over the course of the past decade. The boats and people seem to multiply exponentially, as if grown from spores. And most tragically, you see photos of seemingly endless patches of ocean that have dead whales, polar bears, and other marine life floating on the surface. There's a shot of a Russian aircraft carrier plowing through a field of dead sea lions, their bellies turned up to the sun and blown open by the foul gas that was trapped inside. You can see the seagulls feasting on the carrion. You look at this floating mass of death and you think to yourself that they died to make room for us. There are no more stones to overturn. There is not a swatch of land that doesn't bear our footprint. We are everywhere— and we are increasingly alone because of it.

When the movie ended, Solara looked to my printer. I have a laptop with a scrubbed IP address, and that's the one I use to print out new documents for our mock end specialization clients. The official U.S. government site I use to create the documents is monitored. But the fifty thousand illegal Russian mirror sites are not. Sitting in my printer tray was a fresh plug-in license for Katie Baker. She turned back to me.

"Is this stupid?" she asked.

"What?"

"All this stuff you're doing for me. Is it stupid? We're all gonna die soon anyway."

"You'd be surprised at what people can live through and how much of it they can live through."

"Do you have kids?"

"I had a son. He was killed by the insurgency."

"So that's why you became an end specialist."

"No, I became an end specialist because I like it. What about you? Kids of your own?"

She placed a hand on her stomach and made a little circle.

I was floored. "Get the hell out of here," I said.

"Fourteen weeks."

"Who's the father?"

"Some asshole who'll never get to see what comes out of this body." She sipped a Dr Pepper. "When I was in my thirties, I had abortions. Three of them. After the third the doctor told me I could never have kids again. That was my penalty for procrastinating, for being selfish. Then I got Skeleton Key, and the doctor forgot to tell me that all those little fancy robots would do me the added courtesy of repairing my mangled uterus. He never told me to start using birth control again. It's funny what doctors decide to tell you and what they decide to keep from you."

I stared at her with huge eyes. "It's a miracle."

She glanced at the end credits of the movie. "No, it isn't."

DATE MODIFIED:
6/27/2079, 5:59 A.M.

"This is the next logical step"

Metro was down today. I walked the handful of miles underground, joined Ernie at the East Falls Church compound, and we set out in Big Bertha. On our way to Bethesda, we got stuck in the center of the American Legion Bridge, and I peered over the barrier down into the overflowing, toxic Potomac below. The little dock shanties jutted out into the wide path of gray sludge. I saw men in crude gondolas navigating the river with long paddles, there for God knows what reason. I saw bonfires sporadically lining the banks, with burnouts and addicts standing around the flames, content to stare. All of them were destitute, picked clean by gangs and left with nothing more to ransack. Reams of homeless men purporting to be Arctic War veterans wandered through the middle of traffic, eager to sell dandelions and any other colorful weeds they had found in the ground.

I turned from the river and stared at the dry-cleaning hook above the truck's door. Solara dyed her hair this morning. I chose brown at the store. I don't think I chose it deliberately, but who knows if that's the truth. When she came out of the bathroom and let her new hair unravel, I found myself devoid of anything but primal urges. I thought of Alison as I looked at Solara, and the two merged in front of me into some new, otherworldly lifeform. Something better than anything that came before it. I couldn't be around her without feeling like a hurricane someone trapped in a box, so I made her breakfast and left her alone as quickly as I could. My brain stayed dialed into her frequency every waking second thereafter, and I don't think that'll be changing anytime soon.

"You wanna look at the file?" Ernie asked.

"No."

I let go and gave myself permission to imagine doing everything to Solara that I knew I wanted to do. Vagrants bashed on the side of the plug-in, and I didn't flinch. Ernie had the WEPS radio on, and I heard something about China bombing Khabarovsk by accident while conducting a standard self-eradication. I heard it, but I didn't hear it. I told Solara not to contact me while I was out on duty, and I found myself hating that rule despite its obvious need. Sometime in the middle of this internalized riot, we arrived at the Bethesda compound.

The address was 4912 Cedarcrest Drive, a small split-level house located within the NIH walls. It was a nicely landscaped home, with a white stone-lined path to the door and perfectly manicured shrubs and magnolia saplings dotting the outside. Fresh mulch had been spread, making the garden smell like my shoe after stepping in dog shit. A little black-and-white mutt was tethered to a post in the front on a retractable leash. He ran for the plug-in until the cord had no more slack, and then he started barking, nearly choking himself as he struggled to advance.

I opened the file on the WEPS and saw a little old lady staring back at me. The name on the file was Virginia Smith. She wore glasses with lenses that were no more than an inch in diameter. Dangling from her neck was a thin gold chain and a pendant with a small girl's silhouette. Her birthday was March 1, 1950. She had a cure age of seventy-four. I turned to Ernie. "What is this?"

"It's the file," he said.

"This woman isn't an insurgent. A softie? Matt booked us a softie today?"

"She didn't file an RFE."

"Then what the hell is this? Ernie?"

Ernie looked at me like he had just gone looking for something and returned with no clue as to where it was. "She's just old, man."

The dog barked and jumped onto its hind legs and fell back down, over and over. Virginia Smith opened her front door and looked out at Big Bertha, this orange monstrosity marring her perfect little cottage. She stared at us through her storm door, and I felt myself about to retch. She opened the door and approached.

"Why didn't you tell me?" I asked Ernie.

"You didn't want to be told. You were off in la-la land."

"I'm calling Matt."

"He won't care."

Mrs. Smith knocked on my window. I rolled it down. She looked like a human keepsake. She saw our licenses hanging from our necks. "Can I help you gentlemen?" she asked.

I lied. "I'm so terribly sorry, ma'am. My friend and I took a wrong turn, and we just need to recalibrate the GPS."

"Oh, I could help you. Where are you going? I know the streets quite well."

"You know, I didn't even get the address right," I said. "I have to call my friend and double-check it."

"Can I get you boys some water or some zucchini bread? I just baked it fresh."

"No thank you, ma'am. We'll be out of your hair in just a moment."

"Okay. Well, I hope you boys get where you need to go."

"Thank you."

She turned to the dog. "Momo, no barking!" The dog ignored her and kept lunging. She stood in her yard and watched us.

I frantically dialed Matt. He was painting his deck. "You calling about China nuking Russia 'by accident'?" he asked. "That is some crazy shit."

"What the fuck is this?"

"What is what?"

"Virginia Smith," I said.

"Oh, that. That is our initial foray into the Senior Management Program."

"Jesus Christ!"

"Why are you freaking out about this? We've discussed this for the better part of a decade."

"And I said I didn't want to do it. And you said you didn't want to either."

"That's because everyone says no to everything until they have to say yes."

"What do you mean?" I turned to Ernie. "What does he mean?"

"He means the program is mandatory," Ernie said.

"We don't do it, we lose our license," Matt explained. "All of us. We lose the benefits. We lose the government protection. Not only that, but anyone who says no goes right to the top of the program's 'to do' list. Isn't that neat? I'm a hundred and four, John. I'm too old to make the cut. And so are you."

"They can't do this," I said.

"It passed Congress. What do you want me to say? 'No, that didn't happen'?"

"But millions have already died."

"It's not nearly enough. You know that. Whack one mole, a dozen more spring up. How long was your drive this morning? Eh? Come on, you knew this was coming. This is the next logical step."

Momo the dog pulled up his stake and reached the plug-in at last. He scratched and barked, and I saw the tip of his nose pop up in the window every other second. Virginia Smith stayed where she was and now looked openly suspicious of us. I grew flush, every capillary in my face flooded with hot blood.

"We can't do this," I told Matt.

"We have no choice."

"I've used that excuse before. You only get so much mileage out of it."

"So this is the imaginary line you draw, Johnny Boy? This is where your appetite for this sort of thing goes sour?"

"It's murder."

"My God, it's all the same shit at this point. They all bleed together. If I'd painted the old lady green, you would've blown her brains out by now. You're just drawing lines in the sand to comfort yourself."

"I won't do it."

"Then I have to fire you."

"That's it? Twenty years and this is where we end up?"

He bit into a pretzel and spoke with his mouth full. "Yep. How can I keep you around if I know you won't do what I need you to do? What's the fucking point, John?"

I sat there with the little dog trying to tear his way into the plug-in and Mrs. Smith now dashing into her home and picking up her WEPS to call someone. I looked at her—a small, frightened woman who had apparently overstayed her welcome—and thought of Julia, the first person I personally killed. I killed her at her behest, and who knows if her relaxed and happy face dead on the pillow meant murder or mercy or whatever came in between. It was all death, ugly and exposed. I turned back to Matt. I took his image in fondly, knowing it would be the last time we'd speak.

"Fine," I said. "I'll do it."

"See? That wasn't so bad. Oh, and I never signed away Solara Beck's file."

"Why not?"

He cocked an eyebrow. "Because you're a crummy liar. I don't blame you. She is somethin' to look at. I gave you that mulligan. Not this one. Call me when it's done." He signed off.

The dog yowled. Mrs. Smith grew frantic. I had no way of safely contacting Solara, and suddenly I felt the Potomac widen to the size of the Pacific between us. I turned back to Ernie. "I lied to Matt."

"I know that," he said. "He knows that too."

"You're really gonna do this?"

He gave a flat smirk. "Here's the deal. I've got the wife and the kids and the new kids and the grandkids and the new grandkids to think of. You don't. We're not in the same boat. I have a world of my own I need to protect. I don't like it, but that's what it is. You have more freedom than I do on this one. For me, having principles isn't particularly realistic anymore. It's all about craftsmanship."

I formed a limp plan and committed to it fully, without bothering to play out the endgame. "This is what we're gonna do," I told Ernie. "We're gonna drive away from here, and you're gonna tell Matt that I drew a gun on you and went crazy and forced you to flee without killing that woman. Throw me under the bus. Then I'm gone for good."

"What's the point? There's a stack of Virginia Smiths five miles high after you crap out."

"I don't care. You do what you have to do after this. I won't begrudge you. But don't kill *her*. That's all I ask. Please, Ernie. Just tell him that happened so we don't have to play this out for real. You're my friend, and I don't want that."

Mrs. Smith stared at us through the window in what was now a state of terror. She screamed at the dog to get away from the car. Begged him. Ernie thought it over and brushed aside the arbitrariness of it all for my sake.

"Okeydokey," he said. "She lives to play another day."

He fired up Big Bertha, and we drove back out into the morass, leaving Virginia Smith alone with her little dog, forever confused as to why two end specialists would linger outside her house for so long. I hope she never has to find out the answer. She's one hundred and twenty-nine years old.

DATE MODIFIED:
6/28/2079, 5:03 P.M.

"A very urgent feeling"

I sat in the way back of Big Bertha as Ernie called Matt to tell him that I had stymied the end specialization. Matt shrugged it off. I lay in the back and tried to will myself to telekinetically transport home to Solara. I failed.

The plug-in barely moved along the Beltway. I heard the usual knocks against the side and shouts from crazies bobbing between cars to sell and demand things. It was like being in a car graveyard on a busted conveyor belt. Ernie turned up the WEPS radio, and we heard more bulletins about Khabarovsk being blown to bits, the same updates repeated every half hour. A huge book of tragedy waiting to be filled in. I'm so inured to it all that it may as well have been a report about circus seals. Ernie changed the station and Allan Atkins was busy demanding that we nuke Russia while its back is turned. Ernie tuned to the liberal station, and they demanded the same thing. The voices had become unanimous, as they do only under the strangest of circumstances. My mind played tricks on me. I felt the plug-in rolling forward, only to look up and find us stationary. I began silently counting to a thousand. Eventually, we moved.

At the exit to Route 50, Ernie gave the signal to drop me off. I climbed to the front and shook his hand. "Thanks, Ernie."

"Keep your license around your neck," he said. "No one out there knows it's worthless."

"I will."

"I'll work with Matt to file your termination as a resignation with two weeks' notice. You won't get severance, but you'll get a head start."

"You think Matt'll do that?"

"Yeah. That wasn't as easy for him this morning as you think it was. Now go. Save who you gotta save."

I grabbed two pistols and a box of SoFlo shooters; then I busted the door open and leapt out and sprinted down the exit ramp. Dusk was approaching sluggishly. The compound was five miles away. I tore down 50, running around every derelict and impromptu dead-car camp. The sun was melting into the horizon, and every movement and action I took was with the singular purpose of getting me closer to Solara. My throat grew raw. The compound came into view, and I broke into a gallop, as if trying to run out of my own body. I outran the sun and made it to the gate just before nightfall. My apartment was a mile inside. I walked to rest, then ran, then walked again, then ran the rest of the way.

I reached my building, and when I stopped, sweat began gushing out of me. Little rivers of perspiration built up in fast currents and fell off my face and onto my bright-orange company shirt, making a large dickie of wet material from the collar downward. I went to the water machine and spent the twenty bucks for a bottle. It was empty before I even had the sensation of it touching my lips. I took the elevator up and paused at my door, dying to see her but reminding myself of the idea that she could be long gone—girding myself for disappointment.

I opened the door calmly, and the living room was empty. The bathroom door was open. I looked to the kitchen. No one. I went to the bedroom, and Solara lay on the bed in her jean skirt and a cheap new top, aiming a gun at the door. She saw it was me and lowered it. I wanted to embrace her but fought off the urge.

"You're here," I said.

"Where else would I be?" She looked at my drenched clothes. "What happened to you?"

"We have to go."

I began to pack everything worthwhile.

"What's going on?" she asked.

"Your file wasn't closed. You're still on the cloud. And I quit my job."

"Why?"

"Because they want us to kill the elderly."

"Jesus."

"We have to go. There will be a hard ES order out on me in two weeks. Possibly sooner. We have to get away from here. Our meeting in Fredericksburg is a matter of public record now. Someone could snap our photo in this compound and we'd be boxed in. Pack what you need to pack."

"Why should I go with you?"

"I have an armored plug-in. I have guns. I have supplies. I have money. Not enough to rent an electroplane but a good amount of money nonetheless. I can get you wherever you want to go. Mexico. Canada. We'll move slow, but we'll move."

"I've done Mexico," she said wearily. "I've done Canada. I've done my time out in the wilderness."

"There's nothing left but wilderness. This is what we have to do."

She grew angry. "You lied to me."

"What do you mean?"

"You lied. It's so obvious. You said you never mix love and death, but that's all you do. They're the same goddamn thing to you. Answer me this: Why do you *really* want to help me so badly? Out of all the lives you've taken, why choose me, why choose my child to protect?"

"Because that's what people do, Solara. They go along in life and they figure out who's worth giving a shit about and who they can let fall by the wayside. And all they can do after that is hope against all hope that they cast their lot with the right kind. And that they didn't let slip away someone they desperately should've held onto. So I pick you. It's a gut instinct and nothing more."

"I don't buy that."

I let the curtain fall. "You're right. I did lie to you. But I'm not just drunk on my own hard-on. The truth is that I have a very urgent feeling around you that I haven't felt in lifetimes. Something I thought was dead that's come back stronger than ever. And now I know why I've clung to this rotting planet for so goddamn long."

She sighed. "I told you. I'm tired of men falling in love with me."

"I don't give a shit."

I moved to her and began kissing her. Engulfing her. I wanted to squeeze her until her brain popped out of her head. She kissed me back, and the sky fell down and the universe got sucked into a black hole until it was just the size of us and so dense that a trillion years couldn't even begin to erode it. I threw her on the bed and tore open her shirt and kissed her nipples and licked the numbers and slashes on her belly. She took off my shirt and pants, and I hiked up her skirt, and soon we were connected and I felt as if we were incinerating. I kissed her more and more and wished that one moment could be the entirety of forever so I could throw the rest of forever away. I fell beside her in a naked heap. She took the bottom of my shirt and wiped the sweat off me. Her body radiated.

"I don't wanna die," I told her.

"I don't wanna die either."

"I know there's no heaven. I know it all turns to nothingness. But I fear there will be some remnant of me left within that void. Left conscious by some random fluke. Something that will scream out for this. That one speck of my soul will still exist and be left trapped and wanting. For you. For the light. For anything."

She let her fingers dance on my chest and smiled. She spoke to me, and her deep voice ran through me like a salve, loosening my muscles. "It won't be there, John. Take what you can get now."

"All right." I kissed her. "We better finish packing."

She grew concerned. "So we have to leave right now?"

"We'll be fine. No one's ever gonna touch us."

I went to my old foot locker. My father bought it for me when I went to sleepaway camp decades and decades ago. It was a big, blue, imposing thing, with brass buckles and a locking piece that felt like a paperweight when it swung down into your hand. Two fake leather strips were studded down left and right of the center, like racing stripes. The locker itself was made of a cheap material, something stronger than cardboard but not by much. Carrying it required two men, both of whom would inevitably suffer deeply bruised shins any time the locker decided to bash into them, which was often. I undid the massive lock and threw open the top. The crude top shelf was full of loose bullets. I lifted it up to get at my little armory. I took out a pump-action and showed it to Solara.

"You know how to use one of these?" I asked her.

"Vaguely."

I pumped the shotgun. "You get six shots."

DATE MODIFIED:
6/28/2079, 11:58 P.M.

An Unwelcome Dawn

We were out of the Fairfax compound by 10:00 P.M. and riding off into the endless exurbs straddling I-66 and beyond. My little plug-in would be wiped off the road by Big Bertha, but it still possessed reinforced doors and windows. Most angry vagrants and D36 members were happy to pass it up for weaker, more-penetrable cars. We passed by fires and squatters who lived along the highway wall and decorated it as if each section were the single wall of an open bedroom. Coffin-quiet electroplanes above, discernible only by their lights tracking low and fast through the dark haze, flew filthy-rich people across the sky. We were twenty miles outside Fairfax when I realized my battery was low. There was a safe-house compound five miles on, with a charging station inside. I drove off at the exit and the gate swung open for us.

Inside the compound were rows upon rows of plug-in trucks, hooked up to charging stanchions and parked for the night. I parked the plug-in and hooked it up to a stanchion. The meter gave us seven minutes.

A mini-mall was open in the center of the compound, with food and drinks and VIRGINIA IS FOR LOVERS shirts for people passing through and requiring the easiest gift that came to mind. I brought Solara inside and bought her the six-pack of plastic Dr Pepper bottles and box of Cheerios she picked out. There was a faux-sushi stand inside. I resisted it and got a hot dog instead. Back in the plug-in, we dined in private. She guzzled the soda, and I kissed her when she pulled the bottle from her lips.

"You're very sneaky," she said.

I held nothing back. "I want to marry you. I want to marry you and be that child's father. You don't have to agree to it. I just wanted to say it to you because it feels good to say it. It's all I say in my head when I look at you now."

She laughed. "Who *are* you?"

"Not who I thought I was."

She kicked back in the seat and ate a fistful of cereal. "You make me feel my age, John."

"I'm sorry if I do that."

"No, it's a good thing. No one makes me feel that way. You look at me like you wanna share a lemonade with me."

"I can go back in and get one right now, if you like. Finest lemon-flavored high-fructose corn syrup you'll ever taste."

"I'm fine with the soda, thank you." She swilled the rest of her bottle and opened another. "When I was in my twenties, I always dated older men. Randall, obviously. But others too. I changed my name and moved back to LA after breaking up with him, and I dated a bunch of older guys. Not just old in years but old in looks. If a guy was forty but had a cure age of twenty-five or something, I didn't bother. But if he had a cure age of forty or forty-five, that was right up my alley. I'm sure it was a daddy thing. One of them was this big producer named Bobby. He was, like, fifty."

"Did he get you work?"

"He offered," she said, "but I didn't want to be ID'd. LA back then was . . . I don't even know how to describe it. Everyone who ran out there after getting the cure wanted to be a permanent movie star, but those jobs were already spoken for. The audition lines would wrap around the buildings three, four times over. No one had any money, but everyone was young and gorgeous. People were hooking up in restaurant booths and on street corners. Just this wild, massive, intermittent orgy that creeped you out and drew you in all at once. That whole town reeked of stale sex— the sweat and wet hair and everything else. I got so tired of being around it that I didn't bother going out, even when Bobby had some premiere."

"Was he a really big honcho?"

"He was. He was a *great* bullshitter. He'd always say, 'Baby!

I'll make you a star in this town!' Like it was 1942 and I was some ingenue or something like that. He was a nutjob. But he looked older, so I felt like things were more defined with him. I don't know if that makes sense, but that's how I felt. You're like that, even though you look young. You have that old-man air. But you don't look too shabby, which is nice."

"Why didn't you stay with him? Why didn't you stay in LA?"

"He couldn't keep his hands off anyone. That's men. Even when they find exactly what they want, they'll always ditch it for the sake of variety. As for LA . . ." She lowered her head. "My sister and I were twins. Are twins. Were twins. It's difficult to explain."

"Try me."

She sat silent, as if to summon the strength. "She went true organic, which is funny, given that I'm the one who is now considered a pro-death fugitive. But that was her thing. She refused the cure, and she shacked up with some crunchy eco-lawyer she met online. Every time I saw her after that, it was like looking at my own picture stashed away in the attic. And she'd press the issue. She'd look at me with these judging eyes and say, 'How does it feel?' She'd taunt me. She'd ask me why I wanted to live forever. What good did I do? What purpose did I serve? I didn't have an answer for her. All I said the last time I saw her was that I can't stop living. I just can't. We never spoke after that."

"I'm sorry."

"It's so weird. When we were growing up, we were inseparable. The twin thing. We spoke our own language. Read each other's cues. She was my clone. That's what twins are: clones. I was closer to her than anyone else because she *was* me. And when Dad left . . . Jesus, she was everything. I never thought that would go away. I thought, of everything in the world, we would be the one constant— the one thing I could count on. Then she changed, and it felt like everything else could crumble at a moment's notice."

"What happened to her?"

"She's in a home. Alzheimer's. They post her picture every week on the home bulletin, and I only look at it out of the corner of my eye. I can't stand the thought of her like that. Of me like that. I suppose people like your boss will go hunting her down soon. Blast the old folks' home to smithereens."

"And your brother?"

"Dead. Hit by a plug-in."

"Oh God."

"Eh, he was an addict. There was barely anything to him by the end." She looked up at me. "Everyone I've put my faith in has let me down, John. But I don't know what else I can do but keep trying. Hope to find that one person who'll never go away." She put her hand over mine and squeezed tightly. "I don't know that anyone like that actually exists."

"They do."

"Where are yours?"

"They all died," I told her. "Twenty billion people on this earth, and the only ones that matter are the ones that aren't here. And you."

"Well, ain't that a bitch and a half?"

Just then the WEPS started going berserk. I threw up the screen in midair, and we saw the headline flash under the video feed:

THREE U.S. MISSILES DETECTED APPROACHING RUSSIAN AIRSPACE

The doors of dormant electro-semis opened up, and the truckers began streaming into the mini-mall. I saw screens pop up all over the compound and folks by the dozen making a beeline for the center.

I turned to Solara. "Food."

"Water," she replied.

She grabbed the shotgun. I grabbed two handguns and a plastic bag. We jumped out of the plug-in and ran into the food mart, which was already being pillaged. All the water and milk had been taken. I saw parents with babies in their arms knocking each other over to get at powdered formula and diapers. Truckers who had already gotten what they needed were waving their key sticks at the cashier and telling them to charge them whatever. I saw a case with bottles of some fruity protein drink and threw what I could into the bag before another man elbowed me out of the way and began stocking his own supply. Solara grabbed boxes of candied popcorn and little individual cereal bowls and held on while others tried to pluck them from her arms. She ran out with a meager supply, and I joined her as we dashed for the plug-in. The line out of the compound was already growing. Everyone had gotten what they could get and wanted to flee.

Then the power went out.

Everything at once—every grid down, not just the usual handful. The invading glow that had been the only night I'd known for ages snapped off, and the stars above blasted to life as if thrown on by a light switch—as if the earth had been stripped of its atmosphere entirely. People screamed. I heard a window break in the mini-mall. We got in the plug-in and pulled out into the line. My WEPS.8 network had gone blank. Everyone's had. The satellites weren't working or had been blown away. For the first time since I was a child, the world had shrunk back to my immediate surroundings. Solara. Me. Everyone trapped inside the safe house. That was it. The plug-in was charged for the full forty-eight hours. The crummy food inside would barely last that long.

The line crawled out to the highway. I kept one hand on the wheel and the other on my gun. Solara held the shotgun between her legs, the barrel kissing the floor mat. We made it eight miles, then the road began to choke. Maybe some folks were holding fast in their compounds, but the rest were spilling out onto the road in their plug-ins and scooters and bikes and skates and anything else that would propel them forward and farther away from the coast. After an hour or two, many of the plug-ins died in the road. Everyone began driving wherever stationary objects were not. The median filled with cars, as did the shoulder. Walkers zipped past us and made us feel as if we were besieged. Some knocked to be let in. All were refused.

There was a violent whomp on the passenger-side window,

and Solara jumped in shock. A young man in desert camo was bashing the window with the butt of a gun. I honked and brandished my handgun. He continued pounding away. Clawing. Scratching. Another RMU soldier joined him. They bashed and hammered at the window. Solara raised the shotgun and held it fast at them. I saw one of them break away, jack another car, and quickly eat everything stashed in the trunk. He inhaled the food, as if it wasn't even there. He came back and, together with his buddy, redoubled his efforts on us.

"They can't get in," I told Solara. "They'll give up."

"Then why won't they stop?"

The two soldiers backed off and began conferring. I felt my stomach sucking itself dry.

"We have to get out," Solara said.

"That's just what they're trying to get us to do. Stay calm. Stay cool."

"I can't. I have to get out of here."

"Solara, don't."

"They're gonna shoot!" I saw one of them turn his shotgun on our car and give it a pump. Everything froze for a second. Then I heard a jarring thud on the window and saw the fucker drop from the ricochet. The window was cracked, and now the other RMU soldier was incensed. He took his gun and began laboring at the crack like it was a prison wall.

I ordered Solara to hand me the shotgun. She passed it over, and I traded her the pistol. She gripped it for dear life as the soldier worked tirelessly on the window. I saw the cracks spreading, the glass like a sheet of brittle candy banged against a countertop. I lowered my tinted window and he didn't notice. Solara talked to me but kept her eyes on the growing web. She whispered to me, "What are you doing?"

I unbuckled my seat belt, reached out the window, grabbed the roof with one hand, and hoisted myself up so I was sitting on the car window with my feet resting on the driver's seat. I took the shotgun and aimed it right at the soldier. He looked up just as I was firing. His head blew apart and he fell from view. I heard

Solara yell "holy shit!" and I sunk back into the seat and rolled the window back up. The crack was still there, the window dabbed with blood and unidentifiable bits of human shrapnel. I moved the car forward and squeezed Solara's knee.

"Jesus Christ, John."

"It's all right," I said. "No one will mess with this car after that. There's a Kevlar vest and some duct tape in the duffel. Take it out and maybe we can reinforce the window."

She did as I requested and frantically patched up the window. It wasn't two hundred yards before the road clogged up again, with no passage within eyeshot. She monitored the power meter nervously. "We can't stay in here," she said.

"We have a couple of days."

"Not if we're not moving. I can't stay boxed in like this. I feel like I'm gonna miscarry. There's gotta be a compound we can go to. Somewhere safer than out in the middle of this."

"Okay. Why don't you rest, then? Rest now, even if you can't sleep. Just close your eyes, and when morning breaks, we'll go. We'll have the light." She nodded and closed her eyes. The parade continued all around us, but the car stayed serene.

"Still wanna marry me?" she asked.

"Yes."

"But time is running out."

"I know. That's why it's all that matters."

She opened her eyes. "Okay."

"So we're married."

"Yeah. We're married. I'm your wife, and you're my husband. Does that work?"

"Yes." The car remained in park. I leaned over and kissed her. "I won't leave you," I told her.

"I know."

I heard a growing scream and saw the first RMU soldier on his way back to the plug-in, with a scorched dent in his bullet-proof camo, cursing and shrieking like a rabid animal and unwilling to take no for an answer. He took a tire iron from another plug-in and lashed the window again and again. No more honeymoon. I felt no fear. Doubly strong. I rolled down the driver's-side window again and propped myself up with the gun, but he knew in the nick of time and raised his own handgun up at me.

"Put your fucking gun down!" I screamed at him.

He didn't budge. "Gimme your food and gimme the fucking woman!"

"I'm going to count to three."

"FUCK YOU!" He cocked the gun. I held fast on him. Then I felt a pair of hands grab my vest from the back. In an instant, I was thrown to the ground by another RMU soldier. He rolled me over and pressed my face into the sand, and I heard the first soldier circle around the car and try to get through the window. I heard a blast from the passenger seat, and the fucker fell right beside me. I stared at the hole in his head, the little flaps of bloody skin, moist and glistening and exposed. His head cracked and oozing, like a dropped egg. His colleague sprang up and shouted at Solara. I felt another set of knees pinning me to the earth as the second soldier threatened my wife. He screamed at her, "You fucking bitch!"

She didn't flinch. "I am pregnant and I will fucking shoot you if you don't back off!"

He drew his gun on her. "Give me your food!"

"I SAID I WILL FUCKING SHOOT YOU!"

The soldier walked two paces to the left, out of Solara's firing range. He took out his gun and extended it with his left hand. He could shoot her, but she couldn't shoot him. I struggled to get up, then felt a boot on my temple. The soldier cocked the hammer. "You asked for it, honey."

"NO!" I screamed.

And just then—whiteness. A sickening flash of white, as intense as the back of your eyelids after you've stared at the sun for too long. A white that absorbed everything in its path and turned it inside out in a blinding squall. Like being welcomed to a heaven you know can't be real. Then it began to fade, and I heard the monstrous clap of burnt thunder—as if all the clouds had converged on the world at once. The ground pulsed, rippling like water in a disturbed reflecting pool.

I felt the knees burking me lift away and saw the RMU soldier fall to the ground, clutching at his eyes. A hot gust rolled over us, and I didn't dare breathe it in, thinking it might set my insides ablaze. It passed, and the whiteness receded to reveal an artificial and unwelcome dawn—a Bengal-orange glow on the eastern horizon that signaled to my brain and guts that something was now irrevocably wrong and horrible.

The other RMU soldier fell to the ground. I got up and reached into the plug-in for Solara, who was shielded from part of the flash by the tinted windows. She grabbed my hand, I pulled her out, and we began to run. I looked back and saw a flat, white, billowing corona in the far distance, like the scalp of a star twenty times larger than the sun. The angel of death's halo. The rest of the sky grew darker by the second, and my rods and cones were slow to adjust as everything in front of us appeared only in darkly obscured shapes and blobs. My eyes still strobing from the flash, I viewed the world as if staring through a broken nickelodeon. I tripped and got back up repeatedly. I looked back again and the sky grew sour. Under the orange, a thick black bar emerged. Convex. A rolling, expanding wall of dust and ash.

We sprinted, and I held Solara's hand hard enough to shatter it. Along the way I saw people still bound to the ground, and I reflexively helped them up and prodded them west. Entire families sat in front of their plug-ins, grasping at one another and seemingly incapable of movement. We moved away from the highway, squeezing through the dazed throng and stepping over the blinded and catatonic. At the bottom of a steep embankment we came to a strip of woods and stepped over the dry and cracked branches as best we could. Solara rolled her ankle and screamed in pain. I took her arm and held it fast around my shoulder, carrying her through the mess of brush and rocks.

I looked back, and now the blackening rift had consumed the horizon entirely. I thought of the people I knew who were probably trapped inside. Matt. Ernie. Virginia Smith. All of them burned down to the pure carbon. The thought zipped away, and we came to a wire-mesh fence with no razor wire on top. Beyond, a planned community of tiny Monopoly houses. A loosey-goosey compound. We scaled the wall, along with dozens of other refugees eager to abandon the highway. All the homes were dark. Most of the parking spaces were empty. We bolted for a seemingly abandoned house and others followed suit. A family of six joined me as I busted down the door to the house, and we piled inside. Others came from behind and flooded into the house, as if trying to catch a train about to depart. I pulled down the shades in the living room and searched for a basement entrance. There was a flimsy wooden door next to the kitchen, and I grabbed the loose knob and turned it to no avail. Three of us kicked at the door, and it split in half. We ran down, and a dozen people were already there, making the basement a temporary habitat, cowering in fright.

I apologized for the intrusion. They said it was okay. I found a corner for Solara and me to huddle in and the basement packed tighter. She sank against the conjoined walls, and I offered her the nasty drink tucked inside my vest. She drank most of it, then gave me a look as if to offer me the rest. I shook my head, and she finished it.

We all waited. Someone asked if it was a nuclear bomb that had gone off, and the room replied yes, that's precisely what it had been. A roaring pulse of atomic wind blew over the house, and I could hear the bits of dust rapping on the windows and roof like a plague of locusts eating their way through the countryside. There was a light tremor and people screamed. I held Solara tight and pressed my lips into her hair. I will never leave you. Don't let this be the end. Not when I've just figured it all out.

A bright light emanated from the basement staircase. I

wondered if the power had come back on. A man in the kitchen screamed down to us all. "It's another one!"

The sky howled, and we all sank down, and here we remain, paralyzed.

DATE MODIFIED:
6/29/2079, 6:09 A.M.

The Human Wave

The real dawn arrived, but few of us trusted it. Solara fell asleep for seconds at a time, while I stayed tight beside her. The basement was unfinished, and my legs and butt grew numb from being bolted to the dusty concrete flooring. Moms and dads consoled their screaming kids. Those without children deliberated about what had happened and what to do next. Do we go now? Is everything radioactive? Is the bombing over? What if there were bombs dropped on the nation's midsection? Is there anywhere safer than right down here? One man constantly checked his WEPS screen to see if a connection had been restored—something to let him know that things could be set back in their proper order. His wife badgered him to put it away.

Solara and I shared a box of stale popcorn that she had had tucked away in her pocket, the caramel fused together from the noxious flood of sudden heat from the bombs. She broke off chunks and handed them to me. My hands grew sticky and dirty, and I knew they'd probably stay that way for a good long time. A handful of people left the basement to venture outside. Others came to take their place. A teenage boy went up and came back down to report to his dad. He said there was an exodus in progress. The father said they should wait for it to subside. I did not share his opinion.

"Do you want to leave here?" I whispered to Solara.

"Yes," she said.

"You sure you've got the strength for it?"

"Yes."

I wrapped her ankle with a torn-off shirtsleeve and jammed it back into her sneaker. She handed the rest of the popcorn block to a boy next to her, and his father thanked us. I stood and ges- tured to Solara to help her up, but she waved me off and rose on her own, using the shotgun as a cane. We said our goodbyes and good lucks to the room and ascended.

As we reached the kitchen, I could hear a cacophony of voices. I looked over the kitchen sink, through the cheap, sheer curtain covering the window, and saw a bedraggled army of the living staggering by. I moved the curtain aside, and the tension rod holding it up fell to the counter. The sky was dirty and gray, as if belched up from a smokestack. A dull rain fell on the window, wet soot suspended within the big drops, like water carelessly thrown onto a grease fire. Other people milled about the kitchen and looked out the window with us. Few said much of anything, besides "Jesus Christ" and "holy shit." I didn't mind hearing it or saying it multiple times.

Solara and I walked out of the house and into the human wave. From the east, a rolling mass of humanity flushed out from the trees and roads crept along the landscape like raging flood-waters. The air was thick and choking, as if the atmosphere had been swapped with that of Venus. Thousands upon thousands of people were moving farther inland, compressing the population. Teeming. Swarming. Stretching to the horizon, like a rock-festival crowd waiting for a show that will never go on. Most everyone was armed. Those not on the move were either sleeping on top of plug-ins or on rooftops in the subdivision. Hanging in makeshift rag hammocks from the trees. Dangling there, like large, overripe fruit. Others slept in the tree branches, and the old oaks now appeared to have been built with living masonry.

The crowd lurched west, and I found an odd comfort and secu- rity in its enormity. The limp mesh fence of the compound had been trampled. Solara and I joined the gallery and moved forward, never letting go of one another. I breathed in and the air felt liquid, like I was inhaling everyone else's sweat. Everything seemed precarious. Packs of stray dogs squeezed their way through the bodies, like mice through cracks in drywall. The fuselage of an electroplane lay smoldering half a mile away, papery and broken open like a split cigar. Large circles of fresh sheep-flu dead dotted the landscape like crop circles. Every open spot was covered with humanity—a topography of flesh.

I saw bonfires and groups of drunken people dancing around them. I saw one guy, buck naked, holding up a sign that said WELCOME TO THE END. Another guy, with blond hair, drunk and stoned on hydro, sidled up beside us. "Where are you going?" he asked.

"We don't know," I said.

"Why don't you just stop and chill, brother? Enjoy the time you have left?"

"I don't know."

He took a swig of Popov and yelled at me. "Don't you fucking get it, man? Don't you understand? We're rock stars, man. We are *all* rock stars. We've lived fast, and we're all gonna die young. *All* of us! We're all going out at our peak! We're all gonna be legendary. FUCKING ROCK STARS!" He tripped over a sleeping woman and didn't bother catching up with us again.

We came to a major freelands thoroughfare, and I saw all the plug-ins frozen in place. The ones with any juice left were boxed in permanently and good as dead anyway. Every chain store and restaurant had its windows broken and doors kicked in. We passed secessionist forts with armed men perched atop the walls, defending them from intrusion. Tiny city-states, home to citizens who fancied themselves independent but were ruled by us all anyway, whether they liked it or not. I motioned to Solara to move west by southwest, away from the complexes. We began jagging to the left through the crowd and over the curbs. I looked up, and the sky grew darker and more haunted.

Then we heard gunfire. It came from back east, and I saw a herd of gang members mowing quickly through the crowd, a self-contained riot. Little green heads dotted the mosh. Those in front of them turned to look and fled in panic, pushing forward. The trampling began. Anyone frail or poorly balanced was overrun, and people tripping over them got trampled in turn, until the area swelled with large mounds of the dying. Mountains with no king.

I took my gun out of my waistband and began cutting through people to get us out of the gang's oncoming warpath. I felt the crowd push behind us and grabbed Solara's upper arm to keep the gap between us negligible. In the distance we could make out a small COM compound, and I knew that was the next logical spot on the chessboard. A crowd thirty deep already ringed the wall, and I saw men stacking themselves upon each other's shoulders to get to the top, like a wobbly tower of wedding chairs. Two men held their hands out for another and attempted to catapult him to the top, like clumsy cheerleaders.

The collectivist officials stationed at the top of the wall begged people to stop and either pushed off those who would force the issue or shot them in the shoulder. We were fifty yards away and kept advancing, despite the clear rejection waiting for us. The COM wall guards fired off enough rounds to clear out certain sections of the wall before they filled again with humans scaling. I pushed through with Solara and rounded the compound to the west side, where it faced a patch of woods. The gang was still closing in, but ignoring the COM compound in favor of a business park to the right that was also besieged. The gang bulldozed ahead, scouring its way through the living and the dead.

We touched the wall of the compound, and I looked up to see a guard manning his rifle and aiming it directly at my shoulder. I yelled to him. "Do you know who David Farrell is?"

"David Farrell?" he asked.

"Yes," I said. "David Farrell."

"Yeah."

"I am David Farrell's father. Can you help us?" I held up the ES license that was still dangling from my neck.

"You're an ES, for shit's sake."

"I quit! I swear!"

He rolled his eyes and disappeared behind the perimeter for a moment. A car blew up about a block away and everyone recoiled.

"Think they'll let us in?" Solara asked.

"I think they're about to pour boiling oil on us."

The guard reemerged and set his rifle on the wall. Discreetly, he dropped a crumpled ball of paper at my feet. I rushed to pick it up and backed away with Solara into the morass. Others tried to climb the wall and were turned away. Confident no one was looking, I opened the paper and we read the instructions to walk to a white Chevy plug-in, three hundred paces west and three hundred paces south. I looked at Solara with renewed hope. A temporary reprieve awaited us.

"We're in," I told her.

"Then let's go."

We turned around and found ourselves face-to-face with a short, bald, green man. Dressed entirely in black—shoes, socks, pants, belt, and a dirty long-sleeved tunic that looked like a formal jacket worn backward—he grinned at me maniacally, as if he had been waiting for me this whole time. A new and old face. I felt a tight pinch in my ribs and looked down to see the thick blade already burrowed to the hilt in my side. He pulled the knife out and I saw blood come spilling forth as if I'd been uncorked. He bared his hideous busted teeth and laughed shrilly.

"You look so funny right now," he said.

Then he continued on his way, slashing indiscriminately through everyone else in front of us. Solara raised the shotgun and blasted at him. I saw a little eruption burst from his shoulder, as if a blasting cap had been planted inside. He hurtled forward, ripping and tearing, and soon the bodies swallowed our view of him entirely, leaving him to some undetermined fate best left to my bitterest imagination. I heard screams and cries, but everything inside me soon felt plugged up and I felt an immediate wave of lethargy and dropped to one knee.

Solara grabbed me and jerked me back up. "No you don't."

For three hundred paces west she dragged me through the woods, occasionally resting her body and mine against the backs of those pushing in front of us. We came to a rock and the pain in my side detonated. I writhed like the subject of an exorcism as my blood drained and my insides sparred with one other. Solara hooked my arm round her shoulder and began the slow gimp south to the plug-in. The people moving west knocked us off course, and I could feel her weakening as she tried to battle through them. Dust flew in my eyes, and I could barely see through the sheets of tears flowing out. I felt my right foot soaked and looked down to see my shoe drowning in red. I felt Solara's grip coming loose, as if I were a boat sloppily tethered to its moorings. People flowed across and around us like snakes, and soon I was separated from her entirely and watched with bleary eyes as the undertow brought me down and the human rip currents swept her seemingly continents away. I cried out for her, but my pathetic yelps were no match for the collective's incessant roar. I felt bodies tripping and falling on top of me, one after another until all the light was shut out and I was buried alive by the living. Thick blood oozed from my side, then stopped when I was forced to fold up like an accordion under the weight of the pileup. I tried squirming under the suffocating bodies but was locked in place.

Then I heard the shotgun. Third shot.

Solara was yelling. "Fucking get off of him! Get up!"

Fourth shot. The heap loosened.

"John!"

"Solara!"

Fifth shot. The bodies above began to wiggle, and I was free to bleed again. The pain dug in like Satan's heel.

Sixth shot. I felt Solara's hand grasp my shoulder and bring me back upright. I saw her face, and all I wanted in that moment was one free minute in one square yard of free space. That was all I wanted for the rest of this lifetime.

She dragged me to the Chevy plug-in. Four people were asleep inside, but Solara knew instinctively that the inside of the car was irrelevant. The Chevy was parked against the curb, beside an open storm drain, the gutter rich with blackened rainwater and piss and blood. She slammed me against the side of the plug-in, then let me slide down and tucked me halfway under the car. I looked into the drain and saw the guard from the COM compound peek up from inside. He beckoned to me. I began to roll toward the drain, and was under the car completely when I heard a gunshot.

Solara cried out in pain. I turned. She was twisting down beside the car like a weakly spun toy top, and I saw a pair of black motorcycle boots standing still beside her in the ongoing stampede. The shooter stepped on her back and rejoined the procession without a word, disappearing into the slipstream. I grabbed Solara and dragged her under the car, and there we lay, protected momentarily.

I looked at her face and saw she wasn't gone. The bullet had entered her chest, and her cheap shirt became so overwhelmed with blood and grubby street sand that it appeared to have dissolved. I felt around her body and found that the bullet had exited cleanly out her back, just inside her shoulder blade. I pressed on the exit wound and kissed her on the cheek. I looked at her face and saw relief, as if she had unloaded a terrible burden once and for all.

She held up the shotgun and pushed it down to her feet. "No more shots."

"We're almost there," I told her.

The guard was still waiting for us. I grabbed his hand with my left and cradled Solara in my right as he dragged us quietly into the gutter and we fell on top of him in the shallow, dark cavern below. He shined a flashlight in our faces. "You guys don't look so good."

"Leave me here if you need to," I told him. "Just make sure she's okay."

"No," he said. "Someone's eager to meet you."

I felt a strong set of arms wrap around my torso and pick me up, wringing out whatever little blood was left in my body. The long drag to the compound began. I looked to Solara. Another COM official had hoisted her up and was dragging her along. I stared at her feet as they scraped along the bottom of the sewer, then looked at her face and saw her smile knowingly. I felt royal for a moment, as if the man dragging me was my rickshaw driver. Then my guts churned and brought me back to reality. I began to sweat violently, and the guard had difficulty holding on. Every few feet he'd stop and hoist me back into his grasp. Meanwhile I felt like a boa was slowly working my insides out of me. Others ran past us in the tunnel, in both directions. Whether they were COM members or normal people looking for a way to anywhere, I don't know.

I heard a door swing open and saw my feet being dragged into a clean hallway. The shine on the floor, bright and fierce as the first nuclear blast, made my eyeballs run to the back of my head. The arms holding me up loosened and gently laid me down on the floor, like an infant about to be changed. I looked over and saw Solara. She was still there. Still holding on. I began to pray. Not to any god or man. Just to the air. I silently asked that we both get just a little more time. Just the time we needed.

A stern-looking man with red hair, dressed in khakis and a denim shirt, came into view and knelt beside me.

"You're John Farrell," he said.

"I am."

"I'm the Reverend Samuel Jeffs. I'm sorry to tell you this, but we have no doctors available."

"She's pregnant."

He raised an eyebrow. "Really? How long?"

Solara strained, "John, don't . . ."

"Fourteen weeks," I told him.

The reverend leaned back and scratched his chin. He signaled to a man passing by. He pointed to Solara as he yelled at the man, "Chuck! A doctor for this one."

I heard Chuck run to get a doctor. Solara reached out a hand and brushed it against my side. I felt disinfected.

"There is something I want to tell you, Mr. Farrell," said Jeffs. "Your son saved your life. I don't know if you realize that. For twenty years, our chapter in NoVa has watched you. Monitored you. Watched you kill untold numbers of people, make untold violations of the human vessel. These were mortal sins, and we were primed to punish you for it. The Reverend Steve Swanson told me he had many times been on the verge of taking you away somewhere very deep and dark. Did you know that?"

"No."

"But he didn't do it. Do you know why he didn't?"

I did. "David." I said his name like I was trapped awake at 4:00 A.M. in a hotel room in the middle of nowhere.

"That's right," he said. "Your son was a hero. He died for his fellow men. And his memory bought you the past twenty years of your life. You never would have gotten to live them otherwise. Think of that gift. You're a very blessed man, and I thought you would like to know that. You raised a wonderful boy."

I turned away from the reverend in shame. He handed me a bottle of water, and I thanked him and took a sip, though I knew I was unworthy of it. I looked to Solara and saw her shivering. I turned to the reverend urgently and coughed out the words, "Marry us."

"What?"

"Please marry us."

He looked at both of us with surprise, and then amusement. "Of course." He rose to his feet and assumed a formal air, as if standing upon an altar. "By the power vested in me by the State of Virginia, and with man as my witness, you are now husband and wife. Congratulations."

"Thank you," we said to him.

He knelt back down beside me. "I have to go back upstairs and make sure this church isn't destroyed. I'm sure you understand. The doctor will be down here shortly for your wife. Rest here, for now. I can't promise you'll be undisturbed, but hopefully this will be the time you need."

I thanked him a final time. A pair of hands dragged me to the wall and propped me against it. I grabbed at my side, and it was sticky with coagulating blood. I bunched together the fingers on my left hand, then tried to see if I could separate them. I couldn't. They put Solara next to me and joined our hands. I looked to the floor and saw parallel trails forged in blood. Above us the hard progression of humanity continued, impossible to deter. She rested against me and leaned into my body because she hadn't the strength to prevent it. I could feel my body slipping down to the right, and there on the floor we settled, Solara on top of me,

watching our blood intermingle and collect amongst the filth.
She kissed my bloodied ear.

"Only you can hear this," she whispered. "This is ours and no
one else can find it."

"Okay."

"You didn't let me down, John. You were right. They couldn't
hurt us. I've been looking for the right man to do this with. You
were a good man for the job. Everything's gonna be all right now.
I'm not leaving you."

I shook my head. "No. No. You have to go. You have to run
from me again."

"No, I'm done."

"You're not," I told her. "You get a chance to keep on going,
you take it. You keep on living. That's how it works. Because you
don't know what's coming."

She began to cry. She sounded like she wanted to go to sleep
and never be disturbed again. "I don't wanna know anymore."

"God, I never saw you coming, Solara. And that's what makes
you so fucking perfect. Please, Solara. You have to go."

"I won't."

"Please. In the past eighty-nine years, these four days are the
only thing I got right. Don't let this all be for nothing."

She let out a sigh and nodded consent. A doctor came and
stood at our feet. He took her vitals and told her, "I think we can
do something for you, Mrs. Farrell." He stepped away. I kissed her
a final time.

"I love you, Solara."

She buried her head in my neck. "It feels new when you say it."

The doctor dragged her away, and she didn't bother trying
to resist. I turned and saw her fading down the hallway. I willed
myself to envision a perfect future for her and her child—one I
knew couldn't possibly exist. But I could see it anyway. I could see
the wonderful things we all want to see when we first set out
down the road. I saw that, and the promise of it was all I needed.
She was flawless, forever.

The ground pulsed a third time.

I once met a traveler who told me he would live to see the end of time. He laid out all his vitamins before me and told me he slept seven hours every night, no more or less. All the life you want, he said. It's all within the palm of your hand now. He said he would outlast all the wars and all the diseases, long enough to remember everything, and long enough to forget everything. He'd be the last man still standing when the sun decides to collapse upon itself and history ends. He said he had found the safest place on earth, where he could stay until the gateway to the beyond opened before him. A thousand generations from today. I pictured him there, atop a remote and snowy mountain. The heavens opening and God congratulating him for his perseverance. Asking him to join Him and watch as the sun burns down to a dull orange cinder and everything around it breaks its orbit and goes tumbling, tumbling away, everything that once seemed permanent pulled apart effortlessly, like a ball of yarn. A life into divinity.

But I knew it was a lie. I've always known it was a lie. You cannot hide from the world. It will find you. It always does. And now it has found me. My split second of immortality is over. All that's left now is the end, which is all any of us ever has. The WEPS battery is dying. I have a shot of SoFlo at the ready. There is no dread. There is only certainty.

DATE MODIFIED:
6/29/2079, 10:01 P.M.

Acknowledgments

People who write books are incredibly annoying. All they talk about for months on end is their stupid book. "I'm making great progress on the book!" "Ugh, I hit a roadblock with the book." "I'm sorry I forgot to give Timmy his insulin, dear. I was thinking about the book." There is no more selfish person on earth than some writer who spends all his time obsessing over some book that no one else could possibly end up caring about as much.

Unfortunately for those around me, *I* happen to be one of these monstrously self-absorbed jackasses. And so I'd like to take a moment to thank my wife and children—to whom this book is dedicated—for putting up with me over the span of the past two years. They are far more patient and loving than I deserve, and they're all that matters to me. I'd also like to thank my parents, my brother and his family, my sister and her family, and my wife's family for their never-ending barrage of love and support. I'd also like to point out that I love all of them so much that I even made sure this book has no penis drawings in it.

Professionally, this book wouldn't exist without the support of two men. The first is Byrd Leavell of the Waxman Literary Agency, who supported me from the very first version of the manuscript and challenged me to make this book into a real novel, instead of a masturbatory idea dump. Poor Byrd read this book four times. Four times! I can't read any book four times, even if one of them happens to be my own. This man is a saint. The entire second half of this book was rewritten based on Byrd's expert guidance. Without that rewrite, the end product would have been a waste of my time and yours.

The other man to whom I owe everything is editor Tom

Roberge at Penguin, who fought for weeks to get this book published and eventually succeeded. The book would be dead in the water without him, so to Tom I say, "That's great hustle, sir." Tom edited the book along with Allison Lorentzen (in the United States) and Amy McCulloch (of Harper Perennial in the UK), and Ted Gachot handled the copyediting with remarkable care and attention to detail. I thank all of them for their judiciousness. This book would have been written in 46 percent capital letters without their efforts. Special thanks also go out to Kristian Hammerstad for the main cover illustration and Gregg Kulick for the cover design, as well as Jim Cooke, who drew the first version of the Dead Reaper icon.

Several people read this book (or parts of it) before it was sold and either gave me valuable input or were nice enough to tell me they liked it. I appreciate both gestures in equal measure. So many thanks to Will Leitch, Justin Manask, Matt Ufford, Stefan Fatsis, Justin Halpern, Evan Wright, Neal Pollack, Jon Wertheim, David Hirshey, Howard Spector, Kate Lee, and Jesse Johnston. I'd also like to thank the lovely and talented Spencer Hall for telling me which cities China would nuke within its own borders. He barely took thirty seconds to provide the answer. That man knows China. Or he's very careless. Probably the latter.

I'd also like to thank everyone at Deadspin, particularly A. J. Daulerio and Tommy Craggs, who have been fantastically supportive during my time at the site and are the two hardest-working men in athlete dong blogging. I also owe a great deal to my brothers over at Kissing Suzy Kolber, including Matt Ufford, Jack Kogod, Reed Ennis, Josh Zerkle, and especially Michael Tunison, who covered for me for two months during the completion of this book. He's a remarkably talented and funny man, and I'll be in his debt for a good long time. Jarret Myer and Brian Brater are the Uproxx overlords who purchased Kissing Suzy Kolber three years ago and have remained great bosses through every cheap dick joke I've tossed up on the site. Special thanks also go out to John Ness and the NBC crew.

And any mention of Deadspin and KSK must include a hearty

dose of thanks to the readers. They are all exceptionally hand-some and sophisticated people, and I apologize to them in advance for this book not being a collection of poop stories. Next time around, I promise.

I'd also like to thank Matt and Bruce (and Ernie) for hiring me back in 2004 and providing me the resources I needed to fin-ish this book when I left advertising in 2009. The bulk of this book was written in the summer of 2009 at the Maryland public library. I'd like to thank the library for having a special quiet room that annoying children are forbidden to enter.

Finally, this book was written in memory of many people in my life who passed away long before I was ready to see them go. They include Charles and Eileen Bane, Betty and John Mayher, Alan and Joan Magary, Alex Phay, Rex McGuinn, George Man-gan, and Heidi Spector. I miss all of you very, very much.